PRAISE FOR *THE DARK W*

"S.C. Parris weaves a beautiful story within
you breathless. *The Dark World* is a refreshingly new take on the
Vampire and Lycan war that has slathered the dark fantasy realm
since *Underworld,* and will take the entire community by storm.
Xavier Delacroix could very well be the new Lestat."
– Kindra Sowder, author of *The Executioner Trilogy*

"Parris flawlessy weaves vampire lore into this refreshing
new twist. *The Dark World* series is a mesh between Rice's
*Vampire Chronicles* and the *Underworld* films with a hint of
magical enchantment. This is something
every vampire fan needs to read!"
– A. Giacomi, author of *The Zombie Girl Saga*

"S.C. Parris may be a young writer, but in *The Dark World*
series, she reaches for something remarkable: a vision of horror
firmly rooted in the great gothic tradition of vampire literature,
but completely original. *The Dark World,* populated by mixed
monstrosities, magically gifted humans and the descendants of
Count Dracula himself, will be instantly recognizable to lovers of
vampire tales but accessible to those new to the genre. Some great
story-telling here, with something for everybody.
S.C. Parris is a talent to watch."
– Jamie Mason, author of *The Book of Ashes*

# THE DARK WORLD

## S.C. PARRIS

A PERMUTED PRESS BOOK

ISBN: 978-1-68261-079-4
ISBN (eBook): 978-1-68261-080-0

THE DARK WORLD
The Dark World Book 1
© 2016 by S.C. Parris
All Rights Reserved

Cover art by Christian Bentulan

PERMUTED
PRESS

Permuted Press, LLC
275 Madison Avenue, 14th Floor
New York, NY 10016
permutedpress.com

*To my mother, Patricia Henriquez, and Leah Winfield
for being there for me when this book was in its infancy.*

# Chapter One

# THE FIRST DEATH

The full moon shone in a bright circle of silver, spreading a dim light throughout the night. On the ground below, hushed footsteps hurried along the forest floor, crushing dried leaves and twigs beneath their weight. Both men, draped in dark cloaks, walked along without speaking a word. Only the sound of broken twigs destroyed the steady silence that passed between them. The taller man spotted it first: wispy, gray smoke drifted lazily into the dark air from a stone chimney attached to a shabby cabin.

One removed his hood, his narrowed eyes upon the old wood ahead of them, his long black hair and equally-black traveling cloak trailing on a slight breeze. "This is it?" he asked the other, whose hood still rested low over his face, casting it in deep shadow.

The second man stood silently, his gaze on the cabin, deep thought tilting his chin upward, for the smell of Lycan was thick on the air. There was no denying it. The scent filled his nose freely.

"Are we going to speak to her or not, brother?" the other said. "I don't see the reason for coming all this way just to stare at a diseased cabin!"

*How can he not smell it?* the second man wondered, seeing the Vampire's black eyes glisten with hunger. *Hunger*, he knew, *begets impatience*.

"Christian," he said smoothly, releasing his hood from his face as to better see the Vampire's hunger. Yes, the eyes were shifting slightly, a red hue beginning to cover the black. "There are matters... that must be taken into account before one can go barging into a rundown cabin."

"Like what?" Christian said dryly. "Checking the wind for specks of Lycan stench?"

*Ah, good. His senses weren't all devoid of danger.* "Something of the sort," he said quietly, and after a short pause, "have you fed for the night?"

His red eyes appeared to shine with sudden intrigue. "I haven't," he admitted, staring upon the second man suspiciously then, "why do you ask?"

The thick scent of Lycan filled his nose with greater presence now, and as he stared at his brother through the gloom, he wondered how on Earth the Vampire could not smell it. "No matter," he said, "I just think it foolish for you to accompany me when you have not fed. It would be most...bothersome for you, I imagine, if you...ran into... misfortune or some other matter and you were...ill-equipped to deal with it...."

"Xavier," he said, sternly, and his stare was full of incredulity, "if you think me to wander off for my fix of blood and miss whatever Dracula has sent us here for—"

"I shall inform you of whatever you believe you may have missed," he said, his voice deadly serious. "It is my duty."

His eyes seemed to lessen in their shine although they remained quite hidden from light, shrouded in the dark protection of trees whose trunks twisted darkly and whose branches hung low, brandishing black leaves. Xavier hoped the Vampire would take the hint and leave, for something was very strange here, and he would not see his only brother harmed because of it....

"Very well, Xavier," Christian said at last, and Xavier could not help but feel the Vampire was most relieved to tend to his nourishment. "Thank you." He turned, stepping swiftly through the trees, his back quickly lost in the overwhelming darkness of the woods.

Xavier's mind not able to venture far from the guilt the younger Vampire must have been feeling, for it had been Christian's doing, after all, that they were the Creatures they were—

He smelled her. The rich scent of lilac and freshly drawn blood reached his nose in the cold air, the ever-lingering scent of putrid beast... He turned just in time to see the door swing open, and there she stood, a hand wrapped around the old handle, a strange, dark blue cloak over her shoulders. She stared through the night, and her brown eyes found him the smile slow to grace her lips. "Alone?" she whispered, her voice reaching his ears quite easily as he stepped into the clearing.

Her beauty, her hunger... Yes, she was quite the formidable Vampire, Eleanor Black.

Xavier understood immediately why Dracula had sent them to her. "I believe so," he said softly, stepping forward into the cabin as she turned and walked toward two tattered armchairs that faced a small fireplace, the fire burning low within its grate.

He watched as she took a seat in one farthest from the door and closed her eyes. She waved a hand, allowing the door to close behind him, but how curious it was the smell of the cold night air dispersed as she did this, but the horrid stench of Lycan did not.

"Xavier... Christian wished to feed?" she whispered, bringing his mind back to the here and now.

He gazed upon her, seeing her closed eyes, her long wavy black hair resting against her shoulders and chest as her head remained back against the chair, exhaustion radiating off every pore. What on

3

Earth had she been doing to cause such utter depletion? Did she not acquire blood?

"Yes," he said after a time of staring, knowing full well she could have heard their entire conversation if she so chose.

"It's for the best…he would not take kindly to the news I have prepared…."

"And that would be?"

She opened her eyes, and yes, even against the small light of the fire, her weakness could not be denied: she was starving. "What we need to fight these beasts that threaten our quiet existence with the human world," she answered.

He stepped forward, stopping just beside the vacant armchair, mind rapt with just what that would be, when she said, "Forgive me. I haven't fed all night. I am feeling…a bit out of sorts."

"A Lycan… Did you fight one, Eleanor?" he asked. Surely, a Lycan had remained here—the smell was quite overpowering now.

She stared at him, the disbelief within her eyes apparent as she sat up in the old chair. "No," she breathed, "no, I didn't. I just… I haven't fed, that is all."

Xavier's mind rang with her words, before he decided that she had to be telling the truth; Eleanor Black never lied. "Very well," he said. He moved to sit in the free armchair beside her, pulling back the sleeves of his cloak and white shirt. The pale of his skin illuminated further by the orange light of the low fire, he rested it over the chair for her to see. "Take my blood."

A shaky hand flew to her mouth, and she stared at his arm, the veins quite clear under the skin, and said, "You know I can't. I can't. Not anymore." But she could not look away.

He stared at her, taking in her eyes, the tremble of her hand… Even famished, she still held her beauty. But of course she would— all that had changed was their title. Yet how drastic a change it proved to be.

Turning his mind from disturbing thoughts, he raised his arm off the chair. "Please," he said, and raised his wrist slightly. For no matter their standing now, he would not allow her a permanent death.

And the hand was lowered from her lips as the stark desire to taste him overwhelmed her. Her eyes had slowly begun to change their color, going from a soothingly cold brown to a most mesmerized red. "Are you sure?" she whispered, her voice thick with hunger.

"By all means," he answered, having no time at all to realize it before her hand had reached forth, settling his wrist before her lips. She opened her mouth, the fangs there gleaming in the light of the fire as shadows danced across her pale face.

Before he could say another word, she had bit down across a vein. The blood leaving him in earnest. He fought back a wave of pleasure the more she drank, knowing he should not feel it, not the exact desire filling his dead heart, for they were over—there was nothing there, nothing there at all.

*So why do I love this so?*

He managed to watch her as she drank. She could know nothing of his pleasure, know nothing of his desire, for hers was being fulfilled. And to a Vampire so lost in their bloodlust, that was all that mattered.

She drank for moments more, and when the wind outside the old cabin made the wooden walls groan, she released his arm. His blood spilled down the sides of her mouth with her greed. She had taken far too much, far too much indeed, but he had been far too preoccupied to care.

He stared at her closely now, rubbing a hand over his closing wound, noticing the way she would not meet his eyes. *Of course,* he thought simply, *racked with guilt. She always was one for rules.* "Eleanor?" he said, watching as she blinked, her eyes returning to their regular state, and the smile was slow to grow upon her face, but there it was.

"Yes?" she whispered absently.

"What news have you for me?"

She blinked incoherently and then dawning realization found her eyes. She stood with swiftness from the old armchair and turned, stepping into the darker reaches of the cabin where the low fire's light could not reach.

He stared after her, bemused, prepared to open his mouth once more, when she said, "Dracula has told me he long ago fathered a child...the daughter of whom has had a child of her own. He has watched this family closely in the hopes that one of their offspring will possess his blood, undiluted by the blood of humans."

Xavier heard her footsteps as she moved along the old floorboards. Her sudden silence allowed him to assess what words just left her lips.

She continued after several minutes:

"He has finally come across one such offspring. A girl...well, a woman. Her name is Alexandria Stone. She has shown considerable... 'talent' is what he said, although he wouldn't expand on what that talent happened to be. He himself has kept his eye on her for the past twenty or so years, watched from afar as she's grown, and for whatever reason, he has finally decided to tell us about her. He needs her, as her blood is his, and as we know, any human with the blood of a Vampire in their veins must be turned before they suffer a most unsightly death. She is nearing this state, Xavier, and he wants you to find her and bite her. Give her your blood and she will help stop the Lycans once and for all."

"A human woman commands such power?" he asked, disbelieving.

Her brown eyes gleamed at him from the darkness of the cabin and he could see the faint glint of the silver necklaces she kept around her neck. "Apparently," she answered him, a note of contempt hidden beneath the word.

He narrowed his eyes. It was highly uncommon for Eleanor Black to disagree with Dracula. "And you? What do you think of this woman?"

"I don't know what to think, Xavier," she admitted. "He has not told me what she must do to save us from the Lycans, only that she must be tracked down and turned into a Vampire."

He folded his arms, brow furrowed as he thought. "If he has watched her, why can he not turn her himself?" he asked after a time.

"Marvelous question. I asked this myself when he informed me of what he wished me to tell you."

"And what did he say?"

"He didn't…well, not exactly, anyway." The glint of the many rings upon her fingers caught his eye through the darkness, and he knew she was interlacing her fingers, thinking deeply, just as he was. "He only told me he would not be here for long to continuously watch over the human as he has done before. Something about journeying elsewhere, for what he would not say."

"How odd," he whispered, rising to stand, not understanding what would cause the Vampire to leave them to their own devices. Dracula was not known for secrets; of this much, Xavier was aware.

Eleanor stepped forward into the light of the fire, but remained quite a distance from him and the armchairs he now stood by. "He… has been acting strangely as of late. Surely, you've noticed it."

He thought of anything strange he'd noticed from the Great Vampire, but could not pinpoint a precise thing. However, he'd never before sent him, Xavier, to gather information from another Order Member instead of telling him himself. It was strange, but it was hardly enough of a strange request to warrant any feelings of distrust toward the Vampire, Xavier thought.

"No," he said simply.

Eleanor stepped an inch closer to him, the back of her still caught in darkness, her front only grazed by the light of the fire, giving her an ethereal glow. "I have," she said at last.

"What have you noticed?"

She stared at him, no words leaving her lips.

"Eleanor," he tried again, staring at her curiously, "what have you noticed?"

Silence still.

His eyes narrowed. He noticed now that her eyes appeared glazed, her lips trembling with what had to be fear. "Eleanor, what's wrong?" he asked.

She stood as still as stone, seemingly glued to the weak flooring. When she did not respond for moments more, the air inside the cabin beginning to crawl, he moved a hand to the sheath settled on his waist, sure to exhale what little air remained in his lungs, and squeezed the hilt of the sword. "Eleanor."

The figure in front of him did not move or make a sound.

Xavier drew the Ascalon. The long sword shone in the light of the fire. A deep line ran along its center—one that carried straight down to the tip, the silver hilt gleaming underneath his hand. As he kept his eyes on her, he tapped the blade of the sword to the cabin floor, pressing a thumb against the sharpened edge, allowing his blood to spill into the groove with ease. Yes, before he knew it, he felt his blood burn with preparation, his gaze turning a deep red. He allowed the cold cabin air to fill his lungs, his dead heart pressing against its cage with apprehension, for he knew something was gravely wrong here. He had smelled beasts, and a number of them, and now Eleanor...she was...what? What was wrong with her?

Steeling himself, he took a single step toward her before it hit him, causing him to cease his movement.

There it was: the putrid Lycan scent once again. Much more concentrated, much stronger. It made no sense. He half-expected an overgrown dog to appear at the cabin's door, the smell was so intense...

And then the blood spilled from her lips, a fountain, falling all over her front and splattering onto the old floor as she lifted an arm and stretched her fingers toward him, as though accusing him of some great wrong. A low, rough voice issued past her blood-drenched lips. It was mangled, as if forced to sound against a throat that did not want it to speak. The sound made his skin crawl: "Xavier."

He stared in disbelief, rooted to the spot by her deep dark eyes. They were completely black now. A strange, blank black. And it was a long time before he lifted the sword, it was a long time before he allowed thought to break his transfixion: He knew he would have to harm her, for the smell of Lycan grew stronger, stifling his every sense.

He was not prepared for what happened next, indeed:

Her black, curly hair fell from her head, the skin from her face beginning to peel, revealing not the bloody skull underneath, but thick, bloody fur. He lowered his sword as astonishment captured his hand.

Beady black eyes appeared over the long snout that had now formed, pushing the rest of her skin from her face where it fell to the floor just as loudly as her blood had spilled. It was a sound that echoed on in his ears, even when he lifted the sword at last, trying his best to keep his eyes from the bloody pile of flesh at her feet as the rest of her was removed. The large, overgrown dog shook itself impatiently from her skin. Her many necklaces had fallen to the floor some moments before, not able to withstand the strain of the beast's large neck as it stared down at him from its hind legs, its large head bumping against the cabin's ceiling.

Before he could say a word, it bared three rows of long, sharp teeth; its entire mouth filled with saliva, which now dripped down the sides of its open mouth, the smell of its horrid breath brushing past his face.

He chose not to inhale.

He turned his gaze to its long black nails as it lifted a massive paw, preparing to bring it down upon his head. He moved swiftly, avoiding the attack, the long claws slashing against air.

He squeezed the sword, shock dispersing, as he knew Eleanor was no more now. It was a beast before him, a damned bloody dog and nothing more. He would have to strike it down. *But how was any of this possible at all?*

The Lycan lunged forward. It ripped up the old floor of the cabin. Great snarls left its throat as large drops of saliva flew from its mouth—

He lifted the sword in one swift movement, the blade striking it dead in its large, thundering heart: The fur began to wither, a sound much like a mixture of panic and pain left its mouth, and Xavier turned his head, knowing what would happen next. The beast melded into thick, black ash. All of it dropped abruptly atop the pile of skin and blood, the necklaces atop them.

He reached a hand inside his cloak despite its unsteady tremor to pull forth a small white cloth, wiping the sword of remaining blood before inhaling deeply. The thing that had stifled his senses since he had arrived was gone and so was she. *But it made no sense. How could a Lycan burst through a Vampire's skin?*

Tearing himself from the sight of the ash and blood, he turned toward the door, sliding the Ascalon into its sheath, his mind unable to form anything more than the question: *How?*

And he smelled it, the calm scent of the wise Vampire, it was the smell of cold wind and fresh blood.

He placed a hand on the knob of the door, wondering just what the Vampire was doing here, and turned. Cold, crisp air greeted him as he left the cabin and closed the door softly behind him, canceling the heavy scent of Lycan and blood, the lingering, faint scent of the Vampire that was Eleanor Black.

The light of the moon illuminated the clearing and he thought of

Christian, how the Vampire was fairing with his quarry... How right he was in telling the Vampire to leave....

"That was no normal inquiry, was it, Xavier?" the smooth voice asked, then.

Xavier looked up between the trees and watched as the tall Vampire appeared from behind one, the silver cloak shimmering in the moonlight as he took a silent step forward with polished black boots. With his appearance, the wind picked up ever the slightest and it sent his long, pale, equally-silver hair across his charming face. One violet eye stared at Xavier calmly, knowingly, and made no attempt to allow both eyes to be seen, but rather allowed his hands to wave softly through the air: The wind ceased before he took another step toward the Vampire.

"It wasn't, no," Xavier responded quietly, allowing his joy at seeing the Vampire again to dissipate with the wind. He turned his thoughts to what he'd just left, his dead heart sinking further. "Something...terrible has happened."

The Vampire stepped forward silently, his boots making no sound against the dry leaves, the twigs beneath his feet. "It smells of beast..."

He knew his gaze to turn to the ground as his voice found itself stuck hard in his throat.

"Xavier?" the Vampire asked, the voice much closer now, causing him to look up, to see that the Vampire had indeed stepped across the rest of the clearing and stood just before him.

"Victor," he whispered, barely able to allow the thoughts to rise, for how could he tell anyone, how could he begin to explain what he, himself, could not fathom? "Eleanor is dead." And with the words uttered plainly, he found he could not match the gaze, could not see the look of disbelief that would surely be etched upon that face. "Before she died she spoke to me...a name. The name of a woman. Alexandria Stone."

11

"Alexandria Stone?" Victor repeated, and as Xavier stared back upon him with his words, he saw the violet eyes darken slightly as the subtle hint of deep thought lined the slightly aged face. "How did Eleanor die?"

"Lycan."

"How?"

"I cannot... I cannot say."

"Xavier, what do you mean you 'cannot say?' If she died by the hands of a beast, where is it? Did you kill it?" Victor's eyes were wide as he searched the cabin for any sign of forced entry, or, perhaps, any remnants of brown fur that may have flown from the Lycan before it was sliced by Xavier's sword.

"It was inside," Xavier said, watching as Victor turned his gaze back upon him.

"Inside? How is that possible? It does not look as though there were any Lycan Creature in there—was it in human form?"

Xavier painfully recalled the all-too-fresh sight of Eleanor's skin falling from bone. Stalling the shudder that arose, he locked his eyes on Victor. "No...it was Eleanor."

The shock on his face was paramount: The spark of bewilderment in his eyes would not be swept away. "What?"

"Not here," he decided aloud, not wishing to be near the place that still held miniscule traces of her scent. "Another time."

"Xavier—" Victor started, but Xavier could take no more, he had to clear his head, had to figure out what had happened. He had to see Dracula. He did not eye the Vampire as he stepped past him into the woods once more, doing his best to ignore the Vampire's voice as he continued to call: "Xavier! Xavier, wait! What is this?"

*What is this?* He thought, stopping near a tree, the stretching trunk of it twisting as to cover him in black leaves, casting him deeper in the shadow of the wood. *I hardly know.*

He turned back to eye him, his thoughts turning to a most dismal reality. As he continued to stare from between the black leaves, Victor took his chance to ask, "What of this name? Alexandria Stone?"

"Consult Dracula, Victor," he said quietly. "He was the one who sent me here. He was the one who could not tell me face-to-face that a mere woman must be looked after."

Victor pulled the hood over his head, still staring incredulously after him. "But Xavier, who is this person? What of Eleanor Black?"

His red sight returned before he could stop it: the scene unfurling endlessly within his mind. He had felt an unease near the cabin, that was true, but he had not sensed anyone else but Eleanor inside, so how was it possible that a Lycan resided inside her?

"I don't know who the woman is, Victor," he said at last, "but I am quite sure Eleanor is dead."

The complete realization of this seemed to hit the silver-haired Vampire at last, and he did not speak again. Using this time to gather his thoughts, Xavier said the only thing he knew would equal sense, the only thing right for a Vampire to do. "We must go to Dracula."

Victor nodded, seemingly resigned to the lack of answers now. "I shall get the others—"

"No."

Victor watched him, nonplussed.

"Don't call them," he said quickly, and as the Vampire scrutinized his expression, he quickly covered with, "I wish to speak to Dracula on the matter privately before the entire Order is involved."

"But that is not *done*!" he told him, brow furrowed in question.

Xavier stepped into the light of the moon once more, his red eyes placed carefully upon Victor Vonderheide. He stopped just before the Vampire and said, "I need time to figure out what just happened. I am not sure, myself."

Silence cloaked the night. Victor said no more, merely staring at him through the darkness of his hood. After a long while, the hood nodded. "Of course, my friend. I will still my tongue."

The red hue left his sight. His mind traveled to the thought he had held whilst within the woods, the thought that had meant he would be acknowledging what he secretly knew when she had descended into a Lycan Creature.

Victor nodded again, sending the wind to stir once more as he disappeared from the clearing.

His gaze fell upon the old door of the cabin, the scent of the beast's blood filling his nose once more. He knew, as he stared at its peeling, cracked wood—remembering the sight of her, remembering the sound of her blood hitting the floor, the sight of her favorite silver necklaces falling atop the pile of her skin—that nothing would ever be the same. And whatever had happened to her was only the beginning of more absolute strangeness.

Letting a slow, cold sigh leave his lungs, he turned his thoughts to the Vampire City before any more thoughts could disturb him further, and disappeared into the night, leaving the pale moonlight to shine upon untouched ground.

# Chapter Two

# CHRISTIAN'S TRAINING

The massive mountain of fire lit up the night sky before quickly disappearing underneath a thick fog, but the manor's high stone wall remained ever-visible as he neared it.

*The Dragon still remained.*

It was this thought that propelled him forward with haste. He stepped soundlessly across the soft ground, pressing past the remaining tall trees. He had passed several Pixies, Fairies, yes, but he paid no mind to the buzzing blue and gold Creatures, for the thought of seeing the Dragon at last would not hold itself at bay. He had not seen the magnificent Creature the last time he was here, indeed, he had only heard, while he rested within those stone walls, the terribly loud roars every night. *Perhaps*, he thought, *tonight I will win the Vampire's favor to greet the Dragon.*

When he reached the long stone bridge, he stared at the manor for a moment, taking in its high black doors, the silver knockers shining in the moonlight above. *Let us see how he takes this news*, he thought warily, letting a cold sigh leave his lips. He reached the tall black doors at last, lifting a gloved hand to touch the silver knocker nearest him.

He tapped it against the strike place twice before he heard the faint footsteps beyond the doors. "Who," the rough voice said once the footsteps stopped just beyond the black wood, "dares venture to my home at this ungodly hour?"

He smiled, despite himself, and cleared his throat, smelling the blood of the Vampire quite clearly. "My Lord, the moon graces us with her glorious presence and you dare call her ungodly?"

The doors opened with ease and there stood a dark man with jet-black hair that settled upon his heavily cloaked shoulders. The brown eyes explored his face as though searching for his reasoning for venturing here, and it was a while before he said, "Christian Delacroix. I should have known. Something has happened?"

"Yes, my Lord," he said with a short bow, hand over his dead heart. "Something has happened to another."

"Another?" he repeated, severe question lining his brown eyes. When Christian would say no more, he softened his gaze. "I see. Well then, Delacroix, come in." And he turned from him, stepping farther into the long hall.

Christian followed him through the tall doors, trying to forget the last time he had passed through them, slung over the dark Vampire's shoulder.

*I am not here to feel sorry for myself*, he thought darkly. With a squaring of his shoulders, he matched the Vampire's footsteps, keeping his eyes on the long red traveling cloak the Vampire wore, how it swayed around his finely tailored boots. But Christian had made only several strides before the massive doors closed, causing him to whirl around in bewilderment. No one else was there.

A soft chuckle arose from the down the hall, followed by the rough voice behind it. "I've enchanted my home since you've last been here, with the aid of Madame Blavatsky...it just so happened that a few Orcs were ruining her garden. I got rid of them for her and she protected my home." He turned from Christian once again, a dark hand gesturing toward the large room at the end of the hallway. "Now, please, let us continue."

Polished shields, beautifully crafted daggers and swords gleamed in the light of torches along the walls, Christian eyeing them in earnest.

"Funny that you should come with news now, Delacroix," the dark Vampire said as they walked, "we've come to a decision regarding your training," and after a brief pause, "they've chosen myself for the job."

"It took so long to come to *that* conclusion?" he asked, knowing fully that he wanted only the Master of Weaponry to train him, should he be inducted into the Vampire Order at last. "I would have thought they would have chosen you sooner, Lord Damion."

Damion chuckled, stopping just before the entrance into the main hall. "There was a bit of back and forth on who would do it, but ultimately since it was I who...saved you before...even Xavier could not see a better choice."

Finding this quite hard to believe, he merely gave a short hum, but quickly smiled, for there was a terribly loud roar that shook the foundation of the manor. "Dammath, correct?"

"Correct you are," Damion said. He walked farther into the main hall, bidding Christian to continue with him. "I know the last time you were here you didn't get the chance to meet her. Granted, that damn Dragon cannot control her thirst for blood—you'd swear she was a coldblooded Vampire herself...able to withstand the sun, shoot fire from her nostrils..."

Christian grimaced, remembering vividly the time he indeed was not able to walk through the doors. Damion had carried him on his shoulders, blood pouring from his severed leg, making quite a mess of his home.

17

Christian had been urged not to speak before being given fresh blood from dark hands. After a time, when all was in order and Christian was able to stand once again, the Vampire had then given him fresh clothes and a brand new traveling cloak.

He'd been grateful beyond words, but deemed it important to know the Vampire's name. "Damion Nicodemeus," the Vampire had simply replied, "First Seat to Lord Xavier Delacroix."

Christian had taken in the Vampire's dark skin, the regal coldness to his countenance forbidding evasion. "You're...a part of the Order?" He'd heard that the Vampires chosen for the Order were of profound strength, skill, and standing—he could scarcely believe at the time that one would help him, never mind that he was Xavier Delacroix's brother.

"Yes," had been the reply.

He'd knelt with reverence then, not knowing what more to do, but to this Damion had said, "Christian, I assure you, there is no need to show such formalities."

At this, he'd looked up in shock. He had never told the Vampire his name. "How do you—"

But Damion had gestured for Christian to rise from the floor. "I have known who you were from the moment I saw you, Vampire—I would be a fool not to know my superior's brother."

"Ah," he'd managed to breathe, ignoring the apparent slight on his person. After a few more nights, clinging to Damion's every word, his every movement, Christian decided it was time to leave. He never did ask to meet the Dragon that roared ever so loudly every night. He was simply fascinated by Damion's headstrong demeanor and his skill with advanced weaponry, a grace unmatched by the severity that seemed permanently set upon his face.

A large library opened up before them. The set of spiral stairs in the center of the room shined underneath the grand chandelier that loomed overhead far, far away from where they stood.

Christian turned his gaze to the vast number of books nested in the walls around them.

"It has been a long time since you were here," a voice said quietly, startling him: as he strode to the books, he'd momentarily forgotten that anyone else was in the room.

Damion walked to a desk in a corner where a low table sat. A lit candle shed dim light there, its wax dripped steadily down its long holder. He touched the globe that sat on the desk beside it; Damion let a dark finger trail around the many countries and seas as it spun. With a sudden sigh, his voice almost a whisper, he said, "I have been to many, many places. I have travelled the world in a few years' time. And do you know what I have witnessed in all of my adventures, Christian?"

He continued to stare, *The Art of Time Travel* open in a gloved palm. "No, my Lord."

Damion sighed again, his eyes appearing nostalgic in the faint light. "I have seen a stunning amount of death and destruction. Creation yes, but more death than birth. Mankind has learned nothing from their forefathers. Their ancestors. It is true what they say: history does repeat itself, Delacroix, and those after history are left to make it, but how can they," he removed his hand from the globe, waving it thoughtfully through the air, "when it has already been made?"

Christian closed *The Art of Time Travel* and placed it back on the shelf. "Was that a rhetorical question? Because, I assure you, I know not the answer you seek."

Damion let out a rough laugh. "Of course it was rhetorical, you fool. Do you think, being the Creatures that we are, that we know why humans continue to destroy themselves? It is a mystery that boggles the mind of any man—any Creature at best!" He chuckled to himself again as another terribly loud roar filled the manor. "Ah," he gasped. "It appears Dammath grows hungry. If you'll excuse me, Christian..." He moved to open a door that led to another room.

Christian saw his chance. "My Lord, could I possibly accompany you? I've never had the pleasure of meeting the Dragon."

Damion stopped abruptly, his hand still on the door. His eyes shined with thought before he said, "I don't see why not. Dammath hasn't seen any other Vampire besides myself and Xavier...another friend would be fine."

Christian followed him through the living room, where more books lined the walls. It was dark except for a bright fire in the fireplace. They passed two armchairs at the center of the room, and more beautifully crafted shields and swords were placed carefully upon the walls, their shadows dancing in the firelight. He eyed an empty spot on the wall where the Ascalon was rumored to have once rested.

"Xavier has it," Damion said simply.

"Of course."

Damion opened another door, which led to what looked like a training room. Swords of all kinds were placed on shelves, their shields on another shelf right next to them. Blood could be seen along their bodies.

"I have never seen this room before," Christian said. "You train here?"

"Train, sharpen the blades of my favorites, what have you. This is my personal room. I come here to think and I come here to train those who hope to one day break the Armies' many ranks."

"I had no idea there was such desire for—"

"Protection?" Damion interjected with a curious look. "But of course you wouldn't, Delacroix. Women are more your calling."

He said nothing. The Vampire spoke truth.

The corners of Damion's mouth stretched upwards. "That shall change once you get a taste of Lycan battle, my friend. Now come, we cannot leave Dammath waiting any longer...and afterwards we can talk business."

He stepped with ease from the Vampire, turning toward a stone wall, and without another word, stepped straight through it.

Christian stared at the mass of stone before him. He walked toward it cautiously, looking for any sign of Damion beyond its exterior. "My Lord? Sir Damion!"

The laugh was rough, though slightly muffled, followed quickly by the deep voice, "Christian...this is no time for games, walk through the wall with your head high and all will be fine."

He studied the wall, never having encountered this kind of magic before. It was a full minute before he exhaled and did as Damion instructed. Holding his head high, he walked straight into the wall. A stinging coldness claimed him and then dispersed, and he opened his eyes. A bright torch blazed near the Vampire's head. The high orange light illuminated a stone staircase that headed down into what looked to be utter darkness.

"Shall we go then?" Damion asked, not waiting for a reply. He lifted the torch from its stand and headed down the staircase into nothingness Christian in tow.

They walked quickly down the narrow steps and Christian felt they were indeed heading nowhere for quite some time.

Damion held the torch aloft, shedding light over the next few steps below them.

Christian had just begun to think they were never going to see ground again when his companion reached the last step and said, "You first, Delacroix," gesturing towards a well-kept wooden door the size of the narrow passageway.

He steadied himself, stepping toward it, allowing himself a small, needless breath before he pressed down on the silver handle and pushed it open.

The night air was crisp. A sweeping, cold breeze churned in the tunnel, blowing out the torch, throwing them into complete darkness, save the faint starlight above.

An array of trees, tall as they were dark, spread out before him. A steady glow around them, faint enough for one to notice if one looked hard, gave him the feeling that magic was at work here.

"I suppose you have enchanted this forest as well," he said, watching the Vampire who had remained in darkness behind him.

"I see nothing escapes those eyes," Damion said lightly, settling the blackened torch on the mount most near his head before approaching him. With a wave of a hand, he closed the door they had exited. "We should hurry, Delacroix. This way," he said, already walking ahead of him into the line of trees.

Christian hesitated for a moment before giving pursuit.

Several Orcs, Fairies, Pixies, Gnomes, and Goblins appeared, but upon seeing Damion, they hid once more behind their trees.

Before long, they came to a massive wall where the source of the loud roars seemed to be loudest. Just as Christian began to guess what the Dragon would resemble, a large stone door appeared in front of them.

"Are you ready?" Damion yelled over the low grumbles.

"Yes," he said—although he wasn't sure if that was entirely true.

"Let us go, then." Damion stepped forward and grabbed the impossibly large handle, pushing it open.

The dark Vampire walked through the archway toward a massive beast whose scales glittered green and black against the night. Its gaze held on them, a steady blackness, and when it eyed Damion in earnest, it rose from where it lay atop stone, and spread its massive wings. A huge gust of wind blew up around them as they stared.

With one massive flap, it rose into the air, climbing higher and higher, swooping into low circles around them, its yellow underbelly barely scraping the ground.

Damion extended a hand to the Dragon.

It spun in circles around them, until at last it slowed, landing smoothly atop its large silver claws.

Christian's hair blew away from him, as did his clothes. When the wind died, he saw Damion running a careful hand along the Dragon's long snout.

Opening his mouth to ask how on Earth it allowed him to touch it, it was abruptly closed when the Dragon let out a burst of black smoke directly toward him.

"Come now Christian, she is quite the baby once you get past her deadly exterior," Damion said, the black smoke billowing his traveling cloak and hair across his body and face.

"It's a girl?" he asked incredulously, never once realizing a Dragon could be more than solid scale.

The stare Damion placed him with caused him to shut his mouth yet again. He realized his outburst unwarranted, indeed, and he reluctantly stepped toward the Creature now submissive in Damion's hold.

She let out a particularly powerful gust of wind as she gazed upon him, and he did not move, not even as the Dragon jerked its head away from Damion's hold, her stare never wavering.

His eyes fluttered to the Vampire at her side. *What was she doing? What...do I do?*

"Dammath," Damion said after a few awkward moments, "meet Christian Delacroix."

Before he could say anything at all, Dammath lifted her head and let loose a large burst of fire, before returning her intense gaze to Christian. "He is a friend of yours, Damion?"

Christian could not be sure of what he just witnessed. The Dragon before him opened her mouth and spoke. *Words.*

"Not *only* a friend, Dammath. He is here to train," Damion said, and he looked at Christian once more, "in the hopes that he may one day be as powerful as his brother."

She grunted her disapproval, turning away, nearly hitting him with her dangerously sharp tail, its end littered in silver spikes.

Damion said, "Ah, come now Dammath, there's no need for such a green face. Mister Delacroix is only here for training; he will leave as soon as it is done."

She swished her tail dismissively before ascending into the air, sending another large gust of wind to spread past them both.

He watched her fly away, her large wings beating the night air mercilessly as though she desired nothing more than be far away from here. Yet Christian could only begin to wonder how it was she could fly freely without being seen.

Damion walked across the massive yard toward a door Christian saw nestled within a stone wall. And as he reached it, it flew open, with Damion disappearing inside it for a few moments, then emerging with two human corpses resting on each shoulder.

Christian said nothing, the Vampire dumping the bodies on the ground at his feet, venturing back to the door, emerging moments later with two more dead bodies. Damion did not cease in this labor until ten corpses littered the ground.

Christian looked down upon them. They were drained of all of their blood.

Damion said, "I feed on them and give Dammath their remains. It makes the cleanup far easier."

"I see," he muttered, thinking only of the Dragon munching happily upon her owner's leftovers.

Without another word to each other, they stepped together through the forest, and back up the narrow staircase, darkness clawing at their backs as they returned to the training room. Once inside, Damion said, "I believe you had something you wished to tell me, Delacroix."

"Yes, that I do, my Lord," he said, eyeing the dark Vampire, turning his thoughts from the Dragon to a more serious matter. "Most recently, a Vampire by the name of Eleanor Black was murdered in a cabin not far from here."

"*What?*" came the delicate, whisper. "What happened?"

"Xavier was sent there to receive information from Miss Black. I left early, my Lord, so I am not at all sure as to the events that followed..."

Damion looked around the bloody room as if trying to make sense of what was supposed to be there and what wasn't, and then at last he spoke, although he did not stare upon Christian anymore. He shifted his gaze to a particular bloody sword. "What did he tell you? Did he even tell you anything specific? Details?"

He hesitated. "No, my Lord, I was only told to tell you of what happened. I myself know nothing more than what I have said."

Damion's eyes were no longer a light brown, but now a deep, crimson, and his voice was low, the anger clear. "I'm a Member of the bloody Order and *still* I am told nothing. How much longer do we have until he tears us apart?"

"My Lord?"

Damion turned, giving him his back, the touch of finality not to be denied. "Find a place to lay your head. I must feed." And he was gone.

✳

Christian awoke later that night with an intense thirst for blood. He found his way to the dungeon Damion had placed him during his last visit, and though cold and dark it was, he decided it fitting for his absolute ineptitude as a Vampire.

There was a small opening within the wall, high above where he sat and he stared at it, remembering how he had struggled to remain alive whilst the moon's light beamed past the two black bars that formed a cross within the opening.

*Xavier knew of the Dragon... He knew of the sword... He knows everything, and I... I know nothing of...of anything. Why did I leave that night? For bloody blood?*

Christian rose from the stone floor, feeling overcome with the immense desire for the liquid all at once. His mind throbbed madly within his skull.

*Where is he?* he thought as he journeyed up the stairs to the door at the top. It opened easily. He pushed through and blinked in the light of the chandelier before moving past the spiraling steps in the center of the large room, stepping for the door the dark Vampire had walked through, the door that led to the book-lined room, its two large armchairs just before the high fire.

He sank into one without seeing, mind lost on thoughts of Lycans, Dragons, and most-upsettingly, Damion's reaction to the news of Eleanor's death. *Why had the Vampire reacted so strangely?* But as soon as the thought reached him, it was gone, for how could he expect the Master of Weaponry to tell him anything, indeed?

*I am no one,* he thought. *No one worth spilling secrets to, no one worth the kindness Lord Nicodemeus showed in seeing me healed, housing me, allowing me to gain my strength.*

He raised a shaking hand, removing the glove still on it, staring at his deathly white skin, doing his best to still the tremor, but failed wonderfully: It shook far too much to be controlled. "I must feed," he said quietly, although he remained in the chair, never wanting to leave the mesmerizing fire that blazed on in front of him. His mind was moored to a past most dour.

*Xavier,* Christian thought, *do you blame me for becoming what we are?*

If he had never seen the enigmatic man, he would have never have been bitten, killed, given the Vampire's blood for his own. And Xavier would not have had to follow suit....

A door opened and he heard the familiar footsteps moving to where he sat, but he did not turn. He had little desire to face Damion after the night's words (whatever the news he relayed had done to the dark Vampire), and his head ached. He needed fresh, warm blood. It was with a cold sigh that he closed his eyes, sinking deeper into the armchair, imagining the flames against his skin.

"You are a fool to welcome such thoughts, Delacroix," the deep voice drifted from overhead.

He did not stir. He remained motionless, feeling his body drain of all energy and hope, for he knew he could not match his dear brother in skill, in cunning, in maddening charm...

And then he smelled it, right underneath his nose: thick, warm blood. With a start, he opened his eyes. The chalice the dark Vampire held before his face was full. The golden ring upon the Vampire's dark finger gleamed in the fire's light. "Take it," Damion commanded.

He did not need to be told twice, he moved to grab the cup, sure to throw his head back and inhale the liquid in one large swallow. He did not look up at the Vampire as he placed the cup in his open hand and returned his gaze to the fire, only listening as the Vampire's heels clicked against the hard floor as he left the room.

He sank back down into the soft armchair. His sharp eyes wandered the room, catching the swords that gleamed with a yearning to be used in battle. The feeling of hopelessness engulfed him with ease again, and he stood, walking out of the living room, past the tall bookshelves and down the great hall, the Vampire nowhere to be found. When at last he reached the large doors, he took one last look toward the marble staircase before opening them, stepping out into night.

Without stopping, he began his walk back into town. Having not been able to fly, for he had no amount of proper human blood in his system, he sighed, knowing himself wholly unworthy to train with the likes of Damion Nicodemeus. He drew his hood up over his head and made his way into the woods.

An eerie silence greeted him. It was not long before he knew something was wrong.

The Pixies weren't flying about his head. The Gnomes weren't trying to knock him over with stones. The Fairies weren't fighting with the Pixies. It was all was far too quiet.

Twigs beneath his feet snapped, causing disturbing echoes to ring out into the night, and yet, no Orcs sprang out of the darkness to scratch and bite the cloaked stranger in their territory.

"Odd," he muttered to himself as he walked further.

A loud roar exploded through the air, causing Christian to stop dead in his tracks, his whisper instant: *"What on Earth...?"*

The sound came from the clearing directly in front of him. He took slow steps forward, more out of plain curiosity than anything else. He peered around a tree and gasped at the sight.

Every possible Creature in the forest was here, it seemed, and they all stared at the human that stood in the middle of the clearing.

Her eyes were closed, her face directed at the moon, her dress torn and dirt-stained. She did not to move. All eyes looked upon her, and yet, no Creature dared step nearer than the trunks of trees they stood behind.

Christian took in her features intently. Her hair was dark brown, long and wavy as it fell along her back. She had a delicate chin graced by the light of the moon, which only softened her features further, and Christian was sure if she opened her eyes, he would find them just as fascinating as well...

"You have found her, Wengor, very good job indeed," a loud, haunting growl boomed through the forest.

The Creatures surrounding the clearing stood still, every heart seemed to stop beating as a massive beast standing on its hind legs walked forward. Its beady eyes took in the woman in front of it, and with a low growl, it opened its mouth, revealing several rows of long, sharp teeth.

At once, a surge of great disgust filled him. A horrid stench pierced his nose, something he had never smelled before: He found it quite revolting.

28

But before he could think more on what this beast was, another sauntered forward, right behind the larger one, and dropped on all fours, hissing and growling at the human in front of it.

Christian was astounded further to see she never moved, her face remained directed toward the moon, and her eyes never opened to the lunar light.

His fingers pressed into the hard wood he hid behind. His blood steamed with an insurmountable desire to kill. His gaze took on a familiar red hue, his dead heart beating a mad rhythm against his chest. And all at once, he remembered the words Xavier had bequeathed some time before:

*"Your blood will warm, your rage will overwhelm you, and your gaze, brother, will redden. It is the way of the Vampire to despise the—"*

"Lycans," he whispered aloud, remembering in full what Xavier had said was the name of the hairy beasts. *Lycans, here. But why? Why had they been looking for the woman?*

His thoughts were broken abruptly, the larger beast having reached toward the woman with large claws and a sudden snarl left his lips.

But before he could even think about stepping forward, a burst of red light blinded him and a buzz pierced his ears. He raised an arm to block the light from his eyes. And when at last the strange light died, he stared at the scene before him, confusion gripping his senses.

The larger Lycan had done the same, blocking its eyes from view with a hairy arm, but not before staggering backwards in clear alarm. It had even fallen to the ground, arm still raised.

It was quite alone, the other Lycan nowhere to be found, the rest of the Creatures running madly in other directions, growls and feverish mutters of fright leaving their mouths.

And the woman had fallen to the ground as well, though she looked quite peaceful.

*She could be mistaken for slumbering,* Christian thought, though his enraptured mind told him otherwise.

His gaze was pulled from the woman as the Lycan staggered to its rear legs, its head jerking erratically, and he had the strangest feeling the Creature knew he was there.

It was not long before it sniffed the air deeply, and growled low, turning its head toward him, a moment of remarkable fear marring the bloodlust under that bemused gaze.

"A Vampire?" the Lycan growled.

The voice snaked into his mind, almost mesmerizing in its horridness. He felt as though he were being pinned to the ground with that voice, but his blood boiled, his desire to kill higher than it had ever been—

He was flying through the air before he knew it, mind gone. His only focus was the large, snarling beast—

And he was brought back down to Earth with the intense pain of terribly sharp teeth, the rip and crack that sounded in his ear quite loud as he felt a sudden release. He felt the ruinous tear, and he flew backwards through the air, the vision of blood, hair and clothes flying before his face amidst the maddening pain—

His senses turned black when he came to an abrupt halt, the smack of his back against a rough, hard surface issuing a scream from his lips. He felt his body crumple to the ground, slack against a tree. A pain still pulsed at his right shoulder. He could not look to see the damage done, but knew it vast. His side, as well as the ground, was slick with wetness, and he could smell the blood in the air. His blood.

*Damn.*

A fresh burst of wind blew past his face next. The thick scent of Lycan reached his nose, causing him to cough, and against all thought—against all reason indeed—he opened his eyes against the disturbing pain.

The dancing figure of the large, hairy beast stalking toward him seemed impossible, if only for a brief moment. Yet a raucous laugh filled the air after he thought this, and he was returned to sobering reality with the sound.

*I am a fool*, he managed to conjure as he stared up at the doubling figure of the beast that loomed over him. Its breath thick against his face. He could no longer feel the persuasive hate burn within him, gone with the pain that coursed through him. And he knew he had acted wildly. He had not done what Xavier would have done. He had not assessed the situation. He had not realized the massive size of the beast, the quickness with which it would move...

The black eyes covered his vision of the night sky. No words able to rise to blood-drenched lips, they were lost was in his throat and the fountain of blood that filled it.

How he wished to scream, to cry for help—

"Christian!" a startled voice yelled.

Before he could know who it was, a white arrow darted through the sky and struck its target.

The beast stood straight, and then fell to its side, its eyes still placed on him, unmoving.

His eyes closed with the lack of blood, his vision unable to keep on the frozen beast just at his boots, despite the movement of the Vampire (for who else could it be) at his side. It was only when the hand graced his shoulder softly that he opened his eyes.

"Christian," she whispered, "why did you attack him?"

His black eyes grazed over her face. Her dark blue eyes returned the look with clear concern, yet he could not bring himself to speak. Blood left his lips in earnest.

She nodded.

A strong gust of wind blew up his hair and bloodied clothes, and he felt her hand tighten on his collar. He looked at her, her gaze upon the dark sky, and it was a while before he saw it clearly.

The massive Dragon hovered above them, its large wings flapping slowly to keep it airborne. It snorted, and as waves of thick gray smoke filled the air, something like relief covered Christian's pain. *Dammath.* He managed to keep his gaze on her as she descended, the dark Vampire leaving her back before her large claws touched ground.

There was a strange ringing in his ears. The dark Vampire moved swiftly toward him, a strangeness upon that face he had never seen before—a look of stark apprehension. It was then that he wondered, indeed, if his injuries were truly so bad. He had lost the ability to feel his pain when the Dragon had appeared, the relief the sight had given him had never gone.

"Lillith," Damion said, and the brown gaze would not leave his own, "how long have you been here?"

"Only a few minutes. I was able to stop the Lycan from tearing off more than his arm and shoulder."

*What?* He examined his shoulder at last, and indeed, where his arm should have been there remained only a gaping hole. A slim trail of blood leaving it, creating a greater puddle along the soft ground. He stared in horror until a glint of gold caught his eye, and he turned his gaze to the black and white rags most near the Lycan's head. He watched them for a moment, recognition not reaching his numbed mind, until he saw the golden ring planted atop the ash that spilled out of the sleeve's opening. *My ring. My arm.* And just as greater horror reached him, he was pulled back into a deep sleep, the glint of gold the last thing he saw before all went black.

✳

Damion stared at the mass of Lycan, disbelief marring his greater senses. *Felled a Lycan. Impressive, Miss Crane.*

"We must leave quickly, the spell is wearing off," he said, eyeing the white arrow lodged deep in the beast's side.

*It will not last. They never do...*

Without another thought, he lifted an unconscious Christian carefully over a shoulder, Lillith's gaze on his actions dressed with bewilderment. He felt her glare with his every step.

He placed Christian cautiously in-between Dammath's neck and wing blades, and then scanned the clearing for anything more, a strange scent reaching his nose. He gestured to the human woman lying motionless some feet away from the Lycan's body. "Who is that?" he asked Lillith.

"I've no idea, my Lord," she said, and it seemed she only just realized the woman had remained there. It was so surprised her blue eyes appeared through the gloom.

Before either of them could say a word, a weak growl rumbled the ground at his feet, and he stepped away. The Lycan's growling growing louder the more the arrow's spell faded.

"Damion," Lillith said in a fear-gripped voice; it shook as her hand reached for a fresh arrow.

"Hold, Miss Crane," he whispered, never tearing his gaze from the Lycan's trembling body.

It dug a clawed paw into the dirt as it attempted to stand, though for every slow rise, it fell back down to earth.

"You're the one," it said at last, gaze hard on Lillith, whose hand was still frozen on an arrow at her back, "that struck me?" It then lifted a claw and pulled the arrow out of its side. Blood poured forth and Damion watched as it swayed on its knees.

Lillith lifted her bow, spurred by the beast's voice. She pulled back another arrow. "It was me, and I'll do it again."

*Damn it, Lillith*, Damion thought, *hold!* He moved toward her. Yet with his movement, the Lycan's sights shifted. He stared upon the black eyes, their gaze never leaving his own.

It said, "More of you?" But as it spoke, it attempted to rise to trembling legs once more, much more blood leaving its wound, dousing its brown fur red.

To his left, he barely saw it, the swiftness with which the young Vampire released the arrow, letting it fly, the sharp point ripping the air in two.

He moved toward it before it could hit its target, ignoring the sting of its tip in his hand. "No more, Miss Crane!" he said, eyeing her, the arrow clenched tight in a fist, his blood dripping down its glowing body. His back was to the Lycan as he moved toward her. "We must secure Christian, the sooner we do so, the sooner—"

"Damion," she whispered, her eyes glued to something behind him, and he knew what had happened before he turned around to see.

It had fallen to all fours, having lost a lot of blood, but it did not seem concerned. It seemed to be shrinking. Its fur began to disappear. Its long face became a more human mask and its appendages lost their sharp nails, lessening into plain dirt-filled fingers. The only hair gracing him was that which covered his head and stopped at his tanned shoulders.

He lifted his head, human-sized, yet still twisted into an expression most animalistic, indeed. From the ground, the man glared up at them, his brown eyes deep with a terrifying wildness before he threw back his head and howled, desperate and loud, the sound filling their ears. And it was all they could do to take several steps backwards against its threatening call.

It was not long, indeed, before the low rumblings shook the ground.

Lillith's gasp was what made Damion turn his sight from the man at last. The black eyes of many more Lycans around them held his shock. His hand moved to the sword at his waist without fail.

"Bloody hell," he whispered, grand hesitation keeping him from pulling the blade. There were far too many, far more than he'd ever faced alone, indeed. "Lillith, grab the human and let us go. We've over-stayed our welcome here."

"You are not leaving bloodsucker!" the man yelled, and Damion released the sword from its sheath.

The man was rising to his bare feet, and at his voice, the Lycans surrounding them prodded the ground in earnest, moving closer as to encircle him. "I can't let you leave." His stare was resolute.

Damion narrowed his own eyes upon him. *What the devil was he?* For he had never seen a Lycan show its human face.

The man moved a hand to the gash at his side where the arrow had struck, blood pooling past his fingers, but still he spoke, his voice belying the weakness he must have been feeling. "Stay your sword, Damion. I come not for you."

"Silence," he hissed. He stepped forward, ignoring the surprised gasp of the woman behind him, the warning snarls of the Lycans around him. "How do you know my name? Why are you here?"

The laugh was rough as it shook the air, the cough that soon followed it hard, splatters of blood leaving his lips. A Lycan nearest him whined, but the man merely wiped his mouth with a free hand. "How I know your name is not important, Vampire, but what you have is."

"What do you mean, 'what I have?'" he whispered. "Christian Delacroix?"

"Do not patronize me, Lord of Weaponry!" the man said, his lips curled into a horrible grimace. It was clear his pain was far too much now. "The woman. Dracula's granddaughter! Your kind are not the only ones that know of Dracula's descendant!"

Damion blinked. His sword lowered, but only an inch, and he eyed Lillith Crane, her bemused expression matching his own.

"You don't know, do you?" the man said with a cough, the noise bringing Damion's gaze back around. "You don't know that that woman is Dracula's only living relation?"

The ground trembled again. Even more large Lycans appeared from around trees, growling and howling threateningly. Their eyes scanned the human woman in the middle of the clearing, the Dragon who paced nervously in her place.

The man did not bother to stand. He remained upon one knee, breathing heavily still. "Damion, you must learn...to take notice of what surrounds you...but of course," he breathed with a painful-looking grin, "that must be hard with those rings the Vampire has given you."

*What on Earth?* He snarled and tensed.

Lillith raised her bow again, and in reaction, the Lycans bared their rows of fangs, daring the Vampires to strike first.

"No," the man shouted to the Creatures, and much to Damion's continued surprise they recoiled. "We won't do battle here."

"Won't," Damion snarled, anger brewing deep in his dead heart, the Lycan spoke far too easily for his liking, "or can't?" For he had noticed how pale the man was becoming, the blood still spilled from beneath his hand, staining it red.

He growled and said, "We are leaving." And at his words, the Lycan nearest him bent its head and body low to drape him across its large back. Without another look to its brothers, it turned from the clearing and ran through the trees, picking up speed as it moved. The remaining Lycans followed suit, howling as they disappeared into the night.

"Damion," Lillith whispered.

He faced her. She still held the bow aloft, her hand trembling greatly.

"At ease, Miss Crane," he said, his own sword still tight in his grip. *What the bloody hell was that?*

She lowered the bow before she exhaled. "That—that is what it's like?"

"Unfortunately," he answered, knowing the youngest Vampire

of the Order had never laid eyes on a Lycan Creature, let alone one with the power this particular Lycan had shown tonight. "I must admit, I have never seen that beast before, I've never seen one brave enough to show its true face."

She placed the bow along her hip and withdrew a dagger that hung from her many sheaths. She looked toward the human woman on the ground, deep in sleep, it seemed. "What do we do with it?" she asked.

Damion turned to face the woman, realization sparking. "Dracula's granddaughter?" he said, staring upon the woman's closed eyes. How curious things had become. "We take her."

"You're not serious?" she asked incredulously, her voice rasped with thirst.

He glanced at both her hands and saw no golden ring nestled upon any finger: She was most unguarded.

"I am," he said, hating himself for it. If it turned out she was nothing more but a meal they were wasting... "You heard what that beast said. If we drink from her and she turns out to be Dracula's relation it'll be on our heads."

He cast his eyes to Christian atop Dammath's back and the Dragon turned her long neck to meet his gaze.

"He is losing far too much blood...it won't be worth the dive into a lake that I must take to get rid of his stench if he dies for good."

Damion nodded, knowing they had no time. They would have to worry about the human woman later. Christian Delacroix was much more important—it seemed the Delacroixes often were. He told Lillith, "Take the human woman to my manor. Ride Dammath if you must, as I know you have no energy to fly. I am the same."

She moved to the woman on the forest floor and lifted her over her shoulder, her blue eyes turning red as the smell of human blood reached her senses. "Damion," she groaned.

"Deal with it," he commanded, yet he gritted his own teeth at the

S.C. PARRIS

smell of her, a taunting curse indeed, and for the first time, perhaps, Damion Nicodemeus ached for the damned ring that would stifle his very nature. Anything to be rid of the heavenly scent.

He was broken from his reverie with the words, "Are you not coming?"

He blinked. Lillith had nestled herself atop the Dragon, settling the woman beside Christian, secured against the Dragon's other wing blade, her red eyes pressing.

"No," he said at last, "I would rather walk…there is much I must think over."

"What shall I do for Christian?"

"Several goblets of Unicorn blood—don't worry about running out, I have ways of collecting more."

She nodded and patted Dammath's back. The Dragon beat her massive wings and several trees bent away from their roots as she lifted into the air and shot off toward her home.

Damion felt his blood continue its incessant boil, and knew it would not fade, not for some time. How odd for so many to be in one place. How odd for one to seem to control them all. How odd an effect those beasts had on their blood. How daring that one Lycan was to allow them to see his true face.

Who was this mysterious beast revealing himself? And for a human woman—a woman he claimed was Dracula's descendant?

He recalled the smell of the woman's blood. It still burned his nostrils. He almost shook his head as the memory of it hit him. Power. There was definitely power in that blood. Delicious, yes, but could it really be the blood of Dracula? Diluted, of course, with the passing of blood through humans…but truthfully?

*No*, he corrected himself, *that is not my focus—it is the sword. It is always the sword.*

But how thickly the thought of Eleanor would wrap itself around his dead heart, a great grip of grief.

38

He was only told of Eleanor Black's death hours ago, and still he found it amazing Xavier was the last to see her alive.

*What had happened? And why,* he thought for the millionth time since Christian told him of what took place, *was Xavier ordered to go see her? Was their relationship not over? Were they not finally at rest?*

The skip of his cold heart had nothing to do with the remaining aroma of Lycan now. He had always known that she had never truly gotten over him, —had always known she'd reserved a special place in that presumed emotionless heart of hers. She had always looked upon the Vampire longingly, lovingly...never did she look at *him* that way. Never. And now she was dead and Xavier was the only one to have witnessed it?

*Deceit.*

Damion had always harbored a feeling of resentment for Xavier, but it had transformed to incredible rage with the smell of the beasts' blood. Lycans be damned, the Vampire was always in the know— where Damion should have been, indeed. There was no doubt in his mind that Xavier knew all about this human woman, that he knew just what the Lycan had been talking about, that he'd known of Dracula fathering a granddaughter.

Of course he'd have known! He was bloody Xavier Delacroix. Dracula's boy, his pet, his ever-strong soldier.

*And I am the dirt beneath their boots, the Master of Weaponry.*

He sighed, his warm blood never cooling. Ah, yes, he licked his lips, remembering the taste of Eleanor's blood on his own, how many times they had shared in the forbidden practice.

But she was gone, and he needed warm blood now. She was gone, and how funny it was that the world seemed to fall when she had. Lycans showing their face, strange human women, Christian Delacroix attacking beasts... *Dracula's granddaughter...*

Damion shook his head free of the strange thought. He was not

S.C. PARRIS

prepared to face what it meant, for he knew it something terrible, and instead focused on the smell of human blood through the trees, stepping through the puddle of Lycan blood that remained in the middle of the clearing.

# Chapter Three

# XAVIER DELACROIX

Xavier stepped out onto the balcony, feeling the sun press upon him as a cool breeze blew past, sending the curtains across the doorway behind him to billow into his room. He stared out over the ocean, the waves crashing loudly against the jagged, rocky shore.

He thought, for the hundredth time, of Eleanor, how he had noticed the smell of beast that night, but to think it came from her. And how aloof Dracula acted upon questioning. He had traveled the many days to the Vampire City, only to be told the matter would be looked into. He found this answer a most displeasing one, and if he had a say in it, it was not an answer at all.

*What happened to Eleanor Black?*

It had been a month since he witnessed her skin fall from the muscle, a solid month since he had last smelled her scent. Of course, he could recall it anytime he wished, but there was nothing, absolutely nothing, like the real thing. And he found, now that she was gone, that he missed her more than he had realized when she was living.

But he was the one who ended it, he was the one who called it off all those years ago. Not able to afford the energy love desired he

41

expend. And wasn't she wrapped up in Dracula's training? Wasn't she lost in learning all she could from the Great Vampire? As such, he had not been able to take time from his own battle-worn schedule to love another. To love another just as his father had done. And where had that gotten the man?

*Dead*, Xavier thought grimly.

True, many things had happened in the commotion of that dark night, but he found his memory would always fall most painfully on the vision of his father's death. He had not seen his mother fall, no, he had heard the screams of his father from outside and he had rushed there, hadn't he? But she was already gone. She was lying in a pool of her own blood, wasn't she? And then his father was next, yes, Xavier could remember it clearly, although he had to have been no more than ten years of age at the time... The other Lycan jumping upon his father, ripping and tearing his face apart.

Christian had not seen the violence. He had been sleeping, hadn't he? Soundlessly, only eight years of age, only able to walk, call his brother's name when he needed something, anything.

He turned to see the looming figure hiding deep in the shadows of his room. "My Lord, I apologize greatly for the intrusion but... Christian has been injured."

Xavier withdrew, burying his thoughts. "What?" he asked the Vampire whose dark skin hid him perfectly amidst the dark of his room.

"Injured," Damion repeated, stepping forward, although never entering the light of the sun. "A Lycan attacked him near my home last night."

Xavier's eyes widened. "How could you allow this to happen?"

He remained silent, his light brown eyes dancing behind the curtain. And then, "I left him alone to his thoughts after he...fed, my Lord." He shifted his footing. "And when I went for him again, he had gone. I knew something was wrong. I mounted Dammath and went looking for him. He was unconscious when I found him. Miss Crane had already arrived—struck the Lycan with one of her arrows fixed with a Sleeper Spell."

"And?" Xavier pushed, feeling there was much more that the Vampire wished to say.

Damion's stare was cold. "There was one particular beast that seemed different than the rest," he said.

An eyebrow rose.

Damion said, "This Lycan showed us his human form, my Lord."

"Really?" he said. "What was this Lycan present for? Why was it near your home?"

"There was a human woman—"

"There?"

"Yes. He was there because of her, he said. He said such strange things—"

"What did he say, Damion?"

"That the woman is Dracula's only living relation…that she somehow…holds the blood of Dracula—"

Xavier started, marching past him and heading into his room, striding straight for the note Dracula had been so discreet to slip him when he was heading out of his office those weeks before. It lay atop a dresser near his bed and he picked it up and examined it before asking the Vampire, "You kept this woman with you? You did not drink from her?"

"No, no, I would not think of drinking from her, if it turned out she was indeed Dracula's blood relation—"

He waved a hand to silence him. He had to get to the points that mattered. "You have kept her in your home, I trust?"

Damion appeared bewildered, but Xavier would not falter. It was with a steady glare that Damion finally said, "I have—"

"And has she awoken? Has she said anything, anything at all?" he pressed.

"She has remained sleeping."

Xavier thought he were eyeing him suspiciously, but that did not matter. All that mattered was that the damned woman had been found.

Xavier folded the small note and placed it inside a pocket of his breeches. "Damion," he said, "I trust that you shall take excellent care of my brother. As for the woman, send me word when she wakes—immediately."

Damion's stare was inquisitive, but Xavier did not dare to think the Vampire would do more than he was told. After all, he was nothing more than a placemat for the Vampire that should have joined the Order, indeed.

Damion nodded again—although Xavier saw his eyes spark with dark question—and replied, "Of course, my Lord."

"Good. Take your leave."

He left with the wind that blew into the room.

Xavier's thoughts ran over Christian's brush with a Lycan Creature (*What in the Dark World was that about?*), and over the human woman the Lycan tried to capture. Was she really who Dracula requested? Was she really the Alexandria Dracula discovered still lived, that he had told Eleanor of the very night she died?

The wind blew into the room again, and the freshness of it was no longer felt. His eyes had considerably darkened as he thought of such things. It was maddening.

He sighed and pushed the thoughts from his mind. He moved to his dresser and fished for a clean shirt to wear, and before he knew it, the thought entered his mind, unlike his own...

*"I would like to have a word. Request presence upon your beach. I am here."*

He froze as his hand fell upon the blouse he had chosen at last, and then, with a blink, he swung the blouse through each arm and buttoned it, only just fixing his cufflinks when he heard the knock on the door. "Enter," he commanded.

He turned as the door opened, a young man's head appearing around the wood. Xavier said nothing as the man's brown eyes roamed around the room before stopping upon him, the flicker of surprise existing there.

He smiled, knowing the effect he had on his servants, knowing they would never truly know the truth of the Masters they served, for Dracula had seen to it, and quite well.

The man stepped into the room upon seeing his smile, and said, "M'Lord, Lord Vonderheide awaits your presence on the shore."

Xavier nodded, although he had already known that Victor was there. "Thank you, Addison," he said all the same.

James Addison remained there, and Xavier thought he knew why: this was not the first time the man could not peel his eyes from him. This was not the first time the man was so in tune with the charm the Vampire possessed.

He eyed him, a curious eyebrow raised in feigned question. "Is there anything else you wish to tell me, Addison?" he asked, knowing if he were to speak any louder, the man would lose his sense of self.

He blinked and ran a shaking hand through his shoulder length brown hair before he opened and closed his mouth. He stammered. "I-I will send word to Master Victor that you're on your way."

Xavier watched as he turned from him after a curt bow and stepped from the room, although it seemed his shaky legs were to give way at any moment. And when the hand was placed upon the door's wood, Xavier saw the man's knuckles were white with fear. He could not suppress the small smile as the man gave him one last apprehensive look before stepping through the door, closing it quietly behind him.

※

He found Victor on the beach as he'd been told he would, his boots digging deep into the sand as they stared at the high waves that slammed against the black, jagged rocks.

Victor was the first to speak. "It's been a month and we have yet to find her."

Ignoring this obvious remark, for he'd guessed a while before that this was what the Vampire would come to him with, he said, "Damion has just told me some interesting news."

"Damion?" the silver-haired Vampire whispered, turning to eye him now.

"Yes. He told me of Christian's most unfortunate meeting with a Lycan last night."

"Christian? He fought a Lycan?"

"It was not that he fought the beast," he said, a note of disapproval clear in his voice, for it was ridiculous that Christian would be fighting any Creature without proper training, "it was that the beast injured him."

"Why would a Lycan be near Damion's home?"

"I asked this very question to the Vampire." He sighed. "He would only tell me that a human woman was found there, that the Lycan—who showed his human form—had been searching for her, had found her."

Victor folded his arms across his chest as the wind picked up again. "A human woman? The Lycan had shown his human form? The only Lycan we know brave enough to do so is—"

"Lore, yes, I know," Xavier said darkly. "Why Lore was searching for the woman and how he knows that Dracula has a descendant who shares his blood is beyond me."

Victor gasped. "He knows?!"

"It is why he was there—why else would Lore be searching for a human? He has long since abandoned killing them, hasn't he?"

"Yes, he only turns them when necessary, but how could Lore have figured out about the woman? Were you not careful?"

He glared at him sharply, the Vampire's mouth closing abruptly.

"Careful?" he queried. "Of course I was careful. When I went to Dracula, he would not tell me anything, only that he believed he had a descendant. A granddaughter, that she was human, unaware of her blood, and that she must be procured immediately. He would not tell me why, of course."

"How odd."

Xavier allowed a frown to grace his face with these words, before the Vampire continued, "And his manner? He did not seem perturbed when you mentioned Eleanor?"

"When I mentioned her, he would only tell me that the matter would be looked into."

"What?" Victor gasped again. "But that doesn't make sense. For as long as I have known him, he would never brush off any such matter concerning his Vampires... Especially Eleanor."

"Well, he has. He would only ask if Eleanor told me anything I might deem strange. I told him what I knew."

"And what did you know?"

"I told him that our conversation was no stranger than usual," Xavier said. "He would only scribble things furiously atop pieces of parchment."

"That is entirely unlike him."

"I know," Xavier said. He moved a hand to the pocket of his breeches where the note rested, wondering if Dracula had shown Victor the letter. He lifted it from his pocket and handed it to Victor without a word.

He made it a point not to stare at the Vampire as he read, for he knew the look of shock and bemusement that would exist upon the Vampire's face when he'd finished. After all, the very thing had existed upon his own face when he'd looked upon the letter whilst leaving the Vampire City.

"Xavier, this is impossible," the low voice said against the sound of crashing waves.

Xavier agreed. "So you can see my dilemma, Victor. If she is not obtained soon, we may lose our only chance of ending the existence of those beasts."

"A human possesses such power?"

"Apparently," he repeated the very word Eleanor told him that night, and he found the irony appealing. Taking the note back from a confused Victor, he returned it to his pocket and said, "I cannot let this pass. Eleanor...what happened to her was...maddening, and with Dracula, there is more he is not telling me—us. Would it not be my duty as Lord of Vampires to get to the bottom of all this?"

Victor said nothing. He stared out at the ocean and the waters crashing against the jagged, black rocks that made up the shore.

✳

The afternoon sun was high in the sky when he sat at the dining room table and the head maid stepped in "Pardon the interruption, my Lord, but Miss Crane is here. She wishes to speak with you."

Xavier looked up from the stacks of paper before him and stared at the frail woman whose white hair flew in all directions from scrubbing the staircase. "Send her in," he said.

She hurried out of the room, apparently eager to be free from the intense gaze he had fixed upon her.

Xavier heard several voices outside the dining room. He shifted his attention back to the papers before him along the table, though it wasn't long before, "Hello, Xavier," reached his ears, causing him to look up once more.

He set aside a thin sheet of paper and stood, facing the beautiful young woman. "Lillith Crane, what brings you to my place of rest?" He took note of the embroidered lavender gown draped over her slender body. It complimented her pale skin with the utmost ease, he and turned his gaze to her dark blue eyes as she spoke.

"It concerns Christian," she said.

He gestured for her to take a seat and sank back into his own chair, lifting the paper in front of him again, although he no longer read it. He was quite aware her news would render his work even more uninteresting than it already was. The mess in various Vampire cities was quite tedious, having seen the same kind of reports over and over, most recently something about several Vampires losing their calm when doing the most ordinary tasks.

"Concerning Christian," he began, not tearing his gaze from the hastily scribbled words, "what about my hard-headed brother?"

She cleared her throat. "Well...it is about the Creature that attacked him. I am not sure how much Damion made clear..."

With this, Xavier's eyes found her. He leaned forward and did his best to give her a comforting air. "I was told it was a fight with a Lycan that gave him such wounds. Is that not the truth?"

"Yes, that is the truth," she whispered, before falling into a remarkable silence, her blue eyes wide with what had to be fear.

*Fear of the situation, or fear of me?* Xavier wondered, knowing the young Vampire was not accustomed to the smell of his blood— blood that was not guarded, for he did not wear the ring.

"It was Lore that attacked my brother, Lillith," he said, watching her expression spark with confusion.

"Lore?!" she screamed.

He nodded. "Damion told me earlier that the Lycan showed his human form. The only Lycan I know that is so bold, Miss Crane, is Lore."

"But I had no idea!" she whispered. "I thought he was just another Lycan!"

Xavier stared at her and then sighed. "It's fine. You did not know who you faced, but, I am told, the arrow hit its target wonderfully."

The smile was weak, but it was there. "Thank you, Xavier. But what will I tell Dracula when he requests to see me? For he surely will under these circumstances—I was at fault! If Lore was present, he will want to know why you were not called—"

"Lillith, I will address him myself on the matter. I am fully aware you and Damion had no idea who it was you faced."

She stared at him, apologetic. "I am terribly sorry. Terribly sorry, Xavier, I shouldn't have come to bother you—"

"Enough," he interrupted, the word leaving his tongue a bit faster than he would have liked.

She inhaled sharply and moved two fingers to the golden ring nestled upon another finger.

"Things are not easy for me Miss Crane," he said, after watching her for a moment, knowing he had scared her with his words. "With Eleanor's death and Christian's...foolishness...I am second-guessing living life amongst the humans."

She was quiet as she stared at him again.

He returned to the papers, mentally prepping himself to write out his responses to the sudden madness in Role, Evior, and Chrisanti.

"What happened that night, Xavier?" Lillith asked suddenly, pulling his gaze from the papers again.

"What night?" he asked, thinking of strange Vampires in the City, Role.

"The night...the night Eleanor died," she said.

He blinked as the words reached him, a sigh leaving him. "Right. That night," he whispered, not desiring to talk about it, but knowing the young Vampire deserved at least to know a little of what he knew. "Eleanor...told me something interesting."

"What did she tell you?" she asked, fingers still touching the golden ring.

"She said the name of a woman. Alexandria. Apparently she's human, but that was all I could understand..." he said, his voice trailing.

She watched him after he spoke. "My Lord...a human woman was there when—"

"When Christian attacked Lore," he interjected, "yes, I am aware."

"Well, could that woman not be this 'Alexandria?'" she asked.

"It is a possibility," he admitted, "one I have thought of myself." He looked at her curiously, then. "Miss Crane, what did you feel from the woman, if anything at all?"

She blinked, clearly caught off guard by the sudden question. "I...I wished to bite her. Her blood was quite intoxicating, my Lord."

"Really?" he asked, disappointment filling his dead heart.

"My Lord?"

"No matter, Lillith. Now, please, I must finish these papers Dracula has sent up from the City." He gestured toward the stack of papers and rolls of parchment that cluttered the table before him.

She stood and nodded, managing a small smile as she turned from him and walked through the large doorway that lead back to the main entrance of his mansion, leaving him to his work and, most notably, his thoughts.

With her departure, the dark Vampire's words returned to him, and his brow furrowed at their meaning. The attacks in other towns and cities were, perhaps, a result of what he had uncovered those many years before.

*"You are fairly new to this World, Xavier. You would not understand the darkness that befalls the hearts of those who wish to gain more."*

※

He pulled the curtain closed. Darkness engulfed the room for the third time that night. He knew how he looked in the eyes of Damion, but that was the one Vampire he vowed he would never tell what happened to her. He would surely overreact, he would think Xavier had something, if everything, to do with her odd death—and he, knowing Damion, would act accordingly.

He shuddered, leaning against a wall, thinking on what his next course of action was, for nothing seemed clear.

One of his friends was dead, the Lycans knew of Dracula's human relative, and he was meant to rein it all in.

He sighed opening the doors to his balcony. He stepped out, gripping the banister; the cold he should had felt did not reach him at all. He had been numb the moment he'd been turned into a Vampire, but this was a different kind of coldness—he had no idea what to do next. He knew the deaths could very well increase, but he wasn't at all sure when or where. *And that was the problem.*

Dark thoughts all but clouded his mind. He blinked rapidly, focusing on the sound of the light waves, and indeed, it was a clear, dark night. No moon above to bring forth beasts. He could take solace in that, at least.

He pushed himself up to stand on the railing, and he watched the waters below, wondering when was the last time he had gone for a late night dive—

"I hope my Lord is not intending to jump to his death," the voice came from below.

He looked down at the sand.

Damion Nicodemeus stood a few feet in front of the balcony, his brown eyes cold as usual, but Xavier could not fail in noticing that something was wrong.

He blinked, staring at the dark Vampire face-to-face, and quickly took notice of Damion's eyes now that he was much closer to see them. Tainted with hunger though they were, his face was colder than usual. He had half the mind to wonder what more had happened in the World, when he eyed one of Damion's hands—there was no ring.

"Oh come, Damion. You thought me to 'jump to my death' as it were?" he whispered, almost smiling in the dark.

Damion returned the favor, revealing sharp fangs. His hunger was all too apparent to anyone who wished to see a Vampire at his most dangerous. A low snarl escaped his throat as he replied, "No, my Lord...it is just...one has to wonder what can be running through a man's head as he is standing atop a balcony, clearly able to fall to his death."

"I am no mere man," he said, the smile fading, "and I cannot die. What more has happened?"

Damion shifted his footing atop the sand. "To send your brother to do your dirty work for you...she must've been quite the state."

Xavier did not speak, he merely watched the Vampire before him closely: Damion looked ready to kill.

"Why have you come to me?" he repeated.

"To get answers," Damion said, voice unrecognizable, the pain and hurt he'd suppressed giving way along with his uncontrollable urge to feed.

Xavier looked the Vampire over once more before he decided to say, "I cannot help you."

Damion's eyes turned crimson as he glared at him, his face turning away as though slapped, and his blood the salty air with his indignation. "You cannot help me?!" he whispered harshly, the wind picking up around them, sending Damion's red cloak to fly away from him. "You were there! You saw her die!"

He did not say a word.

Damion growled, turning his back, his hands clasped tightly there as if to restrain himself from doing anything he may indeed regret. "What," he said, voice ripped with thirst, the desire to retrieve answers, "took place that night?"

He closed his eyes, saw her skin fall, her necklaces drop, the sound of them falling against the old floorboards echoing.... "I do not know," he answered truthfully.

Damion's head drooped and he chuckled, the sound of metal sliding against leather reached Xavier's ears and Damion whirled, brandishing a long sword of his own design, swinging to strike Xavier's chest.

He lifted an arm and parlayed the blade, but his skin was not a shield, and his blood fell in large drops to the sand below. He kept his eyes locked onto the Vampire's red ones. "You really thought you were to strike me, Damion?"

"I did," he growled. "If you will not tell me what happened to her—what you have been hiding from me—from the Order—" He lifted his sword again and brought it down in another swing, one Xavier blocked with his other arm, the first arm already healed "—then your death will be a glorious answer. I'm not picky." He charged forward, swinging his sword fiercely, all former skill removed through his rage.

The scent of new blood reached Xavier's nose and he turned his head toward the manor, which was more than enough for Damion to slash him clear across his chest.

He let out a cry of alarm, the flash of the Lycan filling the air of the small cabin, the scent of its putrid fur, returned to his mind. But he blinked and there was Damion, the tip of his sword wet with his blood, a haughty smile upon his dark lips.

"It seems the great and powerful Xavier Delacroix can *indeed* be cut. What is the matter my Lord, have you not fed for the night? Or is it simply your precious blood? The only blood similar to Dracula's—"

He narrowed his eyes.

"Oh? Did he not tell you? Fine. I shall do the bloody honors, then," and Damion pointed the sword at Xavier. "You, my Lord, have the most peculiar blood of all of us," his words slurred, drunk with hunger, "yes, yes, and it's quite the surprise isn't it? You were new to this life and had no bloody idea how to handle a sword before Dracula took you in. I thought it peculiar then, but I was in the Armies. I decided to brush it off...not my place and all that. What tipped me off were those damned rings. *We* had to wear them, while you, newly appointed Head of the Order was free to roam in the sunlight without one. That's when I knew. I knew you weren't like us. Next in line to take over the bloody throne. Next in line to rule us all."

Damion dropped to his knees, clearly weak from immense lack of blood. "So, my *King*," he mocked, "shall you lead us to victory against the dogs, then? I'm sure no one would object to your greatness."

Xavier smelled the blood, heard the fear, great in the thundering heartbeat, felt the eyes from the shadow of the manor wall. *James.* He was watching and listening to everything Damion said, yet what in the world it meant, he could not know. All he knew was Damion was mad with grief, with hunger, and he would not allow one of his servants— his best, if he thought it aloud—to be the Vampire's next meal.

He moved on the air, toward Damion, pushing against the Vampire's blade with both hands, his blood spilling in earnest down his arms. "Still yourself, Damion!"

The Vampire's brown eyes widened. He pushed with the sword, low snarls leaving him. He would not relent.

Xavier waited, staring Damion in the eyes, willing him to disperse, waiting to hear that James had come to his senses—had returned to the safety of the manor.

"Hell," Damion whispered in defeat, releasing his sword.

It fell to the sand, and Xavier dropped his hands.

They stared at each other, and only when he felt the faint wind brush his back, heard the door close ever the slightest, did Xavier snarl. "Vampire, leave my grounds and tend to your nourishment. I cannot help you."

Damion's eyes darkened with rage, but he knelt, gripped the sword, and disappeared with a new wind, marred greatly with a grief Xavier knew all too well.

# Chapter Four

# LETTERS

Victor stood and walked to the large window of the vast living room, pushing aside the royal-blue curtain that had shrouded the room in darkness—the way he liked it—and squinted against the sun's bright rays.

Holding up a hand to block the light, he caught the glimpse of the gold band upon his finger. He stared at it for some time, the thought of Xavier Delacroix's words resounding through his mind the longer he stared, *"There is obviously more he is not telling me—us..."*

*Take your pick as to what it is,* Victor thought dryly.

The Great Vampire was, and he knew it well, adept at the keeping of secrets. Indeed, if Victor hadn't been the Vampire's first, he could have had the blissful ignorance others held close to their hearts. But he knew. Dracula was, for lack of better word, a liar.

But what those lies were...

He turned from the window, shrouding the room in darkness once more, his gaze darkening over the room. He'd inhabited it for many years, shared blood in it, held grand conversations with other Vampires, the few Enchanters....

"My Lord," a tall man with an overarching nose said from an open doorway.

Victor, lost in thought, had not smelled the man enter. How troublesome. He felt the metal clamps within his finger pulse painfully.

The man continued after a brief nod, "A letter has been received from a—" the man held the envelope up to his glassy eyes "—Count Dracul."

Ignoring the pulse, he strode the length of the room in less than a second, the man blinking in the wind created, and with a careful hand, he pried the closed envelope from the wrinkled fingers with ease.

He said nothing to the man who bowed his leave with something of a sniff, and when he was gone, he eyed the envelope in exasperation.

*Dracula's secrets.* The thought passed and died as quickly as it came, the seed of anger in his dead heart sending his blood to grow hot just for a moment, years of practice keeping it at bay. *No. I needn't subject myself. Xavier... Xavier will figure it out when it's time.*

With reluctant fingers, he tore open the envelope and unfolded the small paper inside. He eyed the neat calligraphy that dressed the letter, wishing what he was about to read was as nice as the writing he now saw:

*Victor,*

*I will cut right to the chase, my friend. It appears the Etrian Elves wish to hold a meet with the Vampire World. Regarding what this means for our people remains to be seen. As of now, I see it in the best interest of our two breeds if we are to ever stop the Lycan hold on the human world. Seeing as how the human woman has yet to be obtained.*

*As you may be aware, the Elves despise the overgrown beasts as much as we do, I believe we should hear what they have to say. Naturally, I will need all remaining Members of the Order to return to the City as soon as possible. The Elves will arrive here in a few days' time. Those involved should leave their homes on the surface and to tend to this important matter.*

*Victor, I have not notified the other Members of this meeting with the Elves. Only yourself. I leave it up you to tell them immediately. I have also arranged several carriages, if needed. Of course, you are free to ride horseback if you wish. Just get here as soon as you can.*

*Please send word in a letter before you leave.*

*Your Oldest Friend,*
*Count Dracul*
*P.S. – I have had newer rings made. I shall give them to you all upon arrival.*

Victor read the letter again, this time finding the words "newer rings made." He threw the paper down onto a nearby table in disgust, the pride—whatever there was of it—that came with being a Vampire diminishing all the more. *Being dragged back to the City for the bloody Elves... No, no, Dracula had more up his sleeve than just that.*

*But what that was...*

He sighed and rubbed his hands anxiously together. *It never ends*, he thought, staring at the curtain, shining as it was against the sun's light. *But wasn't it my fault?*

He'd retrieved Xavier Delacroix once the newly-made Vampire had been healed, turned, and admitted to fathering the Delacroix men. And he'd moved quickly to ensure the Great Vampire had all he desired in order. For he'd wanted yet another Vampire to rise up—yet another Dark Creature to take the place that many others had failed in taking.

And Victor had stepped in and helped Dracula secure these

Vampires, watching them fail in the impossible (unknowable) pursuits the Great Vampire had desired for them. And he had been compelled, bidden, indeed, to move as Dracula wished.

He, tied to the Great Vampire more than most...

But it had not mattered, that connection, that tie. The more he moved to cover up the Great Vampire's secrets, the less he knew of what the Great Vampire did. He was kept, maddeningly, out of the room whilst meetings went on—kept far away when strange Dark Creatures would arrive on Dracula's doorstep, begging for help, or screaming in rage.

He stared at the gold on his finger, the day the Great Vampire had given it to him sharp in his mind. It had been in Dracula's office, just after a particularly tiring journey back from the Vampire City, Lane. He had revealed he was relinquishing the necklaces they'd worn before and replacing them with enchanted rings, a special magic imbued in them to still their bloodlust, allowed certain Vampires to walk in the sun. Of course, this had brought to mind the few Vampires, Dracula included, who could walk atop the surface as they pleased.

He had wondered, many a time, how they were able to do that without the enchanted jewelry, but he had never voiced this concern. He was quite sure to do so would draw unwanted attention upon himself. He already obeyed Dracula's every word, and he had seen, far too many times, the cruelty with which the Vampire would move to ensure his commands were obeyed.

A light breeze blew up around the room with his thoughts, and with it, the letter landed lightly on the floor, bringing him to the here and now. He stared at it for a long moment before cursing silently, lifting it from the floor. He read it one more time, unable to shake the tremendous sensation the Great Vampire was dragging him into madness yet again, and he, whatever he'd felt, would do the only thing Dracula's first could: Obey.

❋

He swept from the room where the Vampire screamed his pain, grimacing as he closed the door behind himself.

The Unicorn blood was fresh, as always, but terrible in taste. Still, it did its job well. It would be a matter of time before the Vampire truly healed, indeed.

"M'Lord," a young man said from down the hall, running up to him with a thin envelope in a sweaty hand, "a letter from Lord Vonderheide. Just arrived." He drew level with the Vampire, doubling over once he'd stopped, his free hand upon his thigh, the envelope stretched out.

Damion took the envelope, trying his best to ignore the sweaty fingerprints all across it and recognized Victor's handwriting. He offered a terse, "Thank you," to the boy and took the letter before moving down the long hallway to his room.

He pushed open the two large doors and stepped into the bedroom, smiling at the red that covered the walls, the floor, and the vast bed in the center.

He strolled over to a small desk in a corner of the large room, letting the letter linger idly between his fingers, wondering what it could hold. With a wave of his free hand, the single candle atop the desk sparked to life. It shed light on the dark wood, the quill in its ink, and the fresh parchment.

He sat and flipped open the letter.

*Damion,*

*Dracula requests the Order's appearance in the Vampire World immediately. He stressed the importance of arriving there as fast as possible. Apparently, the Etrian Elves wish to speak with us, so you can see why our presence is requested. Such a matter is delicate.*

*I have sent letters to the others. We must meet tonight. We will meet in the City streets. Do not bring anyone else with you. Dracula has arranged for horses to carry us there. There will be no need for you to bring your ring, we are having new ones made and will be given them upon our arrival into the City.*

*I agree this is a rather troublesome request, but bear with it, Damion.*

*Secondary Lord of the Vampire Order,*
*Victor Vonderheide*

*Ah. Such short notice*, he thought. He had no time to venture back to the Vampire City—it was a place he didn't desire to travel to at any rate. But for the Elves? Absolutely not.

Damion folded the letter slowly, his fingers sliding across the edge. He eyed the small flame atop the candle, the cry of pain issuing through the walls. *How on Earth am I to get more Unicorn blood to see Christian fully healed?*

Another cry cut through the air and he started, staring seriously upon the blank parchment.

*Damned Dracula*, he thought, the candle's flame sparking briefly in his anger. *No prior notice, indeed, and we are just expected to pack up and come home when called? I am no dog.*

But, as soon as he'd thought this, his furrowed brow broke in two and he almost laughed. Ah, yes, he *was* a dog. Dracula's dog. As were they all. Except for Xavier...but he would not—nay, *could not*—bring himself to think on that Vampire, the damn calming control in his green gaze the night before...

No, he could not bring himself to think on Xavier, not at a time like this.

The woman. The image of the curious woman atop the ground, serene in all her ignorance, returned, and his brow furrowed deeper with thought.

There was interest in that prospect, yes.

He had returned home last night to find Lillith had seen to it the woman be placed right next door, that she still slept soundlessly... He'd marveled at her sheer beauty. But it was not until he'd bade Lillith leave of his home that he entered the room of the woman once more and stared in earnest upon her pleasant frame.

Her mouth, all at once, had drawn his attention. He admired its curt shape, its slightly curved frame, and it seemed she smiled while she slept. Yet the dirt upon her red dress, her cheek, her forehead, and the leaves and twigs caught in her long dark brown hair gave him the impression he stared upon a woodland Creature.

She was no normal human, this he could agree to with ease, for her blood was strong, and her frame tense, although she appeared to be in the deepest of sleeps.

All at once, he heard the whispers of excited voices; they danced through the thick walls and drew him out of his mind.

"Warn the master," an elderly woman's voice sounded somewhere farther down the hallway, one he recognized as the head maid's. "The woman's awake!"

He rose from the chair, Victor's letter falling out of hand. The flame dispersed and darkness consumed the room once more. He moved to the silken red wallpaper just beside the desk and placed a hand upon it, not blinking as the wall disappeared. He stared down a long, narrow stone tunnel. Torches along the high walls sparked to life the longer he stared.

*She's awake*, he thought, taking his first step into the narrow passage, *she's awake, but is she truly Dracula's relative?*

The torches' light threw great relief over the stone passage; it stretched further onwards, Damion not slowing in his steps. The stone wall resolute where the passage ended, drawing close. He waved a hand as he approached and it disappeared as well, and in its place, the familiar room showed itself.

He stopped just near the entrance, for he heard voices on the other side, and he tempered his urgent desire to see this woman as he listened.

"D'you need anything, Miss?" a young woman said.

"Nothing, no," a quiet, shaky voice answered, and this voice caused Damion's eyes to widen at its sheer sweetness. "I just wish to know...where I am." "Oh, well... The Master has been called...he shall arrive shortly. If you'll excuse me, Miss..."

He heard the woman step from the room but he did nothing until he heard the large door close.

She remained atop the large bed, the canopy curtains drawn to their tall posts, her pleasant face still pointed at the door the woman had left through. It allowed him more time to eye her now-clean frame, the white gown she wore, and he realized the maids must have cleaned and changed her during the morning.

He stepped farther into the room, waving a few fingers, the secret passage returning to wall immediately. "You must be flustered," he said, "waking up in a strange place."

Her head whipped around and he was rather surprised her neck did not snap from the movement.

The gasp left her lips, her brown-green eyes widening, her stare one of bewilderment. She drew the white sheets to her chest, hiding the white dressing gown from view. "I-I... Who on Earth are you?" she whispered, breathless. "Where did you come from?"

He stepped further into the room, suddenly aware he could not smell her fear, although her eyes were wide her chest heaving with apprehension. It was at this that he grazed the golden ring on his finger. *Perhaps the bloody rings were doing their job after all.*

"I am Damion Nicodemeus," he said, "you are in my home."

Her gaze softened at his words, but her hands were still tense as they gripped the sheets. "Damion...Nico—?"

"It hardly matters," he said, desiring to save the woman the difficulty of pronouncing his last name. "What is more important, surely, is yours, Miss..."

"Stone," she said. "Alexandria Stone."

"I beg your pardon?"

"Alexandria Stone. My name," she said a bit louder.

"Alexandria Stone. How...pretty." He placed a hand around a tall post at the foot of the bed. "Can you remember anything before waking up here, Miss Stone?"

Alexandria's expression turned to one of concern. "I don't understand."

"Please try."

"I'd like to know why I'm here...and where *here* is. I don't even know who you are." *She is different from most humans*, Damion noted, casting away the hint of anger that danced in his gut with her ability to ignore his command. *How interesting.* "Then you remember nothing of last night?"

She stared at him curiously. "Last night? I... What happened last night?"

He hesitated, curious as to whether or not he should tell her that he had saved her life from a Lycan. He watched her alarmed countenance for moments more before deciding she need not be bothered with such information. And, at any rate, if she could not remember, then it was possible she wasn't Dracula's relative...

And suddenly, she pulled back the heavy covers to reveal long, slender legs.

Ring or no, Damion was very aware such a sight would send his blood to burn with the desire to taste her blood, but still, no such smell canvassed his nose.

Distracted by the fact that he could not smell her blood at all, not even a slight trace of it, he did not realize that she had stood and turned to him.

"Well, my Lord, I will thank you for allowing me to stay here for the night, but really, I believe I'm well enough to be on my—"

He moved in one swift step and caught her before she'd truly fallen. He swung her back on the bed, waiting for the urge to feed to fly through his blood, but it never did come.

*What a curious human,* he thought, staring at her closed eyes, releasing his hands from underneath her, a slight breath leaving her lips.

No trace of blood, of anything at all reached his nose. *What on Earth was this?*

※

She stared at the young woman who seemed to float into the room, a silver tray with an envelope and a small cup atop it in her hands.

"Oh, miss, I figured you were still in bed. Although it isn't becoming of a girl your age..."

Lillith smiled, brushing blonde tendrils of hair off a shoulder, her gaze upon the envelope the closer the woman drew. "A letter?"

"Yes, Miss Crane," the woman said, striding up to the bed. She placed the tray at Lillith's feet. "It came earlier this morning, but I figured you needed your sleep. Now that it's nearing the afternoon, I decided I'd wake you with your tea."

Licking her lips absently, she stared at the sand-colored liquid within the white porcelain cup, but could not bring herself to bring it to her lips. Could not, regretfully, drink what was not red.

"Miss Crane," the woman said, "this dress for the day, hm?" She held out a ghastly sea-green day dress, its many skirts thickening its bottom.

Lillith could only smile her approval, what truth it held pointless, indeed: It no longer mattered. None of it truly mattered.

She swung her legs over the side of the bed, resolved to get on with the matters at hand, for as always, there were many. She allowed the maid to dress her quickly, the dark-green bodice drawn tight around her ribs, then she snatched up the envelope.

The woman approached with a smaller tray, atop which silver, gold, and diamond rings were laid. "Which would you prefer, Miss Crane?"

"None of them, Amy," she said, staring at the tight cursive on the letter. She ignored the memory of her servant's blood as it reached her, a finger preparing to slice open the envelope. *Lord Damion... what could have happened?*

Amy gave the gold ring a look that suggested she didn't much like it. "Miss Crane, I'm sure you fancy that ring, but it is rather bland, and it doesn't match your dress at all." She picked up a ring encrusted with diamonds, waving it before Lillith's eyes. "See this one? It would make you shine even more than you already do."

*"It may be harder to convince humans in your household of your need to wear this ring,"* Dracula had said when he'd given it to her upon her coronation into the Vampire Order, *"but I'm sure you can think of something, as resourceful as you are."*

The words set her mind with ease, and she squared her shoulders with the thought. "I'm afraid I won't be parting with this band, Amy, none of the other rings will do."

She watched with a slight smile as the human sighed and set the tray back upon the table. "Very well, miss." She extended a hand to the cup. "Don't forget to drink your tea. I'll bring your breakfast up shortly." And she swept from the room.

Lillith Crane ran a nail over the edge of the envelope once the door closed, her thoughts running to a suitor or some such, perhaps an invitation to yet another harrowing party, and she almost stopped herself from opening it. *If I have to suffer through yet another night amongst walking blood banks...* Her eyes widened as the letter fell open, the seal of Vonderheide Manor breaking apart as it did so.

She felt her blood run colder than normal.

No letter was received from Victor Vonderheide unless it was news straight from Dracula.

*Dearest Lillith Elizabeth Crane,*
*The Elves...*

She read, never once stopping, the short jutting script filling the page.

Once done, she sank down in the chair closest to her, her mind racing with a myriad of questions. And how was she to tell the man and woman appointed to her that she must up and leave them for who knew how long in order to hear about the damning Elves?

"Damn," she whispered

Amy returned with a smile, a tray of food in front of her. Once she placed it on a small table opposite the bed, the woman set about preparing her food.

Lillith pulled the curtains closed and removed the golden ring from a finger with a slight wince, the surge of the woman's blood rushed to her nose. She closed her eyes, as she knew she would see nothing but red now, and she allowed herself to think, something she would not have been able to do with the ring on.

"Miss Crane?" Amy said.

*Good Lord, can I just get a minute to myself?* Lillith thought darkly, irritation rising as Amy's blood filled her nose. She knew the woman had turned to eye her, had an air of curiosity about her.

She opened her eyes, turning to watch the woman, the red veil of her sight blanketing the woman in blood. A short sigh of desire left her before she spoke. "Amy, I have been called."

"C-Called, Miss?" she whispered.

Lillith watched as she took a quick seat atop the bed, the movement sending the scent of the woman's blood toward her. A low snarl left her lips.

The woman covered her mouth.

"Yes," she said. "One of my suitors is heading out of town and wishes for me to accompany him. He says the trip itself will take quite a few days. I shall need, clothes and food, of course. I trust you to prepare these things for me."

"B-but the Lord and Lady, Miss Crane, do they know of this sudden trip?" she asked. Lillith could not know if the woman had heard the snarl or merely ignored it. "And when does this suitor plan to leave? Who is he?"

*My, how I have such a quick tongue.*

While it was true she had created such a tale in only a matter of minutes, she had forgotten how...inquiring the woman was. Yes, the smell of her blood had distracted Lillith from remembering she would need more than mere words to quell the woman's questions.

"Miss Crane?" Amy said again, confusion and apprehension marring her plain features.

Lillith took a step toward her, keeping at bay the desire to move forward and take from her what was never hers to begin with. *"Restraint, Lillith, is the key to mastering your urges,"* the deep voice of Dracula reminded her. *Yes, restraint. Restraint.*

"Y-your eyes!" Amy stammered in horror.

Lillith licked her lips with the surge of the woman's fear. "Yes." She breathed, closing her eyes, the words of Dracula repeating within her head. "My eyes."

"But what...how? *They're red!*"

"Yes," she said, stepping closer to her.

Amy seemed glued to the bedding. She gazed in fixed terror. "They're red."

As she moved, the letter fell from her fingers, her ring clanking against the floor, long forgotten—the smell of blood moved her so. "I did not want it to come to this, my dear. But I'm afraid you leave me no choice." She stopped just before the blue sheets and lifted a hand to the woman's face, though she could do no more before the voice said, *"Control is worth more than the consequences we suffer for our actions."*

"W-what are you?" Amy asked, her voice shaking, recoiling at Lillith's touch.

The cold startled her, Lillith knew, and she pulled away, taking deep breaths that did not need to be taken as she allowed the voice to tell her what must be done, to control...*control*...

She opened her eyes, vision normal, the woman clear now. The hunger still there, yet it did not control her senses so.

Turning her gaze to the ring and the letter on the floor, she moved for it, ignoring the woman's flinch at her step. She slid the ring onto her finger, a cold sigh escaping her as the metal clamps found her skin, stifled her blood. And, yes, soon all extraordinary senses dimmed considerably, the rush she desired nowhere to be found.

She faced Amy, who had let a tear leave an eye, and said seriously, quite prepared for the consequence of this level of control, "I will tell you what I am. That you value your life long enough to keep quiet is, however, another story."

✳

He had received word of their late-night rendezvous to the Vampire City. There were two courses of action he could take. He could either ambush them as they gathered in the City, or he could strike them where it hurt, at their manors, leaving them with nothing to return to.

Cup of tea clasped in hand, he looked up to find her staring down at him.

"May I?" she asked, her frazzled hair swung over a shoulder.

He gestured for her to take a seat. "Why have you come?"

"I'm worried about you, Thomas. Truth be told, this fascination with Xavier and his friends isn't healthy," she said through red lips. She removed his hand from the cup of tea and brought it toward her.

As she took a drawn-out sip, he replied, "Healthy or not, they are a threat to us, and I shall not sit by while they go about their plans to destroy all we have built."

She placed a slender hand on his arm. "Fine. Do what you must, but remember, when the dawn breaks, what you really are beneath all that fur and animalistic behavior." She lifted a finger to his chin and gazed into his eyes before answering for him, "A man."

He took her finger and kissed it. "Thank you, my love. But you must understand what the moon makes me."

"It can't be helped, can it?"

"No, it can't." He gazed out the café window as the sky grayed.

"Thomas?"

He could not help but notice how distant her voice sounded, although she sat right across from him. The only one that wanted to be next to him after seeing his true form, and for that, he loved her to no end.

"Do you want your tea?"

Thomas looked at it and frowned. "No, you can have it."

She grabbed it with a hunger he recognized in the humans as base desire, and when she brought it to her lips, he thought of how delicious she must taste. And the thoughts flooded back to him.

*No, she loves you, don't ruin it.*

With a small grin, he sat back and watched her. *All right, I won't.*

# Chapter Five

# LEAVING LONDON

The night air was welcoming, and it was in this that Damion found comfort. He'd removed his ring a few hours ago, his sword on his hip in its sheath. Dammath was tucked away from any mortal eyes with enough corpses to feed her for a month. He walked the empty streets of London, no longer Lord Damion Nicodemeus, but now First Seat to Lord of Vampires, whatever the title meant.

A figure loomed far ahead of him. He decided it had to have been one of the other members (no mortal man would dream of walking the streets with all the murders taking place at night, surely). He placed a hand on the hilt of his sword, only withdrawing it as his steps quickened, keeping the blade pointed toward the cobblestone. "Who walks?"

"Damion? It is I, Victor. Lillith is not far behind," the silver-haired Vampire said, stepping closer.

With those words, he placed his sword back in its sheath and ceased walking. He watched them draw near, the taller Vampire's sharp violet eyes appearing to glow. Victor's silver cloak swayed underneath the street lamps' lights, and once they were within quiet speaking distance, Damion extended a hand. "Your letter was quite the surprise, I must say."

"I was surprised myself when I received Dracula's letter," he responded, shaking it shortly. "It couldn't have come at a worse time."

Damion eyed Lillith, her long blonde locks unbound, her blue eyes deep and dark. "Princess, a pleasure to see you once again," he said, taking her hand and kissing it softly.

She smiled. "The pleasure is returned, my Lord," she said before turning to Victor, her brow furrowed in slight question. "Have you received word from Lord Xavier yet, General?"

Victor frowned. "No. I have not."

Damion let a derisive scoff leave him at the mention of the Vampire's name, unable to still himself.

"*Damion*," Victor warned.

"Yes, General?"

"You will get no argument from me that Xavier was wrong in what he did to you, what he's done to all of us, but for the sake of our world, please do not provoke him in any way."

"I have no intention of provoking my superior officer, my Lord. Although what he did cannot be forgiven, my mind is focused on the matter at hand. We are to travel to the City, are we not? Hear what the Elves have to say, and we are gone. That is my only concern at this moment."

"Very well, Damion."

Before Damion could utter another word, Lillith said, cautiously, "Lord Vonderheide, was there any mention of escorts in the letter Dracula sent?"

"Why do you ask?" Victor replied.

He saw at once what she meant.

Three men walked toward them from down the empty street. Victor pushed Lillith behind him, and Damion removed his sword without further thought.

The Vampires watched the men draw closer, and when they were only a few feet away, Victor decided to address them: "State your names and business."

The man in the middle stepped forward, his smile full of arrogance and power. The other men on either side of him were much more subdued: Neither looked up from the ground.

He was young, Damion saw, young and not at all aware of the dangers that came with such newfound power.

The man in the middle ran a comforting hand through his sandy, short hair, and addressed Lillith first, completely ignoring the other two, "She's the one. Princess of the Bloodsuckers. We want her."

Victor held out an arm, shielding Lillith. "Lore has told you to come for her, has he?"

The man's brown eyes darted from Lillith to Victor, and he seemed to acknowledge the silver-haired Vampire. "We're not to start with you, General Vonderheide. Just hand over the vixen and no one gets hurt." The sword in Damion's hand caught his attention then, his black eyes darkening even more.

He grinned; he wanted the young Lycan to provoke him.

However, the man turned his attention back to Lillith and said, "C'mon then, Miss Crane, we won't hurt you. We've our orders, of course."

Victor stepped toward the young Lycan. "Get away from here, else you won't live to see the sun rise."

He simply scoffed. "Is that a threat, Mister Vonderheide? Sorry, but we know you won't do a thing to us. It's the other 'un that we were told to be scared of, but since he isn't here, I find there's not much that can happen to us."

"Oh? How do you figure that?" the deep voice said from behind the young man.

Damion let a small snarl escape his lips, for there was Xavier, out of nowhere, out of nothing. Of course, he would move to handle the issue as none of them truly could—free of the consequences.

The other two men gazed at Xavier, their eyes wide, unable to speak, it seemed, underneath his gaze.

Damion half-thought the green eyes were glowing with pleasure. *Ugh.*

"Save yourselves," he said, and they ran off into the night, not bothering to look back. The one just before Xavier remained, and Damion thought it was boldness that caused him to turn and eye Xavier slowly.

"You were saying?" Xavier asked him, his voice smooth, calm against the pup's fresh, disgusting scent.

He stared upon the Vampire for a moment more.

To Damion, the Lycan looked quite flustered. And it seemed the thought of being killed by the four Vampires present propelled him into action, for he lifted a fist, attempting to strike Xavier, but he did not get very far before the Vampire's hand wrapped around his wrist.

"It's scum like you that gives me little hope for our young generation," Xavier said, releasing the Lycan's wrist, placing two hands upon his shoulders, turning him to face the members of the Order. "Show me there's still hope for our younger generation. Apologize to Miss Crane."

"No way. I ain't doing that," he protested.

Xavier squeezed the man's shoulders, and Damion heard the bones crack beneath the Vampire's grip.

"Ahh! All right, all right, I'll do it, I'll do it," the man said, and as blood began to trickle down from one of his nostrils, he eyed Lillith and mumbled, "Sorry."

"Good lad," Xavier said, patting the man's shoulders.

It was then that the young man looked up at Xavier and it seemed he no longer had it in him to feign fierceness. Instead, he asked timidly, "Will you let me go?"

Xavier smiled. "Of course not." With one swift movement, he grabbed the man's sandy-brown head and turned it sharply. The crack of his neck resonated throughout the dark street. He threw the limp body onto the ground and stepped over it, turning his attention to the Vampires who stood before him. "I apologize for the late arrival."

"Did you have to kill him?" Lillith asked.

Damion sheathed his sword underneath his cloak.

"I couldn't leave him alive, could I? He'd just become like all the others, growing older with revenge lined in his cold heart, wanting to claim my head so he might cavort about to the other beasts, 'Xavier's dead.' No, I've made far too many enemies in the Lycan Kingdom thus far. Adding another to my collection would be troublesome, wouldn't it?" he said.

Damion stifled a snarl of annoyance.

Lillith said, "Yes, I suppose it would."

"We should move before anymore of Lore's newly-transformed dogs are sent after us," Xavier said to he and Victor.

Damion blinked. "Don't you mean sent after *you*?"

"And what is that supposed to mean?"

"You are the Lord of Vampires. Figure it out," he spat, stepping up to meet the Vampire. With an angry growl, he pushed past him, his boots clicking loudly against cobblestone in the awkward silence that filled the street.

※

Thomas Montague smiled to himself. Everything was going according to plan. Although one newly transformed Lycan died during confrontation with Xavier, he'd heard, things were still moving along. He knew the poor boy had no chance against the Lord of Vampires, especially since the moon was not in the night sky. He'd just needed to know that Xavier and the Vampires were indeed heading back to the Vampire City, and the Lycan's death, although unfortunate, told him that they were.

He sank back into his large chair. "Wengor, they are heading to the Vampire City. Gather your best men and prepare to attack Lillith Crane's place of rest. You will strike in two nights' time."

The tall, stone-faced man tilted his head slightly at Thomas's words. "Two nights' time? We are ready now. We can attack tomorrow night—"

He lifted a tan hand to silence him. "No. We have more than enough time. I have received word from one of my men. It takes several days—at least three on horseback—to reach the Vampire City." He crossed one leg over the other before continuing. "We can take our time destroying their homes." He flicked the same hand. "Now go. And do not tell Lore of what it is I have told you to do."

The man did not budge. "Do not tell Lore? What, what are you—?"

"I have given you your order! Now go," he yelled, and Wengor's face dropped in absolute horror. He bowed low and proceeded from the room.

He watched him leave with little care, and then stood, stretching his arms once the door had closed.

The Duchess of Holden, Mara Montague, set down her cup of tea atop the dark wooden table beside her gray armchair and watched her husband with loving dark-gray eyes. She knew it pointless to ask, but felt she must in order to restrain him from becoming violent, as he often did when "business was booming.

"Darling, you will send your men to ambush the Vampires' homes one by one won't you?"

He turned to her, his brazen features now settling with the softness of her gaze. "Yes, my love. And we shall take our time. There is no need to rush."

She stood and walked across the large room toward him, sure to stare him straight in his dark brown eyes. "Tommy…may I, please…" she began, her voice trailing with clear hesitation.

His features hardened. "No." His jaw tensed as it often did whenever she dared ask. "I will have no wife of mine become a Creature of the Night. You will stay human, my love."

A sigh escaped her throat. "Then I won't be with you forever."

"Oh, but you will. I shall always roam the Earth looking for my sweet Mara. I shall never leave you—nor have another man claim you."

She laughed, a look of devilish surprise in her eyes, her arms wrapping around his waist. "Ever the possessor, Tommy dear."

He growled, and she felt it deep in her own chest. "I take pride in my possessions." And he kissed her, chasing away the breath that escaped her throat before their lips met.

✳

"I see them! They're coming! Prepare the horses!" an excited voice said to the others, who stood next to the four horses. Sure enough, four figures appeared on the horizon, and the men began preparing their superior officers' horses for the long journey.

It was a Vampire with long dirty blonde hair that stepped forward to greet the members of the Order.

"My Lords and Lady, it is an honor to serve you on your journey," she said, kneeling before them.

"Elisa? Is that you?" Damion said, stepping forward.

"First Seat Damion Nicodemeus, it is I, Elisa Stewart of the Second Army's Battalion," she said, nodding. Then she added, with obvious glee, "I've been promoted: Second Captain."

His face sparked with astonishment. "Really? Promoted? That's wonderful, Elisa! It's been far too long."

"Indeed it has," she said, arriving to her feet. "Lord Damion... I-I'm terribly sorry about Lady Black."

The members of the Order, who had been busy settling onto

their horses, looked up at the mention of Eleanor's name; every eye watched Damion's face.

His gaze dropped. "I believe we are all sorry about her death."

Elisa nodded, her gaze moving from the dark Vampire to eye the others, issuing commands as she did so. "All right. We need two men up above, three on the ground. I'll stay on foot. Patterson you're with me. We need one more, who's up to it?"

A young-looking Vampire with a sharp nose and long chin agreed to go on foot, and said to the remaining uniformed Vampires, "You two, then. Fly low. Give word of anything up ahead. We're to protect the Order, understand?"

They nodded simultaneously and proceeded into the air, above the four horses and the Vampires settled atop them.

Elisa stationed herself in front of Xavier's horse and the other two uniformed soldiers took their positions: one stood alongside Lillith Crane, the other, Damion. Once all were in place, she gave the signal to move. The Vampires above pressed forth a few miles ahead of those that walked the ground. The horses trotted along the faint dirt path, for the City streets were now gone, and they entered the woods south of London.

No one said a word, and it seemed like their journey would be a very silent one, until one in the air shouted down, "Second Cap'n, we've got trouble."

"What is it?" she shouted back, stopping short.

The Vampire glided back down to the ground, his face showing the worry he felt. "We've got beasts. And a lot of them."

Elisa turned her gaze to the clear sky in search of a moon that wasn't there. "They can't be Lycans." She turned her attention back to the worried soldier before her, the horses neighed, but she ignored them. "What'd they look like, then?"

The Vampire glanced through the trees as if expecting a "beast" to come bounding through. "They're huge...white as snow...oddest eyes, green like emeralds," he said. "They weren't—"

"There when he left," she headed off, "yes, I know. Damn." She rubbed her face. This was the last thing they needed. She held up a gloved hand to the other Vampires, feeling their gazes upon her. "I'm going up ahead. Stay here." She did not wait to hear their approval. She marched toward the trees and peered around one. It was just as the Vampire said:

Several huge white beasts walked in circles, apparently guarding the road in case any Creatures—or humans—were to lose their way. They were the gatekeepers, the things that appeared when a journey was void of purpose. They held no name; they merely were.

Elisa turned back to the Vampires, addressing only Xavier, "My Lord, there are...gatekeepers up ahead. What would you like us to do?"

His eyes narrowed in apparent question. "Gatekeepers, you say?" His horse padded the ground beneath them. "I see no reason not to push on. Our cause is a noble one, is it not?"

She nodded and caught the roll of Damion's eyes. *Indeed.* She turned her back to him, despite the chill of his glare, addressing the soldier, "Fly ahead. Land quietly. You know how those beasts can be. Hold your head high and tell them that you are there to clear the way for the Vampire Xavier Delacroix. Nothing more. You understand, David?"

He saluted her before flying over the tree.

It was all she could do to keep from meeting Xavier's stern gaze. But Damion, he looked downright dour, his dark skin gleaming in the scant starlight between the leaves above, his brow furrowed deep in dark thought. *Probably Eleanor, shame.*

The Dark World suffered from her loss, this she had felt plainly in the Vampire City. Indeed, it was even rumored that Dracula himself had grown strange. Well, more so than usual, less vocal with his commands, his meetings.

Of course, she had not seen this for herself, she had merely heard it, namely through her captain.

The ring beneath her glove pulsed, and her adamant gaze to all the Vampires before her seemed to darken as the thought consumed her: *What she wouldn't give to be able to walk in the sun without her powers at their weakest, the urge for blood repressed.*

"Captain Stewart," David said, stepping through the trees toward them, "they've agreed to let us pass."

She blinked, snapping from her thoughts. "Of course. Good job." And she turned to the Vampires atop their horses. "We're moving ahead!"

She moved to stand near Xavier's horse once more, and as one, they moved past the large, white, fur-clad beasts. These beasts said nothing to them, they only eyed Xavier, who sat on his white horse, staring straight ahead, careful not to glance any of them in their emerald eyes.

Once the gatekeepers were far behind, and only in fading memory, did their voices return, yet only to relay passing commands and errant warnings to others. And soon, the dark of the night still pressing around them, complete silence fell, only the sound of the horses' hooves padding the ground protruded through the trees.

The silence continued until Elisa heard the faint sound of footsteps, but from where they came, she could not know: it seemed to echo on around them endlessly.

Her eyes narrowed in the dark and she held up a hand to stop them, calling up to the Vampires above, "I hear something. Can you see what it is?"

"We don't see anything, captain," they responded.

She drew her sword, calling to the other soldiers, "Get your weapons ready."

They unsheathed their own swords, the footsteps growing much louder, seemingly endless against the branches of low hanging trees, the dark about them.

A man stepped through the trees in front of them, holding long-fingered hands up in prepared surrender. "I come in peace."

Elisa lifted her sword, the tip pointed toward him.

The two Vampires who once hovered above them now stood on the ground, their swords drawn as well.

Elisa eyed the newcomer seriously. "State your business, Creature."

"Like I said, I come in peace." His voice was a little too high-pitched for his face, she thought. His eyes were dark, but the exact nature of his person could not be discerned, no matter how long she stared. He could have been a Vampire, a Lycan, even, but one could not be sure with the reports of strange Creatures around the entrance of the Vampire City.

She did not move her sword from his chest. "I said state your business."

He dropped his hands to his sides. "I am Aciel. I have come," he eyed the Vampire atop the white horse, "for Xavier Delacroix. I believe I have some news that might be of interest to him."

## Chapter Six

# THE RETURN

All eyes turned to Xavier. He slid off his horse and stepped toward the man, ignoring Elisa's rushed warnings. "You have some news that is of interest to me?"

A smile formed on Aciel's thin lips. "My, my," he began, looking him up and down, "you *are* just as the rumors say. Terrifying, hm?"

"Watch it!" Elisa snarled.

Xavier raised a hand to calm her. "It's quite all right, captain. He's simply a...Vampire like us." Although he said this, his tongue lingered on the word. He was unsure himself of what it was that stood before him. "Is this all you wished to say to me, Aciel?"

The dark-haired man stepped closer to Xavier, and the rustling of leaves suggested even more men were walking through the trees, surrounding them. Aciel lifted a finger and poked his chest, his voice a whisper. "We have come to relay news regarding a certain Vampire. An Eleanor Black. You are aware of her, are you not?"

His mind drifted from thoughts of the human woman, from raging thoughts of Damion's words, and to the one thing that had bothered him most. "Eleanor?" He didn't understand what this strange man was getting at. Eleanor was dead, so what was this?

The thin smile widened. "Ah. So you are aware of the missus then. Well, she wishes to...speak with *you*, and only *you*." His dark eyes darted from Vampire to Vampire through the trees. "No one else."

Xavier stepped back and looked around.

More men emerged from the trees, their eyes watching the Vampires atop their horses closely, ignoring the uniformed soldiers.

"And if I refuse to go with you?" he asked, turning to watch the man once more, knowing full well that he could be lying, and greatly so.

He lifted his arms and snapped his fingers. Two Lycans appeared behind him, their rows and rows of long teeth dripping with saliva.

He tensed, as did the other Vampires, but no one made a sound. The longer they stared at the two Lycans, the more they realized neither would hurt them: Both remained quite passive, merely prodding the dirt ground with massive paws.

"How are they able to transform? There is no moon," Xavier said, a growl escaping his throat.

Aciel turned to the beasts and called them forward with a wave of his long-fingered hands. Xavier thought they cut through the air with a fluidity he could not catch: one moment they were being waved, the next the Lycans stepped forward, lifting off their front paws, bent double, their large heads brushing the branches and leaves of the trees that surrounded them. But still, they remained passive. Neither moved as Aciel turned from them and eyed Xavier once more. "Everything will be explained with time," he said, "now if you will please..." He gestured for Xavier to walk with him back the way it appeared he had come.

His mind racing, he gave one involuntary glance toward Damion, who was staring at the Lycans with terse control. He said to Elisa, "Miss Stewart, watch over the others please."

"My Lord, you won't actually go anywhere with him, will you?" she whispered before looking around. "And his men."

But he was already walking alongside one of the Lycans, Aciel stepping in the middle of the two beasts.

Elisa's cries continued to haunt his retreating back, but he did not turn. His mind reeled with the blinding hope of seeing Eleanor again. *Was she truly still alive?*

They walked straight for what seemed hours. He said, "How much farther?" growing all the more curious as to why in the world he agreed to come with this mysterious man.

Aciel said nothing, but continued walking, the Lycans grunting indifferently. They turned to the left, Xavier following close behind.

Eventually, they came to a wall, jagged and brown, and Xavier swore he heard the sound of rushing water nearby, although he did not remember ever hearing a stream or river when he'd ventured to the Vampire City those many times before. Thinking that he'd been led far away from the others, he tensed as Aciel extended a hand to the wall, pressing his palm against it.

He watched as the wall tore a hole in itself, and before long, the spot where Aciel's palm had touched was now a dark tunnel in which nothing but resolute darkness seemed to linger.

"After you, my Lord," he said.

He spared him a look, hesitating before stepping into the entrance of the tunnel, barely able to see the large bodies of the Lycans as they pressed on in front of him. He turned his head back to Aciel, who was now examining the dirt underneath his fingernails.

A sigh escaped the man's throat. "You are going, aren't you? Eleanor is waiting, Vampire."

"This isn't some trick? She's really there?" Xavier asked, his hopes somehow waning. *How was it possible that she was alive?*

A frustrated sound left him and he pushed the Vampire out of the way. "If you don't believe me, I'll go on ahead," and he stepped through the entrance, his tattered robes dissolving into darkness as well.

Xavier pulled himself through the tunnel with a quick swear underneath his breath. He stumbled over rocks, not being able to see his hand in front of him, let alone the man that walked ahead of him. He could, however, hear the man's footsteps, and reminded himself that each step he took was supposedly bringing him closer to Eleanor.

At last, a faint light up ahead caught his eye, and he could make out the silhouette of Aciel. He neared the light, the tunnel opening up into a small cave. The two Lycans rested up against the damp, gray walls, a small fire burning brightly in the center.

Aciel stepped behind the fire. He spread his arms wide, as if showing him something of grand importance. "Congratulations, Xavier."

Xavier looked around the small cave in confusion. "I beg your pardon?"

The thin smile appeared upon Aciel's face once more. "Congratulations," he said again, "you've come this far and you've yet to question Eleanor's presence. Can you not sense her?"

Xavier tuned into the scents around him, but they all were various earthly objects: dirt, fire, water. Xavier realized he couldn't sense any other Vampire's presence. So that would mean... "What are you?"

Aciel lifted his hands and clapped them together in mock applause. "Bravo. Bravo. *Bravo!* You've finally realized." His dark eyes narrowed. "But what *have* you realized, Xavier? That I am no mere man, nor Vampire, nor Lycan? You see, I am all of those. A Vampire when it suits me." He stepped toward the sleeping Lycans, "A Lycan when I feel like it." He turned to the Vampire once more, smiling his thin smile, "and a man when convenient."

Xavier stepped away not daring to believe what he said. "How is that possible?"

"How is what possible? That I am able to suppress the blood of all three Creatures when I choose to do so? It's quite easy." He expressed a look of discomfort. "Of course, that is...once you can get past the blinding pain of the first initial transformation. After that, however, it's quite," his smile returned, "liberating."

He took another step backwards, trying his best to locate the familiar scent of a Vampire's blood, the disgusting smell of Lycan fur, or the weak aura of a human man. None of these arrived to him at all. "What does this have to do with me? With Eleanor?"

"We've arrived at the question haven't we? Hm. Let's see. It has everything to do with you and Eleanor, for you see, Xavier, she was the one that introduced me to this life, as it were. And she wants you to join us." Aciel's tongue slithered through his lips as he talked.

He forced the sight of Eleanor, weak and hungry, out of his mind. "If she's alive, wouldn't she have come to me herself?"

Aciel walked idly through the small cave, turning when he reached a wall, letting his legs linger before stepping off the ground again. "I'll admit," he sighed, "and this is between you and me, of course—she's a bit theatrical. Wants to show you how powerful she's become. Wants it to be...special." He gave Xavier a most-significant look.

"Wh—?"

"C'mon then, she's this way," he said, ignoring Xavier's puzzled expression, pushing past him, proceeding to walk down the long tunnel once more.

Xavier glanced at the sleeping Lycans, mind rattled with what he'd just been told, when he realized he'd never seen the beasts so submissive before. Usually, they thrashed about, unable to quell their lust to bring death and decay wherever they roamed. It was quite the contrast, seeing them resting there, their fur illuminated by the flames, almost seeming incapable of death.

One of the Lycans lifted its head and yawned, revealing many rows of sharp fangs.

*Almost.* Which begged the question: How did Aciel control them? Were they able to turn from Lycan to Vampire or human at will as well?

One of the Lycans raised its head and opened its eyes, staring at him, and he held the gaze, half-expecting the beast to charge, but the Lycan put its head back down and resumed its sleep.

Xavier let out a flustered sigh, unsure of what was going on at all, and gazed down the tunnel, in which he could see nothing. He remembered that night and how the Lycan burst through her. And yet, here was a man telling him now that she somehow survived. That she was alive—if changed. But how changed? Did she really possess this new power Aciel spoke of?

Yes, he knew the risk of this being a trap was great, but it was a chance he was willing to take if it meant that Eleanor still lived.

⁎

The wind picked up when he stepped onto soft earth.

Aciel leaned against a nearby tree. "Having second thoughts, my Lord?" the man asked, never looking down from the dark sky.

"No," Xavier said, his interest in who this man was growing with each passing second.

"Interesting," he quipped, finally bringing his gaze toward Xavier. "Are you really so eager to see her?"

Xavier said, "Take me to her. I will hold it to you to keep your word."

"Oh? And if I don't? I see you have no weapons."

Xavier cursed himself for leaving the Ascalon with his horse, as he'd assumed he'd have no need for it. "Where is she?"

Aciel returned his eyes to the darkly swirling sky. "She's here now."

Indeed, the wind picked up even more, and Xavier felt the alarm that came along with it. A restless, dangerous feeling that sunk deep into his core and refused to leave. And then...

*"Xavier..."*

He blinked, unsure of what he'd heard. It had been a whisper, a barely-spoken word for his ears alone, although Aciel now stood at attention near his tree. He felt his blood boil the more the wind danced around him, blowing his hair and clothes away from and against his body, and it was then that what he was, a Vampire, seemed so incredibly insignificant against *this*.

He listened hard as the wind howled past his ears, the voice sounding again, a bit louder than before, but still submerged beneath the screaming wind:

*"Xavier Delacroix..."*

And with this utterance of his name, the wind seemed to dance a few feet before him through the trees and he stared as a woman clad in a tattered dark cloak appeared there. Her hair was long and wavy; much longer than it was the last night he'd seen her. It danced in the wind, away from her face, which was slightly longer, he saw, but still held the elegant beauty he knew all too well. She stared straight at him, her eyes no longer a calming brown, but instead, a dark and murderous color he couldn't name.

"Xavier," she said.

He found his throat clogged with a heavy pressure. *She* was *alive*. "Eleanor..." he choked, unsure of what she would do, what more she would say, why she had come—.

She moved lithely, taking her time in walking toward him, shedding her tattered cloak to reveal a worn blouse, ruffled at the collar and cuffs. The many necklaces still remained and fell over her collarbones, dipping onto her chest, and as she stopped near a tree much closer to him, she smiled.

"So you came," she said. "I really didn't think you would."

He stared, quite aware he was able to smell her scent. The familiar fragrance of lilac and fresh blood. "You didn't think I would?" His voice unable to rise higher than a whisper. *How was it possible that she still lived?*

"No, to be truthful, I didn't think you would come. To hear that I was still alive, well, I wasn't sure how you would react, or if at all."

He stared at her in disbelief, only aware that he had to keep talking to her. He felt if he didn't, she would disappear from him, and he'd be left with her voice lingering in his ears. "Eleanor," he began, "how is this possible. How are you—"

"Alive?" Her laugh was still as contagious as it ever was. "There are many things that were hidden from us in the Order."

He didn't know why he didn't notice it before. Her eyes were changing color, going from dark gray to dark blue. All dark colors. "What kind of things were hidden from us Eleanor?"

"Many things," she whispered, shaking her head as though sad, but it was feigned. The way her eyes narrowed upon him, he gathered she didn't feel sad about any of it. "Many, many things. Things that Dracula," her tongue lingered on the letters as she said them, "didn't want us to know."

"What...are you?"

A smile much like the one Aciel still wore found its way onto her lips. "Has he not told you?" she said, gesturing a hand toward the man who now stared at them with much more interest than before.

Xavier's eyes moved from her to him and back. "He's told me interesting tales. I...don't know what to make of it, however."

"Then," Eleanor said, walking closer to him, "allow me to show you the truth of these tales." She pressed herself against him, standing on tiptoe to reach his ear, in which she whispered, "*Vampire.*"

His blood boiled in his veins. He felt her grow colder, watching in bewilderment as her skin glowed white against the strange dark. He could not speak when she wrapped her arms around his neck and leaned away from him, smiling, her fangs clearly visible against her bottom lip.

"Remind you of old times?" she said, sparking within him a desire to kiss her.

The feel of her, the coldness of her skin, the beauty of her, indeed, brought back the memories he had all but suppressed upon her death. And for the first time, he cursed himself for letting her go. For letting Damion take her. "It does," he agreed.

He eyed her lips, feeling her gaze upon him as she leaned in closer, stopping just before his own. And then her voice blew into him, a settling wind, but also tainted, dangerous, the words they carried housing a truth he could not begin to fathom.

"Xavier, we are looking for more...more Vampires...more Lycans...more humans who wish to join us. But, of course, what interests me...is...you."

And their lips met at last.

He was thrilled to find hers were as he remembered, dreamed about, soft and cold against his own. Her tongue slithered through his lips, the pleasure causing his blood to surge within his veins. *She was alive*. For if nothing else could have convinced him the ghost he stared at, held, had truly returned, it was this.

She pulled away from him at last, much to his dismay, and breathed. It was quite possibly the coldest breath he'd ever felt against his skin. She said nothing as she released her grip from his neck and stepped away, her eyes never leaving his own.

He held the gaze, unable to look away, not desiring to look away, to lose her stare upon him.

She licked her lips, her fangs returning to normal teeth. "You have just seen one of my many faces, Xavier. As a Vampire, I was colder than cold, but I could resist the urge to taste you, another Vampire, no matter...how delicious your blood may be. You see, Xavier, I have taken what is owed to us. To you, to me," she outstretched her arms, "to all Dark Creatures, as it were."

Xavier braced himself, wondering, indeed, if she were to show him her other form, that of an overgrown dog.

She shook her head. "Ah, no need to prepare yourself for a fight. I will not show you all of my faces tonight, my love. I have come to ask you to join us." She pointed a hand at him, sure to say, as Aciel watched carefully, "Xavier Delacroix, Lord of Vampires, you will do wonderfully at my side as King of the Elite Creatures."

He blinked, certain she had regained a more human form. Her skin was no longer pale, it held the glow of life, but her eyes were still shifting in their color. Her blood drifted to his nose, but it was no longer the blood of a Vampire, it smelled quite ordinary, quite delicious.

"Xavier?" she said, pulling him from his thoughts.

He stared at her, seeing her outstretched hand, her waiting gaze, and remembered her proposition. "I-I can't possibly, Eleanor."

"Oh, I see," she said, and he noticed how quickly her vibrant features changed. She became livid. "These are one of those matters that require your time. Very well. I will give you...two months to come to a decision." She walked away, snapping her fingers for Aciel to join her. Then she said, "I should warn you, Xavier, if you decide not to join us, I won't be held responsible for what happens to you and your little friends."

*What?*

"Eleanor!" he cried, his voice finding its freedom at the sight of her back. "Eleanor, wait! What about the others? Everyone needs to see you, know you're alive. *Eleanor!*"

She continued walking further into the trees, though he could hear her voice from where he stood, it faded with every step she took, "Don't tell them a thing, Xavier. I only want you to know of me..."

Her voice trailed. His mind raced with frantic question. Had she truly just threatened him? And what was she? Knowing he could not let her out of his sight, he said the first thing that came to mind: "Eleanor! *Eleanor!* What about Damion?! He is distraught by your death—!"

91

He heard her footsteps halt, and then she was flying toward him, sending his words to die with her wild appearance. She was now a swirl of hair and fangs, her red eyes brilliant in the night, the strange darkness surrounding her seemingly keeping her in the air. She looked as though she emerged from within it. "*What* did you say?" Her voice was terribly cold, horrible in its sound.

It was then that he knew she was greatly changed indeed. He could not help but feel, as he stared at her, that she wasn't a Vampire, whatever her appearance would have him believe.

And with a low voice, he opened his mouth and said, "Damion... he isn't coping well with the news of your death. You...you must see him—!"

"*Damion is not of my concern*!" she shouted, her voice sending his to disappear within his throat.

*What happened to you?* he thought as she continued, landing on the cold ground, her red eyes never leaving his, a faint hint of tenderness within that gaze. "I don't care for Vampires that cannot withstand my existence. You recall the feeling of Dracula in your presence? The feverish, blood-boiling feeling he gives others of his own kind?"

He nodded, his voice long gone with the wind that brought Eleanor back to him.

"You are able to withstand it because our blood is the same—the blood of an Elite. Before the Vampire City, there were the select few who held the blood of pure."

He found he could do nothing but stare.

A smile lifted her lips, though it did not reach her eyes, nor did it quell the strange darkness that lingered around her. "He hasn't told you, yet...it is a shame the Vampire continues to keep his secrets from you. It pains me to have to do this, of course, but it is the only way I can weed out the hopeless from the strong."

"What do you mean?"

She stepped up to him and placed a cold hand on his face, his eyes unable to close against that touch. It was not comforting in the least. A strange sensation filled him the more he stared, a great feeling that he should not be near her at all...

"You will know what I mean, my love...but you must join us before the truth can be revealed." Her lips found his once more, his eyes closing with the feeling of them.

It was not until he felt the cold air against them that he opened his eyes, finding himself quite alone in the wood, her tattered cloak several feet from him on the ground.

He walked toward it, mind blank with the dream he just had, for none of it could be real. As he stooped to pick it up, the voice filled his mind, and the swirl of unease reached him all at once:

*"Remember, two months."*

# Chapter Seven

# AN UNSETTLING ENCOUNTER

He stepped through the trees, her tattered cloak in hand. He stumbled mostly, finding it hard to walk against the strange darkness that filled the sky.

*She was alive.*

*But how? How did she survive the Lycan bursting from within her? Was that even* her *that night? What did it all mean? And what,* he asked himself for the tenth time since she'd gone in a cold, brazen wind, *was she*?

He stopped next to an old tree with a dark, twisted trunk and allowed his thoughts to tie themselves together. She wanted him, that much was clear; wanted him and needed him it seemed, for she was trying to create a new breed, wasn't she? A new Creature. And in this Dark World, did one not need a strong leader to rise through the ranks as King? And what better King to have by her side than the illustrious Xavier Delacroix.

It seemed she grew more cunning with power. Her ability to transform from human to Vampire in mere seconds was astounding. It shouldn't have been possible. He had felt her Vampire form was the same—the same Creature he had come to adore and grown to love in the Order. But that wasn't the case. His thoughts dashed to that night, many years ago, in his living room with Darien. How the Vampire had spoken about her, about Dracula...

*"...The darkness that befalls the hearts of those who wish to gain more..."*

But just what were these dark and dangerous secrets? Did Eleanor indeed use them? Was she the result of a painful transformation as Aciel had told him?

Xavier placed a hand on the tree. He stared at the dark of the wood with bleary eyes. Everything he'd been shown, been told to believe, was it all a lie? Recalling what Damion had told him just a night before, his unease grew: *"I knew you weren't like us. The damn special bloody breed. Next in line to rule us all."*

"Special breed," he whispered. A terrible loneliness falling over him.

Christian was to be inducted per his training with Damion Nicodemeus, it was known for a long time that this was what Dracula had desired...but what would happen to he, Xavier, should the Great Vampire go along with the induction? Wouldn't he, Xavier, have to be pushed out? Possibly placed as the Great Vampire's successor?

He shook his head with the thought. No. Dracula would remain King. He had to. There was no question of that. And he, Xavier, would remain at his side, ever dutiful, ever resilient.

*"...Our blood is the same; the blood of an Elite..."*

Eleanor mentioned it, Damion mentioned it. The blood of an Elite. What did they know that he didn't?

The unsettling feeling continued to fill his mind as he moved through trees and darkness, and it was not until he heard the familiar whine of a horse that he turned his attention away from Eleanor, Dracula....

"We can't wait for him much longer, Elisa. We've got to push ahead." And there was no mistaking the annoyed voice of Damion against the strange night.

"I'm sorry, sir, but we are not leaving without him," she countered, her voice determined and upset.

Xavier heard Damion's voice utter what sounded like, "Bloody Xavier."

He rested against a tree. His blood ran cold—colder than what was normal for him, at least. Yes, he admitted, closing his eyes, feeling his body drain clear of energy, his confrontation with Eleanor took out much more of him then he would have liked to think.

It was not long at all before Elisa spotted him through the trees and started for him. "My Lord! Trent, Patterson, fetch me a canteen," she ordered, still staring upon him. "My Lord, are you all right? What happened? What—?" But Patterson returned with the canteen and she took it quickly, popping open the lid and forcing it up to his lips.

"Blood. Drink," she said, her dark eyes never leaving his face.

He felt the opening press against his lips, the blood cold as he drank. He had only swallowed several gulps before Victor, Damion, and Lillith made their way over, almost shoving the Second Captain of the Second Army out of the way.

Lillith spoke first, her face dressed with worry, "Are you all right? What happened?"

He wiped his brow. "Nothing."

"Nothing?" Victor took the liberty to speak now. "Bloody hell, Xavier, you look like you just took on the whole of Lore's army. What's happened? It was that Aciel wasn't it? What'd he do?"

Xavier stood up straight, for the blood seemed to be working. "Aciel...wanted to speak with me. Nothing important." He marched through the three Vampires and swung a leg over his horse, placing the tattered cloak in his saddlebag.

"Hold it," Damion said, much to Xavier's dismay. His brown eyes were leveled at the tattered cloak. "Where'd that cloak come from?"

Xavier stopped moving and turned his attention to the observant Vampire, feeling the gaze of all turn to the cloak in hand. His mind racing, he cleared his throat, saying the first thing that came to mind: "Aciel must've dropped it. We got into a bit of a fight..."

Damion's brow furrowed as he stepped closer to the white horse. "How can that be, my Lord, when Aciel was not wearing a cloak?"

*Of course he would notice,* Xavier thought. But he knew he could not tell them who Aciel took him to. They could not know until he, himself, knew just what was going on.

"Perhaps your eyes were unclear for the man was clearly wearing this cloak around his shoulders when he came for me."

All eyes were now upon Damion, who held his gaze to Xavier's. It seemed he caught the remarkable difference that they'd held just moments ago...almost weak...powerless. Yet now, they were pressing, crushing with power that most certainly wasn't there before.

Damion bit his tongue just the same. "Forgive me, my Lord."

"You are forgiven," he said, glad he dodged that arrow. "Let us ride. We must reach the City as soon as possible." And he dug the heels of his boots into the sides of the horse and galloped off through the woods.

※

Damion stared after him, his mind thick with the strangeness Xavier exuded.

He did not move, even as the others resumed their positions, Victor and Lillith scrambling atop their horses, the uniformed soldiers taking their places next to animal and night sky. But even as they proceeded to follow in Xavier's wake, the voice said,

"Damion?"

"Yes, Victor?"

"Why are you not on your horse? We are leaving."

97

Damion whistled for his horse and it trotted over to him. He pulled himself on top of it, but still, he did not follow.

Victor was now ahead, gaining speed to catch up to Lillith's gray horse.

The uniformed soldier assigned to Damion stood next to his horse, looking up at him with anxiousness. "My Lord?"

"Do go on ahead, I'll catch up shortly."

"But my Lord—"

"That's an order."

The soldier stiffened and nodded once before running off after the others.

Now alone, Damion allowed his thoughts to consume him, free from Xavier's pressing gaze.

Xavier. When he showed up, his hand was tightly clutched around the old cloak, although this was something no one—except Damion—noticed. He'd appeared crushed...completely drained of all his energy. Surely, no Vampire like that Aciel would be able to do such a thing to him. And the length of time he was gone... It was well over an hour at least before they saw him again.

Of course, it was never determined that Aciel was indeed a Vampire. Damion could not feel anything from him. He would have to have been a normal man. But a normal man wanting to have a word with Xavier? Something definitely wasn't right, Damion decided.

He lifted the reins and brought them down, sending his horse after the others, determined to move forward with his plan.

✳

"Duke of Holden, your Duchess grows most displeased by your lack of entertainment in the bed," she said.

"Is it my lack of entertainment that displeases my wife, or is it the simple fact that I will not turn her?"

She slid from the bed, stepping up to him against the morning light from the large window he stood before. "Perhaps, my Lord, it is a bit of both."

"Oh?" Thomas said, turning at last. His eyes were darker than usual, the vast circles beneath them telling the truth he would not admit: He was exhausted. "Well seeing as how I have no intention of turning you into a ravenous, bloodthirsty Creature, I suppose we must settle on the aforementioned 'entertainment.'"

The small laugh escaped her throat, but she could not deny the sadness in his voice. She planted a small kiss atop his lips. "Is it truly so bad?" she asked, pulling away.

"Is what so bad?" he asked, the darkness of his gaze momentarily dispersing with her touch.

"You know what I mean...being a Lycan. Is it truly so horrible?"

He cleared his throat. "You have seen me—"

"Yes, and here I stand, my love," she said. "I'll admit when you showed up on my doorstep covered in sweat and raving of marriage, I did have my doubts about your sanity, but once all was explained..." and she placed a warm hand atop his cheek, "I did fall madly in love with you and the beast within."

He pulled from her, much to her dismay, his gaze upon the floor. "Grateful though I am that you said yes, my love, I was ravenous, still. Once in a saner frame of mind, I saw what I had done. What I had asked of you. It is a guilt that has stayed with me to this day."

She stepped to him, placing a finger atop on his lips, the nostalgic gleam in his eyes most apparent. She knew he felt guilty for showing up on her doorstep, delirious and exhausted, yet the conversation that had ensued had been one of the most interesting of her entire life. It took a while, yes, but she soon fell for Thomas Montague, and quite hard at that. "Shush. The past is in the past. Let it rest there while we focus on the present and the future. You may not wish to turn me now, but you will someday, of that I can assure you." And when he looked up in bemusement, she went on, "I cannot be your Lycan Queen if I am not *one* of you. And I will be better able to help you against Xavier, the other Vampires if I am what you are."

He looked affronted. "Mara, you cannot be serious—you have seen what the moon makes me! All that violence, I cannot truly control it, whatever father will have you believe! Oh, yes, I know you have spoken with him—I am no fool. But he doesn't understand what I've gained in making you my wife—my humanity."

She could say nothing, his words true to her ears: Lore had shown himself to her only once in her time as Thomas's wife, and he'd told her that she would die, that she was a simple human to get involved with his heir. She hadn't listened, of course—set in her love as she was for the man—but Lore's angry, animalistic gaze could not be dispelled from behind her lids whenever she closed her eyes.

Refusing to be scared away, for if she were to be, she would have been when Thomas first showed himself to her, she hugged herself against the sudden cold—the absence of his skin against hers—and watched him step briskly to the door.

Yet before he pushed down on the handle, he turned to her and said, "I make no promises in this mad World of ours, my love, but you will not be turned by my bite, long as I live. I'd rather die before I see it happen." And he stepped through the door, closing it softly behind him.

Mara turned her gaze to the bright sun, the birds that flew past, and did her best to keep at bay the Lycan's black gaze as she closed her eyes, allowing a small tear to trail its way down her cheek.

※

The afternoon sun beamed high above their heads, and Damion slid off his horse, allowing his mind to wander. They had stopped near a small stream after having ridden the entire morning, because

Xavier desired to reach the City, and quickly. The question that would return to Damion the more he thought on it, was *why*.

He knew the Vampire was no more thrilled about seeing bloody Elves than any of them—so why the sudden desire to reach the City? Or was it to reach Dracula?

He recalled the sight of the Vampire once returned from that strange excursion with that Aciel Creature. How completely strange for Xavier Delacroix to look so utterly...defeated.

*So what*, he thought as he began to drag a dagger's blade across the bark of a nearby tree, *what happened to Xavier? What did he see?*

"Damion?" the careful voice called. He looked up to see the tall frame of Victor Vonderheide walking toward him, but before the Vampire could get very far he offered an answer:

"I'm fine, Victor."

"No, you're not," he said. "You're damaging your best blade, for one."

Damion stopped mid-slice as he realized this was true. "All right," he said at last, settling the dagger back within its scabbard along his chest. "I'm not fine, nor will I ever be. Eleanor's death isn't easy to overcome. And Xavier—"

He stopped short upon seeing the Vampire who still sat atop his horse, looking all the more disheveled.

Victor followed his gaze before turning back to watch him. "You still feel ill toward him?"

"How can one not," he said, his voice low, "this 'mysterious' image is really getting on my nerves. He won't tell us what happened to Eleanor, and when he came back from that little trip with that... that...man, he was clearly drained of all energy. *Weakened*, even. There's something else he's not telling us, and I don't intend to sit here while he holds all these secrets in. We're his bloody comrades. We deserve to know what happened...what's happening to our own..." Yet he could not find the words to go on. It wasn't fair, and it would never be, he knew. The reason Xavier was free to get away with things, the reason he was able to decide freely what he would do, what he wouldn't, was because he was Dracula's bloody pet.

"I have been thinking," Victor said at last as several birds landed on the tree above them, "like it or not he is our superior officer, Damion. Perhaps it would be best to go along with his secrecy—at least for now, just until we speak to Dracula about this matter. Besides, Xavier's hurting from Eleanor's death as well. In my opinion, you're being rather selfish—"

"*I loved her!*" he yelled, sending the birds above flying away from their nests, and the immediate silence that drifted through the small camp was awkward at best. Aware of the eyes that now pressed into his back, he gave the Vampire a sharp turn and headed into the woods, mind brimming with anger. *The nerve of the Vampire. Why, it was as if he, Damion, did not even exist! After all he'd done to secure his place—still he was looked over. Still he was pushed aside! Xavier given all the glory, all the attention, Eleanor Black...*

He marched blindly through the trees, thoughts turning to her, thoughts clamoring to her, her brown eyes so filled with pain...pain, but also change...

Yes, something had happened to her before her death, he was sure of it something had destroyed her before Xavier had supposedly seen her die...

He continued walking, not seeing the blue sky churn with a strange wind, not seeing the clouds disperse from above. He did not see the multitude of shadows dancing through the trees, not until he heard the voice that finally caused him to stop in his tracks:

"*Damion...*"

He looked up from the ground and knew the world to cease. He could hear nothing. Not the chirp of birds or the rush of wind, nothing, indeed, but unearthly silence.

*Eleanor?* For he knew that voice was hers. He knew she had

spoken it, but whether it was from memory or not, he could not be sure.

"*Damion...*" the air whispered again, though he could not feel it.

He had just placed a hand on the sword at his side before the strange shadows dispersed, and there before him in front of a large tree, whose branches stretched toward the sun, stood a single dark figure, hood placed atop its head, keeping its face from being seen.

"Who are you?" he called, beginning to step toward it, not sure if it was a Vampire or Lycan. He moved to pull the sword from its sheath when the figure raised a slender hand toward him—and he froze.

His voice died in his throat. Whatever questions he desired to ask now gone, for he knew who this was. Knew it, but it could not be true. Even as he stared at her, a familiar hand placed in front of her as though beckoning, he found her frame to tremble, to shake, and he could not keep her in view...

Then there was darkness, nothingness, and he found himself staring at the leaves of trees, the branches they clung to spreading out above him: Claws keeping him still.

"Damion!"

The sound was distant, as if it came from mountains far away, yet still he would not pull his gaze from her. She was there, just near the tree, the darkness that settled around her never moving. He thought it might be growing stronger with his own uncertainty. He could barely pull together a thought before he heard the other voice again and the impossible muffled sound of thundering hooves against cold ground.

"Damn!"

A rush of wind reached him along the ground. A strong hand gripped his shoulder, and she disappeared: he blinked and she was gone. But it had been her—it *had* been her!

"What's gotten into you?" Victor asked, his hand digging into Damion's shoulder.

The Vampire was scared, Damion knew. Had he seen her as well?

But as he turned his gaze from the tree, he realized the Vampire did not know who had stood there. His violet eyes remained on him, dark with confusion.

He tried to open his mouth, find the words that clawed through his mind now, but much to his surprise, he found he could not speak.

"What happened, Damion?"

With one last glance toward the large tree, he felt his voice return to him. There was nothing he could do except grasp the Vampire's cloak, for his hands shook far too much, but he had to make him see, make him realize who just left their vision. It was with a low, frantic voice, that Damion finally said it, giving life to the strange figure he'd seen, the truth of it reaching his dead heart with the words: "It was Eleanor…she's *alive*... Eleanor's alive, Victor."

# Chapter Eight

# THE FIRST ATTACK

The door swung open and the young Vampire, followed by several others, entered the room and kneeled, their heads down, not daring to look up at the Vampire that sat in his chair against the wall, a red book in hand.

"Your Majesty, we have just received word, the Elves of Etria are nearing the City," the first Vampire to enter the room said.

"Are they now?" the smooth voice asked. "Show them the utmost hospitality when they reach the City, will you? Have the grand welcoming ceremony as they walk through the streets."

"Yes, right away, your Majesty." Then they stood, heads still down, and scurried out of the room, the door closing behind them.

He turned to the book in-hand once the door closed, eyeing the crimson cover. He had no interest in resuming his reading now that things were finally starting to get interesting again. Rising from his seat, he strode to the long table and set the book down upon it, mind lost with thoughts of his Vampires.

He turned from the book and stared across the room toward the desk he'd just left, eyeing the number of papers upon it, the requests from other Creatures...the demands from those bravest...and still he could only think of what Xavier had questioned only weeks ago.

Eleanor Black. The Vampire had wanted to know of her. Had wanted to know who Alexandria Stone was, as well, but he couldn't be told. Not yet, anyway. There were things that he, himself, was not so sure about things that had to be prepared for.

But it was true other Creatures were beginning to see things in the World.... Were beginning to question. And questions, he decided, moving toward the door, were just as dangerous as the answers being sought. It would not be wise to have things questioned.

He grabbed the door handle and paused, for he suddenly remembered the book upon the table. It would be rather troublesome if an Elf or Vampire managed to get their hands on it; what with the content of the book, one could not be too careful that someone might take it too far, but then, he thought, as he lifted it from the smooth wood, perhaps one Vampire already had.

Making his way to the door once more, book clasped tightly in hand, he squared his shoulders, ready to attend to the preparations that had to be made. For of course, in the Vampire City, one never lacked something to do—not even Dracula.

✳

The horse moved quickly, the ground ripping up beneath its hooves as Xavier pressed on, edging it ever forward against the sun's sinking glow.

His hands had stopped shaking some time ago, and he gripped the reins tighter, the smell of lilac and blood reaching his nose as the flap of the satchel jumped against the horse's side.

*Eleanor.* He pressed on faster, the brown of trees blurring as he kept his gaze straight ahead, the Vampire soldier at his horse's side running swiftly. He could barely question why on Earth it was that

Dracula had soldiers accompany them, let alone had them ride on horses when they were very capable of reaching the City on their own, when he heard disturbed thoughts that were not his own ripping through all senses:

"...*She can't have been real...*"

He pulled on the reins, turning the horse around, much to the surprise of everyone else. The other beasts began to whinny and shake their long heads, doubling into each other. He paid no mind to the gazes of the other Vampires as they pulled on their own horses to settle them, and only stopped guiding his horse through the trees when it reached the black one, the dark Vampire atop it looking quite lost in thought.

"Damion," he called, causing the Vampire to look up.

The brown eyes widened for a moment before a veil of coldness replaced the surprise. "My Lord?" he asked, a hint of unease in his voice.

"Your thoughts. Do you care to explain them?"

"Explain them, my Lord?"

The snarl escaped him as the impatience rose. He had always known Damion Nicodemeus was a touch strange, seedy in his air, and spared a place in the Order if only for his skill with sword. Other than that, Xavier hardly cared for the Vampire. "Do not feign ignorance, Nicodemeus. What were you thinking? Who is the woman you were referring to?"

Damion's expression remained blank, but there was a twitch in the dark Vampire's mouth that allowed a flare of dread to rise to his dead heart. *Could he know?* "The human woman, my Lord," Damion said at last, "I merely thought on her."

"You need to question whether or not she is real?"

"I can smell nothing of her blood while she remains asleep."

"Really?" The anticipation died. If he had only *thought* on the strange woman, then there was nothing to fear. *But what would I have to fear if he* did *see Eleanor?* He turned his thoughts away from her with the implication of the Vampire's words. "You cannot smell her blood?"

Damion shook his head.

"Be sure to relay this news to Dracula when we see him, Damion." Xavier turned the horse around once more, catching the eyes of Victor and Lillith upon him. He could not help but feel their gazes cautious, though he could not understand why. "Something wrong?" he asked as he guided his horse slowly past them.

"Just why you would stop the line to ask Damion a simple question," Victor said, a pale hand running along his brown horse's mane, as though to comfort it.

Xavier said, "A feeling overtook me—I had to clarify something. Let's move on." And with a snap of his wrists, the horse took off beneath him, leaving behind the others with their confusion.

*It hadn't been about her*, he thought, relief filling him. *Damion had not seen her. He still thought her dead. That was best.*

For he knew if Damion had seen her, had known she existed, then he would know that she had shown herself to he, Xavier, and there would be no end to the madness he would face, for as far as insecurities went, Xavier knew Damion was filled with them.

*But she had found comfort in him all the same...*

The dread increased and he let the cold blood he'd drunk settle in his veins, washing away any trace of her, of the kiss they shared, and continued on toward the City.

※

The day faded with the sight of the moon and darkness fell over them. Xavier was the first to spot the familiar black, rusted gates as they approached the entrance of the long, damp tunnel.

"Hold!" the commanding voice said, Elisa holding up a fist.

They all skidded to a stop before the high gates, Xavier sliding off his horse, narrowing his eyes upon her small frame. She wasn't keeping her gaze on the gates as she signaled with a gloved hand to the Vampires that had flown above the trees, her other placed atop the handle of her sword.

She was prepared for trouble, he realized, had been the moment they'd left London. But why?

The two Vampires that had flown above landed on the ground without a sound, their wind sending his hair and cloak to billow up around him. Both Vampires walked toward the gates, one snapping the lock that bound the gate together in chains once they reached it, and the other pulled them open slowly to reveal the long tunnel wherein darkness stretched on forever.

As the others left their horses, Xavier watched the soldiers bow low, Elisa included, stepping aside to allow them entry. He narrowed his eyes at the protocol being shown—he hardly felt it necessary. But as he reached the hard stone floor of the tunnel, he realized they remained behind, and, indeed, as he looked over the heads of Lillith and Damion as they followed, he saw the soldiers enter the tunnel, facing outward, swords drawn.

*Awful trouble to go through to protect us, Dracula,* he thought as they began to walk through the darkness, torches springing to life as they moved, *but from what?*

 No one said a word.

Elisa stepped swiftly to walk at his side, the end of the tunnel appearing through the gloom.

Xavier reached out a hand to push the golden gates at the end of the tunnel open. They gave way to a staircase shrouded in darkness. The torches' light could not reach it.

Elisa pushed past him and pulled a torch from the wall. "Trent, Azel, Patterson, grab torches."

The three Vampires moved without hesitation, leaving three

empty mounts upon the walls next to them. Without a word to anyone else, she began to descend, torch high in her hand. As she moved, Xavier noticed it shook.

He followed her, feeling her fear, knowing the others trailed behind him. Dancing orange light illuminated his back as they descended.

They walked for what seemed ages, but then Elisa hit the last step and held the torch up to light the beginning of another tunnel.

They continued their walk, Xavier's green eyes narrowing through the dark, looking for any sign of the large double doors that would mean they had reached the Vampire City.

For a long while, he walked, only able to see the back of Elisa's head, the light of the torch held high above it, until...yes, the glint of golden handles.

Elisa swept her torch across the doors, illuminating the words embedded within the wood:

*The Vampire City*
*Protection, Preservation, and Peace. Always.*

He felt a wave of nostalgia fall upon him and he remembered the last time the Order was together like this: to speak with Dracula regarding the rings that would be used to allow every Vampire to exist atop the surface, excluding Xavier. He remembered the irony in his presence not really being needed for that meeting.

"Ready?" Elisa asked the Vampires.

They all nodded as one, and Elisa moved at once, grabbing a golden handle to turn it, pushing one of the large doors open, allowing a blinding white light to issue forth into the long tunnel.

Xavier could see the familiar small path that lay ahead of them, soldiers of the First Army standing at attention on either side of the dark road that led to the small white building, which blocked any view of the rest of the Vampire City. And it was here Xavier saw the Vampire who stood at attention in the building's open doorway.

He walked down the small path while the others followed suit behind him, the soldiers on either side of the path lifted their swords above their heads in honor. A frown grew on his lips as he drew ever closer to the tall Vampire in the doorway, very aware that the last time he was here, no such attention was shown to him, for he'd arrived fully cloaked, hood drawn over his head, and moved as though a ghost, desiring not to draw any attention to himself, the grief of Eleanor's death weighing heavily upon his heart.

So why all the pomp and circumstance now?

Reaching the Vampire at last, he extended a hand toward him and said, "Such an elaborate welcome. The Elves have arrived, have they?"

The First Captain of the First Army took Xavier's hand, gripping it tight, shaking it before narrowing his fierce dark-blue eyes, while saying in a deep voice, "Yes, they arrived shortly before you." He then turned to the Vampires who strode behind him, and exclaimed, "Elisa! It was you who was ordered to watch over them? Westley wouldn't tell me who had been sent. I should've known when your squad didn't show up to the meetings."

"Hello to you, too, Dragor," she said, starting toward him, a fist over her heart.

Victor smiled. "Hello, Dragor."

"Victor! It's been far too long. And the Princess—ever the beauty."

Damion stepped forward then. "Dragor."

Dragor's blue eyes appeared to darken and his handsome face grew cold. "Damion."

Xavier cleared his throat. The two Vampires had shared a growing dislike for each other ever since Damion was inducted into the Order leaving Dragor to resume his position as First Captain of the First

Army. It was known far and wide that Dragor was overlooked because Damion, who had been aiming for Xavier's position, singlehandedly pushed back the oncoming Elves of Etria who'd somehow managed to infiltrate the Vampire City a few years ago.

"We should press on," Xavier said, stepping into the building, eager to get to Dracula.

"Wait," Dragor said, placing a strong hand on his shoulder as the others walked past into the building, "Xavier, what's this I hear about Eleanor?"

Unease rolled in his gut as he eyed the Vampire seriously. *Was it possible he knew Eleanor still lived?* "What have you heard?" he asked, trying his best to feign vague interest.

Dragor waited until the remaining soldiers headed into the building behind the Second Army. "Between good friends, what really happened that night? News spread like wildfire that you have yet to tell anyone—including Dracula—what exactly happened."

"I never knew you to be one to pay attention to gossip, Dragor."

"Gossip? This isn't mere gossip, Xavier. There is talk of Vampires on the surface seeing Eleanor. Of course, when they return here, they are in a state of pure shock and to get anything from them proves to be ultimately useless. They babble incoherently. I had the impression she died that night when you were sent to go see her. But if Vampires claim to have seen her, I don't see how that is so—"

"How many claim to have seen her?"

Dragor narrowed his blue eyes. "It would be at least ten since yesterday."

"Ten?!" Xavier repeated, attempting to keep his voice low yet not at all succeeding.

"*Ten*, and it's rather odd. I've meant to ask Dracula about it, but he's been terribly busy as of late. He has a lot of meetings with the Council. And these bloody Elves all of a sudden. If you ask me, dragging you lot here just to speak with them was a waste of your time."

"I couldn't agree more," Xavier said. He caught sight of Lillith, who stood inside the building lined with marble tiles, clearly at ill ease, a group of First Army Soldiers surrounding her. She caught his eye and gave him a look of desperation.

Xavier turned back to Dragor. "If you'll excuse me, we must hurry and get to Dracula, can't keep those damned Elves waiting." He gave his friend a nod before heading into the building. As he did so, every Vampire in the great hall turned to stare at him. They had already gotten their fill of Victor, Damion, and Lillith, and now desired to eye the Lord of Vampires as best they could. It would, perhaps, be the only time they'd ever be able to eye him so closely again.

Silence followed as Xavier stepped toward Lillith, the Vampires that surrounded her stepping away quickly with his approach, their eyes glued to his cold expression. "Let's hurry," he said to Lillith, pulling her by the arm as he caught the glares of Victor and Damion, who broke out of their conversation, watching him in confusion.

Xavier jerked his head toward the door on the other side of the building where two paralyzed soldiers stood, waiting for his approach. Moving at his gesture, Victor and Damion followed behind them as they all moved toward two soldiers, their eyes wide with awe at Xavier.

"If you please," Xavier hissed, his mind swimming with visions of Eleanor, the words Dragor relayed.

The soldiers scrambled for the door, bumping heads as they both looked for the handle, and after some useless fumbling and arguing about "who got the handle first," they finally relented and one of them opened the door while mumbling a quick, "Welcome back, my Lords and Lady."

Xavier pushed through the door first, his mind now burning with thoughts of Eleanor and the Vampires she was appearing to. Ten so far, ten Vampires so far, and what the hell was that supposed to mean for him?

He barely noticed the tall man walking toward him along the dark street, oblivious to the attention he seemed to be drawing from other Vampires nearby.

Behind him, several even taller men with pointed ears and piercing eyes glared at him as they approached.

He was only fully aware of this when the man in front spoke, his voice like ice covering his ears, "We've much to discuss, Delacroix, and as you can see," he held out two sweeping arms, gesturing to the men behind him, "the Elves of Etria grow most impatient with your late arrival."

✻

A throaty laugh escaped him as he eyed the bright moon above. "Men," he roared, "leave no stone unturned—leave no human alive!"

The large beasts howled their obedience and charged toward the mansion, breaking down the doors and snapping frightened horses in two.

Thomas smiled as Wengor ran past, a full-fledged beast in its purest form. With outstretched arms to the screams that filled the air, he laughed again. "Destroy it! Destroy it all! Those damn bloodsuckers will have *nothing* to return to!"

Mara watched her husband command the Lycans from afar, and although he held his human form, he was still terrifying to watch. His handsome face was distorted by the pleasure of death. He was a working force in the Lycan world, that much she knew. It was clear that he was known far and wide, for some of the beasts there weren't even under his usual command, but they paid heed to his word all the same.

She remained seated within the black carriage, her hands continuously smoothing the slight wrinkles on her long gray skirt as the anticipation, the desire to be as he was, consumed her once more.

She watched his eyes light up with terrible power, absolute joy as the screams from the mansion flew all around them, and all at once her thoughts returned to the very first time she glimpsed the Lycan known as Thomas Montague—and the man beneath.

Born into a world of privilege, Mara Locke knew nothing of Lycans, Vampires, or Dark Creatures—she was not even aware that any other "world" except her own existed. Until the very night her mother came to her bedroom door, speaking of a duke from a place called Holden who had come—and indeed, was at the very manor door—to speak to her about marriage.

They had both been taken aback by the sudden proposal—for neither of them had ever heard of any Duke of Holden. They swept to the doors, arm in arm, and when they arrived in the main hall of the then-flourishing Locke estate, Mara was flustered to see a handsome man standing there, quite alone, his shirt undone by the third button, absolutely covered in sweat.

He reeked of dirt, something she'd found questionable even as she removed herself from her mother and stepped cautiously toward him.

He looked tired. And it was then she realized he was in the throes of death, for he was so faintly aware of their presence, it seemed, but when she pointed this out to him, he merely shook his handsome head, sending sweat through the air to land upon their well-to-do clothes.

This made a look of sheer incredulity sweep across dear Mrs. Locke's face, but Mara was certainly intrigued. For what man—what duke, indeed—had arrived at her door at such a late hour? And to speak of marriage? Whatever state they appeared to be in?

Sweeping aside her mother's horrified countenance, Mara allowed the man entrance into their home, guiding him, steadily, toward the sitting room where only the most important of guests were taken.

He had almost fallen into the cream sofa, paying no mind to the fact that he was releasing his sweat and dirt upon its once clean state—for they had just gotten it that very day.

Ignoring this, for she had hated the sofa, whatever her mother believed, Mara, instead stared intently at the man as she took her seat beside him on the couch, trying to discern what was wrong.

For it seemed a great many things were wrong with this duke.

He did not speak, and it was then that she wondered if he indeed had told her mother that he desired marriage—for it was a wonder he desired anything more than a good bath and bed.

"Duke," she started, not sure what to say.

He'd lifted a dirty hand through the air as though asking her, nay, *demanding* her to cease her tongue. To which she blinked, bolstered. For how dare he arrive at her home, not saying a word, but merely breathing heavily as though he waited for death to greet him?

It was then that any outburst she could have dared let rise to her sharp tongue fell immediately back into the pit of her gut, for he did speak at last. "I...have come, Miss Locke, to ask for your hand in... marriage."

His voice was so tired, so rasped with pain, but it was the sheer stench that caused Mara to rise from the seat and step away from him.

"Marriage?" she'd spat. "Excuse me, my Lord, but I don't know you at all, yet you wish to speak of marriage?!"

"Aye," he whispered, his deep brown eyes closing as he seemed to drift off into a deep sleep right there on the couch.

She'd let out a grunt of frustration and had stormed over to him, demanding he rise from his slumber—though she kept herself far from his breathing—pressing both hands into his chest as to rouse him. Yet it was not until she'd slapped him clear across his sweat-laden face that she'd felt how hot he was—and how strong he was. For he'd reached up with remarkable speed (she'd hardly seen it happen), and gripped her wrist with alarming strength, her gasp could hardly leave her throat before he'd risen from the chair and pushed her back against a wall.

Fear filled her veins. Besides the strength that kept her glued to the wall, the heat, the anger that radiated off him, was remarkable, tangible—deadly.

"My Lord!" she'd breathed in sheer terror.

"Forgive me, human," he'd said, causing her heart to run cold with the word, "but I must take a wife for my own. I must prove to my father that I can love, that I am no monster."

"What—?" she'd begun, but her throat clenched tight with the gaze of desperation on his face.

*Who...no,* what *was he?* For she'd seen then, in those eyes so deep and dark, that he'd held a terrible burden—one he desperately desired to rip from his being.

"What are you?" she breathed then, feeling her chest heave with fear, yes, but curiosity even more so.

He'd released her at that question, but he did not step from her, and he'd said, "I...I am not human—just please, say yes. Please be my wife. Our kind is known for forcing themselves on others, I wish... I wanted to give you the choice—the choice I never had."

At the time, she'd hardly considered being slammed against a wall and forced into making a choice as profound as that freedom of will, but in time, with more questions and understanding, Mara Locke found herself falling hard for the man and Lycan known as Thomas Montague.

And it was the power he had shown that night, and the power he showed now, that made her wish to be as he...

"Excuse me, Duchess?" a strange voice whispered, lifting her from her memories.

Sweeping black hair that partly covered deep black eyes, the man that stared at her from the other side of the carriage window showed himself. He stared at her imploringly.

"Yes?" she asked him, assuming that he must have been a Lycan her husband had missed.

He opened the carriage door although he hadn't asked, and lifted himself into it, sure to close the door behind him. "Forgive me, but I have always wanted to meet you. There has been talk throughout the packs of your beauty, but I have never believed... Your husband is a lucky man."

She knew better than to blush—this was hardly the first time another commented on her beauty. "Thank you," she said, eyes narrowing upon the man. "What is your name?"

"That is not important right now," he said. "What is important is that you come with me, missus. Your husband is going to try to kill you tonight." He cast a glance through the open window, causing Mara to do the same, despite whatever his words had done to her, and she saw Thomas begin to walk over to the carriage, his eyes still lined with fire, his face hardened with business, anger.

*Was it at all possible the man's words rang with truth?*

She turned to eye the man beside her, confusion gripping her senses, and she managed to whisper, "What? Who are you?"

With no answer, he kicked the carriage door open and grabbed her arm. "You must come with me, Duchess. You are not safe here."

"Who are you?!" she said again, attempting at once to have her arm back, yet his grip was far stronger, and he pulled her out of the carriage with one simple lurch, causing her to cry out in pain.

She stumbled along the ground as he pulled her, hearing the distant yell canvas her ears, causing her blood to boil with hope, for it could not be true that Thomas planned to kill her. Why would he?

"Hey! Hey! What are you doing?!"

And with these words the man stopped walking and dropped Mara's arm, yet as she stared upon him she saw that he had no intention of letting her run back to her husband. Her mind dizzied with confusion. What was going on? She knew Thomas was getting closer. She could feel his heat, heightened by the number of Lycans that stormed the Vampire's manor, the more he neared the carriage. And it was in that painful moment that she realized this man wanted Thomas to draw near.

*He's using me as bait*, she realized in horror. *But for what?*

She stepped away from the man, back towards the carriage, back towards the large street where several Lycans lingered in full form. She ran once clear of the grass where the man remained, black eyes delirious, she ran toward Thomas, who was now running toward her, fear deep in his eyes.

"Mara!" he said, holding her tight once they reached each other, yet his eyes never left the strange man who remained on the grass within the long field that stretched on and on for miles. "What's going on? Who is he?"

"I don't know," she breathed, fear gripping tight her heart even though she remained in his arms. *Why would he say that? Why would that man say that Thomas wanted to kill me? Was it only to use me as bait? And if it was, for what?* "He said... He said you were going to kill me tonight, Thomas."

These words brought his gaze from the man abruptly and he stared deep into her gray eyes, his own marred with incredulity. "What?" he whispered. "He said what?"

"That you want to kill me. Then he grabbed me and told me he was going to take me to safety—"

He tore from her, her words lost in the thundering fire of the mansion behind her. She watched him sprint toward the man, the heat that radiated off his body something like fire –, for she could still feel it where she remained.

She watched in alarm as he reached the man at last and landed a smooth punch along his jaw, a punch the man received with some difficulty, for he stumbled backwards but soon recovered and threw his own punch toward Thomas.

And in the panic, the rage, the death all about them, Mara could not feel the man that stepped up behind her and wrapped a strong arm around her waist before throwing her up, over a shoulder. A scream of bewilderment left her lips, drowned entirely by the howls of Lycans, the snarls of beasts, the laughter of the man who held her.

She felt the man run across the cobblestone road, saw herself leaving the street, pass the carriage, and run straight past a full-grown Lycan fighting the strange man from before.

"Thomas," she managed to breathe, her voice just above a strained whisper.

Yet it was with this whisper that the Lycan looked up mid-strike and faltered at once, the strange man upon the ground moving quickly with the beast's hesitation, rising to his feet, a dark smile breaking his face in two.

As they ventured farther and farther away, Mara felt an impossible heaviness creep over her, a sweeping desire to sleep, and indeed, even the man's footsteps upon the grass below them seemed to be a lullaby, a simple soft *thud thud thud* upon which to find soothing comfort...

But even as her eyes began to close, and the vision of Thomas and the strange man began to blur, she was sure she saw the man burst into a Lycan as her beloved husband shrank back into a man, sitting upon the grass, absolutely stunned.

# Chapter Nine

# CALLING OF VOID

The fireplace bright and warming the room shone a flickering light over the faces of the people who stared at each other, no one saying a word.

Those closest to the fire rubbed long hands together before it, warming themselves as they cast weary glances towards the stoic-looking Vampires across the room who sat around a large wooden table near the tall arching windows.

"Well," the Vampire said, staring at the Elves coldly, "let us begin this little meeting at last, shall we?"

The Elves clicked their tongues together, an odd barrage of noise issuing from before the fire as they turned from it and eyed the Vampire behind his desk in interest.

The Vampires started, their bored expressions dissolving with the Elves' movement.

With a swift hand, Dracula ran his fingers over the paper presented to him previously by the Elves and eyed the words:

### The Elves of Etria
### Request for Freedom

He looked up at them. "Is this not tiring?"

"Alinneis refuses to give up, as you can see, Dracula. Which is why we are constantly sent here." He looked around the room with slight disgust. "And we will continue to be sent here to regain our freedom, until you see it through. Alinneis' orders, I'm afraid," a charming Elf with a higher nose than his brothers said coldly.

"Of course," Dracula said stepping from behind the desk, his long white hair swaying along his back. He leaned against the dark wood, his light brown eyes scanning the room, a small smile upon his lips as he eyed the Vampires within their chairs.

Turning his gaze back toward the Elves, he said, "I'm afraid our dear friend Alinneis will never regain the freedom he so desperately seeks, as I have told you all time and time again. Really, these 'surprise' visits are getting rather routine, aren't they? You all come in with your papers," he gestured to the paper behind him, "and your requests, and you are sent home empty-handed." He eyed the Elves once more and recalled this being the twentieth time he'd had to entertain them. "Time and time again."

Tittering angrily amongst themselves, the Elves turned to each other to discuss what must be done, surely, when what appeared to be the Head Elf, a very tall, red-eyed Elf with a malicious sneer, lifted a long white hand to silence his comrades and stepped forward.

"With all due respect," although his voice was the last thing one would call respectful, "Dracula, this has gone on for far too long, do you not think? Alinneis is growing angrier and angrier and these trips to this godforsaken City are wearing on my nerves. I grow tired of having to venture here, and I'm quite sure you grow tired of having to look at us. Do you not think that all of this would be solved once and for all," and his tongue clicked against the roof of his mouth, "if you would just grant us our freedom and we could resume our lives, never having to lay eyes on each other again?"

Dracula glared at the Elf as the words reached his ears. "I'm afraid, Swile," he said, "your words, as usual, will not change my mind about this matter. Your freedom should've been thought about when your men were ambushing my City." He threw their request at the Elf's feet. "It's taken us three years to rebuild our army to what it was ever since you greedy Elves decided to attack us—for a reason, to this day, I still know not—and until I feel like it, you Elves shall never get your damned freedom."

Victor and Lillith shifted in their seats, causing two Elves to eye them with disdain, yet Swile remained focused upon the only other standing Vampire in the room besides Xavier. His voice was quiet as he spoke, yet still alive with seething anger. "Alinneis has asked for forgiveness for that rather foolish matter that has, as you have pointed out, taken place several years ago. Is it his fault that you would not accept this forgiveness? Or is it the fault of you, dear Dracula?

"We have learned from our mistakes and we have groveled at your feet for what any King would require as the amount of time needed to repent. Are you not a 'King,' Dracula? Are you not selfless?"

Without looking at him, he spoke tersely, his voice commanding, "You will be grateful that I have allowed you Elves to continue your rather useless existence. Stripped of your powers, you are nothing, but men—men with unusually large ears. I could have ordered your deaths right then and there, but no, back then, with the deaths of my men on your shoulders, it would not be the clear course of action for any 'King'," he sneered, "so I sent you all away to live out your days away from other Creatures. Can you not be happy with that?"

Swile's tongue clicked against the roof of his mouth once more, the anger building in his red eyes. He made no attempt to keep his voice low, as he was clearly past the point, "Had that *Vampure*," he pointed to Damion, who looked as if his mind was elsewhere, "not held us back, we would have surely taken this underground City! Your armies were no match for us then—!"

"But they are a match for you now, Swile. Is it you who forgets that my Vampire," and he gestured to Damion who eyed Swile with red eyes, "took all of your men on singlehandedly. An attempt both foolish," Damion looked up at him then, "but all the same, acknowledged by me as an act of grand loyalty to his City, and his own kind, and for that he has been greatly rewarded, and rightfully so."

Dracula cast a careful smile to Damion before turning back to eye the Elf. "Now that we have spoken regarding your requests, Elves, let us turn to the real reason I have allowed your visit." He turned to the rest of his Vampires. "And the reason I have called you all here."

Lillith spoke up then, her voice quiet against his own, "Were we not sent here to discuss the Elves, my Lord?"

Dracula studied her. "And we just have, of course, my dear Miss Crane."

"But it is rather apparent you did not need us for your little chat with the Elves, Dracula," Xavier said, stepping away from the bookshelf he stood near.

His eyes darkened for a second; something was clouding those green eyes so.... "That is quite so, Xavier," he whispered before turning back to all in the room, sure to keep their gazes upon him. "The real reason I have allowed the Elves' visit, and I have called the Order here, is because we need to discuss where the Elves' loyalties lie regarding the Lycans and their growing influence in the Dark World."

"Our loyalties?" Swile spoke up now, outrage sending him to take several steps toward Dracula.

"Your loyalties. Where do you stand?" he asked, glaring into the Creature's dark eyes, a bit exasperated that he had to repeat himself to a being whose ears were the largest of all.

"We should not be asked to take sides! We have come only to speak of our freedom, not to speak of those beasts!"

"No, I'm afraid you have misunderstood the reason I have allowed you here. It was never to speak of your freedom, dear Swile, for my decision regarding that matter was made quite some time ago. No, I have allowed you here to speak about this very matter—a matter most important to all Creatures—as I'm sure you all know."

Their faces dropped to that of defeat, and there was no doubt in Dracula's mind that they were recalling the gruesome incidents regarding the Centaurs and how several of them had been carried off by a few Lycans not at all long ago.

Swile seemed to relent against the dancing flame, for his long face drained of all emotion. "Very well, Dracula, what is it that you want from us?"

He smiled, glad that things were finally going smoothly. "I want your word that you will fight, if need be. If the Lycans were to ever... attack us, you would come to our aid."

"F-fight?! We have no weapons—you saw to it that they were taken from us, Dracula. I don't see how this is fair."

"*Fair?* You speak of fairness now, do you? Perhaps you should bite your tongue, for that damned attack you Elves pulled on my City several years ago was the last thing one would think to call 'fair.' Think of it as a debt you Elves owe to me," he said, refusing to allow the damned Elves to deny him that small favor.

"B–but our weapons... The Lycans are such ravenous Creatures, surely, surely you cannot ask of us to fight."

"Oh, but I can. I can command it if you will not oblige. And yes, I can command you, Swile. Unbeknownst to you, the Council held several meetings regarding the attack, and we have come to the agreement that I can take full reign over your armies whenever need be. But, moving on," he said, before Swile could contest the word of a Council he'd never been to, let alone heard of, "your powers cannot ever be returned to you, but your weapons, those you are free to use if the time ever arises for battle. At which time, I expect the Etrian Order to be there, front and center, ready to defend their lives for our sake."

"Preposterous!" the Elf half-screamed. "We will not do such a thing! Dracula, it is clear you have allowed your position in the Dark World to fill up your head with false...false commands that will not be followed!"

"Think what you will, Elf, but I am quite sure when you return to your cave and tell Alinneis of what I have just told you, he will have no protests or qualms to listening to what the Council says... what *I* say, for that matter. A bit daft, your leader is, but nothing this important will escape his mind, of that I can assure you. He will agree to fight, and that, you bloody Elf, is that," Dracula said, glaring at the Elf, his gaze black.

He seemed to shrivel into a small ball, drawing his gaze away. He said nothing as he snatched up the paper at his feet and stormed out of the room, the other Elves at his heels.

Watching them go, Dracula let a snarl escape his lips, his thoughts turning to how much those Elves had cost him. *How dare they desire their freedom after all they had done to the City...the other Vampires...* Once the door slammed shut, he turned to his Vampires and eyed them all, none of them reaching his curious gaze, for it was clear something was bothering his Vampires, it was clear something was incredibly wrong...but first, "Damion, you have taken Christian under your wing, how is that fairing?"

Clearing his throat and standing at the sudden question he was posed with, he said, "My Lord, he was attacked by a Lycan the same night he came to stay with me."

"Was he now?" he asked cast a quick look to Xavier, eyes narrowing at the blank expression upon the Vampire's face. It was with a frown that he turned back to the dark Vampire. "And where were you when he was being attacked?"

Damion did not meet his gaze. "I was feeding, my Lord. I had just received word of Eleanor's death, and I was in a bad way. I had to clear my mind. I went out and when I returned, with blood for Christian, of course, he was there at the fire, staring thoughtfully into it. I figured he needed to feed as well, so I gave him some blood of the human I apprehended that night and I left Christian alone."

"Continue," he commanded.

Dracula listened as Damion told his story of sensing something wrong when he returned to the fireplace to find it empty. He'd smelled fresh blood not far away and mounted his Dragon—at this Dracula's eyes narrowed—and he went off in search of Christian. When he'd finally found him, Lillith was present, and Christian was up against a tree, his arm ripped off, his spine cracked.

"Interesting," was all he'd said when Damion finished.

"Interesting, my Lord?"

He turned to Lillith, ignoring the Vampire's question for the time being, curious as to her reasoning for being there as well. "Lillith, what were you doing near the woods in which no one ventures?"

She jumped out of her seat and whispered, "I too smelled the blood and rushed forth to see what was happening. When I arrived, I saw Lore preparing to strike Christian once more, and that was when I shot him an arrow."

His eyebrows rose. "Your arrow? So you were carrying your bow, were you? And you had to have been flying above in order to see what was taking place, weren't you?"

Lillith said nothing.

"Honestly. Damion, was it necessary to bring your damned Dragon into the equation? I'm sure you could have flown there just as quickly and taken care of the beast. Lillith, you were flying, your bow in hand, grateful as I am that you shot Lore before any serious damage could befall Christian, it is still a violation of the Vampire Code—which you so rightfully know by heart. What if a human or even more Lycans got wind of you?" he asked seriously.

"I'm sorry," Lillith whispered as Damion bowed his apology.

He sighed, turning from them. "Never the matter. This one event shall be overlooked because it was to ensure the safety of Christian," he said, pausing as it came to him. "Why was Christian attacked?"

"There was a human woman lying on the ground when we arrived on the scene. We think Christian was trying to save her," Damion said.

Dracula's eyes darted from Vampire to Vampire with these words. "A human woman?" he repeated, his mind racing with possibility. "Did you not take her to your home, Nicodemeus?"

"I did," he said.

"She is safe? In your care?"

"Yes."

"And you noticed how different she is from other humans? How the inability to bite her consumes you?" Dracula asked, eyeing the dark Vampire.

Damion shifted his footing, all eyes upon him. "Yes, my Lord," he said at last, "the inability to bite her...was there."

A sigh escaped him as his thoughts tripled. He calmed himself as soon as they spiraled; he let a thoughtful whisper leave his lips. "Really?" He turned to Xavier, eyeing the cold-looking Vampire with dying interest. He knew what the answer to his question would be before he asked it, yet, he knew, it did not hurt to try. "Have you seen the woman?"

Xavier turned to Victor for what seemed to be reassurance. Victor took to staring adamantly upon the fire that burned behind Dracula.

"No, Dracula. I have yet to see this human woman," Xavier said after closing his eyes, as though greatly pained, before turning back to face Dracula.

"It is important, as you know, that you do," he told him seriously, watching as the Vampire nodded his understanding.

Moving once he could no longer bear to eye Xavier anymore, he stepped toward the fireplace, over which several books rested on shelves. With a pale hand, he allowed his fingers to canvas the spines of books, tall and short as they rested upon their shelves, until his finger rested upon a small blue book sandwiched in between books as tall as the shelf, itself. And with a swift sweep of his hand, he removed the blue book from its place, dusting off its plain cover with lazy sweeps of his palm before placing the book on his cluttered desk.

"We must move ahead," he said, not gazing upon them at all, but glaring at the book for moments more. He lifted his gaze to theirs at last. "I want you all to listen carefully, as what I have to tell you is vital to our existence, moreover, the existence to all Dark Creatures."

They all stared at him with vast interest.

He said, "My most recent visit to the Council of Creatures has made it painfully clear we are up against a greater enemy. No mere Lycan or rogue Vampire can do what we have seen. No, I fear we are up against a mixed breed of Creature. A hybrid of sorts.

"We, the Council and I, have deliberated on these attacks and... appearances plaguing the woods and caves of Dark Creatures, big and small. Several Creatures and Vampires have claimed to see these mysterious Creatures. We're not sure what they are as of yet, but according to other Vampires, they resemble our kind. Although our Vampires cannot feel any presence from them. Their intentions are not clear, for our Vampires have not gone missing or dead, they simply return to the City, if only slightly crazed and completely mute."

"Mute?" Victor asked.

"Mute," Dracula repeated. "Apparently, they lose all ability to think, to reason. It has caused considerable concern amongst the Vampires, and most recently the Centaurs..." His voice trailed away, and he was quiet for a time, reflecting on the nasty sight of a few Centaurs that had been attacked by Lycans. "These attacks" he went on, "if they were to escalate in the Dark World, we Vampires would face endless abuse from all other Creatures. Of course, I'm doing everything in my power to stop it from coming to such a thing, but with these...hybrids out there, it's almost impossible to keep a lid on this. We need to maintain order by any means necessary—"

A knock on the door ceased his words and without turning to eye it, he said, "Come in."

The door opened and a Vampire with wavy gray hair appeared in the doorway, his golden robes sweeping around his high black boots as he kneeled, a fist over his heart, his head down as he said, "We have just received word. Lady Lillith Crane's manor was attacked. Lycans appear to have done the job. There were a lot of them when my men arrived on the scene. We cleared them off, of course."

"And the damage?" Dracula asked the Vampire, anger flaring in his cold heart. *Lore never knew when to quit*, he thought.

"There was not much we could do, my Grace. As I said, when we arrived it was a most horrible scene."

Dracula smelled the tension that existed within the youngest Vampire behind him. He did not turn to her, but said, "Lillith, you shall go with him and he will tell you what to do next. I've prepared a 'Plan B' in these cases."

He heard her step past him, the back of her long hair swaying rhythmically in the light of the fire as she stepped out of the room with the Third Army soldier. Her brilliant blue eyes turned to him with fear before the door closed and she was lost to him.

The anger in his heart swelled to new heights. Lillith Crane, his special task, his golden child...how he had broken all preconceived rules to keep her alive. And all at that Vampire's request. She was always to be watched, always to be protected, for she was, he knew, the only thing that would keep that Vampire under tight wraps, under his, Dracula's, consummate command.

"They attacked her manor. Ours will be next, Dracula," the cold voice of Xavier issued from behind him now, clear, precise, exact.

He almost shuddered at the sound, yet forced himself to still— yes, this was the power Xavier possessed. How he admired it...how he needed it...

Turning to eye them all once more, he allowed his gaze to travel to Xavier. The Vampire's face had hardened, the green eyes so alive with anger.

"That may be so," he agreed, "but we will not move with haste. You were all called here to hear of these new Creatures. It is very possible that they attacked Lillith's manor. We must be aware. Things are greatly changing within our World."

Damion ran a hand through his black, shoulder-length hair. "My Lord, it is possible—" and he looked around at Victor and Xavier before dropping his voice considerably, leaning in closer "— it is possible I have...witnessed one of these ...Creatures. Just before we arrived here, I ran into a cloaked figure, and the symptoms that plague others of our kind were there. If Victor hadn't been there, I might've ended up like them."

These words sent a trill of anxiousness up his spine, and as his eyes widened in severe interest, he whispered into Damion's ear: "Why didn't you tell me sooner?"

"I-I didn't know that this was happening to more of us—" he began.

None of what the Vampire said mattered. None of it mattered at all. This could be the break Dracula was looking for...the truth revealed to quell his haunted guesses, stabs in endless dark. "What did you see, Damion?"

He knew the Vampire was more than scared, more than alarmed

at his own anxiousness, his own excitement, for the Vampire whispered, "I...my Lord—"

"What. Did. You. See?" he barked.

He waited as the dancing flame spread its light to break the thick darkness that existed within the large room, where two Vampires stood greatly confused, and two more stood perfectly befuddled, each for their own reasons.

Damion whispered the name that made his eyes shine red, made his heart drop straight through his body, made his mind draw blank.

And then Dracula sighed, for he had known, he had always known she was the one to take what she had been given too far. She had leapt before she'd looked, before she could bother to wait for his word, his next command. But what he did not know was what exactly she had done.

His eyes found Xavier's, so focused upon his own dark expression, yet, there was something undoubtedly vacant about the Vampire's countenance, Dracula thought. He had seen it earlier, yes, but he had thought he'd imagined it...but if indeed it was she who showed herself to Damion...then she must have shown herself to Xavier...and what? What had she done to him?

Red eyes set, he turned back to Damion and asked, "You are sure it was her?"

"I am positive," he said, his own eyes gleaming with confusion, yearning for more than questions by his King. He wanted answers, Dracula saw, answers that he could not be given.

Turning to the Vampire that could receive these answers, however, Dracula said, "Damion, Victor, leave my office please. I must speak with Xavier privately."

When neither Vampire made a move for the door that had opened on its own as Dracula spoke, he waved a hand through the air, and both Vampires found themselves being pushed toward the door by an invisible force.

Dracula ran a hand over his mouth in exasperation once the door closed. There were a number of things she could have done to him, he thought, eyeing Xavier, what with all the spells she had been taught and what more she'd gained from the book.

Studying Xavier's green eyes for a moment more, Dracula looked away, toward the blue book he'd had placed upon his desk minutes before. *Which spell would suffice?* he wondered as he turned back to Xavier, sure to keep his eyes cold, his heart dead, hardened with conviction. After all, one could not decipher a spell if one was not prepared.

"What did she tell you?" he asked the Vampire who had been watching him with slight concern.

"What?"

"I know she showed herself to you, what did she tell you, Xavier?" he pressed, stepping ever closer toward the Vampire.

✳

*Eleanor, he had to be talking about her, but how would he know she's alive?*

And as soon as this thought hit him, her voice, sultry and sweet, drifted through his mind once again: *"I see he's never told you...our blood is the same. The blood of an Elite..."*

All at once, he saw, not the Vampire before him, nor the large dark office they'd frequented, but instead the dark of night, trees all around him, Dracula gone. Yes, the Vampire was nowhere to be found, but there, just before him, much to his growing horror, was Eleanor Black.

Her long hair tangled in the wind just as it did the night before, but her words...her words did not reach him. They mingled with the fierce wind and were lost to his ears.

It was of vital importance that he hear them...hear her voice at all.

No sooner had the desire to hear her voice fill him, did the woods begin to crumble into nothingness, and Eleanor, the vision of terrible beauty, began to fade with the wind that blew so strong, so cold.

Another voice permeated the void. "Xavier. Listen to me. What did Eleanor tell you?"

He blinked once and took in the cold face of the Vampire before him. He was back in Dracula's office, the flames flickering loudly in the fireplace. He blinked again and shook his head: It felt light as the vision of Eleanor burned behind his eyes, yet began to fade with the passing seconds.

He almost did not see Dracula move past him to grab a chair from around the long table. Blinking at him as his head swam with the wind of his vision, he saw Dracula shove the seat behind him, sending his knees to buckle, and at once he found himself sitting just before the Great Vampire, staring up at him in sheer confusion.

*What was going on?*

Xavier watched as Dracula grabbed both arms of the chair and leaned forward, the brown eyes staring daggers into his. "What just happened?" Dracula asked intently.

"I...Eleanor. I saw her again," he breathed, his heart heavy with the horrible feeling that now radiated through his torso and threatened to spread through his arms next, his mind thundering with questions. Questions, mainly, about Eleanor.

"What did she tell you?" he repeated.

"Dracula—" he started. It felt vital he relay all that just transpired, even if he, himself, was not so sure what it was. "She...was never dead. I saw her die right in front of me—I saw her skin rip from—"

"Xavier!" Dracula yelled, his face pained. "What did she tell you?"

He stared at the Vampire in utter bewilderment, despite his pounding mind. Why was it so important what she'd said? Wasn't it enough that she was alive—alive at all?

"Eleanor's alive..." he managed to whisper.

Dracula let out a sigh of frustration. "I believe we've managed that much," he growled. "Where did you go just now? Where did she take you?"

His eyes traversed the Vampire's anxious expression, and he knew that something was wrong. Dracula, the consummate, coolheaded Vampire...was suddenly quite...scared?

Sighing, he tried to recall what happened that night, how she felt against him, it was like a dream. A dream had long ago, a dream fading from memory with time. "What does it matter?" he said at last, his voice low for a reason he did not know.

Dracula turned away from him at last, running a hand over his forehead, and Xavier saw that his face was one of tremendous concern. He watched in bewilderment as the Vampire strode back to his dark desk, seemingly slightly off balance, to place a shaking hand over the blue book he'd placed there but minutes before.

He sat higher in his seat now, Dracula picking up the book with care, and turned to eye him.

It matters tremendously," Dracula finally whispered through tight lips.

His green eyes ran across the small book Dracula held tightly in front of him, and he wondered just what that could be...why it was the Vampire held it so closely. "Why does it matter so much?" he asked, moving his gaze to match that of the Vampire's own.

"That will be determined once you tell me what she told you," Dracula countered, his voice determined, quite commanding.

Understanding the tone in the Vampire's voice to mean an order he must obey, Xavier opened his mouth, but when no sound protruded past his lips, he closed it abruptly, finding it meaningless to speak. It was not what he must do. He had been told not to.

Once more, Xavier found his eyes clouding with dark smatters of wind, and suddenly he stared at a black enclosure, though it was not the woods where he'd met Eleanor. It did not, indeed, appear to be anywhere at all.

*What on Earth was this?*

He moved forward, eager to understand where he was, and why it had happened.

He had felt that he could not tell Dracula what it was she'd whispered to him in the woods, but why? Was his tongue not free to speak what he will? And what did it matter what she'd said as long as she was alive?

As he thought this, as he wondered what was going on, he felt the cold of a finger upon his forehead, just above his eyes, and he froze in surprise as smooth words echoed around him:

*"Clear the path of sight, raise the veil of darkness over the mind. Return to the present, Vampire. Return to the here and now of time. Destroy the darkness. Destroy the spell placed upon this mind. Xavier, return to me."*

He felt as though he was being pushed back, pushed forcefully through the tunnel of an alarming wind, and slowly, surely, the darkness of nothing began to fade and he stared in wonder at Dracula, who kneeled before his chair, the blue book open in a hand, his long finger still pressing against his forehead.

He blinked and the seconds passed, Dracula releasing his finger. He closed the book, but he did not rise to stand. And it was here Xavier saw that the brown eyes looked dark and cold.

"What did she do to you, Xavier?" Dracula asked as he rose to his feet.

"What?"

"Contact. Did you make contact with her? Physical contact?"

Xavier thought back to the sight of her, the flash of pale skin she'd possessed upon showing her Vampire form. "We kissed," he said, trying to ignore the memory of her lips on his own.

Dracula, who now sat behind his desk, raised an eyebrow.

"Kissed?" Though he did not press the question. He folded his hands and said, "She's cursed you, Xavier."

"Cursed?" he repeated, the taste of her lips gone at once with Dracula's words.

"Cursed. And it is a highly-forbidden curse at that. I didn't want to believe it when I first saw you, but as I continued to watch you, it was clear. Calling of Void. It enchants the victim to be completely under the caster's control. The victim is not able to disobey the caster, and if the victim were close to doing so, he or she would be lost in his or her own mind until the spell is removed. It is extremely dark magic, Xavier, which tells me, from my previously asked question, that she does not want you to tell anyone of what she told you that night. Am I correct?"

Xavier ran a hand over his mouth, trying to understand how a Vampire could be controlled by magic of all things. He was never aware it was possible at all.

As if reading his mind yet again, Dracula went on, "As I'm sure you've gathered, Eleanor is no longer a Vampire. This is why she was able to use magic, why it was able to work. We Vampires are brute Creatures. We have no need for spells and tricks of the mind. Naturally, we leave that to the Elves and Enchanters. I'm afraid," he sighed, "that Eleanor has learned something terrible, and that she is using this newfound power to her advantage. Power, as we know, can only breed greed."

Xavier was silent, unsure of what more to think or even do.

Dracula decided to use this silence as an excuse to speak further. "Now that you are free of the spell, Xavier, it would be wise to tell me what she told you. With what she's said, it will tell me if she is our enemy or an ally."

He sighed as the familiar feeling of despair boiled in his stomach, though it wasn't as strong as it had been. "She mentioned blood. Elite blood...and you, Dracula, she mentioned you." He attempted to hang onto the words Eleanor had shared—they were now leaving his mind far too rapidly to catch.

Dracula leaned back in his chair, seemingly uninterested in the small fragments of sentences he was presented with. "Xavier, Xavier...think, think. She must have told you something, something vital. She mentioned me, naturally. I would expect Eleanor to come to hate me." Dracula leaned forward in his chair, his face half-covered by his hair. "This...Elite blood, tell me more about that."

Xavier stood. Something was happening, Eleanor was alive—he still had a hard time coping with that—and Dracula seemed to only care for what she said, and what did that matter if she was alive? He strode to the fireplace, reaching for the mantle, staring into the jumping flames. His thoughts found Eleanor's words.

"The Elite blood," he said after a time. "She said, before the City, there were a select few who held the blood of pure."

"She didn't—" Dracula whispered.

Xavier looked up then. "She didn't?"

Dracula did not speak immediately, no, but he rose from his seat, his hands pressing into the small bare space atop his desk as he let out a miniscule snarl. But a snarl it was.

"She...she...Eleanor...was there anything else? What else did she tell you?" he asked as though if he held in the words any longer he would never receive his answer.

He narrowed his eyes as he stared at the Great Vampire. Something was wrong. The most loved and feared Vampire in history was worried. Very much so, it seemed. Xavier removed himself from the warmth of the fire he could not feel, and stepped toward Dracula's desk. "What does it matter what's she told me, my Grace?" he asked for the third time.

"It matters—"

"Tremendously?" he finished.

Dracula turned away from Xavier's piercing gaze.

"I refuse," Xavier said, pointing a finger to the dark wood of the desk between them, "to tell you anything until you tell me why Eleanor's life matters so bloody much to you."

Dracula sat down and sighed. "Because I took her in just as I took you in, Xavier. She was the first of my kind. The first Vampire in a long time that I could relate to. In a way she became like a daughter to me."

Xavier's brow furrowed. "The first of your kind? Are we not all Vampires, Dracula?"

"We are Vampires, yes, but you and I," and he pointed a finger to Xavier and then himself, "have never been like the others. Surely you have noticed. The odd glances you have received, the crushing power you possess over the others. Xavier, we possess everything the others lack."

"And what is that?" he asked slowly.

He looked up at the Vampire at last, and it seemed he was remembering something, or at least attempting to forget, but he soon said, "The blood of transformation. Power. Passed to us from our mothers, them from their fathers—" He stopped short, as if realizing he said too much.

"...And?"

"No," Dracula held up a hand.

"And yet you wish to know of Eleanor's words to me?"

"Very much so. But I won't get anything more out of you, will I?"

"I'm afraid not."

Dracula smiled. "As expected. I've trained you well, haven't I?"

"You have," Xavier agreed, but he could not find it in himself to return the smile.

"Something more troubles you?" Dracula asked.

"Eleanor was not the only one to mention my blood. Damion appears to have grown rather upset."

Dracula frowned. "Damion?"

"The night before I received Victor's letter, Damion paid me a visit. It was at night, so naturally, he was without the ring. His features were distorted...he was beyond starving, I'm sure."

"What business did he have with you?"

"He wished for answers, answers regarding Eleanor. I'd sent Christian to Damion to tell him of her death. He did not take kindly to it."

"I see," Dracula said.

"When I told him I could not help him, his thirst for blood and his anger threw him into a frenzy. He released his sword and threatened to kill me if I did not oblige to his commands."

Dracula's eyes darkened. Although he was silent, Xavier knew this enraged him.

Xavier said, "And he swung at me. With each attack, his anger grew more and more chaotic. I dodged all of them and told him he was out of order, that his lack of proper nutrition was causing him to go temporarily insane."

"There's more, I'm sure," Dracula suggested.

"Yes. He was able to hit me after I was distracted. He cut me clear across my chest. I, of course, healed, but his words struck me more than my loss of blood. He said I was 'the heir to the throne... the only blood similar to Dracula's...' and with this, he sunk to his knees, for using so much energy when he was so low on blood was clearly taking its toll on him. He called me 'King' while on his knees, asking me if I was to lead against the Lycans. I told him to stop his foolishness and leave my grounds at once. He finally came to his senses, and did so," he finished.

"He's jealous is all," Dracula said as soon as Xavier closed his mouth.

"It had to have been something more—"

"It was simple jealousy, Xavier. You took the spot he aimed for. I gave it to you because of your readiness. Damion was never as ready as you were. And it could also be anger at the situation with Eleanor—sending your brother to tell him that she was dead was very cold, Xavier. Definitely something one would recommend if you wanted to make enemies."

"I understand how it must seem, but at the time I assumed Eleanor dead and her death still shook me. There wasn't any possible way for me to tell the others of how it happened. I felt a considerable amount of guilt for what happened that night. But, of course, now it is all irrelevant," Xavier replied.

"You're wrong," he said, turning his attention to a drawer in his desk. He freed several sheets of paper. Scanning his eyes over the top of the first paper, and quickly skimming through the words beneath the title of the page, Dracula continued speaking. "The relevance to the situation at hand is astounding. I sent a few soldiers to the cabin after you came to me, and this," he handed over the papers, "is what they reported back."

Xavier took the papers and read the words lined across the first page.

*Position: Rendezvous Point 20.*

*Remnants of Lycan ash found in middle of cabin floor. Ash was disposed of immediately after arriving on the scene. Smell of puskreet and Vampire blood sailed through the cabin. After assessing the situation, we determined a Lycan was present and Lord Xavier did away with it. Eleanor Black's location is currently unknown. We fear her dead, as we have found her necklaces buried in the ash of the Lycan.*

*Although the faint scent of the lilac flower and fresh, cold blood remained inside and around the cabin.*

*Silverchair,*
*Craven Winger*

Xavier flipped through the other pages, seeing Craven's name on the majority of the papers. Only a Bronzechair, Westley Rivers and a Goldchair, Armand Dragon signed two other papers.

He dropped the papers on the desk and said, "You sent the Chairs to assess the situation?"

"Yes, I had my reasons. I had to be sure no other Creature still lurked around the cabin, and I also had to confirm my deepest fears," Dracula said, taking the papers back and shoving them in a drawer.

Xavier marveled at the complexity of the situation, his mind alive with odds and ends, Eleanor...the Chairs...the scent of lilac and blood. "The scent of lilac and blood the Vampire smelled in the report, that's how you knew she was still alive, wasn't it?"

Dracula looked very tired as he said, "Yes, it was how I knew she had not been killed by any mere Lycan. Of course, I would have known this even if that soldier did not smell her scent. I trained her, to use her abilities to her supreme advantage. I suppose she ended up doing that in the end." He stood and met Xavier's eyes. "You will tell no one about this, Xavier. Not even Victor. Is that understood?"

Xavier nodded his understanding. "Of course, your Majesty."

"Good," Dracula said, sitting back down. "You may take your leave, Delacroix."

Still itching to know of their blood, Xavier opened his mouth to inquire further, but decided against it. The information presented was far enough for one day. After all, Dracula still wished to know about Eleanor's words to him, and he still wished to know about Eleanor. Whatever it was the Vampire knew. He could give Dracula a piece of information and in return receive another. Yes, he would use this to his advantage.

Xavier made his way toward the door when Dracula's voice stopped him: "Ah, I'd almost forgotten. The Council of Creatures."

"Hm?" Xavier whirled mid-stride, having made it just before the large door to the Great Vampire's office.

"They wish to meet with you, Xavier," Dracula said from his chair.

"Meet with me?"

"Yes."

Xavier raised an eyebrow. "The Council of Creatures. The group of the most-honored and prestigious Creatures in all of the Dark World wish to meet with me? Whatever for?"

A thin smile lined Dracula's lips. "For a little of this, and a little of that. You know. I must confess, I have not kept my tongue still during our meetings. I admit to mouthing off about Xavier Delacroix from time to time. They just wish to...see you...in the flesh. Chat here and there, see you're worth..."

The fade of Dracula's voice signaled that there was more to this than he wished to let on. But, regardless, Xavier knew he could not say no to the Council of Creatures. Indeed, he had never been called by them before, the fact that he now had made him slightly nervous, but he wouldn't dare show it in front of Dracula. "Yes. Yes, of course. When are they looking forward to meeting me?"

"Oh, in about two months or so. You will travel with me, Xavier. We shall move alone and in secrecy. You are to tell no one where we are going, and I shall call for you when I am ready to leave," Dracula said, his brown eyes flashing with certainty in the torch light of the large room.

Xavier let a cold breath escape his lungs. "Two months?"

Dracula nodded.

Xavier closed his eyes and opened them, demanding the thoughts of her to leave his mind. "Can they not reschedule such a meeting, your Majesty?" he asked, hoping he would hear what he wanted to hear, needed to hear. Instead, he was struck with:

"Reschedule? Is there something more important than meeting with the Council of Creatures, Xavier?"

He snarled, his tongue caught between his lips in an internal fight only he knew was taking place. "No, no, there is nothing. I was just curious."

Dracula's eyes danced with disbelief at this response, but he said all the same, "Good, because such a meeting is mandatory, Xavier. Required for all of the Vampires that I have trained personally. Yes, Xavier, Eleanor has met with the Council as well. You will not be the first Vampire other than myself to do so."

Xavier felt the churning blow of these words strike him full force in his gut. Dracula knew no compromise when there was something he wanted. Knowing he had no choice, his mouth moving reluctantly and not of his will, he sighed. "Very well."

Smiling, Dracula dismissed him with a careless flick of the hand. No further words spoken. He had said all he needed to say, and that, as Xavier and other countless Vampires knew, was that.

# Chapter Ten

# DRAGOR'S DECISION

**X**avier returned to his office, a parade of First Army Officers marching in rows of two in front of the doors, blocking entry to and apparently from the room.

He did not break stride as he neared his office door, causing the many Vampires to stiffen upon eyeing him and move hastily to leave a clear path of marble tile that lead straight to the large doors. Walking down this path, Xavier shook his head at the welcome he was presented with. *Dragor was always one for theatrics*, he thought, grinning.

He entered, almost taken aback at the familiar state of the office. Nothing had changed. As long as it was wide, the office was lit with faintly glowing torches that spanned the room every other foot. The dim orange glow threw relief over the dark furniture, and his desk, which remained to the left of the door facing the rest of the room, was just as black and paper-lined as ever.

He closed the door behind him, cutting off the view the First Army Officers had into the beautifully designed room. Regarding it all as rather funny, Xavier marveled at the fact that he was barely here and yet Dracula saw to it that he had the utmost decorations fit for his favorite Vampire: There were green curtains that covered the large, arching windows, blocking the otherwise-splendid view of the large City that lay before the mansion. And, as usual, he thought with a smile, there was the gigantic portrait the Great Vampire had painted himself, which showed a vast valley and Xavier's stallion in the center, grazing on the grass therein, that sat high on a wall, above the small bookshelf kept near one of the corners.

As he walked further into the room, he noticed three doors had been added, most likely leading to Victor, Lillith, and Damion's offices, settled with magic, for the other Order members' rooms were spread far apart within the mansion. Settling himself in a chair placed behind a wooden table, he undid his cloak and placed it on the back of his chair. He had little time to think quietly at all, for the deep voice of Dragor Descant reached his ears, sounding hollow from the amount of space in between them.

"Xavier, you are very hard to keep up with. It appears Dracula kept you the longest out of all the members. I wished to finish our little discussion we had earlier. You recall the one about Eleanor."

Xavier glanced up from the table to see the ferocious-looking Vampire walking toward him. Apparently he had been sitting in a chair in the corner watching him this whole time. "Yes, I recall," he responded, trying to keep the slight annoyance he felt out of his voice. He really did desire the quiet time necessary to think on all the pressing matters that surrounded him now.

Dragor, seemingly not taking the time to realize any of this, took a seat opposite him, his intense gaze never leaving Xavier's face. Folding his large hands together, he smiled. It was a most handsome smile, one that looked incredibly misplaced upon the Vampire's face: His pale skin was slightly wrinkled due to being turned at an old age, and his gray-brown hair swirled behind his head in a short frenzy of maddened messiness. If one were not careful to take note of the gleaming white fangs hidden inside Dragor's mouth, one would assume he were a Lycan in human form.

"The Dark World has not been the same since you were ordered to the surface with the others," his voice husky and unusually low.

Xavier eyed him. "I'm sure it's been just fine, Dragor. I am quite sure my absence is not a problem with your ability."

"Perhaps. But my ability to fight against the Elves when they attacked was most subdued," he countered, glaring at him.

Xavier cleared his throat. "I was not present when that happened."

"I know," Dragor said, his eyes shining in the light of the candle that sat in front of him.

Shifting in his seat, Xavier said, as the question rose to his own mind, "If you know this, Dragor, then why are you mentioning it to me?"

"Because we both know the Vampire that was supposedly the most successful holding the Elves back was not the only one doing so."

"Funny, I was not aware of this," he said, fighting to keep the boredom out of his voice. How his mind swam with straining visions of Eleanor Black...a desperate Dracula.

Dragor cracked his neck. "Oh, you wouldn't have been." His features took on a more dangerous glow as he said, "Your First Seat... has anyone told you that he attacked myself and several others in the midst of battle against the Elves?"

Xavier sat up straighter now, taking in the fierce expression Dragor held upon his face. "He what?"

"You've heard correctly. He took his sword and placed it right here—" he tapped the right side of his chest. "I looked into his eyes and saw nothing but darkness...an eclipse of the light in his eyes. The blade dug so deep, it cut through my shoulder, breaking the bone. My sword dropped from my grip, my arm went limp, splashing blood everywhere. Of course, the City was already littered with the blood and bodies of dead Elves that the others didn't really seem to notice what had taken place. Damion—ever the con artist—ran to Armand, who had just destroyed several Elves, and called him over to me—I had sunk to my knees from shock—and told him that I suffered a serious injury from an Elf and had to be taken into care immediately."

"...Why are you telling me this now, Dragor?"

"You have the power to destroy him."

He blinked. "Destroy?"

"Destroy his career in the Vampire Order, break his ties with Dracula, and let the truth of that event be known to all," his voice rising as he spoke.

Xavier narrowed his eyes at the First Captain. He was never known for making up such fantastic stories, but it was true he loathed Damion and wished for his immediate removal from the Order. To ask him of this now... "Dragor, if Damion did this to you—"

"And others."

"And others, yes, if he did this to you and others, why hasn't anyone else come to me about it? And for that matter, why haven't you told Dracula, told anyone?"

A scornful look graced Dragor's face then. "Do you think Dracula would believe that the First Seat to Xavier Delacroix, Damion Nicodemeus, purposefully attacked myself and several other Officers? You don't even believe it yourself."

Xavier flexed his jaw at this statement. While it was true he didn't completely believe that Damion would attack another Vampire, he still had to take in to account that Damion did indeed attack *him*. The sting of the Vampire's words remained fresh in his mind: "*...heir to the throne...*" *What did any of it matter if Eleanor lived?*

Shaking away the oncoming thoughts regarding Damion's words, Eleanor's demands, Xavier spoke up, bringing himself to the present conversation and the well-known Vampire at hand. "He could be persuaded if one had proof of said attack," he reasoned.

"Proof?" Dragor was incredulous. "Any proof I had any hope of gathering was conveniently whisked away while I was in the infirmary, healing with the many others who fell ill to Damion's hand."

"How are you so sure Damon harmed them as well?"

"How am I so sure?" he chuckled. "You mean to tell me that those bloody Elves could slice through a Vampire's bone? No mere Elf did what I saw that day, I can tell you that, Xavier. Of the soldiers that went in, all suffered broken, dislocated, or fractured bones. And not in the same place, all different places mind you. By the look on their faces, I knew they felt the same way I did." He scowled. "Betrayed."

Xavier sat in silence as he stared at the Vampire, his friend. Almost everyone who met him loved Dragor Descant, and he was seldom in the infirmary, healing from an attack, if at all. The fact that Damion did that to those men, his own kind, it didn't make the faintest amount of sense. "What would Damion have to gain by doing this, Dragor?"

"What he's *already* gained by doing it, Xavier. Power. Prestige." Dragor gestured a hand to Xavier as he said, "A place in the Vampire Order. Yes, he's gained everything I've worked so hard for, for years in mere...mere days."

"And you want me to remove all of this from him?" he asked, wondering if Dracula would allow such a thing.

"Yes." Dragor's eyes did not quiver from Xavier's stare. "I realize I should have done this myself long ago, but when I finally left the infirmary, Damion was already your First Seat, and the other Vampires who were attacked lost any and all recollection of Damion attacking them. As expected of a Vampire with Damion's rank..." His voice trailed away, but he resurfaced with, "This is all I ask of you, Xavier. Speak to Dracula, see what can be done."

It was not long before he said, "Dragor, you say the other Vampires lost all recollection of the attack?"

"Yes. I've asked everyone who laid in those beds with me. None of them remember a thing."

"You must understand how difficult a decision this is for me, Descant. What you are asking of me, I simply cannot do—"

"Why not?!"

Xavier glared at Dragor, who stood, scraping the legs of the chair against the marble floor. "The evidence is miniscule, there are no other Vampires who will claim that such an attack took place, as you have mentioned, and quite simply... I don't believe that my First Seat has done such a thing. This took place three years ago, correct? Then why—even if Damion was already my First Seat—didn't you march to Dracula and tell him everything?"

"He wouldn't have believed me," Dragor replied, his voice quiet in the large room.

"Then why do you expect *me* to believe you?"

"You are my friend, Vampire. If anyone would believe me, I expect it to be you, but I see...your royal blood has already begun to settle..." he sighed before maneuvering around the table, walking up to Xavier. He bent low next to his ear, sure to place a strong hand upon his shoulder. "You will make your choices, my Lord. Just know that everything you decide will have its consequences." Then, giving Xavier's shoulder a solid clasp, he began to take his leave from the room.

Xavier did not turn in his seat as Dragor's heavy footsteps reached the doors. He only said, "The choice I have made now, what is the consequence of that?"

"We shall see."

And then, the sound of the huge door closing, leaving an echo to resonate off the walls, his ears.

Before he could assess Dragor's situation, and his own, any further, one of the doors on the other side of the room creaked open.

He did not have to look up to know that it was Victor. The

Vampire's thick blood could be smelled even with all the other blood that floated through the mansion.

"Xavier."

"What is it, Victor?" he asked, never looking up from the table.

He knew the Vampire remained near his office door, for nothing in the darkness stirred, yet the Vampire said all the same, "Do you believe him?"

"I am not sure. And what difference does it make if I do or don't?" he replied, running a finger straight through the flame of the candle he could not feel, miserable. *What, indeed, was happening here?*

And as Victor stirred, folding his arms against his chest, Xavier was pulled from his thoughts and eyed the Vampire, only able to see the violet eyes watching him from shadow.

"It makes all the difference. He is going to tell Dracula, Xavier," Victor said, "and you shall be called in to settle the matter. Damion is your First Seat—you are responsible for him. Now, I was there when the Elves attacked, I can tell you that it was a gruesome battle. Many of our men were carried through our streets, most of them dead. Permanently. We lost a lot of soldiers that day, and now that I look back on it, it is odd that Damion Nicodemeus was the only one unharmed."

Xavier stared into the violet eyes that never moved from his face he ran a hand over the flame of the candle and darkness plunged through the room before he stood. "Were you were harmed, Victor?"

"Yes."

"Did you see who attacked you?"

Victor sighed before seemingly deciding the truth was better than a small jab at his ego. "I didn't see who it was, no."

It was while before he said anything, a while before he opened his mouth to respond with, "Surely, you noticed a white robe swishing out of the corner of those eyes. The Elves only don their Etrian robes, they would've worn nothing else, or am I mistaken?"

Victor shifted his footing. "They did wear their robes, Xavier. It was foolish, for they stood out amongst the soldier's uniforms. As for who attacked me... I'm terribly sorry that I cannot say. The attacker came from behind."

"I would imagine, Victor, that when the Elves ambushed the City, there was a barrier of sorts, the Elves approaching and the Armies standing guard—"

"No. It wasn't quite in that way. We heard the screams—"

"Screams?" he asked.

"We heard the screams from the civilians inside Dracula's mansion, Xavier. The Chairs were rounded up—Protocol 32—and the Armies were sent out into the streets."

Xavier folded his arms, brow furrowed. *How was it possible that Elves infiltrated Dracula's mansion?* He'd never heard that little piece of information before. "When were you called out?"

"When Armand Dragon ran into the mansion, frantic because Dragor Descant was hurt. At that point, I gathered my things and headed out into the fray."

"What was running through your mind when you heard the First Captain had been hurt?"

"It seemed impossible—improbable for it to ever happen. I was thinking that no mere Elf could lay a finger on Dragor."

"And then?"

"And then I saw him. As I left the mansion, he was coming in. Carried by two other soldiers. Both bleeding profusely. Not sure they made it. Dragor was in the worst shape I'd ever seen him in. His arm dangling off his shoulder, the bone disconnected and loose. He was unconscious at that point," he replied.

Xavier said nothing for a time, mind rattled even more with the news he'd just been given. Damion, killing his own kind... Elves inside the mansion... It made no sense. None of it made any sense at all.

"Xavier?" Victor asked, as it had been so long the Vampire was lost in deep thought.

He blinked and pulled his thoughts from Damion, feeling that Dragor had the right idea, desiring to pull Damion from the Order. "Although I'm rather thrown to hear of this now, Victor, I thank you for your words. Dragor wished for me to make a decision, and I believe I have."

"And what decision have you made?" the silver-haired Vampire asked, violet eyes dressed with concern.

There was not a sound in the room for what seemed an eternity and when Xavier finally spoke, Victor took a slight step back: "I have decided, General Vonderheide, to pay a visit to my First Seat. With the information I have received, there is no doubt in my mind that foul play was a part of the events of that dreadful day. And as we both know, Elves cannot break a Vampire's bone."

✳

Damion waved the young Vampire out of his small office with a lazy flick of the hand. Yet another newly-changed Vampire, yet another waste of precious human blood that could be put to good use fulfilling the Vampires' urge to feed.

Being back here, back in the City, brought on a vast ocean of hatred that Damion forgot existed when he was on the surface. He knew there was much question of his position. He could hear the Vampires whisper when he passed them in the halls, along the streets. It was at this thought that a particularly nasty wave of nostalgia hit him, for there was one Vampire who would surely retain any sort of remembrance on what took place those many years ago. But as fast as it came, he forced it from his mind, for he had dealt with it, it would not return to haunt him, this he vowed a ninth time since he laid eyes on the one Vampire who, he knew, would never forget.

He sat back in his chair, looking at the large pile of papers a young Vampire just dumped onto his desk. *Paperwork*. This was not what he'd had in mind when he wished to join the Order. He envisioned it to be ceremonious, honorable, and he had hoped he could tout his sanctimonious flair to other "lower bred" Vampires, but alas, the reality of the Order was dull, and tedious, filled with meetings about the various events in the Dark World.

He supposed the closest thing to freedom he had was to be able to venture and live on the surface for as long as he pleased. But even there, his true being was suppressed, and he was forced to live like another human, although the subtle pangs for blood would slip through the cracks every now and then.

Yes, it was absolutely not worth what he'd had to do to get there. He'd fought his way to the top and was not even assigned the position he'd eyed for more than a century. No, he was placed as that particular Vampire's assistant. His bloody First Seat. A title that meant absolutely nothing. A mere foot in the door of being truly considered a part of the Vampire Order.

And Eleanor, her presence had eased the ridicule he'd faced, but was that her, truly, in the woods? Could it have been a memory? Staring around at the small office, he knew how ridiculous it could seem…how much he'd desired her to remain living—

The door opened, and in walked Lillith Crane, several scrolls of parchment nestled underneath an arm. "Have you seen a Vampire by the name of Javier Theron?"

"Javier Theron? No. I've never heard of him," Damion said. He pulled the large stack of papers toward him in an effort to show her that he was terribly busy.

She curtsied her apology for the intrusion, and closed the door behind her.

He turned his attention to the large stack of papers before him, desiring to tear his thoughts from his demeaning title and the strangeness of his superior. He reached up, took down one dog-eared paper from the top of the stack, and read.

*Silverchair Craven Winger's Report on Rogue Vampires*

*The alarming rate at which these particular Vampires are growing in number is astounding at best. They were mostly all citizens of the Vampire City.*

*It has come to my attention that this group wishes to attack the Armies and their Captains, targeting specifically Xavier Delacroix. The Vampire we all know as Dracula's preferred—*

Damion threw it down onto his desk just as the door swung open, the large Vampire appearing there.

"Dragor," Damion gasped, rising to stand.

He entered, closing the door behind him. "Did you think I would forget? That you would get away with it?"

"I...beg your pardon?"

"Did you think I would forget?!" he screamed, his voice booming against the walls, sending a shiver down Damion's spine.

*Not now,* he thought, *this was the worst time to bring up the past...to finally act—*

He squared his shoulders, knowing the Vampire would not leave unless he addressed him directly. "I don't know what you're talking about, First Captain."

"You know damn well what I mean," he said, moving toward the desk.

Damion froze, glaring up at the Vampire, quite aware he cut an impressive figure against the tame glow of the single candle atop his desk.

"The Elves, Damion," Dragor continued, and Damion caught the silver of the Vampire's sword at his waist, "I know you had me remember, but why, I cannot fathom. Out of all the Vampires injured in that...chaos, I was the one who remembered. Why?"

And in the darkness of the office, Damion smelled the scent of fresher blood, newer blood. Yes, he knew the Vampire was ready—ready should he be called. A smile graced his face. *The time was near...*

*Just a moment more, Lucien.*

Turning his attention to the Vampire in front of him, Damion let the smile fall slightly. Sighing, he said, "I don't know what you're talking about, Descant."

And in his surprise he was lifted off the floor, the large Vampire having reached across the desk to grab him. He could barely say a word before Dragor was talking, and rapidly so.

"Your goal has been reached, Damion. You are now in the Vampire Order. Are you thrilled to know you slaughtered countless Vampires to sit at your desk? Are you pleased to know others have died for your goal? Three years. Three years and no words have been spoken. Well, my friend, the convenience you have come to enjoy is now gone. I will no longer hold my tongue because of your word. You shall pay for what you have done.

"How long did you think I would stay silent? I don't know what sorcery you pulled over the others, but I have not forgotten. Whether it was your intention or not, my memory remains fresh. You are not with Dracula; this much is clear. You are a traitor, a liar, and you shall be put in your place."

And the rough hands slammed him against the stone wall, his head bouncing against it. And as his vision receded, darkness flickering brighter than the glow of the candle's flame, he let the dim smile lift his lips, for here it was. And he could not be happier.

*You will be mine, Dragor,* he thought, as all went black, *I will know the secrets they did not want to share.*

※

Dragor closed a trembling hand, staring at the Vampire over the desk, watching the eyes close. *He seemed almost happy...but that was foolish*, he thought, lifting from the desk and turning toward the door. *The Vampire would not be happy about this...he wouldn't know where all of this led, surely.*

Dracula's voice entered his mind before he could turn his thoughts to anything else: *"Prepare yourself."*

And the door opened, the wind of their blood reaching his nose. He kneeled as the clean boots walked forward, stopping just before him, the light of brighter, dancing flames flooding the small room.

"You were right to be concerned, Xavier," the voice of Dracula sounded from overhead.

He did not tear his gaze from the floor as another pair of boots entered the room. "What has he done to him?" Xavier asked.

There was shuffling of feet and then a slight intake of breath. He felt the sharp gaze upon him, but he did not lift his head. "First Captain of the First Army," the voice sounded suddenly, "you are hereby stripped of your title, for assaulting my First Seat, Damion Nicodemeus. You will come with me to the Chambers of Question and we will get to the bottom of this event, immediately."

He rose to his feet, feeling the eyes of Xavier and Dracula upon him, though it was Dracula's gaze he lifted his chin to meet. The Vampire's brown eyes were steady on him, the light of the torch he held in a hand illuminating his disproving expression, though the slight smile was there upon those lips.

"He is heavily unconscious," Dracula said to Xavier, and Dragor realized Lillith Crane and a young Vampire he had never seen before remained within the doorway. "We must have the warden come look at him. I don't think any amount of Unicorn blood is going to fix this..."

Xavier nodded. "Right away. Javier, go fetch the warden. Tell her to bring her supplies with her. We cannot waste any time bringing him to the infirmary."

Javier, the young Vampire, nodded his blond head and whispered, "Of course, my Lord."

Dragor watched him turn on a dime and run out of view, his white robes swishing around his ankles. He could barely ask himself who that was when Xavier stepped forward, placing a strong hand atop his shoulder, the glare of anger clear in those green eyes.

He moved forward with the Vampire, giving Dracula one last glance as they reached the door. The Great Vampire looked thoughtful.

*I will do my part, your Majesty*, he thought as Xavier led him down the long hallway, the passing Vampires giving him curious glances, *I only hope the Vampire will do his.*

※

Dracula set his torch upon a mount and stepped outside where Victor was waiting. "You never mentioned Dragor's suspicions, or your own, when those events took place."

He turned in surprise, having just waved away several Vampires that were curious about the commotion ensuing in front of Damion's office. "I was never certain it was Damion who did it, Dracula."

"Dragor apparently believes it was Damion. This is absurd. Three years and he mentions this now?"

"I believe he was just biding his time. Waiting until a Vampire with more power returned. Waiting for Xavier to return, so he could tell him his story. He most likely assumed, as good friends as they were, that Xavier would believe him without question. When that did not happen..." Victor cast a look to Damion's slumped figure against the wall.

Dracula sighed, running a hand through his hair, sure to keep his expression one of exasperation. "Of all the times... In-fighting between Vampires. And in my own bloody home. With the arrival of these Creatures... I wished to keep you all here for a while longer but apparently this will not be so. You must return to the surface, Victor."

"But Damion—"

"Damion," Dracula said, "will be under close watch. No need to worry, once he is at peak health he will join Dragor in the Chambers of Question until I get to the bottom of this matter."

Victor closed his eyes and sighed, Dracula sensing his desire to protest, to stay just a while longer, but when the Vampire opened his eyes, resignation existed within them. "Where is Lillith? I was hoping to tell her she is to stay with me."

"She moved to her own office," he replied. "If you leave now, you will catch her before she enters." And with this, he smiled, the blankness of it reaching his first Vampire with the desired effect: Victor bowed low, though his gaze never left Dracula's face, and nodded, a hand over his dead heart.

Victor headed toward Lillith's office, leaving him standing in the doorway of Damion's office, the faint darkness of the room seeping past his being, joining the greater darkness of the hallway.

✼

The large hall spread out around them as they passed through the doorway. Rows of chairs faced the elevated desk, long as it was wide. It stretched through all four chambers, divided by four pillars every few rows of chairs.

Xavier was glad the Chamber Masters were not yet here, though it was only a matter of time before they were called from their place in the Clearance Committee building, where they oversaw every Vampire's entrance and exit from the City.

He gestured for Dragor to sit in a nearby chair. "That was the consequence for my choice, Dragor?" he asked once the Vampire was seated.

Dragor stared at his feet, head bowed low. "Yes, it was."

"What drove you to do such a thing, to attack him like that?"

There was silence. Then: "I wished to only speak with him. Get him to admit his wrongdoing. But upon seeing that grin—those eyes—he was taunting me. He knew what I had come to discuss. He knew what he did, and it was his intention to have me remember. To make it so I'll never forget. Let it sit in my mind…torture me endlessly. And it has. When it came to that... His life is not worth the title he was given."

Xavier folded his arms. "So you believed you'd kill him?"

"Kill?" he whispered, gasping the word as if he didn't believe he were capable of it. He removed his large hands from each other and stared down at them. "Truthfully, I am not sure what I planned to do with him. I suppose I wished to hurt him like he had hurt me. In the end, I have only ended up like him... No, I will never betray my people, this City, Dracula...."

Xavier took a seat in front of Dragor, facing him. "I believe your story, Descant. You are just lucky Victor has said more or less the same as you concerning Damion. You say he has betrayed us. Well, I would definitely see this as an act of treason against the Vampire City." At this Dragor looked up, and Xavier continued, "I am sure he did not do this to help those Elves, but I am also sure he is not happy with the title given. Just know, Dragor, had you been promoted, you would have received your rightful place alongside me, my friend. I believe it's called 'Third in Command,' not 'Xavier Delacroix's First Seat.' Damion was only given that title because of what we all believed he did for the City, and also because he was in such a low ranking in the Third Army."

This bit of information seemed to put Dragor at ease, though he said, "And my title, my foolish acts have stripped it of me. What's worse is the Chamber Masters will not listen to a Vampire that has attacked his superior officer. I'm afraid I have trapped myself in a corner."

"We shall see what the Chamber Masters believe soon enough," Xavier said, his eyes on the open doorway where four Vampires could be seen approaching.

A tall Vampire with flowing blond hair spoke first, "Xavier? We did not know it was you who called us here." He looked around the empty Chamber. "Indeed, what Vampire has committed a crime?"

Xavier stood, tilting his head toward the Vampire next to him. "Dragor Descant is the Vampire in question, Civil."

A dark Vampire with glowing red eyes and cascading black hair stepped past his colleague, mouth agape. "Dragor?! The First Captain?"

The Vampire known as Civil lifted a pale hand to ease his comrade, his gold-lined robes swaying as he did so. "Now, now, Warren, easy, easy," he said, his soft brown eyes gliding over Dragor's face, taking in his hard features. "We have yet to hear Lord Dragor's story. Perhaps he was wrongly accused..." those same brown eyes darted to Xavier's cold countenance, "...*perhaps*. In any case—" Civil made his way toward the long, elevated desk at the back of the room "—let us get this over with before it becomes unnecessary publicity, shall we?"

Still casting a curious glance toward Dragor, the Vampire named Warren stepped away from Dragor and Xavier and joined Civil behind the long desk, the other two Vampires joining them.

Once all were seated, Dragor and Xavier approached the massive desk, Civil staring down at them.

"Will the Vampire in question make himself known to the Chambers?"

Dragor kneeled and spoke to the floor, "Dragor Descant, my Masters. First Capt—*former* First Captain of the First Army Battalion."

A red-haired Vampire with black eyes spoke up next, "What is your crime?"

"I attacked Damion Nicodemeus, the First Seat to Lord Xavier Delacroix," Dragor said keeping his voice steady.

All four Vampires cast each other shocked looks. Civil turned to Xavier, looking down at him, and asked, "Are you a witness to this event, my Lord?"

Xavier glanced at Dragor, who still kneeled, his head down, and said, "I did not witness the attack, but I have seen Damion's condition, and it is clear Dragor did it."

Warren let out a gasp, and the red-haired Vampire shook her head. An older-looking Vampire, one with a full head of gray hair and glasses he did not need, spoke up next, his deep voice drawing all eyes to his corner of the desk. "You may rise, Dragor. Although your title has been removed, you are no lower than the Vampire you stand next to. Now tell us, what drove you to attack Damion Nicodemeus?"

Dragor obeyed and looked up at the older-looking Vampire. "Thank you for your kindness, Chamber Master Richard. I believe you may recall the ambush on this City by the Elves of Etria."

"We do," Civil said.

"Hard to forget that," Warren chimed in.

Dragor continued, "Yes, well, I was attacked that day."

"Yes, and so many others. I remember, Dragor," the red-haired Vampire said.

Dragor went on, not casting her a glance, "I have strong reason to believe that Damion was the one responsible for every single one of those Vampires injured and killed that day. The Elves do not have such strength. And we had no trouble at all killing them off, although there was a vast amount of them. To my understanding, they retreated after a time?"

"Yes, they did leave the City after several of them had been slain," Richard said.

"But why would you think that Damion harmed those Vampires, his own kind, Dragor? This is all news to me," Warren said.

"I had just slain several Elves, and I turned to Damion, for he called my name, that was when he struck. His blade sliced through my shoulder and dislocated my arm. Of course, I had to be taken off the battlefield, which Damion had no problem drawing attention from other Vampires to do," Dragor said, making sure his every word was heard by the Chamber Masters.

Civil spoke up after a time, though he addressed Xavier. "Has he told you of this story?"

"The very same," Xavier said.

"And what do you think?"

"I had my doubts at first, but Victor overheard our conversation and told me his side, which was fairly the same."

Civil's brown eyes seemed incredulous in the torch-lit room. "And where were you when this attack on the City took place, my Lord?"

"I was on the surface, where Dracula said I should be," Xavier replied.

"...Quite right," Civil observed before turning his attention back to Dragor. "Due to the complications that would arise out of such an accusation, Dragor, you must wait until we hear from Victor and Damion ourselves. We cannot move further unless we have more witnesses and the accused himself present and able to talk. Do you understand?"

Dragor's blue eyes pierced Civil's. "I understand."

"Very well. The Chambers of Question are adjourned. Dragor Descant, you are to be sent to the Chambers of Waiting until we are ready for you once more. Xavier Delacroix, allow me to have a word," Civil said, rising to his feet.

The other Chamber Masters did the same. They filed out of the room, one by one, until only Dragor, Xavier, and Civil were left.

Civil was the first to speak. "What exactly is happening in this mansion?"

Xavier responded, "To be clear, Civil, I believe that is none of your business."

Civil chuckled at the glare Xavier gave him. He was very brave. "If it concerns the Armies and the Order, I believe it concerns me very much. Especially," he cast a look to Dragor, "when a Captain of said Armies attacks a superior officer over something that happened over three years ago. It's ridiculous. Not the kind of thing we need dampening our name with the other Dark Creatures—"

"Rest assured, Civil, this will not reach the ears of the other Creatures. It will remain here, in this mansion, and it will not go past these walls. This is the last thing Dragor needs. Now, I believe him, whether or not you do depends on the accused, does it not? Fair trial and all that?" he retorted.

Civil's sanctimonious grin left his face. He seemed to fight with himself over what to do or say next, his extravagant features strained. He tore his gaze from Xavier's glare and turned to Dragor. "I-I will escort the criminal to the Chambers of Waiting. If you would please proceed," he said to the Vampire.

Dragor did not move, and Xavier stepped in front of Civil. "Criminal? Such a bold word to use so soon. Dragor Descant is no criminal, and you will not be the one escorting him to the Chambers of Waiting. It shall be me. Have I made myself clear, Chamber Master?"

"Crystal," he responded, catching Dragor's amused expression. He scowled and holding his head high, although his eyes were now completely red, he strode to the doors, slamming them behind him.

"Isn't he the nice fellow," Dragor said.

Xavier smiled. "I am sure they are still absorbing the blow you have given them. I believe you will be waiting in the Chambers of Waiting for a while, Dragor."

"Damion's treachery will finally be heard. I have comfort in that." He placed a strong hand on his friend's shoulder. "And you,

Xavier, I should thank you for listening to me even when I did not seem my usual self."

"Attacking Damion... I am sure he had it coming to him sooner or later, yet I know Damion would not allow you to cause such an injury. How were you able to do that to him?"

Dragor cracked his jaw. "He was not disturbed when I picked him up and slammed him into the wall. He did not fight back. Indeed, now that I think of it... No, I wouldn't say...there is no way that would be possible..."

Xavier raised an eyebrow. "What wouldn't be possible?"

"Well, it has only just occurred to me, but I believe this is what Damion has wanted all along. To have me stripped of my title, and go through all of this—have my name tarnished, slandered."

Xavier was silent. And then he began to walk toward the doors leading out of the Chambers. "If that is so, I shall see to it that Damion Nicodemeus is the one destroyed. Completely."

✵

The men stood in the large cave, ignoring the droplets of water that dampened their hair and bodies, yet one man stood away from the others. He stood in the corner, his sandy-blond hair stuck to his head due to the rain that now hammered the soft ground outside.

The images that flashed before his hazel eyes confined him to this corner. He thought of his wife and the man that hauled her away over a shoulder. He thought of the Lycan that transformed so effortlessly before him—how it was possible at all. He thought of all these things, and felt nothing but anger and sadness. His mind so warped from the event that transpired only hours ago, he could not pay attention to the other men who fell silent, as a larger figure appeared in the jagged entrance to the cave.

Lore wore no cloak about his body, instead, he fashioned a torn, ruffled blouse and red vest, his white breeches dirt-stained and wet, his shoes caked with mud. He entered the cave, and all eyes fell on him. Now out of the demanding rain, he ran a strong hand through his dark-brown hair, which bled with the rain. His strong eyes searched the cave for the man he wanted to see. He wished to know what happened that night regarding a human woman and an unauthorized attack on a Vampire's manor.

A low growl escaped his chest as he spotted him in the corner, his face down. Lore thought the man frozen, for he was so still, until he finally looked up, his eyes blank, tears lining his cheeks.

"What is the meaning of this, Thomas?" Lore asked.

Thomas blinked and prepared to take a step back, although the cave wall prevented him from doing so. He wiped away his tears and breathed. "It was my idea. I had them attack Lillith Crane's manor."

"I know it was your idea. No other Lycan would think up such a ridiculous plan. And what of this woman?" Lore said.

"Mara...she was taken by..."

Lore growled, causing several men to gasp and cast each other frightened looks. *"You had her with you?!"*

Thomas growled back. "I had no choice! She accepted what I was! She was involved in everything I did concerning this side of my life!"

"Yes. Yes, it's apparent she was, because she is now missing, is she not? What were you thinking, bringing a human woman to such a dangerous place?"

"They knew not to attack her. They knew not to touch her," Thomas replied.

Lore chanced a skeptical glance around at the men who watched curiously and soon turned back to Thomas. "None of these men touched her you say? Then where is she, Thomas? No Vampire was there to do the job since they were called to their City—which I am sure you are aware of—so what? What attacked her?"

"I do not know, father!" Thomas snarled. "I do not know what I saw."

"Yes...you do know what you saw." His voice dropped. "You cannot keep anything from me, Thomas. Something took her, what was it? Tell me."

Thomas hesitated, then said, "It was a Lycan."

"I thought you said none of my men attacked her."

"None of them did. This Lycan was something else. I am not even sure I could call it one of us."

Lore turned from his son at that moment and eyed the vast number of men before him with narrowed eyes. They stood as still as stone, waiting for him to speak, their gazes apprehensive.

"Did any of you see this Lycan attack Thomas's wife?" he asked.

They all shook their heads, faces bewildered.

Lore narrowed his dark eyes even more. "Do not lie. If you have witnessed something, come forth."

Wengor stepped forward from behind a newly-turned Lycan—who looked as though he wished to be elsewhere—and said, "With all due respect, my Lord, we were all much too busy destroying the manor to notice what went on outside of it. We saw nothing."

"...Fine," Lore said after a careful evaluation of Wengor's words. "You may all return to your lives for the time being, when I need you, I will call."

The men hesitated, never before having been told to leave Lore's side.

Running a hand through his hair once again, Lore eyed the men. "I believe I have told you to leave."

"Not many of us have lives in the human world," Wengor said. "We have never strayed from your side, we would have nowhere to go—"

"For those of you in need of a place to rest, there is the Dragon's

Cavern, located south from here, as well as the Northern Hills. Make due," he said.

"B-but those are *Inns*! You wish for us to reside amongst the humans, my Lord?"

Lore snarled. "You will need to for the time being, Wengor. With your charm and power, acquiring a room should be of no issue. Now leave Thomas and I, we have much to discuss."

Still stuttering, Wengor turned from Lore and out of the cave along with the other men.

Lore watched as they each ventured outside the shelter of the cave into the rain that thundered down. Their silhouettes were visible, if only for a second, before they disappeared into the woods before them, leaving their leader to tend to his son.

Turning back to Thomas, Lore stretched his arms, and it was with a sigh that he said, "You have always had a hard time listening to me."

Thomas said nothing.

"Perhaps now you will do a better job."

His eyes darkened. "That is not fair."

"If you think I am going to nurture your every wound, you have many surprises in store for you. You have disobeyed me; you will suffer the consequences. What happened tonight was not because of me, it was your own selfish fault." When Thomas did not respond, he continued, "What did I tell you a few months ago?"

He searched his mind for anything significant Lore might have told him, but it was not long before Lore cut through his thoughts:

"The human woman, Thomas. Have you forgotten so soon? She has the blood of that damned Vampire. She can destroy us. It is imperative that you kill her."

He gritted his teeth. "She is *one* human. I do not see what the threat of her existence is!"

"She has the blood of Dracula flowing through her veins, you fool. It is a power so strong one simple drop is all it takes to turn our existence to ash. If the Vampires get a hold of her first, we will not stand a chance against their Armies and her. That, Thomas, is the threat of her existence."

Thomas grew silent, as Lore knew he would.

Taking advantage of this, he continued his lecture, "Why did you go against the order given to you, instead attacking a Vampire's manor?"

"The order you gave did not seem important," Thomas defended himself. "It seemed a waste, going after a human woman when there are Vampires out there who are able to kill us. And I thought you'd already found this woman, father."

"I did. But a foolish Vampire interrupted me—"

"Xavier?" he asked at once.

Casting him a disgusted look, Lore replied, "No, it was not Xavier. I believe that bloodsucker was his brother, Christian. He held no power, survived no training. The way he attacked me, it was clear he wished for death." Lore regained his serious countenance. "The human woman...her power is real. I have felt it. The light of her blood—" Lore shuddered "—it burned right through my fur and struck my own blood. And then others came." He rounded on his son. "You will find her, Thomas, and where I have failed, you will kill her. Do this for me, and I shall step down from my throne, and make you King."

He stared upon the man before him as if not believing what it was he said. It was only after a few minutes that he repeated, "You will make *me* King?"

He closed his eyes and sighed, opening them to reveal a softer gaze. "You have my word on this, Thomas."

"Th-Then I will find her, father. I will find her and kill her before the Vampires reach her. You have my word."

"Yes, of course," Lore said. "Return to your home, my son. I am sure you must keep up appearances with the humans."

Thomas nodded and turned to leave. Though he froze as he glared at the entrance of the cave.

Lore noticed this and turned to his son. "What is it?" he said, stepping up to reach him.

At Thomas's side, Lore snarled upon seeing the line of figures that stood there, their tattered cloaks weighed down with the rain. He glared at all of them before deciding that they were not human, but they were not Vampires or Lycans, or any Dark Creature that he was familiar with. What in the hell were they? And why couldn't he sense their presence? When did they arrive?

Thomas whispered, his gaze transfixed on the figure in the middle, "That's him. He took Mara."

"The Lycan?" Lore looked at the cloaked figure. "He is no Lycan, Thomas..."

"Then what *are you*?" Thomas screamed at the cloaked figures that would not move from the entrance of the cave.

One of them stepped forward and removed the hood from his head, revealing long dark-brown hair. His eyes focused only on Thomas, his tongue slithered through his lips as he talked. "Thomas Montague. Son to Lore. Prince of the Lycans. You have been called."

Thomas narrowed his eyes. "Called? Who are you?"

The man smiled. "I am Aciel. And you will be escorted to Eleanor Black. She wishes to speak with you."

Lore stepped forward, his features brazen and dangerous. "Who is this Eleanor Black and why does she want my son?"

Aciel did not appear intimidated at all. He continued to smile his thin smile, and addressed Lore for the first time that night. "This does not concern you, beast. Kindly retreat to the back of the cave like the good dog you are."

"*What?!*" Lore howled, unable to control his outrage. His clothes ripped from his body as he grew hairier, larger, his teeth stretching and growing into massive fangs. "Care to repeat your words?"

"No," Aciel said. "But I will tell you this: *Symbolia Menta*."

"Wh—?" Lore began, but his mouth snapped shut before he could continue speaking and he was thrown to the back of the cave by an invisible wind only targeted to him.

❋

Thomas started to transform, but Aciel spoke before he could get very far. "Careful, Thomas. We were told not to lay a finger on you, but it's best you don't do anything you will regret."

Another cloaked figure stepped forward and Thomas remembered it as the one who whisked Mara away from him. He instinctively stepped forward, his eyes narrowed dangerously. The cloaked figure removed his tattered hood in response to Thomas's stare and revealed a head of black, short hair and gleaming eyes. "Come now, Aciel, can't we have some fun with him? You should've seen the way he cried and ran after his wife."

"Enough," the Creature named Aciel said, lifting a hand to silence the man. "Return to the line, Amentias."

Amentias did as he was told, and with a snaky grin to Thomas, he placed his hood back over his head and fell back in line with the others.

Aciel said to Thomas, "Now. You will come with us, Lycan."

"And if I don't?" he snarled.

"Well," Aciel responded as though bored, "I suppose you shall never see your beloved wife again. Oh, yes, she is alive, Thomas, but not in a pretty shape at all. Oh no. You see, it appears humans cannot survive losing large amounts of blood like we can. She's barely holding on. We know you love her to no end, and we know you are going to listen to whatever it is we say, or else, the death of the Duchess of Holden shall be on your hands, my Duke."

The loud growl ripped through his teeth as he grabbed Aciel by the collar of his tattered cloak. "What have you done with her?"

171

Aciel lifted another hand to the cloaked figures to stay them. He glared into the hazel eyes of the enraged Lycan. "Let me go," he commanded.

"Not until you tell me what you've done to her."

Aciel sighed. "I've done nothing to your precious human, Thomas. Quite the contrary, you are causing her death by asking absurd questions and demanding things that don't exist. Now, if you would please, let me go, we will take you to her."

Thomas stared into his dark eyes before finally releasing him. He stepped away from the man, and turned to stare at his father, who was still in his beastly form, still unconscious, and it was then that he knew he had no choice: If going with these Creatures was the only way to see Mara again, he would do it. "All right. I'll go."

Aciel smiled. "You say that as if you had a choice."

Thomas scowled as he ventured into the heavy rain with the cloaked strangers, partly because he wished to see Mara again, and partly because he knew Aciel was right. He never had a choice to begin with.

# Chapter Eleven

# DEADLY TRAINING

Dropping the tray at his scream, the maid cast a look to the bed. His scream was haunting enough, but his teeth, they were the true reason for her fear. The two sharp fangs that sat in the front of his mouth were terrifying. She thought him to be an odd man, at first, but upon checking on him the day after Damion's disappearance, she soon knew that he was absolutely strange. Whenever she had to enter the room to sweep the dust from the dressers, or make sure he drank that awful smelling liquid upon his bedside table, she was always struck with the nightmarish feeling that this man was inhuman. His cruel stare whenever she entered the room made her feel as though he desired nothing more than to attack her. The only time she welcomed it was when she was free to leave the room, and his piercing stare glued itself to her back.

Picking up the tray with shaking hands, she placed it on the small table next to his bed, careful not to glance at his face. She strolled to the large windows that hid the sun's warmth with thick, gray curtains, lifting a hand to sweep back the curtains of the first window, when the loud voice boomed through the room. "Don't touch them!"

Jumping at the sound, she released the curtain, and turned slowly to eye the man that now sat on the side of the bed, His black eyes gleamed in the shadow of the room. His long hair clung to his shoulders and arms and seemed to be drenched in what was possibly his sweat. His pale face was sharp, handsome, but all the same, disconcerting, and it was here she tried her hardest not to look as he spoke.

"The...sun irritates me. I am sorry to have frightened you. What is your name?"

Such simple words, but spoken with such a smooth tongue. Trying to find words to match such an eloquent voice, she whispered, "E-Emily, my Lord."

He stretched an arm out to his side and cracked his fingers, causing her to wince with the sheer control he seemed to exude. And as she continued to stare at him in bewilderment, he spoke yet again: "Emily? What a pretty name. How long...have you worked for his Lordship, Damion?"

"Since I was old enough to walk. My mother is the Head Maid," she whispered, very aware that she could not raise her voice any higher.

"Hm. You were born into the help, then. Interesting." He stood at last, quite tall, his unbuttoned blouse wrinkled from lying in the bed all day, and a sleeve of the blouse was missing—it seemed to have been ripped off—and dried blood was splattered across it. He did not seem to mind this as he bent over, stretching his back by touching his toes.

Emily could not help but find his bloodstained shirt odd. "My Lord, your shirt, it's..."

He cracked his neck while returning to a standing position. Taking notice of her words, he looked down at his open shirt and saw the blood, the hole where a sleeve once remained. Slipping out of it, he threw it onto the bed and moved toward the large dresser against the wall. He looked around the drawer for a clean shirt and spoke into the bundle of clothes. "Where is Damion?"

"L-Lord Damion is away. He has told no one where he has gone," she said, her cheeks burning red as she gazed upon him.

※

Christian paused upon hearing this, but pulled out a fresh, tan blouse and slipped it on. As he buttoned it, he said, "I take it he has not told you when he will be back?"

"He hasn't."

"Of course," he whispered. *Where on Earth could he have gone? And so suddenly?*

"I-I should leave you I have bothered you long enough. Please, excuse me," she said. And with a steadying breath, she began to walk through the small pathway between the bed and the dresser, keeping her head down as she moved.

He stilled when she swept behind him, her scent drifting to his nose. All thoughts of Damion, of the mysterious woman, left his mind immediately. He was very aware how thirsty he had been for human blood. *Yes, as helpful as Unicorn blood was,* he decided, *there was nothing like human to quell a Vampire's hunger.*

He turned to her, placing a hand upon her shoulder before she could step past the end board of the large bed. The gasp that escaped her lips at his touch sent his blood soaring. He had known she was scared of him, but it hardly mattered whilst he recovered from his injuries in his bed. But now that he was free—and healed he could take advantage of her fear.

"Emily, wait," he said, suppressing a small smile as best he could as she turned to eye him, confusion and apprehension shining in her brown eyes.

"Yes," she heaved, "my Lord?"

He let a sigh escape his chest. He eyed her naked shoulders, smelling in earnest now the blood that filled her veins: sweet, destroying, vital—he had to have her. "You have been assigned to me, correct?" he asked her, trying to suppress the drive to step forward and sink his fangs into her tender neck.

She looked up into his eyes, a sort of dark cloud falling upon her own. "Assigned to you? Y-Yes, I have been."

He lifted a finger to stroke the tendrils of her soft black hair, causing her to wince, his voice low as he said, "Oh? And it is just you that has been assigned to care for me? Because if you are the only one, my dear Emily, I assure you, the fruits of your labor will be enjoyed by the both of us."

"My Lord," she whispered, unable to look away from his gaze.

He lifted her chin. *You are mine*, he thought. *You. Are. Mine.* "Please, call me Christian."

※

She dived underneath the sheets again, the warmth of the day beaming through the open windows, warming her skin through the many layers of fabric.

It had been three days since she'd opened her eyes to find she was in the care of a wealthy man. Alexandria did not know what to make of it, but she decided to take in the comforts of being cared for by maids and servants at her every beck and call.

She was not used to such luxuries having come from a moderately wealthy home. She had had enough gold to her name to afford her a settled life, but nothing more. She rose out of the bed and stepped to the windows, looking out over the land as she had done many times before.

"'Ello dear, it's good to see that you're up and about," the soft, caring voice said from behind her.

She turned, taking in the friendly old woman dressed in a maid's uniform. She carried a tray of tea and steaming oatmeal.

Alexandria smiled, the woman the only friendly face she knew here. "Hello, Mary. Is that for me?"

"Of course," she said, moving to place the tray on a small table in the middle of the large room. "The Master wishes for you to be healthy upon his arrival, of course."

Alexandria swept her dark brown hair away from her shoulders, swaying in her white chemise. "Who is he, exactly? I've never heard of him before," she told the woman whose smile never seemed to fade.

"Oh," Mary began, running her hands over her skirt, "he's Damion Nicodemeus. His mother was Countess Nepenthe Nicodemeus. I can't remember what they were wealthy from, but it's definitely been passed on."

"So his mother was a countess? Where is she now?"

Mary fished around the large closet. "Dead," she said, as if explaining the weather. She returned to Alexandria with a light peach sundress laced with gold thread. "For you to wear around the house. This was his mother's...as was this room."

Alexandria took the dress from her with careful hands. "This was her room? And her clothes?" she asked, confused. "Why have I been placed here? Surely, there are many other rooms around the mansion for me to have rested—"

She began to undress Alexandria from her nightgown, shushing her with her next words, "His room is right next door. I assume that's why he wanted you here, wanted you close to him, I suppose." She stood while Alexandria examined the sundress she was about to adorn, and pointed to a door. "Leads to his room. He used to sneak in here and sleep with her when he was a lad." Her features then darkened. "Terrible shame, her death. Poor woman didn't even see it coming."

Alexandria waited until the dress hung around her body before proceeding with her next set of questions. "What happened, if I may be so bold to ask?"

Mary's pale-blue eyes admired the dress. "Lovely..." she whispered. Then she thought of the question. "That...was never revealed to us, my dear, but from what we witnessed of that night, it was terrible. Absolutely terrible. The amount of blood Damion and Darien returned home with—"

"Darien?"

Her lips pursed as her eyes danced with every notion of saying something she shouldn't have. "Never mind that. It was a long time ago." And she began to move away from Alexandria, still admiring her small frame and the dress that flowed around her body. "It fits you like a charm. You must walk about the mansion, my dear. Meet everyone. They're dying to meet you, of course."

"Y-Yes, of course," Alexandria muttered, still wondering who in the world Darien was and why she was there... Why the image of piercing brown eyes would not leave the back of her eyelids.

With one last smile, Mary walked to the large doors and proceeded down the hall.

Alexandria stared after the old woman, wondering how long the woman had lived here, cleaning up after Damion Nicodemeus and his brother. Finally deciding it was none of her business, and that she was going to leave the moment Lord Damion showed his face again, she eyed her cup of tea, the steam billowing up from the small porcelain cup that sat atop its saucer. She moved for the cup, and just as her fingers rounded the handle, the sound reached her ears and she froze.

She stood straight, replaying the sound in her mind. She couldn't place it; it was like nothing she'd ever heard before. Sighing, for the sound did not resurface, she moved for the tea once more, and then another sound, much louder now, hit her ears and she almost dropped it in surprise.

*Something is going on here*, she decided. She turned from the tray and looked around. She thought of mice knocking something over in another room, but then she realized a house this grand and this well cared for wouldn't have mice. Her curiosity piqued, she forgot about her tea and moved for the doors, determined to see what was making this odd noise.

She blinked the strange brown gaze returned to her mind's eye and she pressed it back into the recesses of the fear she now felt.

It took a bit of effort on her part to get a door open, but she managed and slipped through. She looked around at the large hallway. It stretched for miles to the left of her, the right ending in an abrupt wall, only one set of doors next to her own. She heard a low sound then, and her attention was brought to the room directly across from hers.

She moved out, her bare feet touching the cold marble floor, toward these doors, her heart increasing in its speed as the curiosity, the fear grew.

Raising a slightly shaking hand, she reached for a door's handle, thousands of questions running through her mind.

Another low growl sounded through the doors. It sounded harsh, strange, as if an animal rested beyond them. She wondered what could be on the other side, her hand finally clasping the cold, golden handle. She pressed down, the door sliding open with surprisingly little effort.

※

Christian looked down at the young maid, her hair flying out around her head like a black puddle, joining with the dark blood that now seeped from her stomach.

He wiped off the blade of the small dagger, letting the napkin settle at her body growling for a third time. He could not allow her to be turned, it was against the rules, but now, as he stared at her and the increasing puddle that seemed determined to claim his feet within it, he knew not what to do with her next.

There were many maids up and about, and he could not afford to draw attention to himself by having a dead woman in the middle of his room. He knew he was running out of time. Surely, a maid or two had begun to wonder where their dear Emily had gone....

Christian froze as he heard the door creak, and his eyes darted to them: One was opening. Barely having time to think, he darted for the closet, swinging the doors shut right as the head of an incredibly gorgeous woman inched through the crack of the large door.

Christian watched the mysterious woman look around the room, her eyes venturing to the body on the floor. He snarled as she let out a raucous scream.

✳

"Now tell me again, as clear as you can: What happened?" he asked, looking down at her through thin spectacles.

Alexandria clutched the hem of her sundress; her knuckles white as her hands shook violently. She choked back tears, preparing herself to try to address him again.

"I heard a sound," she gasped, "it was...like a body hitting the ground...heavy. I-I got up to see wh-what it could've been." She rubbed her eyes. "When I opened the door and looked around the room, I saw her there—" Her voice broke off as more tears began to fall.

Patting her back, Mary cast a look to the authorities that very much said Alexandria would not able to answer any more of their questions.

Nodding, the officer turned to the other maids present. "Who else is a guest in this home?"

A young maid with a trembling voice said, "Th-there is another man here staying with L-Lord Damion."

"And where is he currently?"

The maids offered each other solemn looks.

Mary spoke up when the officer appeared ready to ask yet another question. "We do not know. As far as I am aware, Emily was the one made to watch over Lord Delacroix. They did not leave that room."

"Lord Delacroix? *The* Lord Delacroix? Xavier?"

She stepped away from Alexandria, who had finally stopped crying. "No, not Lord Xavier. Master Christian, his brother."

"Really? You say he was in the room the whole morning? Never left it?"

"Never."

Rubbing his chin, the officer's unusual eyes seemed to glow. "Very well. I believe we are done here," he said.

A deep voice sounded from a dark corner: "Leaving so soon, constable?"

The constable turned, as did every other person in the room.

Christian stepped forward into the light of the chandelier overhead, his black eyes watching the constable.

"My Lord," he bowed, "are you aware there has been a murder in your room?"

Christian's eyebrows arched high. "Really? Have you a suspect?"

"No, my Lord. But we have been told it was your room that the maid was found...."

"So naturally," Christian said, walking closer to the table where Alexandria sat gaping up at him with large eyes, "you would suspect me to have killed her."

The constable ran his eyes over Christian's calm exterior. It was clear that he was the one who did it, for no one else in the mansion was a Vampire. "In other cases, my Lord. But for this, we are positive it was not you. How could it have been you when you were elsewhere this whole time?" Before anyone else could speak, he added, "And, of course, such publicity is surely not wanted. Lord Damion would return most unpleased to learn of this...scandal. May we just take care of the poor girl and be on with it?" His eyes seemed to glow as he eyed every person present in the room.

Christian smiled, glad that matters would be taken care of, indeed. "Yes, I believe it is safe to say you are correct, constable," he said, reaching out to shake the man's hand.

The constable extended his hand and Christian took it in his, his eyes drifting to the gold ring nestled on the man's finger. His gaze then returned to the constable's face, and he noticed the constable held a strange smile.

The voice sounded in his head as clear as day: *"Be more careful, Christian, we cannot continue to cover for your poor choices in places to feed."*

Releasing his grip, Christian inclined his head slightly, as if to say the matter couldn't be helped and stepped back.

The constable raised an eyebrow then shook his head in a noncommittal way before nodding his departure to all in the room. His eyes lingered on Christian's before he and his men proceeded down the long hallway and through the large doors.

The remaining maids wiped at their faces, blotting the tears that fell. After a few moments of silence, they blinked and looked to one another with confused expressions.

Mary blinked as well and then waved a hand to the other maids who stood around dumbfounded. "Why are you all standing around? There's a lot of work to be done before his Lordship returns! C'mon then!"

The other maids lifted their skirts in a hurry, running off in opposite directions of the mansion to tend to their duties.

Mary turned back to Alexandria, who hadn't taken her eyes off

Christian since he made his appearance. "Can I get anything for you, m'dear?"

"No, I'm fine. Thank you," she responded quietly.

Mary smiled and patted Alexandria absentmindedly before taking off through a doorway, leaving the two completely alone.

Christian took notice of the human's stare and turned to her. She did not withdraw her gaze. "Hello."

"Hello...Lord Delacroix, is it?" she asked.

"It is," he almost whispered. He watched her amazing eyes. How interesting they were. They seemed to meet his with almost the same amount of intensity—almost. "And who would you be?"

She stood from her chair and turned to him. "I am Alexandria Stone, my Lord," she said, half-curtsying, half-bowing.

Christian stared at her, trying his best to decide who she could be, and then it came to him: She was the one he saw in the woods with the Lycan. Damion did save her, after all. How interesting things had become.

"Alexandria," the name slithered off his tongue easily, "do you know why you are here?"

"I was told that I was saved by a Lord Damion Nicodemeus. I have come to understand this is his home?"

"Yes. Yes, it is."

He looked down at his hands, noticing he held no ring on his finger, and yet he did not wish to bite her. Thinking this odd, he looked up at her again and noticed her eyes had narrowed. "Is something the matter?"

She said nothing, but stepped closer to him. He did not move, although everything in his mind screamed to get away.

She said, "Forgive me, but I believe I have seen you somewhere before."

"Is that so?"

Alexandria seemed to be at work, shifting through her brain to think of where she had seen him. "I am almost positive we have met once before."

Christian wondered whether he should probe her for information or let her be. He decided not to press the situation further, as he had to find the bloody ring Damion removed from his finger, or else he could not feign being human. "Excuse me, Miss Stone, but I must leave you, there is something I have left in my quarters."

And he stepped past her, quite aware their arms brushed as he did so, and still he could not smell a trickle of blood from her. Never turning, he ascended the spiral stairs, feeling her eyes upon his back and he wondered who in the world Alexandria Stone was.

✳

She twirled her many necklaces through her long fingers.

He said, "What if he does not return?"

"He will."

Aciel placed a hand on Amentias's shoulder. "You worry too much, my friend. Eleanor knows how to get what she wants. He will return. We have his wife."

Amentias flexed his jaw. "But even so, did we have to turn her?"

"We did no such thing. If I remember correctly, Amentias, it was you who bit her. We had no choice but to allow the process to finish," Eleanor said from her chair, still twirling her necklaces in her fingers.

"Even so, it was not a part of the plan. Are you not upset with me, Miss Black?" Amentias asked, confused.

Eleanor finally turned away from her necklaces. She looked at Amentias, her words cool, "Upset? Why in the world would I be upset? You have given Thomas to me, and as a gift, we have a new member for our little union. There is no reason for me to be upset. On the contrary, I believe this is cause for celebration."

"Really?" Amentias said.

Aciel patted him on the shoulder. "You are too tense, my friend. We are not like the Vampires who uphold their ranks and titles to the nose. We are all equal here. We are here because we wish to be, not because we are forced."

"Quite right." Standing from her chair, her long hair flew out behind her. "Ah," she said, spotting the two men who entered the small room next. "What news have you for me?"

They both kneeled, their dark robes puddling around them. The man with dark brown hair and a pointed nose spoke first. "We have secured the next phase, Miss Black. Shall we proceed?"

Eleanor stepped forward, stopping just in front of them. "No," she said, looking down at them, "not yet. I wish to see how things turn out before we proceed."

"Very well," the other man said. His hair was an odd mix of black and silver, falling over his shoulders in a cascading flourish.

"Is that all?" Eleanor asked them.

The same man seemed to hesitate before he replied with, "No. It appears there has been a problem in the Vampire City."

Eleanor's face became one of curiosity. "What sort of problem, Specter?"

The man with dark brown hair said, "Our sources have told us that Damion Nicodemeus was badly injured in a confrontation with another Vampire."

Eleanor's eyes widened in surprise. "Who was it? Was it Xavier?"

"No. It appears to have been Dragor Descant."

The voice came from behind her, "Dragor Descant attacked Damion Nicodemeus?"

Eleanor turned. "You know of Dragor?"

"Of course, I, myself, had the honor of facing him years ago," Aciel said. "He is—was—the First Captain of the First Army. Why did he attack Damion?"

# S.C. PARRIS

The man with cascading hair spoke up next, "We have gathered that Dragor never forgave Damion for an alleged attack during the Elves' invasion of the City."

"That was three years ago," Eleanor almost laughed, "why do something about it now?"

Aciel, who stood next to Eleanor, told her, "Perhaps he was waiting for the perfect opportunity? The Vampires are there, are they not? And who better for Dragor to share his troubles with than his great friend, Xavier Delacroix?"

"Hm. I see your point. In any case, it's absolutely absurd. At this rate, the Vampires will destroy themselves without my interference."

Aciel's narrow eyes danced in their sockets. "Are we going to allow them to do so?" Eleanor placed her necklaces about her throat. "Of course not. How can we obtain them if they wish to destroy themselves?" Waving a hand to the two men who still kneeled before her, she dismissed them, saying, "Specters, rise. I will call you when I am in need of you once more. Return to the Vampire City and gather more information."

They both stood simultaneously, their long dark robes flying over the wooden floor. They bowed before her and turned to leave when she said, "Wait. Amentias...go with them."

He folded his arms across his chest. "I am relatively new, Miss Black. I don't think I can control this power for such an amount of time."

She turned to him. "You will. You have proven yourself thus far. I believe you shall find that remaining a Vampire is far easier than maintaining a Lycan form."

He hesitated.

Aciel said, "Eleanor, we have never witnessed Amentias's Vampire form. Who is to say he can control it for an hour, a week, several months at best?"

186

Eleanor glared at him. "I am quite sure he can handle the Vampire form, Aciel. He was a Lycan before you met him, this I know." Her eyes moved over Amentias's face. "I suppose we shall have to run a few tests on him."

Aciel looked at her in shock, his voice a whisper, "Tests? Eleanor, we haven't had to have any tests since—"

"Since you?" Eleanor cut him off. "I am well aware. It is unfortunate that every so often there are the select few that cannot transform successfully at will."

Aciel clenched his jaw, his eyes vicious. "I was the first one you met, Eleanor," he spat, "of course I was not able to transform successfully. But those tests—those tests are obvious suicide."

"Yet you agreed without further coercion. Explain how suicidal one would have to be to risk their life to join me?"

Amentias narrowed his eyes at Aciel. Placing his inquisitive stare back upon the beautiful woman beside him, he asked, "What tests?"

Eleanor's lips curled upward at the question. "Are you willing to put your life on the line to achieve complete control over the power given to you?"

He stared at her. "Yes," he responded, almost amazed he never realized how beautiful she truly was.

"Good." She turned away from him and eyed the two Specters who still stood in the doorway, and she told them, "Take your leave. He will not be joining you now."

They bowed again and took off, closing the door behind them as they went.

Aciel looked away from Eleanor and Amentias in disgust.

Eleanor ignored him, walking to the other side of the small room, towards a wooden door with a rusted, golden knob. She reached out for it and turned, pushing the door open.

Amentias followed in her footsteps, walking to meet her in front of the door. From here, the darkness of the room beyond greeted him. He took a step back, overwhelmed by the cold and roughness of the wind that seemed to emanate from nowhere.

"In order to become a Vampire, you must die and be reborn by drinking another Vampire's blood at the cusp of death's hold. However," she said, gazing into the dark room before her, "an Elite takes a different approach. You gain power by facing your fears. Do you understand, Amentias?"

He shook his head, his brow furrowed. "I am not sure."

"Do not tell me you are unsure, Amentias. You have come this far. You have agreed to my tests. We shall follow through—do I make myself clear?"

He took a deep breath and glanced from the darkness back to the calm woman at his side. "Crystal," he muttered, wondering what he'd gotten himself into, indeed.

"Step through," she said, gesturing a hand toward the freezing room.

Amentias took another deep breath and stepped forward.

Eleanor stepped forward as well, disappearing into the cold.

※

Aciel closed his eyes when the door shut behind him. The pain of such a transformation returned to him, and along with this were the memories of what he'd endured. The crushing cold, the taunting, terribly unhelpful figures that had appeared, the strange voices screaming around him from everywhere, nowhere, the dark land that cast one into a state of perpetual terror. And he had joined those screams when the strongest of all figures had appeared before him, the completely black eyes, leathery gray skin, and large bat-like wings cutting an impressive figure against the strange dark.

This figure had wanted him to join him, yes, he had, but he had not been able—he had failed, unable to take the thing's black-clawed hand. And it had reached for him, tearing at his throat, his scream the loudest in his ears, then—

The scream encased his mind and body, but it was not his scream, he realized. He turned to the wooden door from where the scream erupted and his heart felt like ice in his chest.

He could not move. He listened to the horrified calls of Amentias's voice from behind the weathered door, unable to believe a mere page could create such horrors...

The death of a human soul into that of a feeder, a soulless, bloodthirsty Creature from which there was no return. But Eleanor had found a way. She had found a way to return to life after one had experienced death.

And Aciel hoped for the life of him that Amentias could survive such a horrible transition.

❋

Xavier turned with the voice, the crowd of curious Vampires detouring around him within the long hallway. Armand Dragon stepped toward him, his long black hair swaying, his red robes swishing quickly around his black boots. "Xavier! Xavier Delacroix!"

"Goldchair? Is something the matter?" he asked when Armand reached him.

The sea of Vampires detoured around them.

Armand ignored their curious stares. "It's Dracula. He wishes to speak with you. He says it's of the highest priority."

"What are we speaking here?"

"A level ten," he said quietly.

Xavier pushed the rolls of parchments he held into Armand's hands. "Take them to my office," he said before heading for the place he knew Dracula would be.

He muttered several pardons as he squeezed through the crowded hallway, well aware the Vampires he pushed past stared up at him in sheer awe.

The more he walked, the more the large sea of Vampires began to thin. He stepped briskly, entering the darker corridors of the mansion. Small, and not made of marble or brick, they were pure stone, the amount of torchlight here scarce at best. Only a select few Vampires were allowed to walk the smaller corridors that stretched on for several miles before the intended destination was reached: Dracula's training room.

Xavier knew the level ten priority message he was given would not lead him to find Dracula in his office. A level ten—the highest-level priority message Dracula could ever give—meant that Dracula would be in the only place he and his Vampires could be completely alone. The training room also served as a secret meeting place where Dracula and the Vampire Order, or the Chairs, could sit and discuss urgent business. And at times, if it was needed, other high-ranking Dark Creatures would be directed to the room in order to discuss certain matters with the King of all Creatures.

As he passed the last Vampire patrolling the small corridors, Xavier's smile faded. He had an idea of what lay behind the door. Perhaps Dracula uncovered some sort of information about Eleanor. Perhaps Dragor would be freed. Or even, perhaps, they had found the human woman Dracula required to destroy the Lycans.

These thoughts and many others filled his mind, but when he grabbed the cold handle, they dispersed. He pushed open the door, greeted with blinding darkness. "Naturally," he muttered to himself as he stepped forward into the room, allowing the door to shut behind him.

Torches that lined the large dark room sparked to life, creating an eerie glow throughout the stone dungeon. Xavier turned his attention to the small table that sat in the middle of the room and the

Vampire who sat there, his chair facing the door, a dark look in his eyes. "Come forth, Mister Delacroix," Dracula said.

Xavier moved for the table and when he was near, Dracula said, "You hurried here. I'm glad to see that a level-ten still claims your attention."

"I don't see why it wouldn't," Xavier began, "—what is the emergency?"

He stood, reaching Xavier's level of sight. "Dragor is still in the Chambers of Waiting. While you were resting, he tried to escape. He was not successful. He is fine...for now. The First Army Officers that were standing guard at the Chambers of Waiting stopped him before he could get very far—"

"You placed his own officers in charge of watching him?!"

"Yes. I know how it must seem, but it is for the best. Would you rather I have placed any other Army in guard of the Chambers? Exactly. Now, I am thinking of having Dragor moved away, out of the City. I had a talk with few other Chamber Masters, and Dragor Descant's attack on Damion does not sit well with them. At this rate, if questioned, Damion could very well keep his position in the Order and Dragor—"

"Will be sentenced to a day in the sunlight. Death," Xavier finished.

"Exactly."

"What am I here for?" he asked, not liking where this conversation was going in the least.

Dracula looked away from his eyes for a second before returning his gaze. "I am asking you... I am asking you to escort Dragor out of the Vampire City. He will go to Lane or Quiddle, or any other Vampire town across this world, but he must not stay here."

"Dracula, do you understand what you are asking me to do?"

"Yes," he said. "I am telling you to escort Dragor Descant out of this City by any means necessary. I have spoken with Civil, Richard,

Warren, and Sarah. Warren and Richard are the only members who do not agree with Civil. Sarah—being the newest member to both the Clearance Committee and the Chamber Masters—does not know Civil well enough to know where his true intentions stand."

"And have you mentioned this plan to Warren, Richard?"

"No. If I had, we would be having this discussion in my office with the two Vampires present," Dracula responded. He must have seen the puzzled expression on Xavier's face, for he said, "I do not trust those Vampires as much as I trust you, Xavier. I am telling you to do this because I know you will get it done without hesitation."

"Dracula, to break the very rule you created—can you not just make your word final? Tell Civil and the other Masters that Dragor is not a criminal? You do believe he is not a criminal…?"

He sighed. "With all that has happened here, Xavier, it is clear either Dragor or Damion, or both Vampires, are clearly out of line. Damion is close to awakening, but Victor cannot be a witness. I sent him back to the surface with Lillith. Without a witness to the events that took place three years ago, Dragor is as good as dead."

Bewilderment filled him. "Why send Victor to the surface if he is needed for the trial?"

"Lillith needs a place to reside. I've sent them back so they can work it out between themselves and Victor's servants."

"Surely there are more important things going on here, Victor is needed—"

Dracula eyed him darkly, sending him into silence at once. "Regardless of where Victor is needed, it remains that Dragor will leave this place. Now, can you do this for me?"

He stared at him for a few moments, not sure what thoughts lingered behind the Vampire's brown eyes, but it was clear the Creature had ulterior motives. Trying his luck, he asked, "Why must Dragor leave?"

"Because he must. You will go to him now. I do think it is the right time for you to make your escape. As it stands, the halls are filled with Vampires from other towns and cities here in preparation for the Ball. If you leave now, I'm sure you will return in time to attend."

His brow furrowed in bewilderment. *What was going on?* "Your Ball is not held until the nearing of winter, Dracula."

"Yes, but that does not mean my friends cannot come and linger to their dead hearts' content. Dragor, Xavier."

He stared at him, almost admiring the hardened, cold gaze he was given. He knew all at once that, whatever more was said, Dracula would not let him do anything more without seeing Dragor out of the City.

He bowed, though his mind still burned with thought. "I will go to Dragor, but what shall I tell the Committee?"

Dracula's eyes narrowed. "Oh, I'm sure you'll think of something."

✳

Amentias's nails filled with dirt as he was dragged viciously across the ground. "Eleanor!" he cried, "help me!"

She stared at him, her eyes taunting and cruel, her boots caked with the dirt he sent flying in the air with his struggle. "Claim your thirst for the blood of the living," she said, and it was as though she didn't care what happened to him.

He screamed, the cold hand gracing his hair, spreading even more blood throughout his black locks. The touch like ice, burning against his scalp. His lungs freezing, he gasped for warm air only to be greeted with returning frost.

Through the drops of black blood that sprayed his face, he looked up at her. Beautiful, dangerous Eleanor Black. Was this what he agreed to do? Succumb to whatever this madness was for mere power? What if he did not return? What if he never returned to the way he was—*who* he was?

He gasped yet again, another gust of cold air entering his lungs, and he found her eyes, black with no feeling. It was then that he knew she was no longer human, no longer a Vampire, for even a Vampire's eyes were not so terribly cold. Her eyes held no raging warmth of a Lycan. *What was she?*

When what felt like two burning hands pressed against his back, he searched her eyes rapidly, desperate for any sign of bloody life, finding none.

"Wh-Why?" he coughed, a gasp quickly leaving him, more cold air filling his lungs. The cold unbearable now.

She smiled.

He heard the growing howls of the dead. They pulled at him fiercely, drawing closer to the black puddle of blood. He continued to dig his nails into the ground, unsuccessfully stalling their attempts to pull him under. "What *are* you? Why have you done this to me?" he cried.

She walked alongside him as he slid against his will. Clapping her hands together, her hair swayed in the cold breeze. "I have done nothing. You agreed to my training. You have put yourself here. It seems you are not ready to face power, any amount of hesitation or fear will halt the process, Amentias. You must be confident, strong-willed. You must know you will return from where true power hides." her voice softening, though her eyes did not.

His veined hands wrapped around a long, jagged rock. He pulled himself toward it, even as the hands pulled him harder in the opposite direction. "What is this?!"

She bent her knees to reach his level and grazed a finger underneath his chin, the warmth of her touch causing his skin to sizzle. He closed his eyes at her touch, no longer able to scream. Her voice was warm and caring, although he knew if he opened his eyes, he would find the exact opposite.

"This is the struggle of your courage to hold true power. You fight with the power; you deny its truth. However, if you simply let them take you under," and her eyes danced to the black puddle behind him where more dead bodies broke the surface, "you will emerge a Vampire. The first step to true power."

*First step?!*

She removed her finger from his chin and placed her palm on his bloody face. The warmth returned to his cheek and his eyes shot open with her touch.

The cold of the dead washed away, moving down his body. His heart beat faster, lungs springing to life with blissful warm air. Almost at once did he feel the cold arms and hands shrink from him, and without turning to look, he knew the dead had retreated into the black puddle of blood: The sound of bodies submerging reached his ears.

His grip on the jagged rock loosened and he fell to the ground. His breathing quickened, mind running wild with what she had done to get her power...what she had lost, and with one last glance to the woman that stood over him, his eyes widened.

She was no longer beautiful, her skin was leathery and black, her feet clawed with long black talons, her head long, chin pointed, eyes completely black, and the large, bat-like wings that had appeared upon her back spread wide, sending tufts of fur to fly toward his face.

He blinked, tufts of brown fur, Lycan, he vaguely guessed, catching in his mouth and eyes. He spit them out, the words he wished to scream getting lost in the high-pitched screech that left her large, many-fanged mouth, before he drifted off into a deep sleep, and all, miraculously, was lost to him.

# Chapter Twelve

# DESPERATION

Christian returned to his room for the second time that day. He had been called downstairs to meet with several Vampires who just happened to be passing Damion's mansion when they had heard that Christian Delacroix was residing there. Luckily, no word of the Lycan's attack reached their ears, and he was grateful for this little fact. The less he would have to hear that he was not as responsible as his brother, the absolute better. One could go mad being compared to their sibling for several decades.

A knock on the door beckoned his attention.

"Enter," he said.

He heard the door creak open yet silence filled his ears for a brief moment. It was replaced with, "Sorry for the intrusion, my Lord."

He cracked his neck, shaking the sweetness of the voice from his ears. Although he did this, the pain of the damned ring caused his hand to tense and he wished he could throw it off and be rid of it once and for all, yet he knew that couldn't be so.

Turning to face her, he let a smile fall over his lips, however false it was. "Miss Stone."

She curtsied, lifting the skirts of a royal-blue gown as she did so.

With her dip, he stared at the shining necklace that fell in between her breasts. His throat went dry, with thirst, desire...he wasn't quite sure.

"I have been asked to attend a ball tonight," she said, her brown-green eyes gazing upon him in what seemed blatant interest, "shall you...accompany me, my Lord?"

Christian tilted his head at her benign beauty. Her dark brown hair curled down her shoulders and back, pulling him to the structure of her heart-shaped face: It was hard to look away. "I shall," he said at last, licking his lips, sending a tinge of red to touch to her cheeks.

Alexandria curtsied again and left the room, something like confusion lining her frame.

He stared at the door for a moment, not quite sure what just happened. *She had asked to attend a ball? But who knew she was here?* Something was wrong, he decided then, not at all realizing that the sight of her had sent his blood to burn in his veins until the ring broke in two upon his finger and fell with a pathetic clank to the floor.

"What on Earth?" he whispered, staring at his ring-less hand, mind racing with the rush of blood throughout his body: He barely had room to think about how this could have happened. His thoughts were occupied with the curious Alexandria Stone. The moment she'd entered the room, his mind went completely blank, the aching of the ring growing worse the longer he'd watched her.

Never before had a human woman caused such a reaction within him with the bloody ring on. What was wrong with him?

But who, indeed, was she? They had saved her, that much was certain, but why exactly, he could not say. It was the Lycans that propelled his actions that night, yet the thought of them laying harm to her maddened him. Why?

Shaking his head free of those thoughts, he bent and picked up the fragments of the ring, eyeing them in his palm. Never before had it broken—it was resilient. He'd had it for many years. Why did it break now? And with the sight of a mere woman?

But, more importantly, he snarled, feeling his tongue go dry for the taste of blood: How in the world was he to get through the evening?

※

"The missus is waiting in the carriage, my Lord," a young man said, bowing before him.

He fixed his collar and slipped on the black suit jacket. "Thank you. I'll be down shortly," he said, watching the boy leave the room, closing the large door behind him.

His eyes turned: The room became doused in red, a sigh of relief escaping him. The pain of holding in the urge to tear the young man's head off seared through him, maintaining his natural eye color was terribly painful as well.

He sighed. *An evening of holding my breath every time a human passes, neck exposed, blood surging...* With unsteady hands, he resumed fixing his collar, pausing only when the realization that he had no idea who was throwing this ball came to him. It could very well be a human, but in that case, he would have no idea who this human would be. He was not as outgoing as his brother and the other Vampires. The only people he knew were the maids and servants of his manor, as well as the maids and servants of Damion's and Victor's. In this case, the invitation to a grand ball must have come from a Vampire.

*Perhaps it was not a Vampire who presented the invitation,* he thought, releasing his collar, stepping up to the door. *Perhaps Alexandria's relatives were aware of her whereabouts and wished to see her again. If that was the case, tonight would be an evening filled with humans.*

Closing his eyes, he let his mind dance to thoughts of human blood reaching his nose, freely, unguarded. He opened his eyes, reaching for the handle, mind set on the blood that would be there. He pushed down, the blood of those in the manor, present and unyielding, reaching his nose without abandon.

The woman walked into view, a basket filled with fresh clothes tight in her hands. Her blood slid to his nose, and his red gaze fell upon her neck. She bent low, placing the basket just before the door, and when she lifted herself to open it, he spied the back of her neck. A surge of need rushed through him, and not being able to control himself, he opened the door with more force than he would have liked.

It slammed against the wall of his bedroom, leaving a crack where the edges of the door hit.

She jumped at the sound and turned to face the noise, and Christian smelled her fear, smelled as it subsided with her steadying heart.

"My Lord," she whispered. "You scared me."

"I'm...sorry." He breathed deep, taking in more of her scent, taking his hand off the door, keeping his gaze upon the floor. He could not let her see his eyes. "I figured you could use a hand. Please, let me..." he said, stepping into the hallway, a rush of even more blood reaching his senses. He could not still the snarl that escaped his throat. He moved to her despite her curious stare, and, careful not to touch her, he reached past, turning the handle of the heavy door. It slid open with ease.

"Thank you, my Lord," she said.

He knew she was flustered, he could smell it, now so terribly close...

He heard her heart rate increase and his own soared, pumping against his ribcage just as it had done in the absence of Alexandria Stone. He was careful not to look into her eyes, as he stepped away from her, her racing blood, and allowed her room to pick up the basket filled with Damion's clothes. "You are very welcome," he said, barely able to suppress his need, careful as ever not to show his fangs.

She continued to stare at him for several moments before bending to grasp at the basket at her feet.

He saw the back of her neck, quite bare, wisps of brown hair against her skin, the faint traces of sweat just there.

He seized his chance.

As she rose, he allowed his senses to guide him behind her, he allowed the smell of her blood to propel his hands to move to her lips, pressing them shut. "Do not scream," he whispered in her ear.

No sound protruded past muffled lips, but he could feel the tremulous pulsing of her blood beneath her skin... How it drove him so...

His eyes flashed and Damion's door swung open, and he thought the words: *Enter the room.*

She moved forward as he slowly removed his hand from her mouth, watching her shake, but step into the red room she did.

He followed her, only able to stare upon her back as she stopped walking, placing the basket on the floor before her feet as though her body was not her own.

And it wasn't.

He waved a hand and the door closed behind him, his command stretching across her body: She stiffened as though a cold wind had blown through, striking her where she stood. He took a slow step forward, her blood filling his nose, sending his mind to empty, nothing but the taste of that sweet blood driving him toward her—

"Wh-What are you?" she breathed, her soft, shaking voice filling him with confusion.

He had not allowed her to speak.

"Never mind what I am," he said, wondering how she had

spoken. He stepped to her quicker still, watching her eyes widen, marvelous fear clear within them. She inhaled sharply, slow tears forming, and he stopped just before her, her blood pulsing, finding a home in his eager brain, the hand that lifted to touch her skin...

He could only vaguely register the stark apprehension on her face, when she opened her mouth and inhaled, and he blinked, regaining his mind, for he knew what would happen long before it did.

He moved behind her, pressing a hand to her lips, the scream dying before it had a chance to shake the air, and he, slipping a shaking hand around her waist, allowed her blood to propel him. He pressed his fangs against her neck, slowly breaking the skin, the gasp of pain leaving her beneath his hand.

His body not his own, he sucked, knowing nothing but the taste of her warm blood as it seeped past his lips, sliding down his throat with familiar ease, filling his veins with renewed power, greater control....

He released her before long and watched her slump to the floor, quite cold, very dead, and he wiped a trail of blood from his chin, scolding himself for his dangerously wild acts of desperation.

✳

The rapping on the steel door caused his head to fly up, dark thoughts leaving him with the sound.

"You've a very special visitor, Descant. Make yourself presentable," the voice mocked from the other side of the door.

"Although he is in these Chambers, Vampire, you will not address Dragor in that manner. He was indeed your superior officer before he was placed here. And as I remember it, you honored the very ground he stepped on," a second, cool voice commanded.

He stood from his chair, recognizing the Vampire's voice, and silently thanking him for defending his sullied honor, he wondered what Xavier Delacroix was doing in the Chambers of Waiting so soon. He had forced himself into thinking he had at least a week in the Chambers before Xavier was called.

The steel door slid open, and Dragor watched the two Vampires push it against the dark stone wall, his eyes meeting Xavier's green ones.

He stood in the doorway, a small smile upon his face. "You must be surprised to see me."

Dragor nodded.

"How are you feeling?" Xavier asked, stepping into the dungeon, the two Vampires pulling the door closed behind him.

A sigh left him and he rubbed a hand over his face, sure to feign a look of great apprehension. "I feel like I look. Tired. Worried." His voice dropped as he whispered, "Scared."

Xavier reached forward, placing his hands on his shoulders, guiding him gently down, back into the old wooden chair before kneeling at his side. "What do you fear?" he asked, green eyes shining with sympathy in the many torches' light.

"I am no fool, Xavier," he said, his voice raspy with little use. "I know what they are planning to do with me—what will happen. I messed up. I messed up fantastically."

He felt the grip tighten on his shoulder before Xavier asked, "So you know you will be sentenced to death?"

"I've heard the guards talking. Damion is nearly awake, isn't he? I already look terrible in Dracula's eyes, don't I? Sent here... waiting for the sun to claim me."

"You will not die. Not here, not now... Dracula has ordered me to escort you out of the City."

*Truly. So soon? What was Dracula thinking?* "What?" he whispered, only able to stare at him, wondering how much, if anything, Dracula may have let slip...

"He called me into the training room moments ago. This is what he requests of me."

"So he believes me—you've convinced him that I'm innocent?" He kept his own voice low, the implication of something more beneath the words.

"No," Xavier said, "I do not know his exact reasoning, but he fears your life is indeed in danger. As it stands Damion has more power—"

"But he's lied to us all!"

"I know," Xavier said. "Which is exactly why we must act, and quickly. Damion is healing as you have said. We cannot afford to waste any more time."

Dragor did not move from his chair as Xavier rose to his feet, questions filling his mind, for why would the Great Vampire send him to the Chambers and not tell him what was truly going on?

Watching Xavier, he asked, "But how will this be done? The mansion is heavily guarded, not to mention the Clearance Committee's rules, regulations. They would not allow you to let me leave."

He saw the Vampire's brow furrow in bemusement. "I'm not sure. We must think of something."

Another knock on the steel door called their attention and Dragor tensed, not knowing who it could be on the other side, for he had only ever expected Xavier. "You've another visitor, my Lord."

"What is the caller's name?"

They heard low voices sharing words behind the door, and then the original Vampire to speak responded: "A Joseph Gail. King of Winfield."

Dragor noticed Xavier mouthed the name, "Joseph Gail" as though he'd heard it before, but could not place where, when the steel door opened, the same two guards pushing it. They watched the tall Vampire who stood in the doorway, his long black hair lying against his shoulders, his gleaming green eyes searching the small dungeon with little care. He wore red robes that swayed around his black boots as he entered, the steel door closing with an echo behind him.

"Xavier Delacroix," he said in acknowledgement, his voice deep, "Dragor Descant."

"What brings you here, Mr. Gail?" Xavier asked, staring at the newcomer.

Joseph smiled. "It is in regards to Dracula, Lord Delacroix. I believe he has grown increasingly desperate, given certain circumstances that have emerged in the Dark World."

Dragor narrowed his eyes at the Vampire.

"Explain yourself," Xavier said.

Joseph moved a hand to the pocket of his gold and red vest and pulled out a note. Flipping the small paper open, he read it aloud, "And if Dracula were to carry Xavier Delacroix to the Council of Creatures, it can only mean that Dracula will soon meet his end." He then handed the note to a soundless Xavier. "That was written by someone close to the Vampire City."

Xavier looked down at the small paper in his hand. "Who wrote it?"

"For me to tell you that, I'm afraid it would betray a mighty sense of trust I have instilled in the Vampire who told me this. I'm sure you do understand, Xavier," Joseph said.

Dragor fought the urge to rise to his feet, for this Joseph Gail knew far too much. He kept his seat as Xavier asked, "Why are you giving me this now?"

The Vampire smiled again, dousing his fangs in the one orange light from a nearby torch. "My Lord, you are aware of the Creatures that have shown themselves recently. Naturally, you would be. Well, let us just say, and I believe we should keep this between ourselves—" he eyed Dragor "—that the Vampire who gave me this note knew that Dracula would pull you aside and tell you that you are to go to the Council with him, although these odd...appearances have just started..."

"So what?"

Joseph turned away from them, and it seemed he was taking notice of his surroundings for the first time, his expression that of disgust. "So it must mean that Dracula does not wish to...remain in office for much longer." He turned to Xavier. "Has he mentioned taking you to see the Council?"

"He has not mentioned taking me to see the Council of Creatures—"

"Whatever it means," he interrupted rudely, "I do think it is an interesting thing to look into. Wouldn't you say so, Mister Descant?"

He blinked, not knowing what to think, for if it was true that Dracula had not talked to Xavier about the Council of Creatures, then the Great Vampire was far behind on his own plan. So what was really going on? "What?" he asked a bit too harshly, his patience with the noisy Vampire was quite near its end.

"I said it is an interesting thing to look into, Dracula taking Xavier to see the Council of Creatures," Joseph said, voice loud, apparently taking the snappish retort to mean Dragor had not heard.

"He is?" Dragor blinked, feigning perfect confusion.

Xavier scowled. "He is doing no such thing. Mister Gail, you have overstayed your welcome. Dragor and I are very busy—"

"Busy?" Joseph laughed. "My Lord, the Vampire is in a bloody dungeon. He's a prisoner in his own home. What in the world could you have to do with Cap, er, *Mister* Descant?"

He closed his eyes, opening them after a moment, figuring he had to force himself to ignore the Vampire's mocking air as well. "Mister Gail," his voice softer, less cold and commanding, "I am not sure how things work in...Winfield, Middle Country, but here, in the main Vampire City, it is rather rude to barge into Dracula's mansion and talk of such nasty rumors. Added onto it, you have questioned me and insulted my dear friend. Now, Mr. Gail, I am sure you are King elsewhere, but here you are just another Vampire. I am not sure how you even gained entrance into the Chambers of Waiting, or how you knew where to find me, but it is clear you have overstayed your welcome. On what business do you come to the Vampire City? Was it only to tell me of a small rumor or is there more?"

"I am here in preparation for the ball, as are other Vampires from all over the World," he said, the smug look no longer upon his face, "I've only just received the note, my Lord—the Vampire who gave it to me did not give me a name, he only told me to give it to you. I am doing as I was told."

Xavier narrowed his eyes in skeptical disapproval. "You are a King, and yet you are listening to strange Vampires who give you pieces of parchment, telling you to hand them out freely?"

Joseph snarled. "This Vampire was no mere Vampire. I cannot explain it, but I had to listen to him. It is hard to explain—"

"You'd better start."

His eyes seemed to dim in the light of the torch. "He told me," he began, as though rather scared to speak the words, "about Dracula—about the Creatures appearing all across the woods here. He mentioned Dracula's...need...to take you to the Council of Creatures. He mentioned that if he had said something about this to you, that the Great Vampire would soon meet his end. No longer King of the Vampires, King of all Creatures, as it were.

Xavier's eyes turned red for a very brief second, his hair beginning to lift from his back and shoulders, a snarl escaping his lips. "I demand to know who told you this! What did he look like?"

The Vampire looked away and stared at the stone floor beneath his feet. When he began to speak once more, it was very slowly, as though his tongue was weighed down by the pressure Xavier exuded. "He never gave me a name—"

"His appearance?"

206

"He was tall, about my height. His face was long, his hair a mixture of silver and black, my Lord. His eyes black. I found even I could not stare into them."

Xavier's eyes drifted to Dragor's and lingered there for the slightest of seconds.

Dragor saw that the Vampire knew not what to think.

When at last Xavier turned back to Joseph, it was to say, "Vampires are here from all over the world, correct, Mr. Gail? Well, I presume you shall track down this mysterious Vampire and bring him to Dracula. I am sure with a Vampire of your...standing...this will not be a challenge."

Joseph's eyes became a misty blue for a fraction of a second before returning to their natural green. Dragor watched as he glared at Xavier, before turning to him, bowing low, a hand over his dead heart.

And all at once, Dragor knew that Joseph knew his place against Xavier's, a small smile tearing his lips in two: Xavier truly was the right Vampire for the job, Dracula's inane tests be damned.

"My Lord," Joseph said before rising to his feet, nodding to them both. He moved to the door and pressed his knuckles against them.

The door swung open, and Joseph Gail stepped through the doorway. Dragor eyed Xavier's back, not sure at all what Dracula was planning to do with the Vampire or who gave Joseph Gail the bloody note and why.

The door closed, bringing him to the present, and he rubbed his hands together. "You do not have to listen to him."

Xavier turned. "But you would have me listen to Dracula?"

"Would you not?" he asked, standing. He had to get the Vampire to stay on Dracula's side, no matter what. And it was here Dragor cursed Dracula for not telling Xavier at least what it was he intended to do for him, to give him a little piece of mind. But no, Dracula had wanted to wait for the right moment. *The right moment, my arse,* he'd thought time and time again. "Come now Xavier, that Vampire could have been lying. We've only just met him—who knows what or who he really is. But Dracula, there is a Vampire you have known your whole death. He has looked after you. He has watched over you, protected you. Do not let your judgment be clouded by a Vampire you have never met—"

"But I have met Joseph Gail once before. He was no King then, but we created a small friendship for as long as I was around him." Dragor stared at him seriously, having never heard this story before. "It was a part of my training with Dracula, to go about the World and meet other Vampires, see that this City was not the only haven for Vampires to flock to when other Creatures were up in arms.

"I knew the Vampire had some royal standing, in both the Vampire World and the human one. It was his choice to pick which world he would rule. He was tormented by such a great burden for many nights. He would keep me up most mornings and tell me of his longing to rule over the humans. Have them under his control. But he knew he could not keep up such a charade, for how would he explain to the humans that he remained the same while most of their children had grown into full-fledged adults? Yes, I see now. He chose the path we all walk."

Dragor was silent for a while, and then he said, "So he was like you, Xavier, able to withstand the sun?"

"No, he always bore the necklace—as it was back then—if he wanted to train with me in the light. He did most of his training at night. I believe he was rather envious of me, always seeing how exhausted I was from my day in the sun. Then he would get up and train with the moon as his guide. Our paths were very different: he, training to become a formidable King, defending his people, whatever they may be, against foes human or not. I was simply there because Dracula wished for me to be. I had no real reason for training, and I had no idea what I was training for, as Dracula would never tell me.

It is only now, years later, that he tells me of my blood—even if it is not in great detail."

Dragor massaged his neck. The Great Vampire had told Xavier of his blood? But not in great detail? How much did he know? "Xavier," he started, trying to keep Xavier's mind good on thoughts of Dracula, "he must've changed over the years. I mean, do you really recall meeting a Vampire with black and silver hair as Gail said?"

"No. I don't, but in any case, I will get you out of the City, as Dracula has ordered me to."

He nodded, glad the Vampire was finally talking sense. He watched Xavier move to the steel door and knock, sure to yell, "I am taking Dragor Descant to my quarters."

As the doors opened, a small Vampire draped in the standard First Army uniform had the nerve to say, "Dracula has ordered no one to take Dragor Descant out of the Chamber."

"He has given me different orders," Xavier said.

He watched the First Army soldiers he used to command fall into confusion over whether to listen to the King of Vampires or the Lord of Vampires. It was several minutes, indeed, before one of them decided to let Xavier pass.

He turned to Dragor, and although he had accomplished the first part of his task, no smile graced his face. "Dragor," he said.

Dragor blinked before assessing the situation at hand, a smile forming on his lips as it came to him. "Yes, my Lord?"

"We are leaving."

And he let his smile deplete into the recesses of feigned sadness, before running a large hand over his eyes, his work not done, not in the least. It was only just beginning.

"Of course, my Lord."

# Chapter Thirteen

# THE ESCORT

He watched from the balcony the two Vampires he'd hired for the night as they walked through the crowd. They did not stop to speak with anyone, as it should be, and the suits they wore completed the disguise nicely—they couldn't seem too obvious. Yes, they had to blend in, and as far as Victor Vonderheide was concerned, they did so wonderfully.

"My Lord, all is well below."

"I am aware." He turned to eye the Vampire when the question drifted to mind, "Has Christian arrived yet?"

"No, my Lord."

He placed a hand on the railing and turned back to the humans and Vampires. He had had no desire to throw a party, since he and Lillith had just returned from the Vampire City, but he wished to know if Christian was fully healed. He wanted to know more about this human woman rumored to be living in Damion's home. If he could lure Christian, then surely she would follow. If she did not, well, Victor could just retire to his room. He had no need for blood. All he wished for was rest. The ride back to London had been tiring, as they did not stop once, not even for the watchers. There were no soldiers to aid them, so they were indeed on their own.

Victor had felt it best to arrive in London as soon as possible. It made it easier to assess Lillith's situation and easier to return to his bed. Nevertheless, it was not only until he reached his home did he think of the human woman living in Damion's. And was Christian not still there? He knew he could not pass up the chance to meet the woman. Yes, it was quite the risk, if she indeed was the one they were looking for. All of the Vampires present would fall prey to her blood. There was no telling how they would react, or if at all. But it was a risk Victor was willing to take if it meant that he had acquired the woman before Xavier.

He sighed, turning away from the boring sight of humans fawning over Vampires and Vampires teasing humans. Taunting and tricking the poor creatures might have seemed intriguing to him many years ago, but now it all seemed pointless. What did it matter how you played with them before you killed them? Was it not just as well to kill them quickly, saving yourself the time and anticipation for the taste of blood that was far too often lacking in quality? Yes, over the years, Victor found he'd grown tired of the games. It did not matter in the end. It never *mattered*.

When he reached the doors to his room, Lillith was exiting hers. She'd changed quickly, he noted, her white blouse and vest gone. She donned a light-blue gown instead, which flowed over her thin legs. Her boots were gone, replaced by equally blue heels, and her hair was done up in a fashion Victor could not begin to fathom. Yes, Lillith Crane was indeed the Princess of Vampires, having a beauty many women would kill for. Unbeknownst to these women, Lillith Crane had indeed killed to gain such beauty.

"Are you not going to join the festivities?" she asked.

Victor stared toward his door. "I am...weary from my journey to and fro. Returning to that world only to return to this one, it is like stepping through two different doors. Places that require completely different faces. It is tiring." He looked at her with a weary smile upon his lips.

Lillith smiled as well, though Victor noticed it was hesitant, as though she was not sure she should be smiling at all. "I will leave you to your rest then, my Lord," she said, curtsying.

Victor nodded and reached for the handle of his door, pulling it open, preparing to step inside.

"And thank you," she said, causing him to turn with the words, "for allowing me to stay in your home."

"I am only doing what is required of me, Miss Crane."

"Of course," she whispered, sure to curtsy again.

He watched as she moved down the hall, her many skirts swaying around her legs.

Victor pulled himself into his room but stopped short, remembering the reason he'd thrown the bloody party in the first place. "Lady Crane," he called.

She turned.

He did not eye her, but stared upon the smooth wood of his door. "Send Christian to my quarters when he arrives. If he brings with him a lady, I want you to watch over her, please."

Lillith was silent for a few moments, and then she moved down the hall.

He closed his eyes, hearing her footsteps on the marble floor, and for the first time since he'd been turned, he felt ancient. It seemed as if the years were falling all over his body, reducing him to his true age—an age as numerous as the lies kept. Yes, he'd held his tongue for Dracula more times than he could count, but just as well, he thought, closing the door, it was the nature of his being. To obey the one who made him. It was the same for others, he knew.

He closed the door to his room and walked over to his bed. He relaxed and spread out his aching limbs, his aching shoulders and back. He closed his eyes and let the worry drift from his mind...

Then he sat up.

Since when did he feel *old* since being turned? Of all the years he'd lived as a Vampire, Victor Vonderheide never felt so...human. What could be causing such symptoms?

He lifted his hand to rub the back of his neck and felt it: the gold band Dracula had given him just before he'd left the City. He brought his hand to his eyes to better glimpse the ring. "I don't believe it," he whispered, knowing he had felt his power diminish greatly whenever he put the ring on, but to think it had a lasting effect... It would have never crossed his mind.

He bit his bottom lip, squeezing the ring, the metal clamps retreating from inside his finger, and he felt his power return. Once the metal clamps were safely hidden inside the ring, he slid it off his finger and placed it beside him on his bed.

He stared at it, wondering what that ring had been doing to him all the days he'd worn it. Was it possible Dracula knew the lasting side effects? If he did, why would he allow them to be mass-produced for other Vampires to wear? No, it was impossible...

He massaged the fading weariness from his temples and stood, stretching his arms and legs. The music from the party downstairs pounded against the reinforced door and his blood warmed. Yes, he felt much better now, having taken off the damned ring. He wished to never wear it again if he could help it. But, it was necessary if he wished to manage living on the surface. Or was it?

His thoughts were interrupted by a knock on the door. "May I?" the voice asked.

"Who calls?"

"It is I, Christian. Please, may you open the door? The smell of these humans is driving me mad."

He moved to the door and opened it, stepping aside to allow

the Vampire entrance. And when Christian was in the room, his eyes turned crimson, something Victor could not ignore. As he closed the door behind them, he watched the back of the Vampire's head, smelling greatly now the blood that drifted off the Creature. "You reek," he said.

"I had to have a quick feed."

Victor folded his arms across his chest, glaring at Christian's black hair. "Who was it? A passing maid? The cook? The servant boy?"

Christian snarled, finally turning to face him, his eyes widening. "A passing maid."

"You disposed of her corpse?" he asked, knowing Christian's affinity for leaving the bodies where they lay.

"I did my best given the circumstances."

"You did your best? And what does that mean, exactly?"

"What does it matter? It never would've happened if that damned woman hadn't destroyed my ring."

"What?"

"Alexandria Stone," Christian said. "She invited me to the ball tonight, but her stare..."

He stepped forward, ignoring the rest of the words except those that had caught his interest: *Alexandria Stone.* "What are you talking about?"

Christian sank into a chair next to Victor's desk and did not look up. "This woman Damion saved..."

"So she *is* staying at his home?"

"Yes," he replied, "she is staying there. She is downstairs now. I was told you wanted to see me so I ran up here as fast as I could—"

"Christian," he said, cutting his words, the realization that she was downstairs tearing his mind in two. "Christian. *Christian!* It's been done! She's been found! Tell me, tell me how you felt when you first laid eyes upon her."

"I felt... I felt like I could not bite her."

At these words, Victor ran from the room, completely oblivious to the voice that called after him: "Victor? What in the world? *Victor?!*"

He was already halfway down the hall, his feet flying underneath him. *She's been found.* But what that truly meant remained to be seen. He had to see her, had to witness her for himself.

He reached the end of the hall, his hands crashing against the railing of the balcony, causing the Vampires standing nearby to jump at his sudden presence. "My Lord?" they asked in alarm.

He scanned the Vampires and humans below with unflappable eagerness. "Where is Lillith?"

As one Vampire responded, "She's down there, my Lord," another took notice of his bare hands. "You do not have your ring!"

Victor thanked the first Vampire to respond before turning to the other. "No. No, I do not."

"Wh-Why not?" the Vampire asked, but he was already making his way down the long flight of winding stairs.

When he reached the bottom, he scanned the large room full of people and Vampires, his first step hesitant. He lingered on the ball of his foot: The smell of the humans' blood filled his nose. He was a full-fledged, unguarded Vampire in a room of vibrant, very-alive humans. He had always controlled of his urges, but he realized he had not fed at all since he'd returned from the City. They had not even stopped for blood during their journey back to London, and now he was cursing himself for forgoing what he needed in lieu of rest.

He stopped one of the Vampires he'd hired for the night, "Take me to her at once."

"Yes, my Lord," he said, not bothering to question what it was the Vampire meant. He turned and moved through the crowd, Victor sure to follow close behind, ignoring the other important Vampires

215

and humans they passed. His focus was to secure the woman immediately.

And when they finally reached the main doors, there stood Lillith Crane and a very beautiful woman who seemed quite overcome: Her brow was furrowed, and as he stepped closer to her, Victor saw her eyes were a, interesting brown-green. Her brown hair fell in curls around her face, spilling down her shoulders and back, over the elegant blue gown she wore.

He extended a hand. "My Lady."

She hesitated, but took it all the same, and he saw that she noticed the cold of his skin. It seemed as though she was prepared to gasp or scream but then her confused gaze met his own and his eyes flashed, forbidding her the notion of doing either. With relief, he saw her beautiful face break into a pleasant smile instead, and he moved to kiss the back of her small hand, glad that she was not immune to a Vampire's charms. It would not do if she caused a scene in front of all of his guests.

He stared at her, releasing her hand from his own. She was different from most humans; this was clear. It was not in appearance, for she looked like any other rather beautiful human, but it was something within her skin...her interesting eyes...

"My Lord," she said, curtsying.

"My Lady..."

"Stone. Alexandria Stone."

"My Lady Stone," he continued, aware he could not smell her blood, "it seems you are new to London. Please. May you accompany me to my quarters for a talk as to better educate you on the way things are done here?"

She appeared flustered by his bold proposition—as she should be, he thought with a small smile—and she stared uncertainly around at the number of people that watched her with great curiosity. "I...I don't know what you mean, my L-Lord."

Victor gazed deep into her eyes. It most vital he get her alone, see what she really was. "Please, I insist," he whispered.

Her gaze darkened, and then, without preamble, her hand reached forward of its own accord and Victor extended his arm automatically, a smile of satisfaction upon his lips as her arm found its way through his.

All eyes watched them as they moved together, uneven in stride and height, to the staircase. They ascended to the second floor, where two Vampires standing watch waited. Victor saw their bewildered gazes, but nodded to them and brushed past, guiding Alexandria toward his room.

He caught her hesitant expression once they neared the door, but he gave her a comforting smile and opened it all the same, allowing her to see his bed, his desk, and the cold Vampire who stood near the windows across from the door.

Her expression darkened once she eyed Christian and hesitantly stepped into the room.

Victor followed, closing the door silently behind them.

Christian glared at them in alarm. He stepped closer to the wall and snarled. "Why did you bring her in here?"

"I had to be sure," Victor said, gesturing for Alexandria to take a seat at his desk.

"Well," Christian snapped, "are you sure? Is she the one he wants?"

Victor's gaze floated to her. She stayed near the door. "Yes," he said at last, "I am quite sure it is her. Her blood does such strange things to me."

Alexandria blinked, staring at them in clear confusion. It was not long before she cleared her throat and said, "My Lords, why am I here?"

They both eyed her, and Christian spoke first, although it was to Victor he spoke, not Alexandria: "What will be done with her?"

He watched her. "We must take her to Dracula, of course."

Alexandria did not move, her brown-green eyes widening with confusion. "What is going on? Who are you?"

Victor placed a careful hand on her shoulder and she shuddered, but with a stern glance into her sharp eyes, she calmed and he said, "Please relax, Lady Stone. No harm will befall you under our watch."

With his words and kind stare, she seemed able to move to the chair at last. She sank into it, eyeing both Vampires, and it was clear to Victor that, although his charms worked, she was still perturbed. She still desired to know why she was there. Indeed, she had a will he'd never seen before in a human.

Alexandria said, "Why did I wake up in some Lord's manor, privy to a murder, only to have the law enforcement dismiss it as child's play?"

Victor stirred. "What murder?"

Alexandria eyed Christian. "Ask him," she said at once, gazing upon the Vampire as though he knew more than he had been willing to tell earlier.

Victor marveled at how cold her glare upon Christian was, despite the charm placed on her only seconds before. Why, she wasn't calm at all.

She said, "He seems to know more about it than anyone else."

"What is she talking about, Christian?" he asked.

Christian's eyes shifted from Alexandria to Victor, his face miserable, his eyes blood-red, and at this, Alexandria gasped, but he merely snarled. "When I awoke, fully healed, the maid assigned to me was fixing the room, and she went to open the curtains to let the blasted sun in. That was when I shouted at her, for I did not have my ring, Damion removed it so my healing could not be slowed. And, naturally, I was very...hungry." His gaze moved to Alexandria's confused expression before he set his stare on Victor. "She was young and I was unguarded, no longer held back by those damned rings. I took my chance like any other Creature would."

Victor was silent, but Alexandria appeared blank, her knuckles white within her lap: She held tight to her skirts. "My God," was the slow whisper that left her lips, forcing her blank stare to turn to Christian. "It...it was you. You killed her."

Victor remained before his bed, staring daggers at the human and Vampire. *Perfect, even more explaining would have to be done to calm her frantic nerves now.*

Christian met her eyes. "Yes, I did."

"Oh, my God. Why? Why would you do such a thing?" Alexandria said, glued to her seat, although Victor could eye the rise and fall of her chest as the Vampire's words dawned upon her.

Victor spoke up next when it was clear Christian would not be able to answer her. "He had to."

Alexandria turned to him. "Excuse me?"

"Although Christian is rather reckless, what he did was no different from what any Vampire would do."

Alexandria's brow furrowed. "Vampire?"

"The infamous London murderers," Victor said. "You have read about them in your papers?"

Alexandria nodded, her eyes widening with true realization at last. She stood and stepped back, away from Victor and Christian, who watched her curiously. She pressed herself against the wall, her chest rising and falling, fear wide in her eyes. "D-Don't hurt me," she whispered.

"Relax, Miss Stone," Victor said again. "You are fine. We will not harm you."

"But he," she cast a dark look to Christian, who glared back as though sick of her presence, "murdered a woman in cold blood!"

"Whatever Christian did to that woman... It is all very hard to explain, Miss Stone, but if you would please sit and allow us to—"

"Allow you to what? Bite my neck and drink my blood?"

Christian snarled in annoyance.

Victor allowed his eyes to narrow in exasperation. If it were not for Christian's clear recklessness, he truly believed they could have gone about all of this much smoother. "We shall do no such thing, Miss Stone," he said, his thoughts returning to the fact that her blood did not seem to reach his nose, even while she stood in clear fear just before him. "Please, allow us to explain what is happening."

Alexandria looked at him through tear-soaked, blotched eyes. She did not say a word.

No one moved for what seemed an eternity, the music from below pounding against the door was the only thing that broke the unnatural silence of the room.

When the music died, and the band started a different song, someone finally said something. And to Victor's surprise, it was Christian Delacroix.

"Please, Miss Stone. You said you've seen me somewhere before. Where did you remember me from?"

She seemed to gravitate towards the slightest inkling of kindness in his voice, for she stepped away from the wall, although her chest still rose and fell rapidly. "It was a dream. I remember you from a dream," she said, her voice shaking.

Christian smiled at her handsomely, Victor's eyes wide in surprise. "Okay. Good. What happened in the dream?"

"It was...dark. There were things all around me. They were watching me." She recalled the dark night Christian left Damion's home. "Th–then a large...beast stalked toward me. I couldn't move. The next thing I remember was you flying toward the large...the large..."

She started to cry.

Christian came to her aid at once. He wrapped two arms around her slender frame, and she grabbed at his suit jacket, sobbing into his chest.

Victor's wonder at the situation was short lived: Christian eyed him over her head, his eyes turning back to their miserable black. And all at once, Victor understood: The Vampire had only feigned caring and compassion, just enough to get her to talk—to calm down. And he had not even used his charm to do so. Miraculous.

Christian looked down at the human in his arms and placed his hand upon her head. She seemed to wince underneath his touch, but she did not push him away. It was a few minutes before anyone spoke, and it was Alexandria who did so.

"It really happened didn't it?" she whispered.

Christian, who had taken to running his hand through her hair, said, "What really happened?"

"The dream. It was no dream, was it?"

Victor stared at him, curious, indeed, to see what it was the Vampire would say. He had never moved so quickly before, never acted so...truthfully before. Especially with a human, never mind if she were requested by Dracula, himself.

Christian caught the Vampire's gaze, as if requesting permission to continue on with his little act.

Victor nodded. Whatever Christian did, it was a start to getting to know more about the curious human, after all.

"No, Alexandria," Christian said, not releasing his hand from her head, "it was no dream."

✳

Xavier marched along, Dragor close on his heels, Vampires clearing a path for them through the many levels of the mansion.

When they reached the last floor, several Vampires who sat at tables sipping glasses filled with blood looked up at their arrival, and many gasped, pushing away their drinks as Xavier passed. He strode to the desk against a wall where a Vampire sat dourly.

"Send word to the Clearance Committee," Xavier demanded, "I am leaving the City with Dragor Descant."

The Vampire looked toward Dragor, who had taken to staring around at the high walls of the first floor of the mansion, before turning his apprehensive gaze back to the tall Vampire before him. "D-Dragor Descant is a cr-criminal under word of the Chamber Masters. He is n-not to leave the City b-by any m-means."

"Dragor is no criminal," Xavier snarled, sending the Vampire's eyes to widen. "And the Chamber Masters have no authority over the say of a Member of the Vampire Order. Are you saying you would take the word of Civil Certance over Dracula?!"

"No! Not at all, my Lord! Not at all!" The Vampire nearly jumped out of his chair. "It is just... Lord Certance has made it painfully clear that Dra-Dragor is not to leave the C-City—" he caught Xavier's smoldering glare "—but if Dracula has said otherwise, I am s-sure Lord Certance would n-not obj-object."

"I am sure he would not," Xavier said.

The Vampire, shaking vigorously, grabbed a stray piece of paper and began to write his request. When he had blotched his name at the end, he looked up, and careful not to meet Xavier's eyes, he called for one of the Vampires sitting at the table nearest them. "Frye, take this paper to the Clearance Committee. Run as fast as you can, do you hear me?"

"Y-Yes, sir," the young Vampire stammered, very well aware that Xavier stood next to him, staring him down.

He grabbed the paper and folded it, carefully, as to not let any of the ink smudge. With a quick nod to the Vampire behind the desk, he pushed himself through the doors of the mansion.

Xavier smiled. "Thank you," he said, glad one part of getting Dragor out of the City was over with.

The Vampire behind the desk grunted, pressing his nose into the papers before him, dabbing his quill in the inkbottle. He seemed determined to destroy Xavier's presence by paying him as little attention as possible.

He turned from the desk and motioned for Dragor to follow before pushing through the doors of Dracula's mansion, proceeding down the many marble steps before them. It was not until he'd reach the last step did he turn to see that he was very much alone at the bottom of the staircase. "Dragor?" he called.

But Dragor was staring at a figure deep in the distance, causing Xavier to follow his gaze. Even against the torches many Vampires held in their hands throughout the streets, Xavier could see the one darkened figure in particular that stepped toward them with purpose.

He turned to look back up at Dragor, a haunted expression on his friend's face. "Dragor, what's wrong?"

The large Vampire rushed down the stairs at an alarming rate toward the dark figure that had covered a great distance in the short time Xavier had turned from him.

Dragor marched up to the figure, his expression that of intense, unintelligible, flustering emotions. "Lu-Lucien?"

The figure removed the hood that hid his face, and Xavier saw that he was pale. A Vampire with slightly frayed blond hair that flew frazzled over his face. His brown eyes were sunken, as though he had not slept in centuries, and Xavier could not place who this strange Vampire was.

Dragor stared at the Vampire mere inches away. "Lucien, why are you here?!"

Lucien opened his mouth and said, his voice holding the air of something quite strange over the words, "I am here because a good friend of mine said I should come before you left. It seems he was right in his timing, as always."

Dragor did not even seem to register that Xavier was standing behind him, his deep blue eyes stared into Lucien's. "What friend? How did you know I was leaving? What's going on?"

"In time. I have only returned to escort you to somewhere safe," Lucien scanned Xavier's face, "that is, if it is all right with the Lord of Vampires."

Xavier said, "Who are you?"

"Lucien," he said with a slow, toothy smile, "Lucien Caddenhall."

"Caddenhall?" he whispered in astonishment. "*The* Lucien Caddenhall?"

"The very same," Dragor cut in, quite enthused that his friend had come to pay him a visit.

Lucien looked to the guards that stood on either side of the large doors leading into the building. "Perhaps," he said, "we should walk and talk." With that, he led them away from the marble steps to Dracula's mansion and farther into the streets of the dark, bustling City. The light that peered over the steps and the entrance to the mansion faded from the three men's bodies as they walked.

When they were a far distance from the mansion, and the large fire that roared, suspended by what could only be magic over the steps, that Lucien spoke again. His hood drawn upon his head, his features hidden, save his mouth, which moved rapidly as he talked. "There is not much time to explain, but I was called here because of Dracula."

"What of Dracula?" Xavier asked, glancing at Lucien over Dragor's shoulder.

It was for the slightest fraction of a second that Lucien seemed to hesitate with his words. "I am a Member of the Alliance for All Dark Creatures. As you may have heard, we specialize in the combination of Dark Creatures' powers, hoping to one day bring forth a better world for our kind. Perhaps even living amongst the humans, without the use of special jewelry and enchanted objects."

Dragor nodded, staring ahead. There was no time to grab a cloak for him, so he was left with the clothes he had worn since he'd been put in the Chambers of Waiting.

Xavier listened carefully, ignoring the ogling stares of Vampires as they passed.

"We reside in the County of Lane," Lucien was telling Dragor. "Our Head of Office, Demetrius Bane, prides himself on working with Dracula, but as of late, the Great Vampire has been less of a compliance. It is bad enough I am here—I've managed to slip past the Clearance Committee unscathed—but Demetrius insisted I come, if only to fetch Dragor. He believes you will be safer in Lane. The news of your attack on Damion has spread like wildfire. The remaining Centaurs and Merpeople have passed it along. Of course, they've acquired their information from the Vampires who are entering the City for Dracula's Ball."

Dragor looked to Xavier, extreme unease upon his face.

Xavier returned the glare, only colder in temperature.

They walked along, not saying a word as they passed the odd, stretched buildings built of dark stone. Some of these buildings were pubs, others inns, which the Vampires who now traveled to the City in abundance, occupied fully. The richer of these guests were, as Xavier knew, holed up in the Secondary House.

He cast a glance over his shoulder to the silver building made of material he could not make out from the distance. The Secondary House was a large building, but paled in comparison to Dracula's towering mansion, seen from anywhere in the dark City. The two pillars that held up the Secondary House were illuminated by the torches that passed.

He turned his attention back to the road in front of them. The main road of the Vampire City ran from the Clearance Committee building to Dracula's mansion. But, of course, there were many small roads that veered off, leading to the many houses that made up the large City. Vampires from all over England lived in these houses, but they were not his concern at the moment. His focus was on Lucien Caddenhall.

The Caddenhalls, as Xavier learned through his study of *Legendary Vampires and the Places They Inhabit*, were renowned for their lone war against the Invaders—secretive, darkly cloaked figures that plagued the family for many generations. It was said that the Invaders, as they were known, arrived on the doorstep of the next Caddenhall family, if only to brand the newborn—boy or girl—with the mysterious emblem. Xavier glimpsed the emblem several times throughout his studies, but it was never explained what the emblem stood for.

As for the Caddenhall family, whose newborn was marked, they were powerless to stop the Invaders. Immediately upon entering the threshold, the Invader grew in power and no Creature, no Vampire, nor Lycan, could ever touch him.

Xavier thought this miraculously odd, for it was never stated in his studies of *The Caddenhall Curse*, and he wondered why Dracula had never done anything to stop them.

Xavier looked up to see they had reached the black gates of the Clearance Committee. The white building—such a contrast from the murky darkness that surrounded them—stood erect with its black flags hanging from poles next to the doors.

They were opening and Lucien, hidden fully in his cloak, slid behind Dragor, and became his shadow. The Vampires that were leaving the building stopped, their gazes catching Xavier with curious intensity. It was as if they'd figured him a painting—as there were many of the Vampire—until they realized that it was the real thing standing before them.

A woman, a tall withstanding woman with glassy brown eyes, curtsied upon recognizing him, and then nudged the Duke of Lessingway with her elbow, causing him to hold his midsection, sending him into a sort of half-bow. "My Lord," she said, "I must say what an honor it is to meet you. We've met once before. I'm the Countess of Lane, Catalina Zey."

Xavier nodded his greeting. "Countess Zey. Glad to make your acquaintance. We have met once before?" he asked, not remembering her.

She seemed to blush, except her pale cheeks did not show it. "Besides the hallways of the Great Vampire's mansion," and she gestured toward the mansion behind him, "we have met on more than one occasion. Do you not remember when you were training with Dracula? You visited Lane—but of course, I was a mere girl. I had not yet reached my Age—you've met my sister, the Princess of Lane, Liliana Zey."

Xavier smiled, for the name triggered in him the remembrance of the Princess. When he had known her, she had not reached her Age, but she was still quite beautiful, still quite passionate. "Of course. Liliana. How is the Lady fairing?"

She smiled. "My sister is fantastic. She's here with my younger sister, Joyana. My mother could not make the trip, but she wanted to visit. Is this Lord Descant?" she had taken notice of the large Vampire at last.

Dragor seemed hesitant to respond, and then Xavier said, "Yes, it is he."

Catalina appeared appalled, although curiosity lined her gentle eyes. "But surely it is not true. Forgive me for prying, but there are talks halfway through the country by now of Dragor Descant's attack on your First Seat!" she said, completely ignoring Dragor.

Xavier did not turn to look at him but knew his eyes had darkened in shame. "Lady Zey," he said, "I did not know you to be one to take to rumors."

She recoiled under his gaze. "O-of course not Xavier, but the talks are so thunderous—they nearly surpass the talks of Eleanor Black's revival!"

Xavier must have showed the anger he felt, for Catalina stepped back, now half-guarded behind the Duke of Lessingway, a position the Duke most certainly did not favor. He was sure to take deep, slow breaths, allowing the feelings that arose with the name to leave him. When they were mostly gone, he countered, "They are calling it a revival?"

"Yes. Have you not heard?"

"I do not need to hear. I was there!"

The Duke finally stirred. "Then what, pray tell, took place that night, my Lord?"

Xavier glared at him. "I will not discuss the Order's matters with you—"

"According to my ears around the mansion, you haven't even told the others in the Order with you," Camaril said.

Dragor raised a fist to stop him from moving forward, much to Xavier's surprise, and spoke, his voice rough from not being used since they left the mansion. "Camaril Edinson, brother to the King of Lessingway, Gregory Edinson, you will hold your tongue."

Camaril stared at him, whatever words he had ready to utter pushed back down into his throat with Dragor's next words: "There have been a constant barrage of Vampires who claim they know what is taking place. This is simply not so! Yes, it is true I have done things I should not have, but what business it is of yours—" he pointed a large finger to Camaril and Catalina "—Countess and Duke? You are here in preparation for the Ball, I gather, so let it be. Do not poke your noses in things that are not of your concern. It is a trying time for the Vampire City—for all Dark Creatures! Surely, surely there are much more important things to attend to than gossip and rumor. And how dare you—how bloody dare you—speak to Xavier in such a way?! Are you not aware of his standing, his right?"

The two Vampires had clearly understood something in Dragor's speech Xavier had not, for they held very grave, apprehensive looks upon their faces, and nodding curtly, they rushed past Dragor, not taking notice of the cloaked figure who stood behind him.

Lucien reappeared clapping a white hand on his friend's back. "Excellent job, very well done, deliciously convincing."

Dragor looked most pleased with himself.

Xavier stared. "Why the congratulatory remarks?"

He could not see Lucien's eyes, but knew the Vampire was staring at him. White lips moved underneath the hood, "There is, it appears, a lot you must learn."

"Indeed," Dragor agreed.

"What d—?"

But Lucien's cloak had already swayed, and it was through the small light of miniature torches that Lucien slipped through the door. A short Vampire strode through, not aware that Lucien had passed him at all.

Xavier blinked, and Dragor smiled. "It is his curse, I'm afraid." And Dragor moved to catch up to Lucien.

Xavier stood there, incredibly confused. Lucien Caddenhall was a mystery. Shrouded in secrets that seemed so very important, but at the same time, so very out of reach, and as he approached the doors to proceed inside the building, Xavier could not help but feel there was so much more to what just happened than what he could begin to fathom.

# Chapter Fourteen

# THE IMMORTAL'S GUIDE

Somewhat amused, Dracula turned his gaze from the window. He'd watched closely the Vampires' rendezvous with the Countess of Lane, Catalina Zey, and the Duke of Lessingway, Camaril Edinson. It appeared that Dragor told them something they'd feared and they'd shrunk away.

What he'd found most interesting was the third Vampire that accompanied Xavier and Dragor. He'd kept the damned hood upon his head, and Dracula could not make out who it had been. Indeed, he'd received no word of a Vampire entering the City who wished to speak with Dragor or Xavier. There was something interesting about that...

His eyes peering curiously to his desk for a few minutes, he smiled. *No, of course not,* he comforted himself, but even as he thought this, the small trickle of dread filled him. Walking over to his desk, he removed the dread by opening the bottommost drawers, pulling it out. As he stared at the crimson cover he realized he was simply overreacting. No other Vampires knew about it. Beside Eleanor and Darien, no other Vampire knew of the book, and he knew it had to stay that way.

He stood, bringing the book with him. *There was Eleanor,* he forced himself to think over. *There was Eleanor and she knew everything I'd kept safely hidden behind the crimson cover for decades. And she decided to use this to her advantage... And, of course, there was Darien. Ever the smart Vampire, that Darien. I wonder if he has finally moved to take matters into his own hands—*

His thoughts were cut short as the door opened, and in stepped the Goldchair, Armand Dragon, a long scroll held tight in a fist. Dracula placed the book on the desk, staring at the Vampire's wild stare. He looked quite angry.

The Vampire paid no heed to Dracula's alarmed face; he flicked the parchment open, letting it roll down, allowing Dracula to see what words lay upon it.

*The Caddenhalls—*

*Their true existence currently unknown, I am still as curious as ever to their whereabouts. Dracula's manner concerning the Caddenhalls is most suspicious. I have uncovered nothing during my two years studying this illustrious family from books and letters that Dracula had, for lack of better word, quite simply stolen.*

*My many attempts to question him about their existence and the mysterious curse that plague their family causes me to believe that there are a great many things Dracula is keeping from me.*

*The emblem. A most strange symbol. I have tried to decipher it many a time, but alas, to no avail.*

Dracula's brown eyes lingered painfully on the emblem Xavier had drawn at the bottom of the parchment. The black, jagged cross that adorned every Caddenhall Vampire still in existence seemed to mock him from the weathered page; he was taken in by the thing, unbelieving that Xavier could draw it so bloody well.

"I cannot believe you had him *study* the bloody *Caddenhalls*! Do you understand what you have done?" Armand's outraged voice tore Dracula from the symbol at last: he stared at the Vampire calmly, though his eyes kept flickering to the parchment. "You have piqued his curiosity! The Caddenhalls—a most dangerous family, Dracula—is of his interest! What if he seeks them out? What if he uncovers the secret?"

Dracula stared into Armand's eyes, seeing the pressing fear and rage within them. "No sort of curiosity was piqued here, Armand. Xavier is not curious of the Caddenhalls—" although his voice wavered as he said this "—he is simply taking to his studies, as he should be. I had him study the Caddenhalls so he would gain information, gain a set of knowledge about the Dark World, you see."

The roll of parchment fell from Armand's hand, which quickly tightened into a fist. "The Invaders, Dracula, have you not thought of them?"

"I've thought of them, of course, but the more I do, the more I see no reason to worry."

Armand's chest rose and fell in great heaves, though he needn't breathe. "You are preparing to move on with the plan, aren't you?"

He glanced at the red book atop the desk. "I am preparing," he said, "for him to take my place."

"You do this by teasing him with snippets of the Vampires? Dracula, he is not ready—you know this more than anyone. Indeed, the other Creatures are not yet in place!"

"I have already begun to move the Order into their positions, Goldchair. We will do this soon. You know I've not much time. The bloody birds have grown impatient already—they will see to it I meet my end—it is their way."

Armand took a step forward, his gaze one of concern. "You have spoken with them?"

He nodded, not bothering to elaborate. "As it is, the Invaders, the Caddenhalls, are necessary tools to move forward with our goals, Armand. The Caddenhalls' gifts are necessary to locating my granddaughter, getting her to me before her death. For it is close. As is mine." He turned, eyeing the tall windows. "Now that Lore knows, it is vital we do what we must to secure her."

"Of course, your Majesty, but..." his voice trailing thoughtfully. And it was not long before Dracula turned to eye him, fear quickening his dead heart.

Armand Dragon stared at the book on the desk, his eyes wide upon its red cover. "I don't believe it—"

Dracula stepped up to him, placing a hand atop the cover, as if his palm could still what the Vampire had seen. He slid it toward himself, pressing it protectively against his chest, and took a simple step away, the power of the pages swirling dangerously against his dead heart. He fought its pull with the Vampire's next words.

"You've had it...had it the whole time?" The anger returned, a fierceness in the Vampire's eyes he had only just succeeded in quelling.

He said nothing, the danger of the book dancing in Armand's eyes.

The Vampire advanced. "Dracula, you must destroy it."

"Nonsense. It is the key to my control."

"It is the key to our destruction!" And he brandished a sword from beneath his cloak. Its silver gleamed in the light of the torch nearest the door. "It must be destroyed. You told us it had been, once you'd journeyed through it. Feel free to spread your lies to other Creatures, but not me, Dracula. We work at your back! You cannot keep things from the Chairs! 'For we do the work of the—'"

"I know!" he shouted, clutching the book tighter to his chest. "I bloody well know the oath! The book holds my truths, my journey to the form I hold—"

"And it very well may be the reason we've a new breed running amok," Armand said, waving the sword through the air.

His grip slackened a touch with the words, and Armand swooped, tearing the book from his hand. He reached for it, despite his every thought to drop his hand, for the book had opened slightly in passage.

"Armand," he warned, but the Vampire had seen the opening as well, and his eyes glowed with pressing curiosity. "Don't!"

He opened it, the red ink gleaming, and Dracula looked away, knowing what would happen before it did.

Armand gasped, a flash of red light filled the room and Dracula's eyes—he heard the sword and book clatter against the floor.

Turning to look, he sighed, dispersing the light of the torch, leaving the angry red glow from the book to douse the smooth floor. He knelt just before it, closing it quickly, the whispers from the pages rushing past his ears, but he ignored them. He'd had much practice doing so.

Clasping the book, he grabbed Armand's sword and stood, letting his blood grow cold, but no longer from fear. He had let things get this far, it was always his fault, indeed.

He strode past the burning fireplace to the decorative green curtains hanging against the wall opposite his desk. He pulled them aside with the sword and tucked the book beneath an arm, pressing his hand to the dark stone, releasing it when the door appeared. He opened it, revealing steep, winding steps that led into darkness. He walked despite it and pushed open the wooden door at the bottom of the stairs.

He stepped into the dark room, the torch sparking, settling the room with dim orange light. He looked around and placed the sword against wall where the withered corpses of two utterly drained Vampires remained.

He stared at them, their sunken eyes void of life, emaciated skin clung tight to bone, and a slow, needless sigh left him. He bent before the corpse of the woman, staring at the lingering tendrils of long, black hair that clung to her once-beautiful head. The book trembled in his grip, and he threw it down at his knee, ignoring its warnings.

"Sindell," he whispered to the corpse, "lead Mister Dragon on. I only regret he could not assist me within these walls."

He stared for moments more before turning his gaze to the man propped up at her side. "Mister Dewery," he said, "regrettably."

He stood, bringing the book with him, and stepped briskly through the small dungeon, giving the corpses his back. The torchlight died, plunging the room into darkness. He closed the wooden door and flew up the steps into his office, shutting the stone door, replacing the draping curtain.

He eyed his desk, bare as it was due to his incessant need to finish his paperwork, but even as he moved toward it, Armand's voice drifted to his mind, *"It very well may be the reason we've a new breed running amok in the World!"*

Was it true? Had she somehow gathered a page for her own means? How else would she have gained the ability to take so many forms at will?

Despite this, he could not find it in himself to destroy it, whatever the Vampire had said. It was still needed. Xavier still needed it.

*And now Armand shall join the ranks of Creature within the book to help him.*

The thought troubled him, for Xavier had begun to question him, had begun to doubt, that was clear, but wasn't that what she wanted? *To meet him, rattle him, plant the damning seed of doubt in his heart toward me?*

He strode to the desk, placing the book atop it, new dread forming within him. *She's one step ahead of me, but there's still the Council of Creatures, there's still his coronation, and then it will be done.*

He eyed the abandoned parchment at his feet. Picking it up, his stare fell on the emblem, and doubt marred his thoughts.

*How much did Xavier know? Was Armand correct in assuming*

*the Vampire would seek out the Caddenhalls? Would he demand to know what I wouldn't tell him?*

The more he glared at the four-arrowed emblem upon the parchment, the more he calmed. Surely, he was thinking too hard about the whole matter, wasn't he?

It was Xavier, after all. The Vampire had trusted him much longer than the others had. There was safety in keeping Xavier clueless... Yes, the less he knew the better.

But even as he rolled up the parchment, and placed it beside the book, he found his thoughts turning to the battle the Vampire was to undergo, and in that thought, the sliver of doubt returned.

*Their relationship had been strong, I cannot deny it, and if she's gained what I believe she has, then the Dark World's fate rests upon the shoulders of a soldier burdened by the one thing a Vampire needn't feel: emotion.*

And that, he decided then, was a very dangerous prospect for the Vampire.

The book's cover gleamed in the fireplace light, and the words appeared for the briefest second, dispersing in the next, and he stared at where they had been, the golden letters burned into the back of his eyelids despite the dread burning in his dead heart now:

*The Immortal's Guide.*

✳

Eleanor cradled the golden goblet in her hand, letting the cool metal rest between her ring and middle fingers. Her gaze on the man along the ground would not waver, his pale skin seeming to gleam in the dark. The sheet of aged paper lay atop his chest, the red ink appearing upon the page, word by word, before disappearing just as quickly, and she smiled.

He would rise at any moment, eyes red, hunger driving him

toward her with a viciousness all newly-turned Elite Creatures felt in their blood. Whether they were Vampires or Lycans, the result would be the same: They would run or fly to her, maddened with the pain of their new form, before stopping short, staring into her eyes, a confusion, a fear, filling their own. And she would always smile, for she would feel it in herself. The deeper being within her blood, what had allowed her to shed her Vampire form back at the cabin thanks to Xavier's blood.

He stirred, his hands twitching against the old wooden floorboards, and she stared into the goblet, the red blood beginning to swirl with a tremulous need to be taken.

She recalled the sight of his eyes, the fear within them foretelling the truth: he had seen her true form, the form she aspired to when first she traversed Dracula's mad red book. She needed that power, whatever Dracula had told Xavier, whatever reasons he had kept it to himself. And she would reach it. *All I needed*, she thought with conviction, Amentias rising to his feet, eyes red, a swaggering grace to his movements that had not been there before, *was Xavier*.

Amentias began to run toward her, and she held out the goblet for him, his red eyes delirious as they caught its gold within them.

# Chapter Fifteen

# CADDENHALL MANOR

Victor stared at his bedroom door, knowing there was nothing he could have done but send them both home to await further instruction. He had already written his letter to Dracula. It lay atop his dresser, ready to be sent off in the morning, the thoughts of the mysterious woman not leaving his mind since he'd laid eyes upon her.

Was she truly the one who held the power to fend off Lycans, as Dracula's note had said? And if so, her blood, he admitted he would like to smell it, but not a whiff reached his nose at any point.

*Dracula's granddaughter.*

*Why had he never let slip he had a granddaughter? Fathered a child? How on Earth could he have fathered a child? And never to have told me...*

Victor knew he would not be getting any of his much-desired rest tonight, so thick were the questions filling his mind. *Dracula... Was it possible that he had seduced a woman, making her bear his child? To what end would the Vampire need a child? An heir?*

*Nonsense*, he thought, but he quickly realized that he could not deny Dracula's actions, if this, indeed, was the case. It would not be the first time the Vampire had moved to procure outrageous means of furthering his standing in the Dark World.

Turning from depressing thoughts, he found it much more viable to focus on Alexandria Stone, why she was there in the woods before Damion's home. If she was in London, then why on Earth would Dracula tell Xavier to find her? Why not just direct her to Xavier's door? And why had Lore arrived? To claim her? To stop her from awakening her power, her blood? How much did he know?

Remembering that Lillith had not been privy to the strangeness that had ensued, he felt it best to go tell her. After all, it was she that stopped Lore from sending Christian to a permanent grave, and he was just before his door when he had a wild idea.

Why, indeed, would a human woman be in Damion's forest? And why, indeed, would Damion leave Christian to feed once he'd given the Vampire some blood? Why had he not just taken the blood of the victim he had procured for Christian?

His hand on the door, he did not turn it, for several footsteps sounded from below.

"Is she here, Minerva?" the deep voice called. "Do you sense her?"

He opened the door, the woman answering the familiarly deep voice, "We feel like she's been here, but it has dwindled since then..."

"Yaddley!" the voice called to another. "Come here! We are not to wake them. Get down from the stairs—"

Victor listened. The footsteps ascending the stairs halted and began to descend, venturing back to their caller. It was here he moved swiftly, opening the door, moving to the end of the hallway before sinking to his knees, hiding beneath the shadows the railing created under the chandelier's light. He stared down at the scene below.

Three cloaked figures stood in the middle of the ballroom floor, the doors wide open behind them. "We cannot dawdle any longer. Is she here or not Minerva?" the man covered in a long cloak said to the smaller of the two figures just before him.

He could not see the woman's face under her hood, but knew instantly who she was: Minerva Caddenhall, the only female Vampire under an Invader's power. "No, Demetrius, the woman is not here," she said.

The man named Demetrius scowled beneath the hood that shielding his face from view.

"Victor, what's happened?" Lillith asked, causing him to stiffen in alarm.

But the damage was done.

Demetrius looked up toward the sound of her voice, and glared at him, Victor able to see the black eyes; they shined with a strange presence. "We must leave, the girl is not here," Demetrius said to the Caddenhalls, beginning to walk toward the open doors.

Victor stood, lifting himself over the railing of the balcony, moving straight for the Creature. "Darien!" he yelled, causing the Vampire to turn and eye him with little care.

Before he knew what had happened, Darien lifted a hand with a graceful flourish and Yaddley stepped in front of his Master, prepared to take the attack.

He reached Yaddley, pushing him aside, not paying attention to the loud crash made as his body hit the multitude of trays. They were topped with unused wine flutes, glasses, and gold-lined goblets. "Why are you here?" he asked Darien sharply, staring him down.

Darien did not speak, He stepped back, his cloak blowing in the wind that slipped through the open doors.

And the scream filled Victor's ears.

Minerva Caddenhall, a dangerous expression on her face, hovered above him, ready to strike—

"*Victor!*"

Lillith's shrill scream caused Minerva to freeze, hovering in the air, and then Lillith leapt over the balcony as well, her blue eyes sharp with panic. She shouldered Minerva into the ground at Victor's feet. The marble floor cracked under Minerva's body, and she lay still, Lillith atop her, not moving as well.

Victor heard the laugh from behind him and whirled.

Darien called for the Caddenhalls, "Yaddley, Minerva, let us end this. They are not who I want. Come, we must leave...the ones I am after shall leave the City at any moment, I fear."

Yaddley stirred and arose from the glasses, many shards embedded in his cloak, but he seemed not to feel them as he walked to his Master.

Victor turned just in time to see Minerva open her eyes and push Lillith Crane off her. The dust and rubble tumbled from her as she stood and walked to Darien, much in the same fashion that Yaddley did.

Their hoods removed from their heads, the two Vampires appeared distinctly similar, if different sexes. Yaddley Caddenhall, tall and muscular, towered over his younger sister and Darien, his strong features heightened even greater by the spilling light of the chandelier above. Minerva Caddenhall stood next to Darien and Yaddley, much shorter in stature, her features soft, holding a fierce, almost tormented quality. Her blonde trademark Caddenhall hair was long and spilled down her dusty, marble-cluttered cloak.

"Darien, what do you want with the human?" Victor asked.

Minerva sneered at the name, as though she resented him for uttering it. "Demetrius Bane won't answer to the likes of you."

Darien held up a dark hand, and Minerva fell silent, peering at him with crimson eyes, as though sorry she had spoken. He stepped forward, lifting his arms with the air of a king addressing his royal servant. "I need her," his voice ringing on in Victor's ears long after he'd stopped talking.

"Why?" Victor breathed, not liking at all the ringing in his ears.

Behind him, Lillith moaned in the hole.

Victor could not turn to her, could not tear his gaze from the dark Vampire before him.

Darien said, "She is not safe with the Vampire you adore. She is safe in no one's hands but mine."

"Safe? What do you mean? She is needed by Dracula—"

"No!" Darien yelled, Yaddley and Minerva's faces shrinking into apprehension. "Dracula seeks to destroy our true power. She is not safe in his hands…she is safe in mine."

He merely stared, mind filled with the madness Darien spoke of, but before he could ask just what the strange Vampire meant, he heard Lillith stir from the hole behind him.

"What…is that sound?" she asked, pain in her voice.

And without turning to eye her, Victor realized he heard it the more he stood before Darien and his Vampires, the strange, low buzzing that covered their ears beneath the Vampire's words.

"Tell me where the girl is, Victor. I do not wish to harm you or Miss Crane," Darien commanded, apparently unaware of what bizarre occurrence his voice caused.

He turned back to eye Darien, his brow furrowing the longer he glared. "Are you threatening me? Whose side are you on?"

"My own." And with that, the Vampire gave him a sneer before he stepped away, moving backwards to the open doors.

Yaddley and Minerva remained standing before him, their sanctimonious grins identical across their faces, and it was not until Darien said, "Minerva, Yaddley, let us go, we have severely overstayed our welcome here," that they moved, following their Master's footsteps through the open doorway. As they reached it, a freezing wind blew into the room, sending Victor to raise an arm to shield his eyes. The wind died as quickly as it had come, and he stared through the doorway, where nothing remained.

"Victor," Lillith said, and he turned to eye her as she climbed to her feet, stepping to where he stood. She was remarkably upset:

Her eyes gleamed red in the remaining light of the hall, her clothes ripped by sharp fingernails, and there was a drop of blood sliding down a cheek from a cut that was no longer there. "Why'd she call him Demetrius Bane? Isn't that the Head of Office for the Alliance of All Dark Creatures in Lane?"

Victor blinked, bringing himself to the Vampire next to him. "Demetrius Bane? Ye-Yes, he is...he was..." he whispered, not at all sure what was true anymore.

Lillith stepped briskly to the open door and pushed it closed, shutting out the cold before turning back to eye him. "Do not worry about Darien—Demetrius, Victor." She waved a hand to the crater in the floor. "We must call them; it will take at least several minutes for them to arrive."

Victor looked to the crater in the main hall of his home. "Yes," he whispered absently, before turning back to her. "Thank you, Lillith... Such skill shown tonight."

"Do not mention it. I am just greatly confused. Minerva and Yaddley? Were they not living with an Invader? That is where *The Caddenhall Curse: The Invaders' History* left off," Lillith said, massaging her shoulder.

"Do you not get it, Lillith?" Victor said, his shock from the previous event now fading. "Darien is the Invader that has control over Minerva and Yaddley."

Her blue eyes widened. "That would mean—"

"Yes," he said sharply, "Damion is the other Invader. I read they were close to being caught once, but the older Invader—Damion—got a hold of the baby Caddenhall and branded him."

"But, if Damion and Darien are the Invaders of the Caddenhall Curse, why not just mention who they were in the books? Why let them take up positions in the Armies, the Order?"

Victor began to walk toward the doors of his manor, not eyeing her as he moved. "I do not know."

He reached the door and pulled it open, preparing to step into the cold when Lillith's voice stopped him: "Where are you going?"

"Isn't it obvious?" he said, turning to face her, the wind whipping his silver hair into the house. "To get the Erasers, they do not live far from here."

He closed the door behind him, leaving Lillith clutching her shoulder.

✳

He stepped onto the hard, leaf-strewn ground and stared around at the multitude of trees. *Night already?* he thought in wonder before the blond Vampire at his side said, "Shall you be accompanying Dragor and I to Lane, my Lord?"

Xavier eyed him, seeing a pale hand stretched toward him: Lucien's long nails seemed to gleam within the dark. *Should I really go any farther with this Vampire?* he thought, not sure that it would be best to travel with Lucien Caddenhall, even if he had moved to see Dragor safely escorted out.

And were they to go to Lane? No, Xavier knew he could not take that trip, even if it was to see Dragor truly safe—Dracula had only told him to see the Vampire out of the City.

"No. No, I will stay here, Lucien," he said at last, taking the Vampire's hand, sure to shake it briskly. How disturbing the Vampire's touch—it was as though he had touched something that should not have been. Shaking off the eerie feeling that he was in the presence of something he truly did not understand, he went on: "It would not do for me to travel all the way to Lane when you are with him."

"I see," Lucien said from underneath his hood.

Xavier half-wondered why he had not removed it now that they were free from the watching eyes of Vampires that most feared the Caddenhalls.

Lucien said, "This is goodbye, then, my Lord." And once more he extended a hand, the sleeve of his cloak rising against his arm, revealing part of the four arrowed cross, which Xavier could not help but gaze upon for a moment far too long.

Lucien gave his arm a slight shake, the sleeve fell over it, and he dropped the hand and bowed low, tendrils of his blond hair falling out of his hood.

Xavier thought the Vampire's lips flickered into a sneer as he rose, but the more he stared, the more the expression remained blank, almost bored beneath the hood.

Dragor stepped to him then, and before he knew it, wrapped two large arms around his midsection, and squeezed.

Xavier was sure to return the embrace.

"I cannot thank you enough," Dragor said once they pulled away, and even in the dark, he could see the joy in those blue eyes. "You needn't thank me," he said, but a smile traced his lips all the same, "I was only working on Dracula's orders."

"Of course, of course," Dragor sighed, his own smile widening. He turned to Lucien, who was examining the dirt at his feet, and said, "Well, shall we set off?"

Lucien did not speak.

Indeed, Xavier realized the Vampire had said very little once they were free of the City's harboring security. He nodded his hooded head curtly and a small strand of hair shook against his face with the movement.

Dragor stepped to the Vampire and with another wide smile, they disappeared, Xavier staring at the rusted black gates leading into the tunnel.

Turning on his heels, he began to walk into the woods, when the thought occurred to him. It was awfully late, and would anyone notice, indeed, if he simply transported himself home? No one frequented these woods anyhow.

He had just closed his eyes when the shrill laugh filled his ears.

"Yaddley, we must secure this woman but not like that! Besides, we've no idea where she is! I bet that Victor knows...not telling Master about it...he sickens me! When will these Vampires learn the rightful King of Creatures is Demetrius Bane!"

The man named Yaddley grunted in response to the woman's high-pitched words.

Xavier remained where he stood. They could not be more than several feet away.

And then he began to step toward the voice, entering the trees, for the woman had mentioned Victor, hadn't she? Did she mean Victor Vonderheide?

"And that succubus, Lillith Crane, how dare she attack *me*! At least the hole in that damned floor will take a while to fix—no Eraser can fix such a disaster before the break of dawn."

*Lillith?* he thought, halting behind a tree. And it was a moment before he could see them, two figures, one taller than the other. They walked through the night, away from him toward a large white house that certainly wasn't there before.

Xavier narrowed his eyes, watching them step past the open gate and float up the many steps to the white door. The woman reached for the golden handle and turned it, pushing it open before they stepped inside, closing the door behind them.

Figuring he'd better stick around to hear what more the two Vampires said, he approached the large manor, his footsteps making no sound against the hard ground. Stopping just before the tall gate, he stared at the large window, covered by a sheer dark curtain. A light burned bright beyond it. He heard the wind pick up ever the slightest, and wondered if he should be here when he heard the deep voice speak:

"Lord Demetrius is rather upset, Minerva."

*Interesting*, he thought, knowing full well who this Minerva must be. He almost wondered if Lucien knew his cousins were nearby when she responded solemnly:

"I know; we must be quick in securing this woman. I hear other Creatures are after her."

"Yes, I have heard the same," Yaddley said in response. "We cannot dawdle any longer, especially with what happened tonight."

"I was sure I sensed her!"

"You were sure, and yet, she was not there. What games do you mean to play with Demetrius?"

"I play no games!" Minerva bellowed, and Xavier could hear the crashing of plates against the floor. "I am most loyal to our Lord! If I say I sensed her, then I sensed her! Do not stand there and tell me I mean to play games with Demetrius!"

All was silent within the large house, and against the wind, Xavier heard the low voice: "Keep your voices down. Is this how your master raised you to serve him? Bickering and pointing the blame for what happens?"

There was a gasp, then Minerva's voice: "Ewer, we are most sorry for waking you. We have just returned—"

"You have just returned from the Vampire Victor Vonderheide. Darien told you to return to your home while he ventured to Lane," the seemingly old voice wheezed knowingly.

Yaddley spoke next. "That is not his name, Ewer."

Ewer inhaled a gust of air. "It *is* his name! Darien Nicodemeus he was born and Darien Nicodemeus he shall remain. Demetrius Bane is only a front to keep the others off his trail."

Silence filled the house once more, and Xavier considered leaving, feeling he had intruded far too long when the voice of Ewer arose, spreading throughout the night, "This...human woman, you have not found her yet." It was a statement more than a question.

Minerva's voice floated to his ears, "We have been working hard to find her. Dracula desires her desperately. Lore has no use for her, he only wishes to kill her before she can be used on him. This woman is only safe in Deme—Darien's hands."

"Yes," Ewer's voice hissed. There was a shuffling of furniture, suggesting Ewer Caddenhall had taken a seat. "She is only safe in that boy's hands. Only Darien knows what to do with her. Damion has long since betrayed us."

"And Lucien, Ewer, what of Lucien?" Yaddley asked next.

"Lucien, a special case, is definitely under Damion's hand: He was the one who branded him all those years ago, but with Damion's absence, Lucien is as good as Darien's as he is Damion's. The brand is only strong if the Invader who cast it is present in the newborn's life. Damion, as we all know, was not," Ewer wheezed in his old voice.

More silence. And then, "Sessa...Evan, why did they disobey Damion's entrance? Darien said that they actually fought back."

"I heard the same," Ewer gasped. "Sessa and Evan were fools. They never believed in the Caddenhall Curse. They believed they should've been free. What Renere did was foolish, yes, but we have grown in power from the Nicodemeus family because of his disregard."

The sound of scraping chairs suggested both Yaddley and Minerva had taken seats, and then Yaddley's deep voice said, "What will be done with Eleanor Black? It is said she is searching for Xavier Delacroix."

"Eleanor is not of our concern, nor is that Vampire. Darien has made it clear we are not to harm any of them. We shall let their lives run their courses," Ewer responded.

More silence, and the rustling of leaves beckoned Xavier's attention, but he did not move. With the utterance of Eleanor's name, a heaviness fell over him. He could not move, not even if he desired to do so.

The lights went out, and he stared through the darkness, Yaddley's voice filling the air, "Someone has been listening."

"Who?" Minerva breathed.

The sound of chairs scraping against the floor could be heard from outside, the hurried footsteps scrambling for the door.

Xavier only saw the door open, barely saw the tall Vampire named Yaddley standing there, his eyes narrowed through the night, and he almost thought he saw the gaze move to him before he allowed himself to be carried on the wind.

# Chapter Sixteen

# THE ERASERS

He stared up at his home, the hard pavement of his front yard the only thing keeping him upright.

*Ewer Caddenhall is alive. I thought he'd died in battle with his father, Renere, their fight with Lady Cewenthe, endangering her two and only sons. But that was the name Minerva and Yaddley spoke to, which could only mean, surely, he was alive, somehow.*

*Minerva and Yaddley branded by an Invader. Here. Nothing was safe anymore, not if Lucien Caddenhall could walk freely through the Clearance Committee Building, raise no alarms. Nothing,* he thought, catching sight of a red-eyed James Addison within a high window, lit only by dancing candle light, *is as I thought it was.*

Not wanting to deal with the young man, he had fled his manor once he'd received Victor's letter, hoping the precautions Dracula placed upon the land would go to work, ensuring any human who saw a Vampire without their ring would immediately forget it occurred. It was how Christian had survived a life among humans all this time. Of course, he did not know if the same precautionary spells had been placed on other Vampire homes.

The whooshing of the wind claimed his attention and he looked up just in time to see two large figures flying overhead, their blue and black cloaks flapping wildly.

They landed with no sound at all upon the pavement.

"This is not normally our job—"

"Never been asked to do it before—"

"But General Vonderheide requests your presence at his manor—"

"Instantly, it would seem—"

"Rather important—"

"Very grave—"

Xavier stared at the Vampires, the words, "Mess-Cleaned Section of Powers" emblazoned on the badges pinned to their cloaks.

"Victor requests my presence?" he clarified. It was hard to understand them. They jumped on each other's sentences, finishing the previous one for the other.

"Most grave," the taller of the two repeated.

"Of what priority would you say this is?"

The shorter of the two, with a small face and short red hair, pulled out a small piece of paper from his cloak. He cleared his throat, reading it with the air of someone addressing Dracula himself:

*"Is it not something I can discuss in front of the Erasers, Xavier, but you must go to my home the moment the Erasers have read you this note. Lillith will be there, filling you in on what has happened. I, after acquiring the Erasers to locate you, am heading to Damion's manor. I fear the human woman is in grave danger. And yes, she's been found Xavier. All will be explained by Lillith, I'm sure.*

*"General Victor Vonderheide,*

*"Secondary Lord of the Vampire Order"*

The Eraser folded the small piece of paper and stuffed it back into a pocket of his cloak, and the taller of the two said, "I would imagine, Lord Xavier, that it is of grave urgency that you arrive at Victor's manor. According to the note, of course."

His green eyes flashed and he was just closing them when the shorter of the two spoke, "No my Lord, you must not transport there! We will fly with you. We are not able to transport under Code Twelve of Dracula's Distinct and Direct Orders for all Vampires." Then, as if being pressed to recite Code Twelve, the short Vampire said, "*The Erasers, who reside on the surface, are not to transport—it requires a vast amount of blood not to be expending with exception of dire emergency.*"

Xavier stared. With one last growl, he closed his eyes, and left the pavement of his manor. When he opened them again, he was staring at the familiar manor of Victor Vonderheide, one of the doors open. With no hesitation, he climbed the steps to the doors and entered the large manor.

His eyes widened. He knew a matter most grave had taken place here. He saw the large crater in front of him. He stepped into the large house, eyeing the staircase and the small balcony above. When he reached the first step, he heard the ravenous sound of a Vampire feeding, and turned his head to where the sound came: The blond Vampire's hair shook. She was kneeling, hunched over the body of a maid.

Xavier knew she was dead. He left the staircase and approached the feeding Vampire. When he was near, the smell of the human's blood filled his nose, reminding him that he had not fed in a few days.

His words were soft, for he knew how dangerous a Vampire who fed was. "Lillith Crane?"

Her head turned. Her eyes were a deep crimson. Her mouth held traces of blood she was not able to drink, and although it was not much, the blood still slid down her chin, falling onto the marble floor. "Xavier?" she whispered, her voice no longer sweet.

"Miss Crane, feeding at this hour? What happened here?" he asked her, taking a few steps back.

She stood and stalked past him, wiping away the blood that fell from her mouth with an arm. She knelt at the edge of the crater, staring down into it. "Minerva Caddenhall," and her voice was filled with hate, "that Vampire was going to attack Victor. I had to... What more could be done..."

"She was here?" Xavier asked, keeping a safe distance from Lillith, although the smell of the maid's corpse was close to driving him mad.

Lillith looked up at him again, her eyes still their fierce red. "Oh yes, she was here. Her and her damned brother, Yaddley—"

"Why did they come here?" Xavier asked her, although he had a very good idea.

She stood, and stared past him to the dead maid, and Xavier figured she was recalling the events that just transpired. "Looking for Alexandria," she answered. "I don't know how they got wind of her, but they're looking for her. Minerva picked up her scent, which is strange seeing as how she *has no scent*, but they came bursting through the door hours after she and Christian left—"

"Christian was here?"

"Yes," Lillith said, snapping her shoulder back into place with a grimace. "Victor threw a last minute party. I suspect he wanted to lure Christian out of Damion's home. If Christian came, that meant he fully healed, and the news of the human woman staying at Damion's was fresh on Victor's mind—he knew Christian would have to take her with him. I am sure they filled her in on what happened to her— she left in tears—it was only when I'd finally gotten to sleep that I heard the voices."

Before she could say anything more, Erasers bounded through the open doorway. They spotted the large crater in the floor, and tutted at the broken glass against the wall, and finally heaved sighs of frustration at the dead maid's corpse, dripping with blood.

"Horrible, horrible, most horrible," the shorter of the two muttered to himself, striding over to examine the broken glass and trays that remained spilled out across the floor.

The taller of the two stepped toward Lillith, but noticed the fury in her eyes, and stepped back. From his safe distance, he said, "M'Lady, Lillith Crane, an honor, an honor...but what, I must ask, has happened tonight?"

Lillith snarled at him, her irritation at the sudden influx of Vampires evident. "Just get to your job."

The Eraser stumbled backwards. "Well, I simply wished to know. First order of business when an Eraser enters the home of a Vampire—"

"Be silent and fix this mess!" she yelled.

Xavier was surprised no other maids or servants scrambled to the main hall to figure out what all the noise was.

The Eraser's eyes darted to Xavier's and Lillith's before they dropped to the large hole in the floor. He walked around her and bent down on one knee, ran a gloved finger across the edge of the crater, some loose rubble dislodging from the jagged circle, tumbling into the center of the hole. He turned to Xavier, apparently finding Lillith the harder of the two Vampires to approach at the moment, and said, "My Lord, it is quite clear that this crater was caused by Lillith Crane..." and his eyes drifted to her.

She snarled at him.

Xavier said, "Yes, I know it was she who caused it. She told me that Minerva Caddenhall was preparing to attack Victor, which was when she must've attacked the Caddenhall."

"Minerva Caddenhall?!" both Vampires said, rising to their feet.

Lillith growled, and with a final glance to her dinner, stalked out of the manor, onto the steps.

Xavier cleared his throat, bringing their perturbed gazes back to him. "Minerva Caddenhall and her brother, Yaddley Caddenhall, were present tonight, I believe."

"But that must mean—" the shorter of the two Eraser's began.

"That an Invader was present!" the other finished.

Marveling at their annoying ability to finish each other's sentences, he glared at them. "What can be done about this mess?"

The Erasers blinked, casting glances to each other before turning back to Xavier. They annoyingly, and simultaneously, said, "Everything."

"Everything?"

"Quite right, everything," the taller Vampire said, his blue robes swishing as he approached the dead maid. He peered down at her. "We can take this one to the river, dump her body, or give her to the Dragons." He waved a hand at the crater past Xavier's feet. "We can call the Cleaners to fix that mess, no one else is allowed magic like they are besides the Enchanters. And those glasses," he stood, waving another hand to the glasses and trays on the floor, "can't we just say that they fell over after the party? General Victor got rather clumsy? The humans won't pay it too much mind..."

"Yes, I believe that settles everything quite nicely," the shorter Vampire said.

"Well," the taller Vampire said, bending down to take hold of Lillith's prey, "I'll take the woman to the Dragons. They're not that far from here. Lexington, will you call the Cleaners? The sooner they fix that hole, the better. Quickly now, before dawn is upon us." He picked up the maid's corpse and rested it over a shoulder, her limp legs dangling down his chest.

The shorter Vampire removed yet another piece of paper from his cloak. He read it aloud, his voice smacking against the walls. "The Erasers, Lexington and Wellington, require the Cleaners," he eyed the crater as if considering something before continuing, "Numbers Five, Six, and Three-Hundred Thirty-Two."

An odd sound, much like the slicing of a sword against the floor, reached Xavier's ears, his attention brought to the doors. Before he could understand what was taking place, the large Elf pushed his way through, his sword dragging across the marble floor of Victor's home, and without sparing a glance to anyone else, he eyed Lexington, "You called us here?"

"Indeed I did," Lexington said, his annoyingly high-pitched.

"Well," another Elf slinked through the doorway, his long blond hair traveling behind his head, just as long as his white Etrian Robes, "what is the damage, *Vampure*?"

Lexington stepped aside and gave the Elf a clear view of the large crater in the middle of the floor. Another Elf arrived, looking perturbed. "What has happened? I was just in the middle of preparing myself for Alinneis when I heard the call—" His silver eyes rested on the large crater and he fell into silence.

The three Elves stared at the crater, then at each other. "*Vampure*," they said at once.

"We've assessed that much, what can be done about it?" Lexington asked, looking a bit harried.

"What else can be done in these times?" the tallest of the Elves said, lifting his sword to bring it down over the crater.

The other two Elves took their places around the hole, and Xavier felt he'd better take a step back.

The two Elves, free of swords, lifted their hands over the crater, and before he knew what was happening, a bright golden light spread from the tip of the sword to the Elves' long, skinny fingertips. From this light, several marble tiles formed over the large hole and slipped into their places beneath the outstretched hands and sword of the Elves. The light died and the Elves now stood in a circle around the marble floor that shone just as beautifully as before.

"There we are," Lexington said, rushing forward to inspect it. When all was in order, he turned to the Elves. "Thank you most kindly."

"Charmed to do it, I'm sure," one of the Elves said, annoyed.

Lexington paid no mind to this Elf's words. He was too busy bustling over to Xavier. "Well, my Lord, everything seems to be in order. We shall leave you now, I expect."

Xavier glared down at the Vampire, attempting a smile. "Do what you wish."

The Vampire nodded and turned to the Elves. "Shall we depart all at once?"

The tallest of Elves, Xavier believed him to be Number Three-Hundred Thirty-Two, scoffed, "Really...depart with a *Vampure*? Really?" And he was gone.

The other two Elves nodded to Xavier and the Eraser before disappearing as well. Lexington gave a small bow to Xavier and with the utterance of "My Lord," he was gone.

Lillith entered the doorway. "Have they finally departed?"

"Yes," he said.

"Finally. Victor is here...he's brought Christian and Alexandria."

"What?" Xavier said, watching the open doorway.

He did not have to wait long until his brother's face appeared: he looked rather uncomfortable. Next was the woman Xavier believed to be Alexandria, her appealing face stretched in tremendous fear; she followed close behind Christian, as if he were her lifeline. At last, Victor trekked into the house, closing the door behind him.

He tore his gaze from Alexandria to stare at the Vampire that approached him the most.

Christian stared back, not a word leaving his lips, and Xavier half-wondered if he were thinking about getting cut up by a large dog.

He sighed, a real smile curling his lips. "Hello, Christian."

# Chapter Seventeen

## ARMINIUS'S WORDS
## OF WARNING

He took a single step before the words left him in a hurry: "Xavier, you must forgive me. It-it was foolish of me to attack the Lycan, foolish of me to move so recklessly—"

"No," Xavier interrupted, "I know how hard it is to still oneself from the lure of a Lycan's blood. You need say no more."

The Vampire turned to Victor, who looked prepared to speak, his thoughts lost in question. He had fully expected the Vampire to ream into him for even attempting to fight a Lycan—what was this? "We…must stop Darien before he comes after Alexandria," Victor offered cautiously.

"Darien is not going to come for her, he is traveling to Lane," Xavier replied.

"How do you know?"

Christian kept his gaze on his brother, mind working hard on just what could have happened that was more important than he, the roughshod brother, foolishly moving to get himself hurt by an overgrown beast.

He followed Xavier's eyes when they moved to the woman near the door, fear and bewilderment in her eyes.

Xavier stared back at Victor, sure to say, "Dracula wanted me to escort Dragor out of the City before he was put to death. Upon leaving his mansion, a Vampire approached us. It appeared Dragor knew who it was. Yet it wasn't until the Vampire turned to me that I realized he was Lucien Caddenhall."

Christian stared, nonplussed, as a gasp of surprise left Lillith, and he looked to her, her eyes moving in disbelief to Victor. "How did he get into the Vampire City?" she asked the room at large.

"It seems the Caddenhall Curse is true," Xavier said. "Lucien moved in shadows, his aura most elusive, just like in the stories. He'd told me he was to escort Dragor to Lane, mentioning that he came from some alliance for all Dark Creatures, due to some Demetrius Bane, the Head of Office there."

Lillith and Victor exchanged appalled looks, but they did not speak and Xavier continued: "When we left the City, Lucien left with Dragor. I was preparing to transport home when I heard voices in the woods. It was Minerva and Yaddley Caddenhall, and I followed them to Caddenhall Manor.

"Minerva was speaking of ways in which they could acquire the human woman. And when they entered the house, another voice emerged." But he quite suddenly looked as though he didn't want to go on.

"Who was it?" Lillith said, sounding nervous, Alexandria now the only one left at the doors.

"Ewer Caddenhall," he said after a moment.

Victor shook his head. "Impossible."

Lillith shrieked, "He's dead!"

"No," Xavier said tersely, much to Christian's bemusement. "The Caddenhalls continued their conversation, and Yaddley mentioned Demetrius Bane. Ewer was quick to correct him, saying that

Demetrius Bane was Darien Nicodemeus. That the name Demetrius Bane was only a front."

Victor bared his fangs in frustration. "So it was him."

All Vampires eyed him, but it was Xavier who said, "Darien was here?"

"Yes," Lillith said, looking both angry and scared.

"Well according to Ewer, Damion has 'long since betrayed' them," Xavier said.

"Well what does that mean?"

"Your guess is as good as mine."

Christian, feeling all the more left out kept his thoughts on the only thing that made sense to him. "Well what will be done about Alexandria?"

The Vampires turned to look at her, and she stared back, speechless.

"We should take her to Dracula," Xavier said.

Victor sighed. "So it's another trip back to the City, is it?"

"No," Xavier said.

Christian opened his mouth to speak, when Lillith said, "But you just said we should take her back."

"Dracula has lied to us all avoided our questions for years. He's had us read books on the Curse and here we stand, once believing all of the Caddenhalls to be tucked away safely with their Invaders, only to find that no, that is not so and, low and behold, Darien and Damion Nicodemeus have been the Invaders all along."

"But—"

"It is clear Dracula has been keeping this from us for as long as we have been under his command. There's no telling what he truly needs from the woman. And Eleanor Black, we believed her dead, but she is very much alive, and I believe Dracula knew what she was capable of."

No one said a word for a long time, and then Christian, once more at a loss, offered quietly, "So what will we do?"

"We will resume things as usual. I do not think it is best to draw any unnecessary attention to ourselves...but remain cautious, naturally."

Victor and Lillith exchanged apprehensive glances, and Victor said, "And what of Alexandria?"

All Vampires eyed her, and she shrunk under their gazes, drawing herself up against the frame of the doorway.

He considered her before saying, "Damion saved her, yes, but we cannot give her up to Dracula unless we know what he intends to do with her."

Christian stepped forward, mind intent on what he could do. "I'll watch over her."

"Don't be silly, you need to be able to protect her, not kill her," Xavier said.

"But I can!" he retorted, anger filling his dead heart. It was clear they were all wrapped up in this Caddenhall business—why not leave the woman with him, the only Vampire that had nothing helpful to do? "I can protect her. I won't kill her. Bloody hell, I cannot bite her, none of us can. Why is she safer in your hands than she is mine?"

Xavier looked at him coldly, and Christian almost retreated under that gaze. "I never said I wanted her. She would be rather troublesome for me, I do imagine. If I had her, there is no telling the number of Creatures that would be knocking down my doorstep to snatch her up. And even if I did want her, she would be safe in my hands because I would know how to defend her. You were sent to Damion for training, and you got yourself cut up by a large dog. You'll look after no one—especially no one as important as her—until you can properly protect yourself."

Christian snarled, but he could not find a word to say.

"So who will look after her?" Victor asked.

Xavier turned to him. "I would think it unfair to ask you to do the honors, since you already have Lillith here with you." His green eyes flew to Alexandria. "I believe it would be best to have her decide herself."

Christian stared at her, along with the others, and she blinked, looking from Vampire to Vampire, the fear full in her wet eyes.

"I..." she began, and Christian heard how low her voice sounded against Xavier's, "I don't know wh—"

"Please, human," Xavier said, "you need to choose who you will stay with."

"B-but why?" she breathed, her chest heaving, her breath leaving her in gasps. "I just—I want to go h-home."

"You can't," he said, stepping toward her, and she drew up even further against the wall.

Christian stepped forward. "Xavier, please—"

"She needs to choose and she needs to do so now," Xavier interrupted, stopping just before her.

Her eyes were closed, her head turned away from him, tears leaving her eyes.

"Xavier!" The way he was going about it wouldn't help anything, truly.

"What?" Xavier snapped, turning to eye him at last.

He felt their gazes upon him as he said, "Can't you see you're terrifying her further?"

Xavier's eyes widened; he seemed to realize what he caused in her, indeed, and turning back to her, he asked, softly, "Please, Miss Stone, you will be safe with us."

They waited for what seemed an eternity before she relented, her shoulders slacking as something like release filled her, but release from what, Christian could not know. They said nothing as she lifted a shaking hand and pointed a finger past Xavier, toward a direction Christian could not quite believe.

Xavier followed the direction, his eyes lined with slight disbelief. "That settles it then: she stays with Christian."

※

"My Lord, there is someone here to see you," the man said with a sniff.

Xavier turned from the window, dispelling the notion that his servant had run off; he had not seen him in quite some time. "Who is it?"

"He is a...most odd-looking man, my Lord."

Xavier narrowed his eyes at the clear hesitation in his voice. "Odd looking? Do explain."

"Well..." and the man shuffled from foot to foot, looking perplexed as to how to go on. "He has rather large ears, my Lord."

"Large ears?" he said, wondering why in the world an Elf would decide to pay a visit in broad daylight.

"Yes, my Lord."

He asked no more questions. His servant was intensely confused by the Elf's appearance, as were the maids and doormen no doubt would be. He stepped through the doorway, leaving the man with his bewilderment.

When he reached the main hall, he looked warily for any exceedingly pale man with large pointed ears, but found no one waiting for him near the main doors. He signaled to a maid scrubbing the floor farther down the hall. "Excuse me, where is the gentlemen that came to see me?"

She never lifted her head. "Last I saw of him, he was escorted down into the living room, told to wait there for you, my Lord."

*The living room?* he thought, proceeding past her. "Which living room was the man taken to?"

And now, seemingly aware of the distance between them, she looked up, although no farther than his shoes. "The one not many are allowed in, my Lord," her voice shaking with the words.

He narrowed his eyes. "The white one?"

"Yes."

Xavier stared down at her for a few more seconds before tearing his gaze from her small frame, moving down the main hall, mind thick on just why an Elf was here—and to see him.

When he reached the white doors, he turned the handle, and pushed them open, only to see a tall man standing near the fireplace. The Elf was still. He appeared to be gazing into the flames so intently his head did not move. His long black hair was straight, resting lightly over the long white, gold-lined robes he wore, and only from behind the black curtain of hair could Xavier make out the two tips of the man's ears.

Xavier stepped into the room, closing the door behind him. "Arminius," he said, "to what do I owe this surprise?"

Arminius turned, his black eyes distracted: He looked lost. It was a long while before he stirred at last, if only to clutch the red stone that hung from a golden chain around his white neck. "Xavier," he breathed, and his voice came through oddly strangled in his throat, as if someone was forbidding him to speak, "I hope you can forgive me, but I had to see you."

He took a small step forward, sure to keep his distance from the Elf. "What do you wish to speak to me about?"

Arminius let out a quiet hissing sound, keeping his white lips together. His gaze danced from the flickering flames back to Xavier's eyes. "There is unrest. Great unrest. I am not sure how long we have until things explode in our World."

"What do you mean?"

"Surely you have heard—witnessed even—the crushing feeling that plagues all Dark Creatures?" the Elf said, with a bit of hysteria, as if he could not believe the Vampire's inability to understand. "Alinneis is plotting his revenge against Dracula, all Vampires. He claims that what is happening, the mysterious Creatures plaguing our woods, our caves, is all Dracula's doing. He seems to think that this is part of some grand scheme cooked up by the Great Vampire to do away with all Dark Creatures. These…Creatures plaguing our World have an influence on every Creature, and from what I have gathered, it is never a good one."

Xavier did not speak.

Arminius continued: "What is Dracula planning, *Vampure*?"

He merely stared at him, wondering what the Elf's purpose was for coming here, speaking so freely. "I thought you were not with the Etrian Elves, Arminius."

His face twisted into a smile with the words, and Xavier could only marvel at how odd it looked upon his long face. "Etrian Elves? No. My...leave of that band of Elves has long since taken place. I have you to thank for that," he added bitterly. "I am now with the Elven Wing, a much more serious group. There are many more breeds of Elves than I would have ever thought. But, my reasons for journeying here are not to catch up on old times. I am here to see what the *Vampures'* point of view of this whole… plot to destroy all Dark Creatures is. Well, Xavier? Is Dracula planning to unleash these new Creatures all over the world to satisfy some sadistic urge he has to be on the only 'King' left standing?"

While it was true Dracula was acting strange, Xavier could not be so sure that Dracula had some hidden agenda to destroy all Dark Creatures. "There is no such plan that I can say is taking place, Arminius."

"Hm," the Elf sniffed.

He reached out a long-fingered hand to the fireplace, and for a brief moment, Xavier thought he was to grab for the flames, but his hand clasped a white cane, which was embellished with snakelike, golden designs draped around the long body. The handle was straight, turned at a sharp ninety-degree angle, perfect for grasping, which Arminius now did, looking quite prepared to leave, as if he'd been offended in some ghastly way.

But instead, he kept his gaze on Xavier. "You realize I came to you, not because of our past, but because of your standing with the *Vampures*. I thought if anyone knew Dracula's deepest secrets, it'd be you, Xavier. I can see now...Dracula must be getting desperate, hiding his secrets from even you—"

"What are you implying?" he whispered.

"Simply," he hissed, the stilted pleasure gone from his person, "that Dracula is not, nor has he ever been, what my kind would call a trustworthy Creature. We Elves value trust, and it is clear from the moment you meet Dracula there is something terribly wrong inside that mind of his. It is because of him—placing all of our trust into the hands of one Creature—making him 'King' of us all, that we will soon meet our end." He lifted the cane and bought it down in front of him, stepping with a leg that seemed to drag. He made his way toward the white doors, not looking Xavier in the eye as he limped past.

Xavier was sure to step out of the way, but the terrible blame that exuded off the Elf's body was tangible. *He still held the grudge.*

He wondered if the Elf would ever forgive him for throwing him off the edge of the cliff, foolish he was in his youth as a Vampire.

But he could not think on it for long, Arminius turned to him, pressing the crane against the floor. With his free hand, he clutched the red stone on his chest again and closed his eyes, most likely remembering something very painful. When he opened his eyes, his mouth moved, "You may not see it, Xavier, but the fall of our World is coming. It approaches sooner than we know. Dracula is the key to our survival, but he also must be destroyed before things are taken to a new level. Push aside your love for the Vampire and see what he really is: a murderer."

Xavier could say nothing more before the Elf hobbled down the long hallway, his voice reaching Xavier's ears with profound ease: "I will be back, *Vampure*. Let us hope we have not been destroyed when I return."

＊

Westley Rivers was aware his dead heart was pounding in his chest as he neared it. He could see the silver handle just there, yes, all he would have to do was reach out for it...

It took him a moment to realize he'd stopped walking. Such was the fear that filled him, but with a quick, "Get on with it," he resumed his movement toward the door, and before he knew it, his hand was upon the silver. His blue robes danced around his boots as he pressed down and entered the room.

*For we do the work of the Phoenixes.*

He scanned the large office, the draping curtains against the long, arched windows, the desk pushed in front of the wall.

The desk. Perhaps Dracula had left a clue, a piece of information about where he now was. For how bloody strange he wouldn't dare share a word, now, when he had done so many times before.

He started for it, a dark hand reaching out to grasp the small handle of the first drawer, which he pulled open with ease. He looked hard at the various folders that sat in a messy pile, and he pulled them out, reading the various documents they held within.

"*Haven for Vampires,*" "*Rules and Regulations for Newly Turned Vampires,*" "*How to Keep Lycans at Bay.*" None of it was what he needed. With a frustrated sigh, he dropped the files back into the drawer, turning his attention to the one beneath it.

Here were folders, arranged in a vertical fashion, that held many papers. They were thick, making it rather hard to dig one out, but when he did, he saw the words "Eleanor Black" upon one and his hands began to tremble.

He stared in awe at the black ink that held the name atop the aged folder. He flicked it open, wondering what Dracula had never shared of his Vampire—the one Creature that had returned from permanent death.

267

Upon the topmost page were descriptions of Eleanor, and they seemed to be written in Dracula's neat handwriting:

*Vivaciously beautiful, immensely curious, seemingly no qualms as to her state of being...even seems to enjoy drinking the blood of humans...does not take too well to my creation of necklaces to keep the urges at bay—*

He tore his gaze from the paper. He was reading something not meant for his eyes, and indeed, was he not here to figure out what happened to Armand?

Quickly placing the paper back inside the folder, he slid it back into the drawer with the others, fingers moving, once again seeing names of various Vampires he knew and knew well. Then he saw it: The aged folder was dog-eared, more so than the others, and he pulled it out of its bed, the name written in that same neat handwriting:

*Xavier Delacroix.*

His dark eyes gazed at the name in wonder, for here were, perhaps, the very secrets Dracula held of his favorite Vampire. The one chosen where all others failed. He sighed, throwing it back in the drawer, knowing the matter of the Vampire's truth would come to light, and soon.

He blinked, drawing his mind from the Dragon; he was intruding, his time perhaps very limited. There was no telling who, or what, would come barreling through the dark door at any moment. Yes, he had to find out where Armand was. He could not do his job if he did not know.

Closing the drawer with his boot, he scanned the large office, looking for anything out of place, any book out of line on its shelf.

He maneuvered around the desk, sure to make his way toward the table before the windows. The dark wood gleamed in the light of the torch, and he let out a quick sigh, there was nothing here— nothing here that would incriminate Dracula, nothing here to even suggest that Armand had entered...

Quite prepared to leave at last, his gaze fell upon the thick green curtain draped against the wall, it was in between two bookshelves, which begged the thought: Why on Earth was it draped there, of all places?

Believing this rather odd, he moved across the room and ran a dark finger down its edge, his thoughts turning to the feel of it: it was quite rich, made not of silk or cotton, but of another material, one he could not place, not readily anyhow.

He pulled it aside, the remainder of hard stone appearing, but here, even with the bookshelves placed on either side, he rather thought the space resembled a door...

And indeed, didn't other Vampire cities, their Head Vampires, always hold secret rooms or tunnels leading to or from their offices? So why hadn't Dracula ever let it be known that he too held a secret room? For Westley knew the Vampire must have one It would only make sense.

He was just pressing a dark hand against the stone when the black door flew open, causing him to turn in alarm, the curtain swinging back into perfect place.

"Westley Rivers."

A slight gasp left him, and before he knew what to more to do, the pale hand was raised, and he found his voice stuck hard in his throat. He lifted a hand to grasp at it as Dracula entered the room, closing the black door behind him, the fireplace sparking to life.

Dracula looked quite tired, windswept, his brown eyes sweeping across the large room. Westley could not make out his expression, not a hint of surprise, nor even a flicker of recognition.

"What were you doing in here, Vampire?"

"I," he gasped, finding himself able to speak suddenly, "I was merely...looking, my Lord—"

"Looking?" Dracula whispered, he kept shifting his gaze from his desk to the curtain. "What on Earth were you looking for?"

He took a small step forward. "Ar-Armand Dragon—" he began.

"Armand? What of the Vampire?"

"He is...missing," he whispered, dark eyes narrowing at the Vampire's sporadic eye movements. What was wrong with him?

Dracula took several steps forward. "Is he now?" the Great Vampire whispered, a hand moving to the golden clasp of the thick blue traveling cloak against his lean frame.

"Y-yes," he barely whispered, "under protocol, I—"

"Took it upon yourself to enter my office and do your duty: search for your missing Chair," Dracula said, releasing the traveling cloak from his body, throwing it carelessly atop his desk.

Westley almost thought it was with anger that he Dracula spoke "Well, I assure you, Mister Rivers, Mister Dragon is not here...and he is not there behind that curtain."

*Damn*, he thought, the Vampire's pressing eyes difficult to stand: Their gaze made it quite impossible to move. "My Lord, please, I was not trying to intrude, I was only doing my duty—"

The scoff left him, and Westley fell into silence with the sound. Dracula began to stride the length of the desk, before turning when he reached the end of it in order to resume his pacing, and the more Westley stared, the more he realized the Great Vampire was smiling, although the smile never reached his eyes They remained cruel and lost in dark thought.

"Your duty," he mocked, white hair flying out behind him; he turned to eye him straight on at last. "Is it not your duty to pay heed to my word, my action, Bronzechair?"

"I—"

"And is it not your duty, Westley, to keep my secrets, my truths, close to heart?"

"It is, of course, but Armand—"

"Armand didn't go the lengths you have to ensure my secrets are kept!" He waved a hand to the curtain. Westley turned and eyed it before Dracula continued, bringing his gaze back, "Armand has been relocated, Rivers."

"Whatever for?" he asked, wondering what more the Vampire kept from him, for it made no sense, no sense at all.

"He wished...he wished to take action where I would not allow him to, and you know better than anyone that that...is not done."

He opened his mouth, but as the thought came, he closed it, knowing the Vampire spoke miserable truth. Instead, he said, "The Vampires...they began to whisper of your disappearance."

A hand was lifted to his lips, his brow furrowed in dark question. "As they would," he said behind the hand, "though I hoped they wouldn't notice." Then he had a renewed vigor about him. "Well, I am here now, so—" He gestured toward the door expectantly.

He did not miss his cue, starting forward, he kept his eyes down. He had dodged an arrow, perhaps laced with Lycan blood, for Dracula was keeping something hidden, he had a feeling he had been very close to uncovering it, spared his life only with the secrets he'd been entrusted.

When he reached the door, Dracula said, "I was always here, Westley."

"Of course you were, my Lord."

And with that, he pressed down, wasting no time in tearing himself from the room and the Vampire within.

# Chapter Eighteen

# THE SWORD

He had spent the last three weeks mostly in the white living room, staring at the high walls, his mind working on Arminius's words, the troubling feeling they'd left him with.

It had been years since he'd seen the Elf. The Plains of Witterdell, a place he dared not visit again, and how strange it was that Dracula had not reprimanded him for that action.

"I never liked those blasted Elves," Dracula had said on more than one occasion when Xavier would bring up the punishment he felt he so rightfully deserved.

But what would Arminius want with information on Dracula's "secrets?" It was true that there were things the Vampire was keeping from them all, but to go as far as to say that the Vampire was a murderer... Was he not a murderer by birthright? He was born a Vampire, had the urge to kill since his childhood, this Xavier was told by Dracula himself, so what would bring Arminius to say it with such fear? And their World would soon come to an end? Dracula was the key to their survival but he also must he stopped? It made no sense at all.

He had yet to tell Victor about Arminius's visit. The Vampire was busy taking care of Lillith and her suitors, going on trips to faraway places, and putting on the appearance of a very wealthy human. While he, Xavier, had slipped into the confines of the manor, never leaving either this white room, or his bedroom. It was in this room that he could think, try to make sense of the situation.

The woman's proposal would fill his mind at the most inopportune times: when feeding, when writing his letters to various Vampires. Yes, there Eleanor's voice would be, ushering him into making a decision he was not so sure he wanted to make. And he knew he could no longer ignore it, for he had wasted too much time trying to do so. It was almost two weeks to the day since he had seen her in those woods.

And it was almost two weeks to the day Dracula had said the Council of Creatures wished to see him. He had almost forgotten Dracula's words. How indeed was he to pull this off? There was no way he could visit them at the same time, and he was not even sure how he was to contact Eleanor—if at all he was. But if he did not venture with Dracula to the Council, the Vampire would be disappointed in him, and he would miss what the Council had to say. But, if he did not go to Eleanor...

Bringing himself back to the present, he stood, the overwhelming smell of dread reaching his nose with ease.

*Outside*, he thought, *her Creatures were here already.*

Wondering why on Earth they were here (didn't he have more time?), he grabbed the Ascalon, which had been leaning up against the side of the couch, and moved for the white door, preparing himself for whatever he might see.

It blew open, a burst of cold wind, sand, and sprays of salt reaching his senses all at once.

When he lowered his arm, the dark of the night lingered before him, a foreboding presence in itself, for it could have not have been night so soon.

A man appeared, dark large hood over his head keeping his features from view. Xavier could do nothing before the man had grabbed his shirt, pulling him forward, his strength alarming—he was almost pulled off his feet.

He could barely say a word or lift his sword. The Creature pushed him forward, Xavier eyeing the large rocks before the water, the sprinkle of stars illuminating the night.

"Listen," the man whispered in an ear.

He did not see how he couldn't: The man kept an impossibly strong hand against his shoulder to keep him from running, and Xavier found he couldn't lift his sword.

There atop the sand appeared several cloaked figures, their hoods low over their faces, but the dread they exuded was overwhelming. He almost thought he would fall to his knees with the pressure, but then it was gone, and the air stilled, the sound of the waves against his ears dispersed. Nothing but the feel of the strange man's hand remained.

Two of the figures stepped forward then, removing their hoods from their heads, revealing determined faces. One was a man, the other, a woman. The man's brown hair reached his neck, his eyes hazel, his expression dangerous in the dark, and Xavier knew all at once that this man was a Lycan: The hate that filled those eyes belonged to one kind of Dark Creature.

The woman, however, gazed upon him with an interested glare. A *Vampire*, he deduced, for her crimson eyes and long, cascading hair gave that much away.

He was wondering how they were able to stand right next to each other when the man said:

"Xavier Delacroix, we meet at last. Eleanor has allowed me the pleasure of meeting with you one last time in this form before I am turned."

"Who are you?" he asked.

"Thomas. Thomas Montague."

"The Duke of Holden?"

Thomas smiled and turned to the woman at his side, sure to clasp a hand in hers before he continued: "Eleanor does not believe I can handle myself around you, Xavier. I have wanted to kill you for such a long time, but I will control myself tonight, if not for your sake, then for my wife's."

The cloaked figures behind them stirred, shifting their footing at Thomas's words. It seemed they were there to watch over Thomas and nothing more.

Xavier glared at him, not quite sure what he was hearing. "You are working with Eleanor?"

"Yes," he said. "She...lured me to her, by taking away what I loved..." His voice faltered. "But with my wife's transformation, there was nothing left for me to do but follow suit. And then it will be easier for me to kill you, Nightwalker."

The hooded figures stepped closer to Thomas, the one behind Xavier keeping a steady hand on his shoulder.

"Eleanor is most gracious, but she is not a fool. She wants me to remind you—" his voice rang with disgust at the very idea, "—that you still have time to make your decision. She will come to you in three days. Do not worry about her finding you; she will know where to look."

Xavier's hand lowered the sword, despite himself. "Three days?"

"Three."

His heart quickened its cold beating, the dread spreading through him in earnest. What was she playing at? Could he really follow in her footsteps? Could he really leave Dracula behind? Dracula, the Vampire that held his own secrets...

"Are you actually scared?" Thomas's incredulous voice sounded, snapping him abruptly from his thoughts.

Thomas's laugh was inescapable. "You have nothing to fear,

Vampire—except me, of course, but that is only if you do not agree to Eleanor's proposal and Eleanor does not kill you first."

"She plans to kill me?" he asked.

"If you do not agree."

*Truly?* he thought in bewilderment. He knew his choice would have consequences, but never one so rash, so final, so..."Why won't you just try to kill me now?" he asked, vaguely thinking this course of action most desirable against waiting, waiting, waiting for Eleanor to come to him.

The Lycan in human form expressed a look of severe longing, and his voice was low, the hooded figures behind him stirring as if on cue: "Eleanor wishes for the duty to be her own if you do not accept. I am not to lay a finger on you...unless she does not succeed."

"Thomas," the woman next to him hissed, placing a pale hand on his shoulder. He flinched with her touch, but did nothing more. "That is enough."

He growled. "Fine. But I will have you, Xavier. Mark my word."

She squeezed his shoulder and they all dispersed from the beach, blowing up sand and water with their departure. The sounds of nature returned to him, and he realized he was still clutching his sword tight.

He stared at the spot Thomas Montague had been just moments before and wondered why Eleanor would lure the Lycan to her with his wife. What was she really after?

The wind picked up again and he was greeted with the vaguely familiar scent of lilac and blood.

✳

"We must let him sleep!" Victor's deep voice danced to his ears, sounding as though it were coming through a long tunnel. He opened his eyes and sat up, listening to the unsuccessfully hushed voices outside the door:

"We must speak to him!" Lillith replied. "We've not seen him for weeks, and he ends up on his beach—the Ascalon just inches from him—if his servant hadn't sent word, he could have been found by another human, or Lycan!"

"There are no more Lycans out there," Victor said, his voice calmer than hers. "They have all joined Eleanor and turned into those...Creatures. Now, it is clear something is troubling him, we will find out what it is, but we must let him get his rest!"

Xavier heard the impatient sigh, Lillith's footsteps moving away from the door, and he wasted no time in saying, "I'm awake, Victor."

The door opened, Victor's eyes shining with clear concern. When he swung his legs over the side of the bed, the Vampire asked, "What happened?"

"Eleanor," he said simply, rubbing the back of his neck, marveling at how much it pained him.

Victor raised an eyebrow. "What do you mean 'Eleanor?'"

He stood, immediately met with pain in his heart that had not been there before. Rubbing a hand over his chest, he said, "Back when we were to travel to the City and Aciel called for me...he took me to her."

Victor was silent but his eyes were wide.

"She...is different. The reason these Creatures are plaguing the Dark World. She wants me to join her," he said, realizing how strange it all sounded.

"Join her? Become one of them?" he breathed, incredulous.

"Yes."

"Why didn't you say anything to us before? Did you tell Dracula?"

With this, Xavier forced himself to stare into the Vampire's alarmed eyes. "Of course. Of course, I told Dracula—he knew she wasn't dead. He'd sent the Chairs to assess the situation at the cabin once we'd left it."

Victor was silent, thinking over his words, and then: "Did she come to you last night?"

"No," Xavier said, feeling uneasy at his lack of sword. He looked around for the Ascalon, and saw it, resting against the bed. He picked up it and swung it with his right hand, his mind reeling with the images of what he'd seen hours before. "Thomas Montague and his wife came to me upon my beach."

"The Duke of Holden? He is one of them?"

"He is not one of them, but he is going to be. His wife was turned; he will follow suit," Xavier said, resting the sword on the bed.

"Mara Montague was turned into one of those...things?!"

Xavier could not begin to fathom why Victor was so engulfed in the fact that a Lycan and his wife were working alongside Eleanor, but he shrugged away his confusion to say, "Eleanor has given me two days to come to a decision regarding her. If I do not say what she wants to hear, she will kill me."

"You do not honestly think Eleanor would kill you for not agreeing to her little plan."

He almost laughed when he realized that was what he'd told himself only hours before. "I do."

"But, Xavier, she used to be one of us! She...she was your greatest treasure, your joy, your heart!"

He merely stared, knowing the Eleanor that Victor spoke of was no more. "She is different, like I said, and she is determined to have me."

"What will you do?"

He sat down on the bed, wondering where these painful aches were coming from. "I will wait and see. Hopefully, Dracula's letter will come later than the next two days and I will have more time."

"Dracula's letter?" Victor asked.

"I am to meet with the Council of Creatures," he said, knowing the Vampire would not forgive him for leaving out that bit of vital information. If anything, it was a high honor.

True to Xavier's thoughts, Victor looked cross, but he said, "In the same time that Eleanor will meet you, I take it."

"Let us hope not," he whispered.

"You really should have told me sooner; I might've been able to—"

"To what?" he asked, looking up to see the furious Vampire. "To help me? There is nothing you would've been able to do. It is my decision and it will remain as such."

"But Dracula—"

"Dracula no more cares about Eleanor's existence than he does what she knows. He's made that perfectly clear." Xavier realized that the Vampire had done more harm than good in keeping so many secrets from him and the rest of the Dark World, but Eleanor seemed to have taken things too far.

Victor ran a hand over his eyes in clear exasperation. "Where must you go?"

"It matters not. She will find me. On the day she is to come for me, I will leave. I will not see you and Lillith in harm's way."

Victor did not say a word, and Xavier silently thanked him. The last thing he needed was his dear friend telling him that he was being foolish and that he had to stay within sight, that there was no telling what Eleanor would do.

A knock on the door demanded their attention, and they both glanced toward it, Victor blinking as though driven from a deep sleep. "Yes?" he called.

The door opened, a servant held a tray, a small envelope atop it. Victor moved to greet the servant, his back blocking the servant from view, and Xavier heard the name "Count Dracul" quite clearly.

Victor took the envelope and closed the door, his face paler than usual. "Xavier," he began, apparently not able to finish. Xavier said nothing, striding the length of the room, grasping the envelope, staring at the small scribble atop it. He broke the seal with a nail, working to release the paper from its home, and eyed the page, skimming across words such as *the time, Council, secrecy, hidden, woods, interesting endeavor*—the finality of the choice to be made reaching him in seriousness. He was trapped between the Vampire he once loved and the Vampire he once trusted.

Why did Eleanor and Darien have to stumble upon the Vampire's secrets? Would it not be better if things remained the way they were?

"Xavier." And he felt the Vampire's hand upon his shoulder; apparently he had been reading as well. "Where will he meet you?"

He spared a glance at the words and said, "He already knows I'm here."

Victor removed his hand, a cold sigh escaping his lungs. "I apologize. I should have known what was happening. I should have been there to help."

"Thank you, but there is nothing that can be done about it now."

Reaching out to grab his sword, he realized the black leather strap was not sitting across his waist. "Where is my sheath?" he asked.

Victor blinked. "What are you doing?"

"I am leaving. I cannot stay here." Xavier looked around the modest room for any sign of the sheath.

"You cannot leave! Dracula knows where you are."

"You know what must happen," he said shrewdly, ceasing his search to gaze upon him, "I will not put you, Lillith, my brother, or that human in harm's way."

The Vampire looked as though he wished to say something, but his mouth never opened, and it seemed he'd come to terms with what was happening at last.

Xavier turned from him, spotting the sheath on the floor, just near the wall, and grabbed it, placing it around his waist, settling the

Ascalon into it. He did not eye Victor, but moved to the open closet, and threw on a traveling cloak. He eyed the door that led to the hallway knowing the Vampire would try to stop him if he walked past.

So there, eyeing the old Vampire, he bade him one last nod, and disappeared from the room, turning his thoughts to where Dracula could have gone.

✖

He transported to an unknown place. It seemed to be a forest he'd never frequented before. Soft snow darted everywhere, making it a challenge to see anything but the wooden trunks of trees all around him. The ground beneath his boots crunched against the snow; he took a few steps in a direction he was not sure was north at all.

He looked above him, the sky a thick, swirling blue, the snow drifting to the ground, and it was here he wondered where Dracula could have been. He had thought of him when he'd transported, and here he remained. Dracula must have been close.

He considered transporting again, but found the pain overwhelmed him now. He could barely continue his walk through the woods, so he trudged on, hoping to find a sign of the white-haired Vampire.

He walked, his thoughts unwillingly traveling to Eleanor Black, the idea of her finding him here jarring him where he stood, but he felt as though this place was safe—magical, even. He was almost at ease amongst the swirling snow, at ease amongst the trees. If it were not for the small pit of dread in his stomach, he would have been able to walk along without a care.

He walked for an hour, at least, but he could not be sure. As far as he could tell, the concept of time seemed unimportant here.

The trees began to thin, and soon he laid eyes upon a terribly tall (endlessly so, it seemed) building, hovering several feet off the ground. Its dark stone was easily seen against the white of the falling snow. He turned his gaze upwards, eyeing two towers that stretched on even farther above. Two large wooden doors appeared at the building's base, right before him.

Narrowing his eyes, for he was certain they weren't there before, he stepped forward, a hand on the handle of the Ascalon as he moved. When he reached them, they swung open, a hard-looking man standing there, hands splayed against the wood of the doors, his deep, golden eyes narrowing: He looked out beyond the falling snow, apparently searching for something. His short red hair flew every which way atop his head, a bit of it moving over his eyes despite his persistence in finding whatever it was he was looking for out in the snow.

Xavier cleared his throat.

The man looked down, his golden eyes widening. "Xavier Delacroix?" he asked, his voice fairly light, but filled with something else Xavier couldn't make sense of.

"I am," he said.

The man stepped aside, allowing him entry, and he jumped up onto the hard floor. "Dracula's been here for a few minutes, now, wondering when you'd arrive."

Xavier paid no heed to his words, for he was far too busy staring at the multitude of Creatures that walked around the modest hall:

An Enchanter swept past, his flowing dark-purple robes leaving a faint trail of what looked like dust in his wake. A Satyr hobbled by on its hind hooves, its black eyes gleaming in the light of several torches placed around the room.

The strange man led him deeper, passing a couple of Garden Gnomes fighting amongst themselves over what looked to be a seed.

Xavier laid eyes on a long wooden bar set toward the right side of the room. Behind it stood a gorgeous woman, her long blonde hair falling over her shoulders. She served the other Creatures, handing them cups filled with a variety of colored liquids.

The strange man gestured to her with a finger and she passed a glass filled with a blue liquid to an Elf before moving toward them.

"What'll it be?" she asked the man, blue eyes shining.

He gestured his head toward Xavier, and the woman, seemingly understanding something in that gesture, let a smile grace her face. "*Anima* it is," she said quietly, moving away from them.

And before he could ask what was going on, the man said, "It will make you feel much better—ease your nerves."

"What will?"

The woman returned, a chalice of red liquid in hand. She offered the drink to him and he took it hesitantly, not understanding what he now held. He sipped it, feeling his strength return to him, surprised to find that he drunk very delicious blood.

Once he had taken his full, the man moved away from him and moved deeper into the room, his form getting lost in the sea of Dark Creatures.

Figuring that he had to follow the man, Xavier moved, nodding curtly to the woman, quite surprised when she flashed him a knowing smile: It was as if she was aware of his whole entire life, and what would come shortly within it, and he nearly tripped over a nearby stool, for it hit him so squarely.

She was a Fae. It was obvious now. Having never actually met one before, he could not realize the exact glow that existed around her, but now that he was paying attention, he saw it clearly. She was a Creature that resembled a human woman, if only far prettier. She, like the other Faes in the World, held the ability to discern one's future. He frowned, for he realized she was here in a bar, serving drinks to various Dark Creatures, not holed up with a Goblin or Elf, one of the Creatures that would have a great need for her.

He moved away, passing a few Enchanters, Goblins, and Fairies, his thoughts flying to the fate that often befell the Fae: Forced to divine the future for their captors, they often died quick, untimely deaths, their power not able to sustain them, being used for such selfish purposes.

"This way, my Lord," the man's voice sounded from up ahead, pulling him from dismal thoughts. As he looked, he saw the man's hand upon a knob of a wooden door: He was turning it, prepared to enter another room.

Walking quickly to catch up, he returned his thoughts to Dracula's whereabouts and hoped this man was leading him to the Great Vampire. When he passed through the doors, he saw that the man was indeed doing just that.

This room was much larger than the one they'd left. Tables existed here as well, but not brown and old, no, they seemed to be made of pure gold. The benches that accompanied them were made of the same material, illuminating the Creatures that sat atop them, mostly Vampires, here. He and the man with the golden eyes walked past them, one Vampire catching his eye: Dracula.

The Great Vampire sat on a bench, looking quite calm, a golden chalice in front of him. He spoke to another large Vampire, who appeared to be hanging onto his every word.

"—And, of course the Elves were sent back to me with that damned request for freedom. I've often wondered how Alinneis is acquiring the paper to write the things."

The Vampire let out a hearty laugh and choked on the blood he'd swigged down, his laughs turning to hacking coughs.

The man with the red hair and golden eyes patted the Vampire on the back. Smiling, he said, "Really, Capernicus, you should swallow first."

Capernicus gave the man a rueful look. "Couldn't help mehself. 'Tis not every day you get to share a chalice with the King of Creatures." His eyes then found Xavier, and his playful demeanor disappeared. "What's the meanin' of this?"

The Great Vampire stood, removing himself from the bench. "I remember telling you about Xavier Delacroix."

"A course I remember him...bu–but *now*, Dracula?" Capernicus sputtered. "He in'nt ready! Not with these Creatures terrorizing the Dark World and all...ye' would really do tha' then? Ye' would really put Xavier out there, alone, to, to..." He chased down his lost words with more blood.

Dracula eyed the large Vampire. "I made it clear, Capernicus. Xavier is terribly ready to face whatever is out there, and he wouldn't be alone, he'd have his advisers and the Chairs to help him."

Capernicus seemed to be at a loss as to what to say or do next and drummed his large fingers against the golden tabletop, his misty eyes lost in, Xavier guessed, disturbing thought.

Dracula made a notion with his head to the man with golden eyes and the man patted Capernicus on the shoulder. "Up you go. Dracula must talk."

The large Vampire, casting a weary glance to Xavier, and then Dracula, shrugged off the bench and trudged to a staircase Xavier just realized was there. The strange man followed. When they could no longer be seen, Dracula slumped back onto his bench, finishing the last of his blood.

Xavier sat opposite him.

Dracula said, "Well, Xavier, how are you fairing?"

And with this question, the thoughts on Eleanor's words, Darien and Damion, the Caddenhalls, Alexandria Stone, and Thomas and Mara Montague resurfaced, but all he could muster to say was, "Quite well."

"Really?" Dracula asked, and when Xavier could not find the words to respond, Dracula gestured toward his empty chalice. "Would you like some blood?"

"No thanks. The Fae at the bar gave me some."

"Ah," he said, stifling what looked to be a smile. "Quite lovely aren't they? You must be careful not to stare at them too long, of course. Then your secrets are revealed, and they have the power to destroy you with the mere knowledge."

Xavier said nothing, his words caught on his tongue. His thoughts returned to Eleanor. *Two more days.* It seemed even the serene feeling of the place they were in could not hold back the feeling of dread that bubbled in the pit of his stomach.

"Xavier?" Dracula's smile disappeared.

He looked up from his hands, and he realized he had been wringing them. "Dracula?"

"You seemed perturbed by something."

"It's nothing, nothing at all."

"Hm." The disbelief was clear on Dracula's face but even so, he said, "I see you've brought the Ascalon with you. Worried that you would run into some Lycans on the way?"

Xavier did not answer this question. "What is this place?"

"Cinderhall Manor," Dracula said, his features growing more curious.

"Why are we here? I thought we were to travel to the Council."

"We are, we are. All in time. It is still quite a journey from here, of course, but we will make it with no time to spare, I imagine. First, we will rest here."

"And what is this place?"

"Some think of it as an inn for Creatures. I think of it as a second home. Cinderhall Manor is a place Creatures go when they are to prepare for the journey to the Council. Of course, so many Creatures are usually not in attendance, but the subject of this particular meeting is very...enthralling."

Xavier stared at his hands again, willing the feeling of dread to disappear from his body. Instead, it grew. He sighed. "What is the subject?"

"You."

He looked up, the feeling of dread replaced with temporary shock, and soon found himself almost yelling, "Me?!"

"Yes, yes, you. Keep your voice down," he said, waving a hand. "The Council is most interested in meeting you.... It seems they are in the searching for a new King.

"Not that I am not doing my best, of course, but naturally, I must pass the torch, as it were, to someone with power, strength—someone who is able to take care of these Creatures, Eleanor Black..."

Xavier did not breathe.

Dracula said, "I chose you, Xavier."

"M—Me?! You chose me as the new King?!" he almost shouted once again.

Dracula glared at him to keep his voice down, and he wondered just how he was supposed to do that when presented with such news.

"I chose you, yes. We all chose you."

Xavier could not speak.

The Vampire patted his hand. "I am sure you are overwhelmed at the prospect of it all, but is it not an honor? I imagine when you have rested, you will think more happily about it."

"But I cannot be King," Xavier said.

"What do you mean?"

"I...I just cannot. What of Victor? Is he not your first victim? Your oldest friend?"

"Victor Vonderheide is my dearest friend, yes, but we must face the facts here: he is not what the Council is looking for."

"And what is that exactly?"

Dracula hesitated, and ultimately decided to remain silent.

Xavier stared at him. "You expect me to be King when you cannot even tell me the reason for it? What makes me so damned special? Why choose me?"

"Your blood, Xavier. It is why I chose you. My first choice was Eleanor," he said.

*Again with the talk of blood.* "What about my blood, Dracula? You have told me nothing—"

"I will tell you when I am ready. That time is not now."

"And when will it be?"

"It is not now."

He glared at the Vampire, utter disbelief lining his eyes. "You will not tell me, and yet you wish for me to be King? I have every reason to go back to my manor."

"You cannot leave."

*Was that a threat?* "I believe I can—"

"You do not understand, Xavier," he said, heading him off. "You cannot leave. No one can, once here, we can only travel to the meeting place. Otherwise, we must wait here until the Council's meeting has ended."

He blinked. "What *is* this place, Dracula?"

"Like I said, it is an inn for Creatures who wish to view the Council meeting. There is a barrier of magic around the building and land for several acres. Humans, the Etrian Elves, and Lycans cannot see it, it cannot be penetrated. We are safe here."

"So you would have us stay here until we are to leave?"

"Yes. We leave tomorrow. We should reach the Council by the next day."

The feeling of dread returned tenfold and he did not attempt to fight it. He was to travel with Dracula to the Council of Creatures, a place where many Creatures would be gathered to see his possible Initiation as King of All Creatures, and his hands started to wring once more, Xavier remembered what Thomas had said to him upon his beach, *"Do not worry about her finding you...she will know where to look."*

✳

He awoke to the sound of hooves and footsteps outside his door, but he remained in bed, listening. The footsteps moved down the hallway and down the stairs, shuffling into the large dining hall he had been in the day before.

Knowing the many Creatures in Cinderhall Manor were there to see his coronation as King, he got out of the large bed and grabbed the Ascalon he had propped against a wall, still in its sheath. Settling it around his waist, he turned to the black cloak on the back of the chair of the desk provided for him, though he never did use it.

And now, looking around the room for the first time since he'd entered it, he saw the extravagant chandelier above him, the brightly burning fireplace. Finding it slightly strange that a fireplace existed in a room that led to nowhere, he turned for the door.

Once opened, he laid eyes on Dracula. He was leaning against the wall opposite the door, a dark expression on his face. He could barely say a word before the Vampire said, "Finally. Were you really so worn out?"

"I...is it not morning?" he asked, peering down the hallway to see if any more Creatures existed there: It was barren, it seemed all present Creatures had indeed left their rooms.

Dracula pushed away from the wall, a hand on the hilt of a sword around his own waist. Xavier stared at it, aware the Vampire held his sword only in matters of extreme importance.

"It is morning," Dracula replied, "a little after dawn, actually. Come, Xavier, we must make haste."

And before he could say a word, Dracula had turned from him, the blue cloak flying out as he moved. He was prepared to ask where he'd gotten it (for Xavier had never seen it upon him before), but the Vampire was halfway down the hallway; with haste Xavier moved to catch up.

Together, they descended the stairs, and instead of sitting down at one of the many golden tables, Dracula strode through a back door once they reached the great dining hall. Xavier followed after a brief moment of hesitation and pushed through the same door, but halted on his step, for Dracula hovered above the snow, his hair and cloak whipping in the wind.

"Quickly, Xavier," Dracula said, flying through the trees.

He closed the door behind him and followed the blue cloak, releasing himself from the ground, fairly surprised at how amazing he felt. His thoughts turned to the strange drink he'd been given back at the bar, quite amazed at how invigorated it made him feel.

The swirling sky above was still a misty blue, and Xavier wondered if night ever really fell at all. He passed many tall dark trees and was amazed at how far ahead Dracula was. He pressed forward, the Vampire's call reaching him in the next moment: "Stay there."

He landed atop a branch and watched through the trees. Dracula hovered next to a branch of a tree ahead before moving to stand on it, but it was not long before he crouched, keeping himself pressed against the trunk.

Xavier wondered what Dracula was doing, when the Vampire lifted a pale finger and motioned for him to come closer. Gliding slowly toward him, Xavier stopped near the branch and looked down.

The lake was large and a few miles ahead, white capped mountains were farther beyond it, lining the horizon. Snow fell onto the water's dark surface, only to disappear once it landed. This lake, however, was not what held Xavier's attention, no, it was the massive flying Dragons that glided gracefully through the air above the lake that held his awed gaze.

There were two of them. One a crystal blue with shining scales that seemed to turn white against the snow. Her claws—Xavier felt that this particular Dragon was female— were silver and curved beneath her massive body. He watched her swerve through the air before diving furiously into the lake, all becoming unnaturally still once she disappeared beneath the surface.

The other Dragon, a black one, rested on the bank of the lake and seemed bored. It never lifted its large head to eye its companion's strange actions.

Xavier, still wondering about the female Dragon, began to open his mouth to ask Dracula what was going on, but the Great Vampire raised a hand in protest. He was gazing into the dark lake intently, waiting, but for what, Xavier could not fathom.

And before Xavier could think just what more was going on, what a couple of Dragons had to do with the Council of Creatures, the water rippled, and the long snout of the blue Dragon appeared, her face emerging from the water as well as her body. Dripping wet with water, the Dragon seemed to have held something in her mouth, and upon keeping his gaze there, Xavier's eyes widened, for the Dragon held a Mermaid between its sharp teeth, gargled screams leaving her lips. The Dragon chomped down on her pale body mercilessly.

The Dragon's wings flapped, the Creature swerved in a loop through the air, throwing the remains of the Mermaid into the blue sky, sure to catch her as she fell, swallowing her whole.

He could not still his gasp of surprise, for he had read of the Creatures eating Mermaids, humans, indeed, any Creature it could get its claws on, but he had never before seen it. He was broken from his shock by the intent glare of the Dragon, her long sharp tail swishing dangerously, beady black eyes seeming to gleam through the falling snow. Xavier wondered when she'd known they arrived.

Dracula pushed himself off the branch with ease in the next second and flew straight toward her, leaving Xavier behind. He watched as the Vampire turned in midair, feet from the waiting Dragon, his brown eyes gleaming just as the large Creature's did. "Follow," he said.

Xavier froze. His stare traveled from Dracula to the large beast and he thought the Creature watched him with hunger, though she did nothing but hover there.

"Hurry," Dracula said, throwing himself past the blue Dragon before Xavier could say a word, and Xavier knew he was heading for the mountains.

Letting out a frustrated growl, he left the safety of the woods, pressing past the blue Dragon He felt the fierce wind her large wings made against the sky, but he continued on, just past the edge of the lake now...he had made it...and yet...

He was being pulled back against the falling snow, unable to move forward. He turned to find the large open mouth of the black Dragon that had once rested upon the banks, its fangs glistening against the snow. It inhaled large gusts of cold air, determined to pull him in.

His eyes widened as he stared into the red mouth. He swirled around, drawing his sword, still pressing against the large inhales of the Dragon, going nowhere. He felt his body drag slowly, until he was in between its rows of teeth, and he pushed the Ascalon up, blocking the line of fangs above him. He pushed back against the jaws that were pressing down, trying to claim him in their deadly cage.

He then caught the glint of the Dragon's black eyes and panic filled him. It was tired of playing with its food.

As if on cue, a warm gust of air exploded from its throat, throwing him back against the air. He landed brusquely on the snow-covered ground, the Ascalon flying out of his hand, sliding several feet away.

He could barely get the snow out of his eyes when the terribly loud roar filled his ears and he caught sight of the small ball of fire that was forming in the Dragon's open mouth. The fire grew, seeming to slow as it left the Dragon's mouth, hurtling toward him—

The blue cloak billowed before him in the next instant, the Vampire holding up his own sword, the blade stopping the large trail of fire from reaching him on the ground. Dracula's white hair flew out all around him, his feet leaving the snow, and he was in the air once again, charging straight toward the black Dragon, his sword aimed at the Dragon's heart.

When it struck, a blinding red light escaped the blade, traveling to where Dracula's sword cut through tough scale. They glimmered as the Dragon let out a remarkable scream.

Xavier willed himself to stand, his green eyes widening: The Dragon burst into black ash, which sprinkled across the sky, mixing with the falling snow, and Dracula settled next to him on the ground, sliding his sword into its sheath, the dark red gem in the center of the guard gleaming vibrantly.

"Why didn't you follow me as soon as I left the branch?" he asked.

Xavier stared at him, pulling his gaze from the gem. "Dracula, they're Dragons, forgive me if I hesitated before flying out in between two of them!"

Dracula glared at him before turning away, muttering something about *"not listening,"* and *"troublesome."* He eyed the Ascalon, half-covered by snow, and raised a hand toward it. It left its snowy grave along the banks of the lake and zipped to his hand. Xavier was prepared to say something when Dracula turned to him, sliding the Ascalon into the sheath at his waist and said, "Be more careful next time. And do as I say.

Dracula disappeared, the glint of his brown eyes lingering in the sun.

# Chapter Nineteen

# THE COUNCIL OF CREATURES

The sky had turned a dark shade of violet before they knew it. Dracula had taken to jumping over treetops while Xavier followed on the ground, the thoughts of what others said about the Great Vampire spiraling in his mind.

*"Yet another thing that Vampire keeps from his own kind...what he really is: a murderer...he also must be destroyed..."*

*But what was the truth?*

He ran, looking up, the quick shadow of the Vampire jumping from tree to tree, blocking out the stars like some sort of eclipse, and it was here he recalled what Darien told him in his living room so many years ago: *"I have learned the dark secrets Dracula has been hiding from his Vampires..."*

*Just what were these secrets?*

He decided now was the best time to ask, if he ever were to find out, after all, he might be dead tomorrow at the hands of her. "Dracula," he called to the trees above.

The trees stopped swaying as if a breeze had abruptly died and Dracula appeared before him on the ground, his feet not making a sound against the snow. "What is it?"

He halted, staring uncertainly upon the Vampire's calm demeanor. It seemed quite impossible that Dracula would be a Vampire mired in all his secrets, not desiring to let one slip....

"I must know..." he began.

Dracula raised an eyebrow, his face perfectly blank.

"I must know if you are...keeping secrets from me – from others."

A slow smile formed on Dracula's lips, much to his surprise. "Of course. You did not think I would tell you all everything, did you? There are things you all don't need to know."

"Even if—"

"Even if you are to be King."

Xavier stared at him, wondering how he could go on following the Vampire's word if he would not tell him anything. "Why won't you tell me?"

Dracula shifted his footing, casting a look to the dark skies above. "We must hurry. The Heads of Creatures from all around the World are heading there." He glanced back toward him. "I imagine we'd want the best seats."

He growled impatiently. "Dracula—"

But the Vampire had already closed his eyes and disappeared from view, leaving him standing alone in the cold dark wood.

✳

Dracula was several feet ahead of him, and the sun peeked through the treetops; he grimaced. Eleanor would come to him today, and he hoped she was not able to follow. He hoped that the protection of this place would halt her progress to him and she would cease her pursuit.

But she wouldn't. She would probably attack the other Vampires...once her friends, her comrades, all because she didn't have him. The notion seemed rather selfish, and Xavier wondered if what Eleanor was doing was really for the benefit of all Creatures. She seemed to be doing much more harm than good.

The hurried sound of several footsteps before him brought him back to the here and now, and he picked his head up.

Dracula disappeared behind a large tree, a new voice reaching him against the morning: "My King, it is an honor. My men and I have prepared a trail up to the palace—"

When Xavier rounded the tree, the voice stopped abruptly, and many new voices started chatting excitedly at the sight of him. Dracula turned to where it was the Creatures looked and extended a hand, beckoning him forward.

He glanced around at the Centaurs that watched him fiercely, their wild orange eyes shining. What he deemed to be the Head Centaur, Vimic, stepped forward and bowed low, his front legs getting lost in the snowy ground. Xavier stepped next to Dracula and stared down at the long black hair of the Centaur. "Is this...really necessary?"

Many of the Centaurs behind Vimic laughed, but Vimic stood, lifting a tan hand through the falling snow, and they fell silent immediately. The Centaur's eyes were black, quite different from the others and their orange gazes. "It is most necessary, Xavier," Vimic said, casting a curious glance to Dracula.

The Great Vampire's eyes gleamed with knowing, and in that stare, Xavier saw a command. Indeed, Vimic seemed in quite a hurry to reach the palace, and he turned, his long black tail brushing against Xavier's chest. The Centaurs followed Vimic's hooves, pummeling the ground. They moved with grace and power, yet several Centaurs remained where they stood, staring at him as if they had never seen a Creature like him before. Dracula growled threateningly then, sending them following the trail of trampled snow behind Vimic and the rest.

Xavier was prepared to ask Dracula why Centaurs were their escort to the Council of Creatures, but he seemed quite content on avoiding questions: He was gone from sight before Xavier could get a word across. Sighing, he followed suit.

They reappeared several miles from a large manor that seemed abandoned in the middle of what Xavier thought was nowhere. Two Centaurs left the pack and flanked the sides of the large doors, their dark hair flapping wildly with the wind. Vimic waved a strong arm to the other Centaurs and said, "Disperse." Without a second thought, the other Centaurs rode off in opposite directions, their wild hair blowing violently in between the drops of snow.

Vimic turned his gaze to Dracula. "Welcome back to the Council, your Majesty," and he stepped aside, away from the large doors that were creaking open.

Much to Xavier's surprise, the Vampire who opened the doors at Cinderhall Manor stood here as well, a sly grin spreading across his face and even through the cold, Xavier could make out the strange glint in his golden eyes. He wore a long black robe that fell onto the black tiled floor of the manor and swept out two long arms. "My Lord," he addressed Dracula, before turning to Xavier, seeming to hesitate on his words before saying, "My...Lord."

Dracula, not paying any attention to this, strode forward, passing through the doorway, nodding curtly to the red-haired Vampire. "You beat us here Nathanial, when did you leave the Manor?"

"Just a little before dawn. Decided I'd beat the rush," he said with a grin.

"Hm," was all Dracula said, stepping away from them, heading deeper into the manor.

Xavier hesitated and Nathanial noticed this. "Come in, Xavier."

He obeyed, stepping into the manor, Dracula's long robe quite a distance down the long hallway that seemed to stretch throughout the length of the place.

"...should be a day to remember, once the meeting's over with," Nathanial was saying to Vimic, who gazed into the building with fierce eyes.

"A day to remember indeed," Vimic agreed, casting an interested look to Xavier.

A cold wind blew past Nathanial, ushering snow through the doors, and Nathanial prepared to close them, nodding to the Centaur who reciprocated the acknowledgement curtly.

Nathanial waved his hands and the doors closed, Vimic instantly gone from view as the long hall was swept into darkness. He turned back to Nathanial to greet the golden eyes that peered at him, curious.

"Xavier," he said after a few moments of silence, "Dracula has told you—?"

"That I am his choice for King, yes."

"Well," Nathanial said, beginning to walk down the hall, "I am not supposed to tell you this but the others are convinced you will hold the title next."

They walked, passing the dark brick walls upon which were various swords and shields planted decoratively between portraits of other Vampires.

"The others?" he asked.

Nathanial did not turn his gaze to meet Xavier's, but stared straight ahead, toward an unseen destination. "The Head Creatures. I've spoken to Thrall, usually a nasty little Gnome, but he's seemingly determined you will hold the title with honor. And Wiffle, and Drivor, Peroneous, Axely, Evert, Friandria, Dunley, and Renor, of course. I'm quite sure Dracula has convinced them all, somehow."

"And who are you to this whole Council?" Xavier asked. He seemed more and more to be a King of some far away country.

Nathanial turned to him then, his eyes placed on Xavier's, but he did not break stride. "I'm the...Adviser of Affairs here at the Council. Dracula came to me three years ago with the idea to gather others together to hold a meet for our World. Seemed to think we would need it in the coming years. Can't say he was wrong, of course, what with Eleanor Black flying about…"

The dread grew with the mention of her name, a name he'd forgotten for the few minutes since he'd first laid eyes upon the massive stone manor.

"Where will the meeting be held?" Xavier asked, wanting a distraction from the woman that claimed his mind, his heart.

Nathanial reached a large black door, tattered with age. The worn knob looked as though it didn't belong within the wood. Xavier wondered how long this place had been there when Nathanial said, "The meeting will be held through there." He pointed a pale finger to the door on the other side of the hallway. "But you aren't to see it 'til we're ready to begin. Of course, the other Creatures will have to be filed in before you can enter."

Xavier stared at the larger door across from them, a grand sensation of being terribly small reaching him the longer he stared. *Bloody King.*

The sound of a knob turning, the click it made when the door opened, brought his attention back to Nathanial. He was entering the room, his black robes swaying as he walked. The room was large, filled with drab black furnishings pushed against the walls: A rickety old rocking chair was placed near a stone wall, its legs so old Xavier wondered how it was still standing, a small bed, placed next to the rocking chair, held black sheets atop it.

There was no source of light, nor was there a window in sight, and Xavier walked deeper into the room, the bookshelves lined with cobwebs; seemingly ancient books, never before touched, graced the shelves.

"This place used to belong to an Enchanter by the name of Carvaca," Nathanial said. "She's long since passed away, so we'd thought it be a good idea to use her manor with it being far away from others."

He turned to him. "And where are the others staying?"

"Where they always have whenever meetings are had, upstairs."

"Then could I not have a room upstairs?"

"No. All of the rooms are occupied. And as this is only a temporary visit for you, we've decided that this was the best room available. And it's so close to the place where we shall meet...you do understand the convenience this room creates," the Vampire said.

He stared around the dark, drab room and sighed. "Very well."

Nathanial smiled, his red hair swaying with his head as he spoke. "We should be ready for you in an hour or so. I will call for you when we are." He made his way for the old door but stopped midstride and turned to Xavier. "Dracula was right you know, there is something about you. Make no mistake, when the others see it too, they will not hesitate to make you the new King."

Xavier stared at him, lost for words, but before Nathanial could exit the room, he found them: "Why is a new King necessary? Is Dracula not acting up to standards?"

"Oh, he is," Nathanial said. "He has his reasons, Xavier. This is something not even I can begin to understand, to just up and give his post to someone else. It is not that he is bored, nor is it that he is not acting up to standards, but this is happening because, believe it or not, he wished for it."

"Dracula wished for me to be King?"

"He wished for a *new* King."

"But why?"

The Vampire smiled. "Because he is Dracula."

"How can you—?"

"Because I have seen what Dracula does to those that do not agree with his word," Nathanial said. He could have been explaining the art of horseback riding.

Xavier narrowed his eyes. "What?"

His golden eyes flashed before he opened the door and swept out of the room without another word.

✳

It seemed he'd only just entered the dark room when the door swung open again and Nathanial appeared. "We are ready for you, Delacroix," he said, his golden eyes harder than before.

Xavier stood from the uncomfortable bed and grabbed the Ascalon, placing it around his waist, before striding through the door, grabbing his traveling cloak from atop the old bookshelf. Nathanial had turned to the large doorway on the other side of the hallway, a lot of noise issuing from within.

Xavier glanced toward the red-haired Vampire, but Nathanial paid him no mind. He moved toward the large doorway, and Xavier, gripping the handle of the Ascalon, followed suit.

Once he was over the threshold, all boiling dread and rising fear diffused into the thick air. Many voices converged, creating the oddest barrage of noise Xavier had ever heard: the many, many, Creatures placed about the extremely large room were chatting loudly amongst themselves. The seats rose all around the room, almost reaching the handsome ceiling, and it was here Xavier wondered how the bald, fat heads of the Goblins and Gnomes did not grace the top.

It seemed some sort of magic held up the cascading rows of benches, for there was a space in between one bench from the next. Below the Goblins and Gnomes—who, graciously, were not wearing their dirty, stained pointed hats, out of respect, perhaps—sat the many short, fat, Orcs, who held their strong small fists against their small, bare, dark-green thighs. Their beady eyes scanned the room maliciously. It seemed they wished they did not have to be there with other Creatures, but as far as Xavier was concerned, the Orcs were just as excited as the other Creatures—in their very own special way.

His gaze traveled to the bench below the Orcs, where the Fae sat, their gentle features quite a contrast from the Orcs above. They whispered to each other, no doubt knowing what the outcome of the meeting would be.

Enchanters sat beneath the Fae, and his eyes lingered there most of all: He had never seen so many in one place. They wore long gowns made of unidentifiable fabric, a mixture of men and woman, their eyes all a misty black, much different from the color that existed within the Enchanters' eyes back at the bar. They were not speaking to each other as the other Creatures were; they were all very stoic and stone-faced, perhaps rather uncomfortable at the fact that Vampires sat several benches below. Below them were the Satyrs, their black eyes searching the large room with ill-held impatience. Some even turned to their horned brothers and talked in loud, screeching wails, their black tongues long, rolling out of their mouths.

Below the Satyrs was what seemed to be a completely empty bench, until Xavier caught the gold glint of a Fairy, then the blue light of the Pixie beside it. As his eyes grew accustomed to the size of the Creatures, he noticed the whole row seemed to dance in an odd barrage of gold and blue light, annoying the Satyrs above. The Vampires on the last bench, however, seemed undisturbed by the bright light of the Creatures above. Their stares were placed all about the room, and some even glanced anxiously toward the hovering podium in the middle of the room, centered right in between the curving rows of benches.

Another door on the other side of the vast room opened, and all of the Creatures fell into silence. Their unique eyes followed a line of Creatures that filed into the room, one after the other, Dracula in the lead.

Xavier watched the Great Vampire step up to the podium, and clasped the sides, his hands blending with the white marble on its sides.

When Dracula finally opened his mouth, many Vampires' eyes flashed in admiration.

"Welcome, Creatures of the Dark World, to the Council of Creatures. Indeed, I am not sure if we've ever had such a large gathering here before, but we are determined to go along, business as usual. Interruptions are not to be had." He spared a warning glance to the Vampires along the bench.

They turned their eyes away from his gaze and found the hands in their laps a much more interesting sight.

Dracula then scanned the room. "We are here, as all of you know, to discuss my choice for the next King of All Creatures. A title I have held—officially —for over one thousand years." With his words, excited chatter filled the room. The Satyr's black tongues were visible in their mouths and the screeching stood out from the others' deep speech.

Dracula raised a hand to regain control of the room, and when he'd had it, Xavier realized the other Creatures who had filed in behind Dracula still stood behind him. There was a thoughtful-looking Vampire, a short Gnome who Xavier guessed was Thrall, a tall dark-skinned man who wore the same robes the other Enchanters did, a short, hunching Goblin who stood only three feet in height next to the dark man, and a Centaur whose hair was black, eyes dark. They all kept their hands clasped in front of them, watching Dracula as he spoke.

"...and I am most honored to present, Xavier Delacroix."

A hush swept over the crowd, and they craned their necks to watch Xavier.

He shifted under the weight of their gazes, making it a point to watch only the Vampire before him. He walked to the center of the room, a hand tight around the Ascalon's handle. It seemed an eternity before he reached it, endless thoughts of Dracula's secrets, his lies, his rules, filling his mind as he neared, but when he reached him, he could only stare blankly while Dracula said:

"Xavier. You stand before the Council of Creatures, before me, before representatives of all the Creatures of the Dark World. We are here to witness...your initiation as King of All Creatures."

A loud bloom of applause erupted through the room and he fought to keep his eyes on Dracula only and said, "Do the other Members of the Council not have to agree to my initiation?"

The room grew silent with his words and Xavier felt everyone's eyes on the Vampire before him.

"They have already decided," Dracula responded coldly.

"But do we not need to witness their vote?" an old Enchanter said from her bench.

Dracula stared at her. "We can, but I see no point. We have all elaborated on this matter for far too long, I know what their answers are—"

"But we do not!" This time it was a Vampire who spoke up.

"Yes! Yes! Let us hear their answers for ourselves!" the other Creatures began to yell.

Dracula sighed. "Very well." He stepped down from the floating podium, turning to the line of Creatures behind him, a hand sweeping through the air, gesturing toward a Vampire near the start of the line.

She stepped forward, her red hair resting down her back, the black sleeveless dress quite revealing, and Xavier wondered if she were related to Nathanial, for even her golden eyes were the same. As her hands pressed against the marble of the stand, Xavier forgot about the red-haired Vampire that was Dracula's Advisor: "Speaking on behalf of the Vampire Wing, I, Friandria Vivery, place my vote for Xavier Delacroix to be King of All Creatures."

The crowd roared their approval, and she stepped down, Dracula lifting a hand to silence them before the Goblin stepped up to the podium. An Enchanter waved her hands, lifting him high enough to see over it. He eyed her with thankful, beady black eyes and addressed the crowd: "On behalf of the Goblins—" this met with a rowdy cheer from the top of the benches "—of Edinwire, I, Dunley Dirte, place my vote for Xavier Delacroix to be King of us all." Less enthusiastic applause met Dunley's statement.

The dark Enchanter took his place, and he addressed the crowd, his voice deep, his brown eyes piercing, "On behalf of the Enchanter's Guild, I, Peroneus Doe, place my vote for Xavier Delacroix to be the next King of All Creatures." The applause was more than polite this time around and fewer jeers could to be heard.

The Gnome stepped up and several Enchanters shifted in their seats: It seemed he was waiting for one of them to help him see over it. When it was clear no one would, he pointed to one of the Vampires with a stubby finger and commanded, "Assist me."

The Vampire he'd singled out did not look pleased, but his dark eyes shined, and the Gnome rose, hitting the ceiling. All eyes followed as he fell through the air, landing atop the podium with a painful crash. Cackles of laughter sounded throughout the room. The Vampire received appreciative pats on the back. As the Gnome rose to his feet, he looked quite prepared to scream any number of profanities the Vampire's way, but Dracula cleared his throat and the small Creature addressed the crowd instead.

"I, Thrall Quillington, on behalf of the Mountain Gnomes deep within the valleys of Dunderhurst—"

"Get on with it Thrall," an impatient Vampire snarled.

Thrall looked displeased, but cleared his throat, and said, "I place my vote for Xavier Delacroix to be King of All Creatures." He hopped down from the podium, casting a final, threatening glance to the Vampire who had "helped" him.

Lastly, the Centaur stepped forward, all eyes on him as he opened his mouth to speak—

A loud boom shook the ground and the air somewhere close to the castle, and Xavier moved a hand to the Ascalon. Sounds of panic and surprise left the Creatures on their benches. And before anyone could do anything at all, footsteps echoed down the hallway into the large hall.

Before long, three Vampires filled the doorway, looking both scared and exhausted. "They have...they have Wiffle Citador!" one of them gasped.

Dracula narrowed his eyes as he stepped forward. "Renor, what are you saying?"

"The figures in black. The figures in black! We were arriving here, Wiffle, Drivor, Axely, and I when we came upon them! Horrible Creatures!" Renor gasped, and fell to the floor, dead.

"Close the doors and windows, round up the Creatures who have their weapons and skills about them!" Dracula yelled, not sparing a glance to the corpse.

Everyone left their benches and scrambled to leave the large room despite Dracula's words. Xavier watched as they tried to squeeze through the wide doorway all at once, trampling the newcomers' bodies underfoot.

When he and Dracula were finally alone, he turned to him, but the Vampire was already saying, "You are to stay by my side," and there was a definitive way he said this that made Xavier's blood boil with apprehension.

*Eleanor is here,* he thought quickly, hand still clutched tightly to the sword, *and she was indeed killing all who stood in her way.*

Dracula moved, clutching the hilt of the sword at his waist, toward the limp bodies of Axely and Drivor that lay in the doorway. He pulled the doors closed.

"There has never been death at the Council before," Dracula whispered, "this shall stain these protected walls, surely."

Wanting to know what just he meant, Xavier watched the troubled Vampire eye the large windows surrounding them. He had just opened his mouth to say something when a figure appeared in one of arching windows, Dracula's brown eyes widening. "Michael?"

The figure named Michael—draped in a billowing dark cloak—hovered in the window, his grin increasing with his stare.

With a deep sigh Xavier realized they were trapped in the large room, their only exits blocked off, for he was sure there were many more Creatures outside the doors: He could hear the sound of raucous battle issuing throughout the long hallway.

"Michael," Dracula repeated, this time surer in his conviction. He left the tiled floor and flew toward the window as a blast blew him back, the glass flying around the room, carrying Dracula with it. Xavier was at his side in the next moment, a bracing hand tapping the Vampire's cheek, for his eyes were closed. "Are you all right?" he asked the Great Vampire hurriedly.

The Creature in the window called to others out of view, snow flying into the large room: "They're in here! Trapped themselves in like the fools they are—"

Dracula left the floor and was in the air again, although he did nothing more than hover, staring at the Creature in the window, and Xavier saw a tense hand move to the sword at his waist.

The Creature entered the room with Dracula's bravado, a smug grin across his boyish face. "Well, if it isn't my old mentor, my old King. I see that you have not learned to trust the powers you were given."

Dracula snarled, anger filling his brown eyes. "What are you talking about?"

"You know bloody well what I'm talking about! Eleanor has told us, has shown us what we have been missing from our lives. Something you have never done for us. You, who have lied to us for all these years."

"I have not lied to you!" And with that, a massive burst of air from the hovering Vampire sent him barreling backwards against the ground. When Xavier dropped his arm from his eyes, Dracula's gaze was red, his white hair billowing up from his back, spreading around him in his anger.

*What is going on?* Xavier thought, never knowing the Vampire to show this much anger, this much power....

"Then what were they, Dracula, if not lies?" Michael growled, his grin disappearing.

"I was protecting you, saving you from becoming what you are now!"

"A likely story!" Michael screamed, his own handsome features distorting with anger. "Eleanor has given us new life. She protects us by making us what we are! And you, you have done nothing but guard your book, that damned sword, not giving us what we needed. Not giving us what we need to live."

Dracula seemed shocked by these words: his eyes were wide and his mouth opened, as though he could not find the words to respond. And he was no sooner recovering when another figure entered through the window, hovering just beside his companion. "Michael," he said, "where is Eleanor?"

"Is she not on her way?" Michael asked, tearing his gaze from Dracula's.

He shook his head. "The Vampires are holding her back, surprisingly enough," he said.

"Interesting," Michael said, but his voice did not seem interested at all. "Call for Aciel. He will be pleased to know I have found them."

"As you please," the man said before disappearing.

Dracula's hand clenched the hilt of his sword, and it seemed Michael took notice of this: his eyes caught the red gem centered in the guard and they narrowed in disbelief. "You've killed someone, haven't you?"

"I fail to see how that is any of your business, Michael. You will tell me why you are here—with Eleanor Black of all Creatures!"

"And why should I?" Michael screamed. "You killing another Creature is very much my business—all of our business—it only proves what Eleanor Black has been trying to tell the whole Dark World: you are twisted – corrupt in your ways!"

Dracula snarled and shot toward Michael. The Elite Creature had only a moment's notice to dart out of the way before Dracula appeared where he last stood, eyes wide with his rage.

"Is it I who is twisted?" he roared, and Xavier could not help but notice the weird gleam in his eyes—he stared at Michael with a delirious air. "You know nothing! Nothing of what I have done!"

"I know you have killed! She told us! She told us what happens when that gem changes color!" the Creature retorted, looking quite apprehensive.

Xavier watched as Dracula's hand tightened around the handle of the sword. "You know nothing! Whatever Eleanor told you—"

"Is truth!"

A burst of cold air filled the room and Dracula was zooming toward the Elite Creature, sword held out in front of him, prepared to strike—

Michael waved a brazen hand and plume of black smoke left his fingers, forming a wall in front of him, and when Dracula's sword reached it, a spark of blue light appeared and Dracula was blown back against the cold air. Xavier moved to catch him, but he never did fall.

Dracula caught his balance in midair looking prepared to strike once more, but decided against it: his red eyes darkened, and the sword lowered in his hand. There was a tangible moment of silence as Dracula and Michael stared at one another through the black smoke wall, then Dracula let out a long sigh, as though the weight of the centuries was falling down around him.

"You will not understand this, Michael," he said, breathlessly. "Even if I do explain everything I have done for this World, you will not understand. She has reached you first."

Michael waved another hand and the wall disappeared, and he

stared upon Dracula as though expecting him to attack again. "Make me understand it, Dracula," he said, as though scared he'd never hear the words from the old Vampire's lips.

The sword was raised in the Great Vampire's hand and his eyes lingered on the red gem, how it seemed to shine with a strange light from within...but then Xavier could see the red eyes reflected within it and he turned his attention to Dracula, himself.

The Vampire was weathered, and tired, so much so that Xavier was surprised he'd never allowed himself to see it before. Something weighed him down, and it did not take Xavier long to guess that it was the secrets now threatened to be revealed by this Elite Creature. Would Dracula finally disclose all he'd kept hidden?

"I have killed," Dracula said at last, the sword not lowering. "My last kill with this sword being my Goldchair, Armand Dragon—"

"What?" Xavier said. "You killed Armand?"

Dracula was before him in the next second, sword still in hand, his back to the Elite Creature in the air, a look of terrified realization in his red eyes. "There was a reason, Xavier—"

"Of course there was a reason!" Michael interjected. "You simply wished to keep him from your secrets, didn't you? Couldn't stand for him to know the truth, could you?"

At this, Dracula let out a loud snarl and whirled, the sword swinging wildly in his grip: Xavier moved to avoid getting sliced. "As I remember it, you lived through my word, you were suckling at the teat that is my power, you were in reverence to my every move, my every action—"

"I was deceived!" Michael said shrewdly before the Vampire could finish. "After discovering what you truly hold, I can only say that your words, your actions, are nothing but stains of blood on the floor of deception!"

"Ha!" Dracula was moving toward him now, the sword trembling in his grip. "You speak as if you have lived through it all! You know nothing – nothing of what I must do—have done for this World!"

"And so you say! But we know all you do is trick and coerce—" Michael's gaze found Xavier at last, and a look of realization crept over his face. "Your new pet, I presume? This must be the Delacroix Eleanor won't shut up about. What is he to you, Dracula? Yet another pawn in this game you play with our lives?"

And instead of retaliating, Dracula turned to watch Xavier, his red eyes filled with what looked to be a terrible sadness, yet Xavier did not understand it. He'd never known the Vampire to show anything but perfect coldness.

"Xavier," Dracula whispered, "surely you understand: you are a necessary tool. To have you as the new King would assure that my secrets—our secrets—remain safe within our bond, the veil of blood. You must understand why I have done what I have – why I have kept you safe, free from harm for all these years—"

"And he plans to leave you as soon as you were crowned. Not in the know of the Great Artifacts left over by the Ancients to flourish in our newly-created World," Michael finished.

Xavier stared, unsure of what was happening, or what he should be feeling, and even as he stared at the Great Vampire, he could not find it in himself to believe what Dracula had just whispered.

*Necessary tool...*

"You think me nothing but a tool?" he asked. "Something to be cast aside while you kill Vampires who find out about your secrets? Everything they said, everything they told me, was it all true?"

Dracula swept toward him. "You do not understand...I needed you, and I still do. You can be King. Do not let this deter you from our years of friendship. I have watched over you like a father—" And with the whisper of this last word, Xavier's hand squeezed the handle of the Ascalon tight.

*How dare he? How dare he use that word knowing what it held for me?*

Pulling the Ascalon from its sheath, he stared at the exasperated Vampire before him, not sure if he should move to strike him. The shadow of doubt that had been marring his trust and faith in the Great Vampire thickened as he stared at Dracula, unable to believe what was happening. What did it all really mean?

Several figures flew into the open window, creating a large wind that blew the hair and cloaks of all the Creatures within the room, and Xavier tensed. They landed in unison just in front of Michael. He stared at them, Dracula turning to eye the newcomers as well, his own sword rising in his hand.

One Creature stepped forward, despite Dracula's tension, toward Xavier, and with a slender hand, removed the hood from atop her head.

Xavier almost lost his grip on his sword.

"My love," she crooned.

"Eleanor," he breathed, taking a step from her. The feeling of dread was not to be found, but instead a serene feeling of incomprehensible power left her being.

"You have come to a decision?" she asked.

It was as if Dracula was not even there.

Xavier held the sword awkwardly, not knowing what to do with it in his hand. If he said "No," she would most likely kill him before he could move, but if he said "Yes," then there was no need for the weapon... But Dracula, what he'd just said....

"I... Eleanor, I am not sure."

She did not seem upset, quite the contrary: she smiled. "I had hoped after seeing Dracula's display of treachery to you and other Vampires that you would embrace me with open arms."

He stared from Dracula to Michael and back. "That was staged?"

"Staged? Oh, heavens no. Michael was sent to look for you because I knew Dracula would keep you close. Dracula and Michael go way back, farther than anyone I know. They would speak, and as it has been shown, panic and fear," she looked at Dracula in disgust, "ultimately ends in the abandonment of original plans, the chaotic reevaluation of events, the speaking of secret plans...it would all come into fruition. And it has."

He marveled at her words. The truth they held could not be denied.

Dracula then let out a sound, something of a whimper, and Eleanor snarled. "There is no need for you anymore," she whispered, snapping her fingers.

Michael began to transform.

It was the oddest thing Xavier had ever witnessed. All surrounding newcomers moved from him at once, and now clearly seen, Michael's long face stretched even longer outwards as the long snout formed. His black nose came into view next and the rows and rows of fangs protruded from his mouth, enlarging by the minute. His skin was ripped from his body and, as his cloak was shed, ruffles of brown, shaggy hair graced his body. His feet had grown out of the boots they once occupied, and now large paws took their place. He was tall, but hunched over, his black beady eyes glaring hungrily at Dracula.

And then he charged. In a blink, he moved from his position to Dracula's.

Dracula did not bother to move, or perhaps it was that he could not. But Eleanor's ever-changing eyes had changed to one color—a deep dark red—and Xavier assumed she was placing a spell on Dracula to keep him from moving.

Xavier hesitated. Could he really allow Dracula to pay for what he had done to him? To the Vampires? To Victor?

"Eleanor wait." And Eleanor's gaze broke from Dracula's, the Lycan's large head turning to face him.

"What is it, Xavier?" Eleanor said, flustered by his words, her brow furrowed in concern.

313

"Must he die so cruelly?"

"Pity, Xavier? I never thought it of you." A few guffaws leaving the cloaked figures behind her.

She turned to them, silencing them with her eyes.

"Do I not deserve to know the secrets he has been hiding from me?" Xavier asked, stalling for time.

Eleanor whirled to face him, and she seemed to consider his words before saying, "That you do."

A cloaked figure with the others stirred and the raspy voice protruded from beneath the dark hood, "You will tell him when he is not yet one of us?"

"I will tell him now, yes. Think about it, Jasper, once he is one of us—" her eyes brightened with admiration at the thought "—would it not be best for him to already have an understanding of the life he shall lead with me?"

The one Eleanor called Jasper fell silent, her words seemingly satisfying enough.

"You are not a normal Vampire, my love," Eleanor said to Xavier, "your blood runs thick with the pureness of the Ancient Ones."

Dracula spoke at last, his eyes fierce with anger: "Don't—!"

"You would rather tell him the story yourself?" she asked him.

Dracula appeared flustered. "I would rather," he gritted through clenched teeth, "tell him when he is ready."

"I am afraid you shall not be alive to do so," Eleanor said. "You will die in this very room today; your reign of secrets shall cease."

"My reign of protection and comfort, you mean," he corrected her. "It is you, Eleanor, who has been terrorizing my Creatures! It is you who have killed my Creatures!"

"Silence!" Eleanor yelled. "You know not of what it is you speak! I have killed no Creature of yours! These Creatures—" she raised arms to signal the outside of the castle walls where the battle was continuing "—are slaves. Slaves to their minds – slaves because of you! Their power, although great, is not as excellent as it should be. I have taken what you have hidden from them and used it! Is it my fault that they cannot handle the presence of my men? No! It is yours, Dracula."

The door flew open, and Nathanial, Peroneous, and Friandria stood there, their clothes bloodstained, their breaths short and quick. Nathanial, eyeing Eleanor and the Lycan that towered over Dracula hungrily, gasped. Friandria glowered at Eleanor, and Peroneous kept his gaze on Xavier.

Eleanor, Xavier, and Dracula watched the newcomers with puzzled eyes and no one dared speak.

It wasn't until Eleanor let out a small chuckle did anyone finally breathe. "Lovely. We've more guests. Come, let them in, they need to hear this as well."

# Chapter Twenty
# THE SWORDS OF
# TREMOR THE GREAT

Peroneous moved into the room first, slowly following behind was Friandria, Nathanial bringing up the rear. Eleanor swept a hand and the door closed with a slam behind them, causing Friandria to jump, and Nathanial to scowl.

Ignoring him, she turned her attention back to Xavier. "Where was I?" she asked him, as if expecting him to answer. But her dark eyes flashed with remembrance and she continued on as if three Dark Creatures hadn't entered the large hall with them at all: "The Ancients...a remarkable breed of Creature.... Some say they were the first humans, others sure that they created the humans. Only two of us in this room know differently."

Dracula shifted his footing and grasped the hilt of his sword, while Michael—still in Lycan form—growled.

Eleanor ignored them, determined not to let her words be dimmed. "They were always in existence, living out their lives with the trees and grass, adoring the Earth and giving her what she needed so they could take what *they* needed from her with no discord. But, as it happened, another Creature felt the need to create a different breed...I imagine he felt that life was far too boring with only his lot and the Ancients to accompany him. So he created the humans as we know them today. Of course, such a new race was, at first glance, deemed a threat by Tremor—the Ancient Elder—and he forbid any of his kind to speak with, let alone mate, with the humans.

"But of course," she sighed, casting a knowing look to Dracula, "one of them did. Drifted off into the towns and as it happened, met a man. She fell in love with him. They had a child...the result of which is standing before us now."

Everyone's eyes danced to Dracula whose face could not be seen. His head was down, his hair hiding it like a curtain, his free hand balled into a tight fist.

Eleanor continued: "Tremor, naturally, learned of his daughter's treachery, and confronted her about the child. He cared not for the human man, but only for what the consequences of her actions were. He wished to know what the child resembled. Was it more human?

"His daughter cried and, flustered, answered her father: 'He was a monster,' she'd said. 'Not of their flesh, not of their livelihood, and certainly,' she'd said, 'not of their blood.'

"He'd asked her what she meant and she said, 'He has fangs that are sharp, like the tools the humans used for their day-to-day duties. He has taken to their blood.'

"She'd caught him feeding on a boy after his lessons one afternoon when she went to get him. She pulled him off the boy, but it was far too late, the boy was very dead, but very delicious, I'm sure." She paused with a smile.

"She didn't know what to do with her son—who more resembled a...monster, for he'd killed his father, the human that gave him life, and it seemed Dracula had gone, leapt out of the window, unable to face what he'd done. Soon after, she'd killed herself, mad she was with the knowledge that her son was murdering others—draining them of their blood."

No one said a word. It seemed no one could.

Eleanor went on, far from being finished, "Hearing of this, Tremor had a sword created. A blade that could end the lives of such horrid creations. He'd also wanted his revenge on Dracula for what happened to his daughter. He'd searched for Dracula throughout the land, determined not to rest until he found him, before Dracula could create any more of these Creatures. But Dracula had indeed created more Vampires, as they were later known. I have heard that the Vampire and Tremor finally clashed and battled. The result was what you see before you now: Dracula alive, the sword of Tremor at his waist."

Friandria clasped a hand over her mouth, Peroneous stared unbelieving at Dracula and the sword, and Nathanial stared at Eleanor. Dracula did not move.

"Tremor was not killed," she continued, "as surprising as that may seem to you all. He survived, just barely. He'd retreated back to his palace and told the others of what took place. They all were outraged and set out to destroy this Vampire that had the sword of Tremor now in his possession. One woman stayed behind. She had taken to a human man, and although she never married, she was pregnant with his child.

"My mother gave birth to me in Tremor's palace, without his knowing. She feared I would turn out like the then-infamous Dracula, but I did not. My...urges were suppressed for far longer than Dracula's. It is something, to this day, we do not know the reasons for...

"At the same time, others were branching out and marrying humans, making children with them and moving away from Tremor's failing protection and dwindling power. When the others never returned from their hunt for Dracula, Tremor had aged with the grief and guilt: Countless numbers of his men had died at the hands of the great Dracula, and he would soon rise to power. However, Tremor was wrong about one of these things. Many of his men did not die at Dracula's hands. They all gave up the search. Tired of searching for the Vampire, and they did not care for any sword.

"But it was then that *another* Creature emerged from the womb of a human woman who married a descendant of the Ancient Ones. Lore was born, not as we all know him today, but as a sweet boy who did not seem any different from any other normal human child. And at what we call a Lycan's Age, he began to change. He had short bursts of anger, and as he grew, so did this anger, and soon, Lore was an oversized dog, terrorizing towns and cities.

"Tremor, hearing of this, overcome with guilt as he was, made one last order to his most faithful servant who stood by him after all the years of abandonment. He was ordered to create a sword, capable of destroying these new beasts should they grow in number."

Many eyes then fell to the sword against Xavier's waist, and he immediately removed his hand from the hilt, revolted by it.

"Yes, Xavier," Eleanor said. "The Ascalon was created as Tremor's last great plan to destroy the Lycans—a plan, we now know, that was thwarted by a Vampire who heard of the sword and wanted it for himself. Dracula fought off Tremor's servant and took the sword, keeping it safe under his watch while Lore rampaged throughout towns and cities, creating more of his own kind…. He eventually had a son…a man I believe you have met, Xavier."

At this, he looked up at her, eyes dark with his realization.

"Thomas Montague."

"Precisely," she said. "A rather determined young man, driven by the scent of your blood…. It is an odd thing our blood does to the Lycans, have you ever wondered why this is so?"

His eyes widened, the thought that there was any more of a reason for the Lycans' hatred of Vampires than it simply *being*, reaching him in bemusement.

"Tremor had good reason to fear what would happen to the

offspring if his kind were to mate with humans," Eleanor continued. "Vampires, born from the mothers who were descendants of the Ancient Ones, were tainted with the blood that should have never been mixed. It left the Vampires a starved breed, hungering for the blood of humans…the blood they will never be able to have freely in their veins. Lycans, born from the fathers, descendants of the Ancients, were also tainted with their blood. Their anger fueling their transformations. It is only one who has been bitten by a Lycan that will turn underneath the full moon's glow. The immortality comes from an Enchanter—" at this, everyone's eyes found Peroneous, "—yes, Dracula sought you out, didn't he Peroneous Doe? As disgruntled as he was, he forced you to make him immortal, didn't he? If you did not oblige, I imagine he threatened to kill you."

Peroneous's piercing eyes cast down from everyone's gaze.

Eleanor continued on, smiling. "With this spell placed upon him, Dracula could never be killed. And every Vampire that he bit from then on was given the same spell, transported through blood. And we all know the first victim after Dracula left Peroneous…."

"Victor," Xavier whispered, shock coursing through him.

"Yes, the great Victor Vonderheide was the first Vampire to have a taste of immortality," Eleanor said. "The ones before him were not able to share such a…lucky fate."

Everyone was terribly silent.

Xavier waited for her to continue with her story, and it was only when the howling wind outside and the distance sounds of battle clamored through the room that anyone said anything at all:

"Now that you know, Xavier, will you join me?"

Friandria took a small step forward, as did Nathanial, but Peroneous seemed determined to blend in with the background.

"Join her?! You will join her, Xavier?" Nathanial asked.

"He has not yet decided," Eleanor said, "although I have given him such a long time to come to a decision—"

"But you cannot," Friandria whispered. "You are our new King."

He growled in frustration before he could stop it: Dracula was not saying a word, not defending himself at all, an Elite Creature in Lycan form waiting to rip him apart, Eleanor staring upon he, Xavier, expectantly, her men close behind, and he held the sword of the Ancient Elder, Tremor, at his waist, Dracula with the first one created.

It seemed impossible that this was a dream. But how lovely that would be. To wake up and realize he was merely suffering through some horrid nightmare.

"Xavier," the voice of Eleanor Black drifted to his ears then, destroying his wishful thoughts.

Dracula said, to the surprise of everyone in the room, "How did you come upon all of this knowledge, Eleanor?"

She turned to him, her small smile fading. "After I...read the contents of the book, I paid a visit to dear Tremor. It was rather hard, searching for a Creature that did not wish to be found, but I had many resources...and once I'd found him, it was not a challenge to get from him what I wanted."

Dracula snarled, his eyes a murky black. "You sought him out?"

"Yes. That I did."

"What more did he say?"

Eleanor looked him up and down, as if to see whether or not he could handle the information. Xavier agreed with her action; Dracula seemed quite ready to crumple with the years of lies he'd piled atop his shoulders.

"He seemed content that I could not keep the book in my possession," Eleanor said.

"And why is that, Eleanor?" Dracula asked.

She glared at him. "He would not tell me...after I'd come all that way to know more. Why indeed! What is it about that book?"

"You felt it then? The rushing power from its pages? The truth spoken in a hail of red light? The book sucked you in, and you had to fight your way out, didn't you, Eleanor?"

Her lips clenched together, forming a thin line, and her eyes sparked with indignation. "You made a deal with him?"

Dracula smiled at her. "It was no more a deal then it was a cry for help. When I returned to him, out of spite, curiosity consumed me. I had to see the Creature I had once tried to kill, if only to destroy him. But it did not end that way. He was brittle, as you have said… when I saw him, he'd only just entered his stage of guilt and turmoil. I saw the desperation in his eyes and my pity for the man—my grandfather—grew within me. I had no choice but to help him, for I am forever bound to the one whose blood allows me to stand here as I am.

"With the last of his Ancient, even godly, power, he created a book. But it was a book upon which one could learn the infinite knowledge that surrounds us. A book that was written with the blood that courses through me. My blood helped create *The Immortal's Guide*. And any Creature who would dare read it and walk away alive would ultimately suffer the curse of my blood. You, dear Eleanor, and your men, the Vampires and Lycans who have battled for ages, you have taken what he has shown you and you have used it in the absolutely worst way. It is a book of knowledge for *me*. No other was meant to read it. No other was meant to know it existed.

"I was the one, blessed by Tremor, to carry out his last request. To ensure that nothing like my birth ever happened to another Creature again. No one should have to withstand the years of adolescence I did. No one."

Eleanor's eyes were wide.

Not a soul dared breathe.

"What you have done, Eleanor Black, is destroy the thread that rests between Vampires and Lycans," Dracula said after a time. "Giving Creatures such power…it was never Tremor's intention. We were never supposed to be, but through the Goblet of Existence, we can continue our lives and we can exist, side by side, as Tremor now feels we were meant to. He holds no ill will towards me, and I'm sure for Lore it is the same, but you must realize, Eleanor, what you have done. You have placed, Xavier in a terrible predicament. I made him King because I could then search for the Goblet without the eyes of all Creatures wondering where I had been."

"But you killed Armand Dragon," Xavier said.

Dracula turned to him. "I did not kill him, not through way of my blade. *The Immortal's Guide*, when opened, can be a paradise or a whirlwind of terror and confusion depending on how strong the mind is, how prepared one's soul is to tame the power within.

"With this Goblet, it is Tremor's wish that I end the discord and suffering that has plagued our World since my birth. The Ancients are no more, as far as we are concerned, and being his only living relative, Tremor placed his trust in me, that I would see to it his ultimate wish is fulfilled.

"But," he eyed Eleanor, "through your foolishness and greed you have created this," he pointed a cold finger to Michael, who still stood before him in Lycan form, "something that was never supposed to be.

"Have you ever wondered why Vampires and Lycans of old cannot stand the very presence of you and your Creatures? It is not because you are powerful, it is because you are a curse. A walking curse that plagues whatever you touch. And I will not allow Xavier to become a part of this. I need him. I will find the Goblet of Existence and end your lives before you can destroy any more Creatures."

Eleanor and Dracula stared at each other coldly.

And then Eleanor stepped away, as if scared of his next move, whether it was a slap or a mere snarl of the fangs.

Dracula removed his sword from its sheath and everyone's eye caught the red gem in the middle of the guard. He let the point of the blade touch the floor, running a finger along the edge of it, his blood spilling down the groove in the metal. Nathanial and Friandria turned away from the smell of his blood, but Xavier found it familiar, though he did not remember ever smelling it before—

Michael, in his Lycan form, took several steps away, snarling: he sank to all fours at the sight and smell of it.

Dracula smiled at the Creatures' reactions to his blood, and as soon as it reached the tip of the sword, forming a small puddle against the floor, he lifted it, and before anyone knew what happened, sliced through Michael, who fell in two, his body floating into ash.

His ash mixed with the falling snow, and everyone watched as the wind whirled through the room, carrying the Lycan's ash through the open window.

Many of Eleanor's men stepped away, and Eleanor, not at all pleased, remained where she stood, although her gaze was held on the sword.

"You will know the name of this sword before it slices through you, Eleanor Black," Dracula said.

Eleanor remained quite still, and Xavier was reminded of the time she looked this way before, just before she had burst into a beast.

Dracula ran his finger along the blade once more, and he lifted it, pointing it at Eleanor's face. "Meet your maker, Eleanor Black. The brother of the blade made to destroy Lycans: *Ares*."

# Chapter Twenty-One

# DEATH

She stared at the tip of the sword, Dracula's blood dripping in large drops onto the floor before her feet. The smell of his blood did not seem to reach her nose: She stared past the sword, glaring at him, her eyes foggy with what Xavier thought were oncoming tears.

She never did cry: Her hand flew up instead and she snapped her fingers. One of the cloaked figures standing near the window gave an involuntary jerk, his eyes flashing a clear white. And when Eleanor's eyes changed a dark color, he flew toward Dracula and the outstretched sword.

The man struck the tip of the blade Dracula held outstretched and he did nothing to fight the spell he was under, even as his blood spilled from him, turning a dark shade of red. He then stiffened and relaxed, his head hanging forward over his chest, his body limp, only held up by the Ares's steel.

Dracula stared at the Creature upon his sword. He turned his gaze to Eleanor and brought the blade down, the man's limp body flying across the floor. It came to a stop at Peroneous's feet, and he

325

gave a look of horror, moving away from it quickly. Dracula snarled at Eleanor. "You would harm your own kind for the sake of your life?"

"Is it not the same thing that you do for your Vampires?"

"No!" And he ran another finger across the blade, the blood filling the groove once again. "The Vampires that died on my watch could not be saved, Eleanor. I would never put them in harm's way!"

"You mask your lies with your actions! You kill just as I! We are no different! We are both searching for the things that shall complete us, that is why you continue to live! To find the Artifacts told to you by Tremor. If he did not speak to you, would you still be here?"

"Most likely not," he said, although his eyes were lined with anger. "But I don't care what happens to me, as long as my Vampires continue their existence in peace with the other Creatures, my death can greet me at any time. But before I go, I shall find the Goblet and drink from it. And my blood...the blood that travels through all of my Vampires, shall cease to reject the scent of a Lycan's blood. There will be peace in the Dark World, Eleanor. And if my death brings about this peace, so be it. I will have lived for a great purpose."

"You will have died in vain!" she screamed, an arm lifting into the air. She spread out her hand, the palm facing the Great Vampire. "Let us remember what has happened here, all of you, in this room, remember this day. The day your beloved *liar*, Dracula, died at the hands of Eleanor Black."

Xavier took a step forward, but she turned to him, spreading another palm. "Do not interfere," she barked.

Xavier stared at her fiercely, mind reeling with what she just said: Was she really going to kill Dracula? A hand moved to the handle of the Ascalon as the thought grew: he couldn't let it happen. But he was no closer to releasing the sword from his side when one of the hooded figures appeared before him, placing a strong hand upon his arm, keeping him from pulling the Ascalon out. And before he could utter a word, there was a large explosion behind the Creature's back, and Xavier could not see what had transpired until—

"*Dracula!*"

And with the voices of Nathanial and Friandria ringing out across the hall, Xavier pushed his way past the Creature, his blood freezing.

The podium remained on the floor, broken in two, the top half crumpled beneath the body below several destroyed benches.

*What?* he thought, not understanding it in the least. It was just moments ago that Dracula stood, so sure, so powerful against Eleanor and now, now he was... No. No, he couldn't be…it was impossible—

A shrill laugh filled the cold air as he stared at the Great Vampire's unmoving body, and then:

"You have no choice, now! Dracula is dead and you *will* join me! You will be my King and together we can rule all of the Dark World!"

He barely heard Friandria step forward, barely heard her say the words, "Y-you…how dare you. He did nothing...he *did nothing*!"

He only tore his gaze from the Vampire's body when he heard another hit the floor. Looking around, he saw the limp body of Friandria Vivery, eyes closed, red hair spilled out around her....

Nathanial ran to her and crashed on his knees at her side. "No," he whispered, touching her face as though she would break if he pressed too hard.

Xavier's eyes fogged over. *How was it possible? How was it possible that she had killed another Vampire, so easily, so quickly, just as she had killed Dra—?*

She moved toward Xavier, and without a thought, he stepped from her, rage filling his mind, for what she'd done was finally reaching his senses at last.

Eleanor stopped moving, as if smacking into a brick wall. Her eyes glanced at his hand upon the Ascalon, and she sneered. "So you would kill me rather than touch me?"

"I will never touch you again," Xavier growled.

Her eyes danced with shock and then regained their steel touch. "Such words. Are you moved by your King's death? Are you so enraged by his absence from your life that you would think to kill me, Xavier?"

"I know of your affinity for curses and enchantments," he said, remembering how lost in his own mind he was when he tried to recall what happened the night she'd kissed him...cursed him.

"So he's told you, has he?" Eleanor said, cheerful, as if she could not wait to explain why she did what she did. "I needed you to be silent, Xavier. I could not trust your word alone. Measures had to be taken."

"So you would have had me lose my mind?"

"No, of course not. I knew Dracula would catch on to what I did to you. I knew he would remove it." She appeared thoughtful then. "I wonder what he managed to extract from you."

Xavier kept silent, not daring to give her the satisfaction she sought.

"Very well," and she lifted an elegant pale hand, the fingers stretching toward him, "I shall get what I want from you yet."

Then he felt it: the blinding pain that rested over his muscles, pulling them from the bone.

The sound of a sword sliding against the floor reached his ears, and for the second it took one of her men to fall to the floor, a spurt of blood issuing from where an invisible blade struck, she dropped her hand.

"What—?" she whispered as each of the cloaked men fell, their blood spraying around them before the rest of their bodies turned to ash.

A blur of blue and white zipped through the room, and it came to a stop on top of the broken podium.

Nathanial released Friandria's corpse and whispered, "Dracula?"

Xavier gazed at the white hair that flew before the Great Vampire's face in the harsh wind and snow. It was not until Eleanor spoke that he realized what he was seeing.

"How are you——?"

"You are terribly mistaken to think that such a curse, as deadly as it is, would do away with me. When will you learn that you can never win this hopeless battle as long as I or Xavier exist?" Dracula said.

"But how did you survive? You should be nothing! Smoke!"

Dracula laughed, and Xavier smiled—it was a laugh one could not help but catch. The Great Vampire said, "I am the first Vampire, do you not think through my years of surviving this Dark World that I did not learn the ways to combat any spell that is sent my way? Peroneous tried several on me before I finally got to him, it just so happened that my body grew immune to magic."

Eleanor looked defeated, her mouth closing and opening as though the words to retaliate escaped her, and Xavier thought he knew why. After all, her men were dead, and the others were still fighting outside, but she wouldn't be able to call for them, not with Dracula's speed and power: He would send the blade through her before she knew what happened.

Dracula left the podium, his sword held out in front of him, covered with his blood. He flew straight for Eleanor, who stood quite still, her eyes blurring over as if losing connection to the present.

And then the sword sliced through her body, an instant smile gracing Dracula's face.

"No!" the yell came from the open window where Thomas Montague floated, his skin pale, eyes red with horror—

Dracula blinked and looked at the woman he'd struck now, and Xavier didn't know how he didn't see it before: Her long black hair flew over her beautiful face, but it was not Eleanor's. Her mouth lay open in a wide circle, her eyes emotionless, and when Dracula pulled the sword out of her midsection and watched her blood run a solid red, Xavier let out a small gasp.

Eleanor had tricked him, had tricked them all, for it had seemed as though he had struck Eleanor, but it was only Mara Montague. They all watched her body slump to the floor with a sickening thud and before anything else could be done to stop it, she turned to ash.

Thomas was upon Dracula before he could take his next breath. He flew to him, his hood off his head, revealing even longer, brown hair. Thomas had mastered the art of transformation into a Vampire, it seemed, and he was broken, destroyed in a way Xavier knew well.

There was a hint of sadness in the Creature's darkened hazel eyes as he connected with Dracula, grabbing his blue cloak with strong, pale hands. It seemed no effort was exuded on his part as he threw Dracula back against the floor where he slid until the broken podium stopped him.

"Why must you kill those who oppose you, Vampire?" Thomas screamed, his mouth curled into a perpetual snarl.

Dracula, dazed and slow, returned to his feet, but his hands were empty. The Ares remained upon the floor in front of him, covered in both Mara's blood and his own. He eyed Thomas wearily. "She was not my target."

"*Of course!*" Thomas screamed, eyes flashing with the rage, the grief, that consumed him. "You would lie even now!"

Xavier eyed Eleanor, who seemed content to fade into darkness. She was stepping backwards as though to meld with the plume of ash that remained of her men. He snarled at her cowardice and Thomas turned to him sharply. "You," he whispered, lost in his rage.

Thomas's eyes scanned the rest of the room. His eyes rested on Nathanial and the dead Vampire at his feet, the Enchanter that seemed resolved to blend into the door, and, at last, he turned to where Xavier stared. His eyes fell upon Eleanor and he looked at Dracula, down at the remaining ash at his feet, and back to Eleanor.

"She risked her life to save yours," he paired it all together, staring at Eleanor with a mix of grief and wonder.

Eleanor said nothing, indeed, she seemed rather apprehensive.

It was as if Thomas would attack her for what happened to his wife.

But he did nothing. He turned back to Dracula, who had been inching his way toward the Ares upon the floor, and reached to grasp it before Dracula could, much to his dismay. Thomas's brown eyes stared at the blood on the Ares.

Xavier could not understand why the Vampire looked so defeated. The hopelessness on face only intensified with Thomas's words: "So this is it? You were to kill me with this?"

"Not...when it is in your hands," Dracula said, his gaze held on the sword.

"Oh?" Thomas breathed, stepping toward Dracula leisurely, twirling the handle of the sword in his fist. "Then you are in quite a situation aren't you, bloodsucker?"

The Great Vampire's hand rested upon the broken podium for support. He did not attempt to move as the Elite Creature strolled toward him.

"I would say I am."

Xavier stepped forward. He knew Eleanor did the same, although her face held the look of shock and disbelief.

No one said a word when Thomas ran the inside of his other hand across the edge of the blade, his blood lining the groove with ease.

"Is this how it's done?" he asked, staring at Dracula's pained expression. "I do wish to do it correctly. Killing you should be the greatest honor for any Elite Creature...one of pure descent."

They all watched, partly in horror, partly in amazement.

Thomas drove the sword through Dracula's abdomen. It was so fast Xavier was surprised it happened at all.

Dracula lurched forward, his shock masked only by his long white hair flying forward onto Thomas's shoulder.

Then Thomas seemed to glow. The red light that surrounded him and, indeed, filled him, traveled from Dracula's abdomen, through the blade of the sword, and flashed as it hit the crystal in the middle of the guard.

Thomas then let out a cry of pain, the red light surrounding him turning black, and he was blown away from the sword, hitting Eleanor, who landed with a heavy crash against the floor.

They scrambled to their feet just in time to see Dracula's body dissolve to ash, the Ares falling to the floor where he last stood.

Xavier's hearing was dismantled and it seemed his eyesight was at well. For how in all of the Dark World could such a thing have happened. How could it have been possible? He didn't hear the exuberant cries of Eleanor Black urging Thomas Montague to retrieve the sword. He did not hear, or see, Thomas fly to the sword and take it in his grasp, half-shrinking away from it, terrified of what it might do to him again. Nor did Xavier witness Eleanor's cloak lift into the air, whispering for Thomas to follow her, and quickly, the glint of the red crystal the only thing he was vaguely aware of last—

"Xavier? *Xavier Delacroix!*" Nathanial's panicked voice flooded his ears, and with a jolt, he realized he was lying down on the cold floor. He had fainted.

"Thank Tremor," Nathanial whispered.

Xavier pushed himself off the floor, only able to stare at Nathanial for several painfully terse minutes.

Desiring something to do other than stare at a flustered Vampire, he Xavier turned his gaze to the large pile of ash near the broken podium and felt his blood freeze. *Dracula was dead*. And even as he said it in his mind, it seemed as impossible as Eleanor flying away with Thomas at her heels, the sword in his hand—

"Xavier," Nathanial's voice sounded, turning his attention away from the ash near the podium, the only remains of the Great Vampire, and Xavier looked down to see that Nathanial was on one knee, his hands at his sides, turned into fists as they broke the floor around them. The Vampire's red hair shook, his gaze upon his boot, and with a faltering voice, he asked, "My King, Xavier Delacroix, what is your word?"

# Chapter Twenty-Two

# THE KING

Xavier stared at him for several minutes, not able to process what was happening. "Nathanial, please stand," he forced himself to say after a time.

Nathanial stood, but did not turn his gaze to Xavier's eyes as he had done before. And in the eerie silence that issued between them, the sound of battle could still be heard past the door and through the broken window where snow threatened to fill the room.

"What is your word, my King?" Nathanial asked.

"Nathanial—"

"Vivery, my King. Nathanial Vivery."

"...Nathanial...Vivery...why—?"

"Dracula's intentions were made clear today; you are meant to rule. You are...meant to recover the Goblet of Existence."

Xavier— still having a hard time taking in any of this— said, "I don't even know where the Goblet is. And Eleanor—"

"— is the biggest threat to the Dark World. It is your duty to make sure no more harm befalls the Creatures."

"But I—"

"Follow me," Nathanial said, keeping his head down. He swerved around Xavier and, stepping over his sister's body, reached the large door and turned the handle. It appeared Peroneous Doe had successfully disappeared during Eleanor's escape.

With the door opened, the once-muffled sounds of the battle ensuing beyond the palace walls could be heard. It appeared none of Eleanor's Elite Creatures realized that their Queen had left with Dracula's sword, it also appeared that no other Creatures were alive, save several Enchanters—who were casting the most dangerous of spells on the Elite—and Vampires, who were swiping at the Elite's Lycan and Vampire forms without hesitation. They filled part of the hallway, some of the Vampires grabbing the ancient swords and shields upon the walls while the Enchanters relied solely on their skills. Xavier saw several puffs of ash fall from the sky and turned his head quickly, not wanting to think whether it were Eleanor's men or his.

Nathanial had turned a sharp corner beyond which there was a staircase, hidden if one did not know where it was precisely. He was now climbing the steps with Xavier at his heels and Xavier noticed his black robes were smeared with blood—Goblin by the smell of it. And as his robe swayed, Xavier saw the gash in the back of his leg. "You were harmed," he observed aloud, although he noticed the Vampire did not limp as he stepped up with this still-bleeding limb.

"Nothing to worry about, your Majesty, an Enchanter missed. Simple mistake."

When they reached the top of the stairs, Xavier looked down the hallway that stretched to the left of them. No precious artifacts were to be found here, upon these walls, but there were a vast selection of doors that stretched all the way down the hall. Xavier wondered how this manor could have so many rooms placed together so tightly, but Nathanial stepped up to the one of the doors—a rounded wooden one with a snake as the knocker—and opened it, Xavier sure Carvaca had enchanted her home.

The room was large; it seemed fit for royalty. Xavier was sure this was the room Dracula frequented whenever he was here at the Council...when he was alive.

Nathanial stepped over the black tiles. He seemed guarded, turned to steel by the death of his sister, blocking out the death of the previous King, acting as a servant should underneath the gaze of his new ruler. He walked, with intention and grace, toward a man Xavier realized was in the room with them. He lay across the large bed, his pointed shoes still on, his long golden robes spilling out all around him, his pale face quite peaceful, and Xavier guessed this Creature was indeed the missing Evert that never showed up to the Council of Creatures.

Nathanial tapped the sleeping man rudely on the shoulder. "Wake up, Evert. You must see him— *Wake up!*"

At this last command, Evert opened his eyes: they were the color of the deepest ocean. He sat up, his eyes boring into Nathanial's golden ones. "What's happened?"

The man's long golden hair flew out behind his head and rested upon the mountain of pillows beneath him.

"It's happened. Dracula's gone," Nathanial said, his words quick, it was as though he hoped if he did not linger on them, the truth of it would not strike him so ruthlessly.

Evert's eyes were strong, full of a power Xavier was sure he'd never truly understand, and when they reached his face from across the large room, and something of a deep sigh left Evert's chest, Xavier was sure he was in the presence of a being most unlike any Creature he'd come across.

Evert removed himself from the bed, a large red gem swaying about his neck. He towered over them by several feet.

"Xavier Delacroix," Evert wheezed, his voice weighed down with sweeping indignation and impenetrable power. "You have witnessed the death of Dracula?"

Xavier froze, his mind blank. And then he remembered that he was spoken to. "I...have..." Not at all sure that what he'd seen was, indeed, the truth. *Dracula couldn't be dead.*

"And you are prepared to take on the task set forth for you? To recover the Goblet of Existence?"

"I...I don't—"

"He is ready," Nathanial's voice interjected rudely, Xavier only able to stare at him, bemused.

Evert seemed to not notice the Vampire's words, but remained staring at Xavier, blue eyes shining. "Then we can begin," he eyed Nathanial, "where is *The Immortal's Guide*?"

"Dracula had it in his possession last, Evert."

"Then it must be in his mansion," he wheezed knowingly. "Xavier, go to Dracula's mansion in the Vampire City and find *The Immortal's Guide*, once you've read it, return to me."

Xavier stared at him, not entirely comprehending. "...Who *are* you?"

Nathanial looked quite alarmed at Xavier's question, however, the corners Evert's mouth lifted into a rather mischievous smile. Xavier could not help but take a small step away. It was as though the Creature was to harm him suddenly, and he seemed quite capable of doing it.

"Evert. I am Tremor's last remaining servant. I am the one who has helped Dracula. I took the necessary measures to ensure the Vampire had all he needed to obtain the Goblet, but his death, as I knew it would, became a troublesome affair. That is why I had him choose another to take over...one that would rule in his place, take over the journey left for him by Tremor." He then lifted a very long, sweeping finger and pointed to Xavier. "And that is you, Vampire."

"...You knew he was to die? But was he not immortal?"

"He *is* immortal," Evert whispered darkly, as though Xavier had offended him in some ghastly way. "Dracula lives even now, but not in the flesh as you have known him to. He gave away his physical life when Tremor and he created the book…the blood he spilt to make that book was the blood that ensured his death. The knowledge Tremor passed to him was a part of the reason for his death: the knowledge in those pages…one cannot know it without facing their end…no amount of spells or enchantments can stop that, Xavier.

"And, I imagine, mad as he was with the knowledge that he would die, those that came upon the book frightened him. Those that managed to escape had to be killed before they suffered a most excruciating death at the hands of his blood…so, you understand why he killed the Vampires he did, why he banned the ones who happened upon *The Immortal's Guide*. It was to save them from dying, although it would be by his hand, either way.

"I foresaw his death many moons ago. It was inevitable. It remained unchanged as the years passed. That is when I told him. And that is when you were shown to him, and he took you under his wing: All of this was so the Dark World could be a place of peace and not of endless war."

Xavier felt his mind spin. "But why me?"

Nathanial stepped forward. "You saw what happened to Thomas Montague when he struck Dracula with the Ares. Dracula's remaining soul is in that light: The darkness of his blood. Thomas was never a Vampire, a descendant of the one who was born from the Ancients, yes, but never a Vampire. The light rejected him, and I imagine it will reject Eleanor Black as well, with how tainted her blood as become. But you, Xavier, your mother was an Ancient."

"She was?"

"Yes," Nathanial answered. "Why do you think Dracula singled you out of all his Vampires? He did not wish to tell you anything before you were ready. You hold the blood that can handle Dracula's light. And I believe you can survive *The Immortal's Guide*, it is only a matter of retrieving it now."

And it was here Xavier saw how different Nathanial seemed from the pleased, seemingly carefree Vampire in Cinderhall Manor that he was before. He was serious, his golden eyes deep and hardened with the importance of the task placed upon him. And Xavier realized that he was more than just the Adviser of Affairs, Nathanial was more than likely Dracula's Adviser of Affairs. He'd probably helped the Vampire on his quest for the Goblet of Existence.

Evert, taking advantage of the silence that passed between them, said, "Xavier. You must retrieve *The Immortal's Guide*. This is the duty left over to you from Dracula. Where he has failed, you can achieve success. I believe he was close to gathering the Goblet once."

"We've never come across it, I'm afraid," Nathanial said.

"I see," he whispered. "We must worry about the Goblet later. Xavier must gain the knowledge in order to fully understand what it is he must do. I am sure he does not."

Xavier, amazed that Evert was so miserably correct, said nothing.

"Then is that all?" Nathanial asked the tall, worldly man who towered over them both.

"Yes." Evert nodded. "I believe that is all. You must help him, Nathanial. You, who have searched for the Goblet before."

"Yes."

Evert sank onto the large bed beneath him and lay across it, his golden robes flying about him as if they were the sheets. And when his blue eyes closed and he resumed his slumber, Xavier could not help but feel it was as if he'd never opened his eyes, was never broken from his deep sleep to tell a Vampire what must be done—

"Let us leave," Nathanial whispered, strolling past him and to the door. As he pulled it open, Xavier regained his mind and moved to follow.

The door closed and he stepped through the doorway, the knocker letting out a faint hiss.

They did not speak as they stepped down the stairs, and it

appeared that Nathanial's gash had stopped bleeding, although Xavier was sure that it had not completely healed. When they'd reached the landing, Nathanial strolled straight past the door where Dracula had died, past the door were Xavier remained before he was called into the Council, and straight to where the heat of battle was taking place.

In the long hall, several Vampires had just successfully sliced through two large Lycans when Nathanial reached them, waving away the ash that had spread all around their heads.

Xavier remained near the stairs, and he could tell the Vampire whispered something important, but he could not be certain: The words would not reach him, regardless of how hard he tried to hear. The two Vampires stared at him after Nathanial had stopped speaking, and with a look of reverence and understanding, nodded.

He, not knowing what else to do, nodded back and the two Vampires flew through the long hallway towards the doors, slicing through any and all Elite Vampire or Lycan that remained in their way with ease.

They flew through the hall and killed the Elite Creatures, the other Vampires that were free of foes, joining them in the air. When they reached the large doors, Nathanial motioned to him with a hand. "Now."

And before Xavier could understand what was to be done, Nathanial removed his feet from the floor and flew straight toward the open doors where a few Goblins and Orcs were fighting off several Elite Vampires.

Xavier followed suit, picking up speed. He passed the Elite Vampires, who just killed a Goblin, his stubby body falling to the snow like a statue.

With his death, they caught sight of Xavier and ignoring the Orcs, took pursuit of him.

He gained even more speed, eager to evade the two Vampires who followed him, their eyes gleaming with deranged glory—

Nathanial appeared before them, and with a wave of a pale hand, sent flashes of blue light toward them, and they fell out of the sky.

Xavier watched their bodies, a brilliant clash of light forming in the air above the castle, begging his attention, and his eyes widened. Several Enchanters that had mastered the art of levitation were in a heated duel with an Elite Vampire: An Enchanter sent streaks of lightning from his fingertips to the Vampire, who shook violently and fell out of the sky.

Xavier turned away right before the Vampire burst into ash.

Nathanial flew past him toward a forest, the tops of the trees covered with white from the falling snow. "Hurry," Xavier managed to hear as Nathanial zoomed past.

He moved, the sounds of screams and excitement dying out the more he flew, and he pulled up alongside Nathanial as they passed over the snow covered treetops, thinking briefly on the strong-headed Centaur, Vimic, and whether he was told of the outcome of the meeting. Thinking how much everything had changed since those three hours before, he turned his attention to the red-haired Vampire at his side. The wind pressed against them the more they flew, and he decided to ask, "You can do magic?"

"We're heading back to London," Nathanial said, not bothering to eye him.

"You can do magic?"

Nathanial said nothing, and he relented for the moment, turning his thoughts to what the Vampire had said: *London.*

How could he explain to the others that Dracula was dead? That he, Xavier, was left to go on an impossible search for a goblet that they didn't know the whereabouts of? And how in the world was he to explain to them that he was their new King?

He clutched the hilt of the Ascalon and pushed ahead to catch up with Nathanial, who had taken advantage of Xavier's deep thought and sped up. And when he reached him, he imagined himself as

S.C. PARRIS

Dracula flying alongside the Vampire. The anxiousness to reach *The Immortal's Guide* filled him just as the dread of Eleanor did. He had to acquire this elusive book, a most dangerous Artifact in the hands of any Creature, if Eleanor was any example of its power, and he had to do so quickly.

"Something troubling you, my Lord?" Nathanial asked suddenly, and Xavier realized he had been watching him out of the corner of his eye—had been doing so since Dracula's death. It was as though he, Xavier, were diseased.

"What? No," he said, "merely wondering what secrets Dracula kept that Eleanor discovered to make her so...changed."

Nathanial looked rather uncomfortable as they flew, the Dragons below letting out clouds of black smoke in their direction, and it was a while before he said, "Whatever it was, my Lord, it's in the book, we must focus on that, first and foremost."

*Indeed*, he thought, wondering just what more Nathanial knew. After all, knowing magic, traveling around the World for the Artifacts left to Dracula, the red-haired Vampire had to have vast knowledge on just what all of this—Dracula's secrets, Eleanor's power, this book—meant.

✳

"You aren't authorized to go in there!" the Vampire said, raising a hand. It seemed Dracula had stationed two guards to stand watch outside his office since he'd left for the Council.

"Like hell I'm not," Nathanial said defiantly, his golden eyes bright with indignation.

The Vampire glared at Nathanial, fiercely but Xavier said, "Let us through, please."

At Xavier's words, the Vampire seemed to shrivel into a ball of humbleness, although it appeared he did not know the reason for it.

342

"O-of course, my Lord."

As they stepped through the doorway leading into Dracula's office, Xavier was aware the two soldiers were gazing upon him in apprehension. More so than usual. He did his best to ignore them, perusing the drawers at Dracula's desk, halting slightly as he realized it was now his.

"I don't see it here," Nathanial said, putting back several books he had pulled from shelves, pulling Xavier from his thoughts.

"Something tells me it's not here at all," he said, stepping around the desk, moving to the low table against the high-arching windows.

"Yeah," Nathanial sighed, "I had a feeling it'd be too easy if it were."

"What is to be done now?" Xavier asked, eyeing the high flames within the fireplace, knowing it only burned because he was there.

"I know a number of places he could've kept it if not here."

"Where? What places?"

"There is Cedar Village, a town of Enchanters and Fae, Quiddle of Terry and Mila Quiddle, and at last, Lane."

"Lane?" he repeated, wondering why the second most frequented Vampire City in the Dark World would hold this elusive book.

"Yes, my King, Lane," Nathanial said.

The Vampires at the door gave each other shocked stares at Nathanial's words, and Xavier looked at the desk.

Nathanial ignored them, he moved for the door, and with the movement, Xavier, mind reeling with the sight of Dracula's death, what he'd left them with, followed suit.

Once they were far enough from the two Vampires, he said, "When should I tell the Vampires the news?"

"News?" Nathanial asked.

"Dracula...myself...when is it best to tell them what's transpired?"

"When you have acquired the book, you will know what must be done after you have traveled through *The Immortal's Guide.*"

Xavier kept the burgeoning thoughts of recent events at bay, how immense it all seemed, how maddening it was that only several hours ago a vast history had been spilled.

While he and Nathanial stepped together down the hallway, his mind traveled to Dracula's ash back at the palace, wondering grimly if it had been swept away by a harsh breeze by now. It was with a further grimace that he thought of the book he was supposed to find, mind spinning with the World Dracula had created, a World, he realized, looking around at the tall walls of the hallway as they ventured to the stairs, he didn't quite understand.

How was it that Dracula never bothered to mention the Council? How was it that he never thought it important to mention this book that supposedly held all of his knowledge? That another Vampire could happen upon the book and change drastically, sending the rest of the Dark World into chaos?

*And why*, Xavier thought angrily, venturing down the stairs toward the first floor of the mansion, *did Dracula never tell me he was going to die?*

※

A cold breeze blew past, and they stepped up to the large white doors, all the dread that had been building since he knew he would have to explain all of this rise to his throat; he could not find the words.

"Something wrong?" Nathanial asked.

"No," he said, pushing aside the nervousness. He lifted his hand to the knocker and pressed it against the strike plate twice before the dread could return.

He waited but a minute before the door opened, and Lillith Crane's bright eyes shined upon him. "Xavier!" she almost shouted in surprise, the white lace covered day dress she wore sweeping around her house slippers. "You were gone for two days, where have you been? Who's this?"

"A friend," he said tersely, brushing past her, eyeing the large hall where only days ago the Caddenhalls had attacked, the Cleaners had cleaned up their mess.

Staring around at the spotless hall where a few maids were deep in gossip near the staircase, Xavier felt the wind at his back with the door's close, and Lillith said, "Victor is in his office...we were worried sick about you."

"Sorry to make you worry, Miss Crane. Victor...has he said anything about me? Where I was going?"

"He hasn't said a word. He knew?"

"Yes, I thought he would—" he began, catching Nathanial's golden eyes. The Vampire stood near the doors, looking quite on guard: It was as if he weren't allowed to take another step into the place. "Never mind that, I just wish to speak to the both of you."

"Whatever for?"

Nathanial cleared his throat. "Sorry, my Lord, but we cannot linger."

*Of course.* He turned to Lillith. "I need to speak to the both of you – it's very important."

"I – alright," she said at last, looking from him to Nathanial and back before moving past the stairs toward a wooden door within a back wall.

Nathanial took her place, looking rather unsettled. "Do you need to tell him of this?"

"They both need to know."

"My Lord, there is a reason Dracula never let slip his journeys—"

"A reason he would have you believe is just, I assume," Victor's cold voice issued from atop the stairs.

They looked up in unison, the tall, silver-haired Vampire looking quite formidable, a pale hand clasping the railing, his violet eyes appearing colder than normal, not a pleasant smile to be found upon his stern face.

"Victor," Xavier began, stepping toward the stairs, ignoring the maids: they shuffled out of the room at his movement, "when did you—"

"This is my home," he interjected rudely, stepping down the stairs, "I should know if and when I have... visitors." His eyes lingered far too long on Nathanial as he said this. "Now, what did you have to tell us that this Vampire did not want shared?"

He merely stared. "Victor," he began, not knowing how he could say it at all. "It seems...at the Council Meeting...something... happened."

"Obviously," he snapped, anger burning in his eyes, "otherwise I doubt you'd be here, two days later, stumbling over your words, with this...Vampire at your side. Now, tell me—what is it that's happened?"

*Why was he so angry? Was it possible he knew?* "Thomas Montague," he could barely whisper the words, "killed Dracula...and I-I have been named his successor."

Victor eyes closed with the words, and Xavier had thought he'd barely heard them, it was so low he'd spoken, Victor's grip tightening on the railing as if to steady himself. "I knew it," he said. "I knew he was gone—I could feel it...here." And a hand moved to his heart.

Xavier was aware Nathanial shifted uncomfortably at his side, and he, himself, couldn't find the words. Of course he had already known—he was the damned Vampire's creation—of course Victor had known when Dracula turned to ash...the pull between Vampire and the one turned was immense, strong, unyielding. Assuming, of course, you know the one who turned you.

Xavier kept his gaze on Victor. "There was nothing that could have been done, you must understand—"

He lifted a hand. "I understand completely. I understand that his secrets caught up with him. He paid his price, at last. But you... Vampire...you will... take his place? Lead us in his stead?"

*Was that sarcasm on his tongue, within his words?* He knew himself to feel drastically reduced under that gaze, how condescending it was. "I-I did not choose to take his place, Victor," he defended himself sternly.

"But you take it all the same!" Victor yelled, the railing cracking around his grip with his words. "And to think it was me who was by his side this whole time—to think it was I who put up with his myriad plans, his schemes, never fully knowing what he was doing!"

"I gave him your name!" Xavier responded. "I asked him why he did not come to you with this!"

"And what did he tell you, hm? Said it wasn't my right? I wasn't right for the job? I wasn't chosen, despite being the first one *he* chose?"

*That is exactly what he said.* "He would never say that, Victor. You were his first for a reason, I'm sure!"

"Ha! The damned Vampire took pity on me—an old, decrepit man. He didn't even give me a bloody choice in the matter, did he? I was his first test—his first experiment to see if this immortality business worked, wasn't I? But I never mattered when it came to his real secrets—I never mattered when it came to – being someone like you – someone able to c-carry on his...legacy!"

Victor was miserable now, his darkened eyes were pitch black, the cold air emanating from him palpable at best. Xavier was almost knocked off his feet by the wind. "Calm down, Victor," he yelled, he and Nathanial covering their eyes with their arms, "please!"

"Don't tell me what to do in my own home, Vampire!" Victor roared, and he was in front of Xavier in the next second, a hand tight around his throat. "You don't get to boss me around—you may have taken his place, but you will never be him!"

Before Xavier could say a word, Nathanial had a hand around

Victor's arm, a glowing red hand at that, and Victor relinquished his grip as though burned.

Rubbing his throat, Xavier stared at the astonished Vampire as he stared from Nathanial to him and back, and he opened his mouth to say something when a door opened and Lillith entered the large hall, terribly exasperated.

"I couldn't find him—" But she stopped short upon seeing Victor, a look of relief on her face, it quickly turned to worry as she surveyed the situation closely. "Victor, what happened?"

The Vampire was still rubbing his arm, casting Nathanial a scalding look, but with her words, he seemed to snap back to himself, and rubbed a hand over his eyes. "They were just leaving, Miss Crane."

"But Victor—"

"Get out of my house!" he roared, stepping toward Xavier.

Nathanial was before him in an instant, keeping him from moving any farther, and upon seeing him, Victor relinquished, eyes still dark with anger.

"Victor," Lillith whispered uncertainly from behind him.

"Let us take our leave," Nathanial said, turning for the double doors.

But he did not move. How could he, when Victor was terribly hurt? When he had to make it right?

A hand was upon his shoulder then, edging him back. "Please, my King," Nathanial said, "we have overstayed our welcome."

It was with one last look toward Victor and Lillith, Victor looking furious, Lillith, rather worried, that he said, "I am sorry, Victor," before following in Nathanial's wake.

The Vampire had already opened a door, the afternoon sun clear in the sky. He stepped through the door, the sword pulsing at his side.

Tightening his grip on the handle, he turned to Nathanial. "Is there a chance, any at all, that Victor will come around?"

"He does not understand," Nathanial said, stepping down the path leading to the gates, "it is why Dracula never gave his secrets freely."

"So you think it would be better that I never told them what I must do? Where we must go, what for?"

"You didn't even get that far, did you, your Majesty?"

His lips pursed with this realization. "Yes, well, I just don't understand Victor's reaction—er, I understand it, surely—but... there was something more about all of this that has him bothered."

"You mean besides the fact that he was the first one Dracula bestowed permanent death?"

Xavier scoffed. "Very well," he sighed, seeing he was to get no answers to his qualms from the strange Vampire. Turning his thoughts, instead, upon the elusive book, he squared his shoulders, and, tightening his grip on the Ascalon at his side, said, "Dracula's secrets are in this book, correct?"

"Yes."

"Have you read these secrets, Nathanial?"

"I haven't, no."

"So you don't know the exact nature of the book, then?"

"Only that it has too much power—in the hands of the wrong Creature. Eleanor Black is a nice example of this..."

The sight of her long black hair, smoldering eyes, and chilling smile reached his mind with the name, but the feeling of dread was nowhere to be found.

"Indeed."

They had reached the gates at last, Nathanial pressing a hand to the bars. "Follow me, my Lord."

Xavier only nodded as Nathanial pushed open the gate, and took one step over the threshold, gone to the afternoon air.

Eyeing the barren street before him, the sight of the red sun along the horizon, he turned his thoughts to where Nathanial was, but before he could allow the wind to carry him, he felt the gaze at his back.

Turning to eye the tall manor, he scanned the many windows upon the second floor, searching for the gaze that caught him, and then at last he found it, in a window just above the doors: the piercing gaze of Victor Vonderheide.

And just as he found those eyes so cold, the lights near the front steps went out, and that was when he felt it, the Vampire's anger. So thick, so cold, so resounding, Xavier thought he would suffocate with the feeling if he needed to breathe.

He allowed himself a moment to grieve for the Vampire, all he'd lost, before the sword pulsed thickly at his side as though bidden. He turned from the gaze much against his will, turning his thoughts to Nathanial Vivery, departing on the cold wind, the sword's pulse never fading as he went.

# About the Author

Besides being addicted to vampires, blood, and a good, steaming cup of tea, S.C. Parris attends University in New York City, and is the author of "A Night of Frivolity," a horror short story, published by Burning Willow Press. She is the author of *The Dark World* series published by Permuted Press, and enjoys thinking up new dark historical fantasies to put to page next. She lives on Long Island, New York with her family and can be found writing ridiculous articles for CLASH Media.

# BOOK

IS COMING

# PERMUTED
# PRESS
### needs **you** to help

## SPREAD (THE)
## INFECTION

### FOLLOW US!

ｆ | Facebook.com/PermutedPress
🐦 | Twitter.com/PermutedPress

### REVIEW US!

Wherever you buy our book, they can be
reviewed! We want to know what you like!

### GET INFECTED!

Sign up for our mailing list at
PermutedPress.com

**PERMUTED**
PRESS

# 14

**Peter Clines**

"A riveting apocalyptic mystery in the style of LOST."
—Gran DiLeole, author of The Infection

Padlocked doors.
Strange light fixtures. Mutant cockroaches.

There are some odd things about Nate's new apartment. Every room in this old brownstone has a mystery. Mysteries that stretch back over a hundred years. Some of them are in plain sight. Some are behind locked doors. And all together these mysteries could mean the end of Nate and his friends.

Or the end of everything…

PERMUTED PRESS

## THE JOURNAL SERIES
### by Deborah D. Moore

After a major crisis rocks the nation, all supply lines are shut down. In the remote Upper Peninsula of Michigan, the small town of Moose Creek and its residents are devastated when they lose power in the middle of a brutal winter, and must struggle alone with one calamity after another.

*The Journal* series takes the reader head first into the fury that only Mother Nature can dish out. Book Five coming soon!

PERMUTED
PRESS

## Michael Clary
### THE GUARDIAN | THE REGULATORS | BROKEN

When the dead rise up and take over the city, the Government is forced to close off the borders and abandon the remaining survivors. Fortunately for them, a hero is about to be chosen...a Guardian that will rise up from the ashes to fight against the dead. The series continues with Book Four: *Scratch*.

## Emily Goodwin
### CONTAGIOUS | DEATHLY CONTAGIOUS

During the Second Great Depression, twenty-four-year-old Orissa Penwell is forced to drop out of college when she is no longer able to pay for classes. Down on her luck, Orissa doesn't think she can sink any lower. She couldn't be more wrong. A virus breaks out across the country, leaving those that are infected crazed, aggressive and very hungry.

The saga continues in Book Three: *Contagious Chaos* and Book Four: *The Truth is Contagious*.

### THE BREADWINNER | Stevie Kopas

The end of the world is not glamorous. In a matter of days the human race was reduced to nothing more than vicious, flesh hungry creatures. There are no heroes here. Only survivors. The trilogy continues with Book Two: *Haven* and Book Three: *All Good Things*.

### THE BECOMING | Jessica Meigs

As society rapidly crumbles under the hordes of infected, three people—Ethan Bennett, a Memphis police officer; Cade Alton, his best friend and former IDF sharpshooter; and Brandt Evans, a lieutenant in the US Marines—band together against the oncoming crush of death and terror sweeping across the world. The story continues with Book Two: *Ground Zero*.

### THE INFECTION WAR | Craig DiLouie

As the undead awake, a small group of survivors must accept a dangerous mission into the very heart of infection. This edition features two books: *The Infection* and *The Killing Floor*.

### OBJECTS OF WRATH | Sean T. Smith

The border between good and evil has always been bloody… Is humanity doomed? After the bombs rain down, the entire world is an open wound; it is in those bleeding years that William Fox becomes a man. After The Fall, nothing is certain. *Objects of Wrath* is the first book in a saga spanning four generations.

PERMUTED
PRESS

# A PREPPER'S COOKBOOK

*20 Years of Cooking in the Woods*

## by Deborah D. Moore

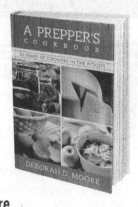

In the event of a disaster, it isn't enough to have food. You also have to know what to do with it.

Deborah D. Moore, author of *The Journal* series and a passionate Prepper for over twenty years, gives you step-by-step instructions on making delicious meals from the emergency pantry.

PERMUTED
PRESS